"And don't you even *think* of throwing my stuff out behind my back while I'm gone. That, may I remind you, would be cheating."

"Don't flatter yourself," Ren said with a derisive snort. "As if I'd need to cheat to get *you* out." Then, with a sharp twist of their heel, they headed for the garden, pointedly leaving Pansy – and her plethora of bags – behind.

Granted, this didn't stop Pansy from calling out after them, the need to have the last word in all things evidently yet another universally halfling trait. "Don't forget to take off your shoes before coming back inside! Remember: dirt belongs *outside*, not in the house!"

We'll see about that, Ren thought with a smirk. Because now they had an idea – a very, very good idea – one that Pansy was all but guaranteed not to like.

Praise for

How to Lose a Goblin in Ten Days

"An adorable delight! This wonderful and charming treasure of a book will warm your heart!"
—Sarah Beth Durst, *New York Times* bestselling author of *The Spellshop*

"*How to Lose a Goblin in Ten Days* redefines 'coziness' in the most romantic and charming manner. Jessie Sylva settles readers into a soothingly familiar world before gently and thoughtfully upending all expectations of it. An utterly lovely and unforgettable book."
—Sylvie Cathrall, author of *A Letter to the Luminous Deep*

"Imagine a honey-sweet enemies-to-lovers story set in a high fantasy world of halflings, goblins, and wizards. Cozy-fantasy lovers will tuck into this lovely story and want to savor every last morsel."
—J. Penner, author of *A Fellowship of Bakers & Magic*

"*How to Lose a Goblin in Ten Days* is an adorable story that will fulfill your cottagecore dreams—and also carries a poignant message about acceptance, belonging, and community. This sweet, cozy tale is the perfect escape for anyone seeking comfort, warmth, and a dash of magic."
—M. Stevenson, author of *Behooved*

How to Lose a Goblin in Ten Days

JESSIE SYLVA

orbitbooks.net

This book is a work of fiction. Names, characters, places, and incidents are the product of the author's imagination or are used fictitiously. Any resemblance to actual events, locales, or persons, living or dead, is coincidental.

Copyright © 2026 by Little, Brown Book Group Limited

Cover art direction by Sophie Ellis
Cover illustration by Raahat Kaduji
Author photograph by Jessica Hassett

Hachette Book Group supports the right to free expression and the value of copyright. The purpose of copyright is to encourage writers and artists to produce the creative works that enrich our culture.

The scanning, uploading, and distribution of this book without permission is a theft of the author's intellectual property. If you would like permission to use material from the book (other than for review purposes), please contact permissions@hbgusa.com. Thank you for your support of the author's rights.

Orbit
Hachette Book Group
1290 Avenue of the Americas
New York, NY 10104
orbitbooks.net

First Edition: January 2026
Simultaneously published in Great Britain by Orbit

Orbit is an imprint of Hachette Book Group.
The Orbit name and logo are registered trademarks of
Little, Brown Book Group Limited.

The publisher is not responsible for websites (or their content) that are not owned by the publisher.

The Hachette Speakers Bureau provides a wide range of authors for speaking events. To find out more, go to hachettespeakersbureau.com or email HachetteSpeakers@hbgusa.com.

Orbit books may be purchased in bulk for business, educational, or promotional use. For information, please contact your local bookseller or the Hachette Book Group Special Markets Department at special.markets@hbgusa.com.

Library of Congress Control Number: 2025942128

ISBNs: 9780316585910 (trade paperback), 9780316585927 (ebook)

Printed in the United States of America

LSC-C

Printing 3, 2025

*For Mama, who encouraged me to dream big,
even as her own world grew smaller*

How to Lose a Goblin in Ten Days

1
Pansy

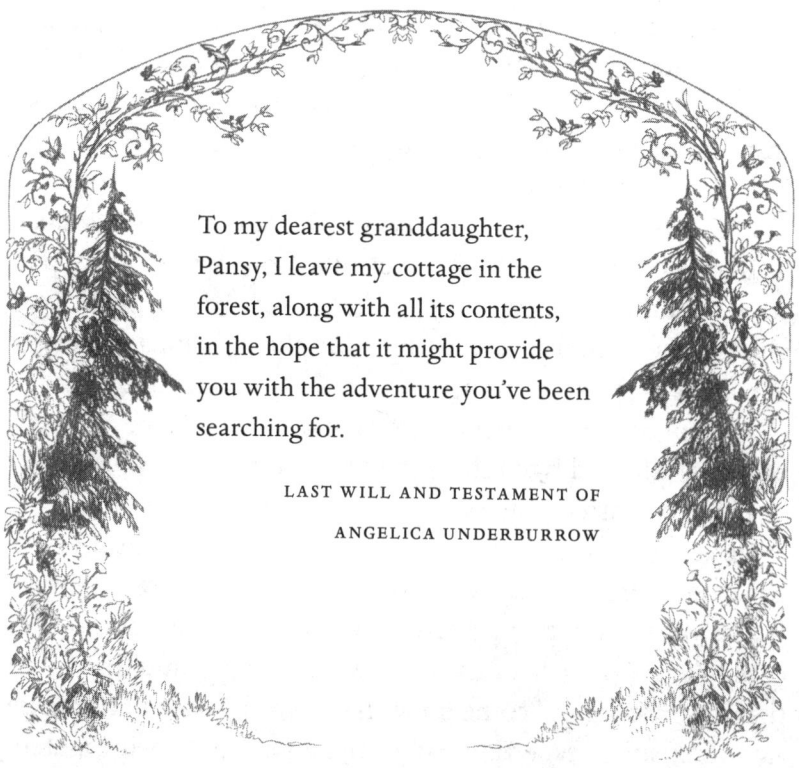

To my dearest granddaughter, Pansy, I leave my cottage in the forest, along with all its contents, in the hope that it might provide you with the adventure you've been searching for.

LAST WILL AND TESTAMENT OF
ANGELICA UNDERBURROW

T he problem with mushrooms, Pansy decided, half-squatting in the damp forest earth, was that far too many of them looked alike. Take the crop of orange fungus blanketing one side of the fallen log before her, for example. Was it the delicious, yet rare, Phoenix Tail mushroom she'd spent most of the morning searching the forest for? Or was it the far more ominously named Bloodletter Shroom? Gods only knew the answer to that one. Because Pansy certainly didn't; not even with a borrowed copy of *Fatleaf's Fungal Fancies* clutched in one dirt-stained hand.

At this point, a more prudent halfling would have backed away and left the mushrooms to carry on as they were, undisturbed. But the thought of leaving behind what could be the greatest culinary treasure this side of Giant's Reach made something inside Pansy shrivel. Not to mention she would be coming home empty-handed – on tonight of all nights.

No. Pansy shook her head. She couldn't do that. She *wouldn't*.

Blowing out a breath, she tucked a stray ringlet of copper-colored hair behind one large, rounded ear and squinted closer at the finger-like frills jutting up from the log's mossy surface. Well, it was certainly orange. But was it the "burnished orange of a warm hearth", as Elwan Fatleaf had put it? Maybe. Though how that differed from the "dull orange of an overripe pumpkin" Pansy wasn't quite sure.

Perhaps her friend Blossom would know. She was a florist by trade, so mushrooms weren't precisely her area of expertise. But it *was* her book that Pansy had borrowed. And if Blossom couldn't give her a firm answer – well, Pansy would throw out the mushrooms and come up with something else. Better to be safe than sorry, especially when the alternative meant potentially poisoning your entire family.

"The things I do for a good quiche," she muttered, retrieving a small paring knife from the folds of her apron. There were probably blades better suited for this: foraging knives or some such. But like most halflings, until today, the closest Pansy had gotten to foraging was visiting the local grocer, who did not deal in anything other than the very ordinary. And Phoenix Tails were anything but.

Even with only a paring knife at her disposal, the mushrooms came away without much fuss. Soon, Pansy was rising to her feet, her potentially-poisonous-but-hopefully-not haul tucked safely inside her wicker shopping basket.

As much as she would have liked to keep searching – just in case – the hour was getting late. The sky overhead, glimpsed in narrow snatches through a wild, thick canopy, had already deepened to a soft lilac, edged in equally delicate pinks and golds that continued to thin as daylight waned. Pansy estimated that she had a couple of hours before night set in. Plenty of time to walk the winding trail back to Haverow – *if* she left now.

As luck would have it, she managed only a few steps in the direction of home before a new treasure caught her eye: a truffle, white and plump, rising just above the carpet of dead leaves blanketing the forest floor. Had some animal unearthed it, only to abandon their plunder in a moment of panic?

"Huh. Well, you won't find me complaining," Pansy said, hopping off the path once more.

It took a little bit of maneuvering on her part, the ground here more gnarled roots than dirt, but soon she reached the shallow divot in the earth the truffle called home. The white bulb was enormous, nearly the size of her fist. With it, she could make enough truffle butter to fuel dozens of recipes, from truffle-butter mashed potatoes to a wonderfully soft white truffle-butter bread she'd always wanted to try. None would be as extraordinary as the Phoenix Tail quiche she'd been hoping to prepare, but the truffle butter, at least, she could leave behind. It would be a piece of her heart for her parents to keep close, a reminder that her love for them could never diminish, no matter how much distance might come between them.

Warmth bloomed beneath Pansy's breastbone at the thought. Perhaps tonight would not be such a disaster after all – even if the mushrooms in the basket *did* turn out to be poisonous doppelgangers.

Squatting down anew, Pansy reached for the truffle. However, before her fingers could so much as graze its pockmarked surface, a pink blur darted out in front of her, and the truffle was gone.

"Thief!" she cried, watching as a conspicuously well-fed pig made off with her would-be prize. "Piggy thief! Bring that back!"

Her demands fell on deaf ears. But Pansy would not give up so easily.

She surged to her feet, dress hiked pre-emptively around her knees. No need to give herself any more things to trip over; the forest already had her covered on that front. Still, even with a sea of uneven terrain before her, Pansy managed to keep pace with the pilfering swine. In fact, soon she was *gaining* on the creature.

"I've got you now!" she shouted, legs pumping harder still.

Pansy's vision had condensed, leaving nothing but the rotund, pink mass ahead of her – plus, the truffle clamped between its jaws. When the pig released the truffle in apparent concession, she gave no thought to what might be around her. She dove.

No sooner had her fingers closed around the squat bulb than another set of fingers, longer and greener than her own, found hers, pressing nails like flat shards of obsidian into soft, unguarded skin.

For half a breath, hazel eyes met yellow in complete and perfect stillness, where even the world itself seemed to pause on its axis. Then, the moment passed, and both Pansy and the unexpected interloper broke apart, each relinquishing their hold on the truffle in favor of scrambling back several paces (and, in Pansy's case, letting out a less-than-dignified squeak).

A goblin? Here? Pansy hugged her basket close, heart kicking hard against her ribs.

In truth, this shouldn't have been such a shock. Just as the forest bordered Haverow and several other halfling villages on one side, it abutted a vast network of caves on the other, all inhabited – or "infested", as the neighboring dwarves might say – by goblins. No doubt this was one of them, having temporarily abandoned the dank, festering darkness they loved so much to – what? Scavenge? Steal? That's what goblins did. Provided they weren't too busy slaughtering halflings in the name of whatever dark lord or necromancer they volunteered to serve.

This goblin, at least, seemed to be unarmed. Granted, the claws they sported at the end of each finger could do some damage with the right application; the tiny, pink pinpricks dotting the back of Pansy's hand were proof enough of that. But even those claws seemed to have diminished slightly, as if they'd been retracted. Like a cat's.

Still, it was difficult to know anything for sure. While Pansy had stumbled backwards in a straight line, the goblin had taken a more strategic approach, seeking cover behind the same knot of overgrown roots they had popped out from. If Pansy squinted, she could just make them out. But in the ever-waning daylight, who knew how long that would last.

In many ways, the goblin appeared exactly as Pansy had imagined: dark green hair; green skin; clothes in varying shades of brown and gray, all held together by scraps of fabric and a prayer. And yet, their features were also softer, rounder, even when doused in the gnarled, twisting shadows of the forest. With sharp cheekbones and an intense, lash-lined gaze, the goblin was almost – *dare Pansy say it?* – cute.

To think, she had an entire bookshelf's worth of Wolf Banefoot books at home, and none of them had prepared her for this. But she could hardly expect stories about the greatest halfling hero to wax poetic about the very goblins he was fighting.

Speaking of: was this goblin going to fight *her*?

The goblin was still frozen in a strange half-crouch, their muscles pulled bowstring-taut beneath the gray weight of their cloak. While one hand gripped the curve of an immense tree root, the other extended behind them, palm flat and out, almost as if they were telling someone to wait.

But who? Pansy sucked in a sharp breath, panic squeezing around her throat like a vice. Her gaze swiveled away from the goblin, searching, instead, beyond. There, she found not another goblin as she'd feared, but a familiar thief, pink and potbellied, its head cocked slightly to one side. A goblin's accomplice. *Of course.*

Had the goblin stolen the pig? she wondered, only to nearly scoff at herself for having deigned to ask such a silly question. They were a goblin. Surely, that was answer enough.

No sooner had Pansy glimpsed the creature than the goblin left cover and came back into her line of sight. *Don't you dare*, blazed the silent accusation, knife-bright behind a tangled veil of moss-dark hair. No words had been spoken. Yet Pansy heard them all the same.

"I'm not going to hurt your pig," she snapped, the hot swell of her own indignation shattering the uneasy silence between them. "I came out here to gather some ingredients. That's all."

A beat. Just long enough for the goblin's long ears to unpin from their skull. "I didn't know halflings foraged." Their voice was surprisingly soft – almost pleasantly so – but oddly devoid of inflection, particularly when compared to the way Pansy's neighbors in Haverow spoke.

"I'm making a quiche," Pansy declared, canting up her chin at a defiant angle; anything to eke out a few extra millimeters against a goblin who thought her so low as to hurt a defenseless pig – thief or not. "A very halfling thing to do, mind you."

The goblin's eyes flicked down to Pansy's basket, still clutched to her chest, the narrow slits of their pupils flaring ever so slightly wider. "You know those are poisonous, right?"

"What?"

"Those mushrooms. You can't eat them. They'll kill you."

Heat flooded Pansy's face, rushing all the way up to the tips of her ears. So, they *had* been Bloodletter Shrooms, after all. Just her luck. She'd spent the whole day slogging through these woods, all for the privilege of accidentally poisoning her parents with what was supposed to be the greatest meal they'd ever had. And worst of all, a *goblin* had been the one to tell her just how badly she'd mucked it up.

"I-I knew that!" Pansy stammered. "I wasn't going to eat them."

An awful lie by any measure. The goblin clearly thought so, given the way their nose wrinkled. Still, they asked, "What were you going to do with them, then?"

"I—" Pansy floundered, her cheeks burning hotter and hotter with every second wasted scrabbling for some halfway-believable excuse. As if there could ever be one! She knew it. The goblin knew it. Perhaps, even the pig knew it. And still the goblin continued to wait for her answer, their expression an inscrutable, unyielding wall.

"Decoration," she forced out at last, managing to keep a straight face.

"Decoration," the goblin repeated flatly.

"Yes." Pansy sniffed. "Decoration. Am I not allowed to decorate my home?"

"With *mushrooms*. You decorate with mushrooms."

She shrugged. "I like the color orange."

The goblin blinked at her, long and slow, then said, "Take it."

"What?"

"The truffle." They gestured towards it, still lying between them. "You need it more than I do."

Pansy balked. "What's that supposed to mean?"

The goblin shrugged, their gaze drifting to one side. "I don't want a bunch of dead halflings on my conscience, is all."

At that, Pansy's waning flush roared back with a vengeance. "I told you they're not for eating!" Then, just to really drive home the point, she upended her basket, scattering the lingering evidence of her failure across the dirt. "There! Happy? Now you don't have to worry about us stupid little halflings poisoning ourselves with deadly mushrooms!"

For several beats there was nothing beyond the ragged drag of Pansy's breathing, her shoulders heaving as she stood at the center of an orange halo of her own creation. The goblin said nothing, did nothing. But then they started towards Pansy, pausing to retrieve the truffle, which they deposited in her otherwise empty basket, now hanging limply at her side.

"You should go home before it gets dark," they said, close enough that Pansy could see the smattering of barely there freckles dusting the bridge of their nose. "The forest is thick and hard to navigate without light, especially for someone like you."

As the goblin stepped away, Pansy considered whether she ought to thank them. Good halfling manners dictated that when someone gave you something, you responded with a show of gratitude in turn. It wasn't so easy when that someone had been anything but polite themselves. Still, it was the right thing to do.

Steadying herself with a deep breath, Pansy opened her mouth to utter two words she had never expected to say to a goblin. But before she could so much as form the first syllable, the goblin tapped their cheek and, with a whisper of something like a smirk curling at the corner of their mouth, said, "By the way, you have dirt on your face. A lot of it."

Pansy could have screamed.

Returning to her parents' burrow in Haverow should have been a relief, a much-needed balm to soothe the sting of her encounter with that awful goblin. There was nothing an hour or two in the kitchen couldn't fix, unless someone had beaten her there – someone who, to be clear, was *not* supposed to be there.

"Mum!" Pansy groaned as she set her basket on the counter, the truffle inside rolling lightly across the bottom. "I told you I was going to cook tonight!"

"Oh, honey, it's fine." Her mother waved her off with one oven-mitt-clad hand as she stirred the contents of a heavy red saucepan with the other. Judging from the state of her hair, often wilder than even Pansy's own curls, she had just started: the brown ribbon she always used to hold her hair back while she cooked hadn't even begun to slip. "You were out all day. You can cook tomorrow instead."

There it was – the very thing Pansy had been afraid of. She

swallowed the sigh that welled up in her throat and said, as kindly as she could manage, "Mum, you know I won't be here tomorrow."

Her mother shrugged. "The day after, then."

"*Or* the day after. I'm moving out. We talked about this."

A beat passed. Her mother said nothing, her gaze fixed on the pot in front of her: filling for a pot pie, Pansy guessed, given the smell – warm and homey and full of butter. But her mother's thinking had always been plain to see, etched, this time, in the tightness around her mouth.

Finally, a sigh. "Do you really have to leave?" her mother asked plaintively, hazel eyes in the same shade as Pansy's own flicking over to meet hers. "You'll be so far away."

"Not that far," Pansy corrected, heading over to the basin to wash her hands. Just because her mother had already started on dinner did not mean Pansy couldn't help. "I already told you I'd come visit. Every ten-day. Like I promised."

Her mother would not be placated so easily. She shook her head, frowning. "It's not right. You should be home. *Here*. With family. Even your grandmother recognized that, in the end, when she moved back to Haverow. Not that it made much of a difference..."

"*Mum*." Pansy shot her mother a hard look, her hands stilling on the water jug. "I'm moving into Grandma's old cottage. Not"– she gestured haphazardly, uncaring of the tiny droplets loosed from her fingertips – "running off to fight in some wizard's war."

The notion alone was enough to pull a noise of distress from deep in her mother's throat. No matter that it had been nearly six decades since the last Great War, and that the Realm was, arguably, at peace – perhaps even the most tranquil it had ever been, with the latest in a long line of dark lords sealed away behind powerful magic, his cruel armies of goblins and orcs decimated by the forces of Good. It mattered even less that Pansy had no interest in following in her grandmother's footsteps, whether it meant adventuring with some wizard, killing goblins or saving the world. The fact that she wanted to see more – the slightest, *ittiest* bit more – of what lay beyond the four corners of their cozy little hamlet was enough to mark her as a cause for concern in her mother's eyes, an echo of an old wound that had never truly healed.

At this point, Pansy's father, who had doubtless been eavesdropping since the start, poked his head through the doorway and said, "Your mother's right, Pans. The forest is no place for a halfling. Plus, no one's lived in that cottage for decades! For all you know, the roof could have been blown clean off by now."

"Then I'll fix it," Pansy declared. Her father's favorite nickname for her wasn't going to sway her – not this time. "I know neither of you is happy with my decision, and I'm sorry you feel that way, but my mind is made up."

"But there could be *goblins!*" her mother all but wailed, her lower lip trembling as a ruddy haze mottled her usual golden-brown complexion.

Pansy half-wanted to tell her about the goblin she'd encountered earlier, as proof that her mother's concerns were largely overblown, but that was not what her mother needed right now. Letting out a breath, Pansy wiped her hands on her apron before pulling her mother into the biggest, tightest hug she could muster.

"It'll be okay, Mum," she said, resting her chin on her mother's shoulder like always. "If anything happens, I'll come right back."

A sniffle. "You promise?"

"I promise."

"Good." Pansy's mother pulled away just enough to lightly dab at her eyes. "I get so worried, knowing that there'll be goblins living near by. That cottage is *right* on the border."

"Hopefully they'll stay on their side of it."

"But what if they don't? You know, a farmer over in Halfbough found his pasture ransacked just last week. Not a single goat left behind! The work of goblins, no doubt. He swears he heard a whole pack of them cackling outside his bedroom window. Of course, he was too afraid to go outside and check. Smart man. Who knows what they might have done to him if he had? We all remember what happened to Lillishire during the War." She shuddered.

To be fair, Pansy didn't exactly "remember" per se; not in the way her parents did. After all, they had been alive during the Great War, while she obviously hadn't. Yet she knew exactly what her mother was referring to – any halfling would.

Often described as the "darkest moment in halfling history", the Lillishire Massacre stood as a black albatross over their collective consciousness. Even sixty years later, no one could forget how the dark lord's goblin armies had swept through nearly two-dozen halfling villages to the east, razing them to the ground while putting everyone who hadn't managed to escape to the sword. Now, instead of two halfling provinces, the Realm had only one.

Perhaps her mother was being a tad overdramatic, referencing Lillishire like that. From what Pansy could tell, petty theft was more goblins' speed these days. But, at the same time, could she really blame her? Because while Pansy had learned about all of Lillishire's horrors in the abstract, her mother had seen them firsthand, in the haggard, terror-soaked faces that had flooded Halvenshire in the ten-days and months that had followed, seeking refuge in the only place they had left. That sort of memory wasn't something you could just shake.

Pansy gave her mother a reassuring pat on the arm. "I already told you, Mum, I'll come home. You're acting like the next time I see you I'm going to be telling you all about my new goblin housemate."

Thankfully, her mother let out a little, hiccuping laugh at that. "You're right," she admitted, now smiling as well.

"I usually am. Now what's for dinner? It smells *delicious*."

And like it would go well with some truffle. But as to where that truffle had come from – well, Pansy wasn't going to think too hard about that one.

2
Ren

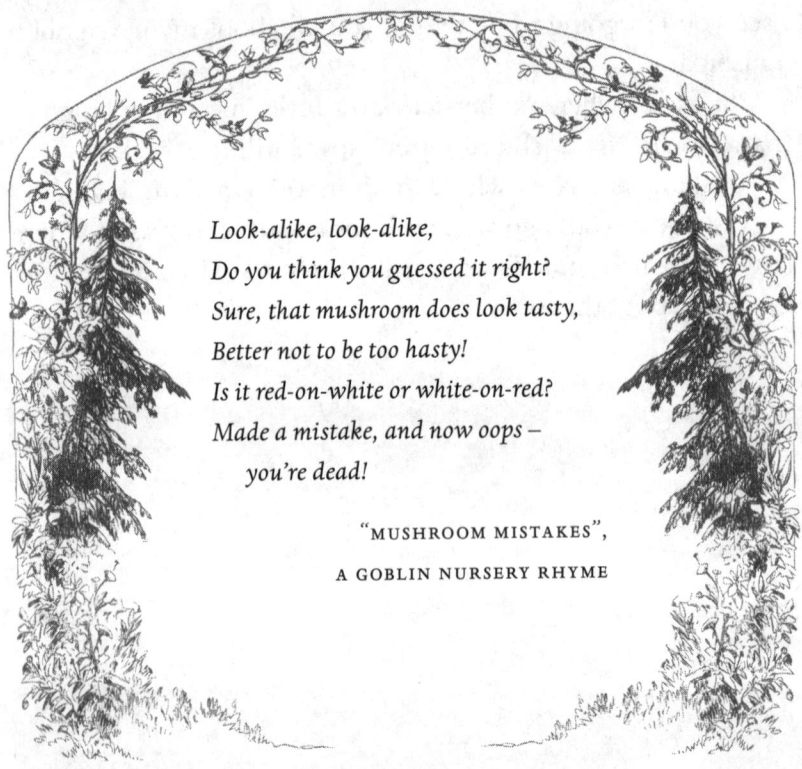

Look-alike, look-alike,
Do you think you guessed it right?
Sure, that mushroom does look tasty,
Better not to be too hasty!
Is it red-on-white or white-on-red?
Made a mistake, and now oops –
    you're dead!

"MUSHROOM MISTAKES",
A GOBLIN NURSERY RHYME

There was a halfling outside the cottage.

And not just any halfling, Ren realized with a cold jolt of nascent dread. But the halfling from the forest, the one who would have baked enough Bloodletter Shrooms into a quiche to fell a full-grown dragon if left to her own devices.

Evidently, she'd taken Ren's warning to heart, despite her less-than-grateful response at the time. Given how mule-headed halflings always were, especially about things they knew comparatively little about (because *of course* that made perfect sense), Ren wouldn't have been surprised if she'd loaded those mushrooms right back into her basket the moment they'd turned their back on her. In some ways, that might've actually been preferable. Ren wasn't particularly enamored with the thought of some halfling tramping around their garden, and quickly discovered they were even *less* enthusiastic about it in practice.

Leave those alone, they thought, eyes narrowing as they watched the halfling prod at the start of their mushroom farm, a number of narrow logs, all stacked in a grid-like formation. Judging from the halfling's expression, she had no idea what she was looking at, rendering her insistence on messing with it all the more infuriating. *Exactly. It's not for you.*

But the halfling couldn't hear Ren – what with several paces' worth of garden and a window and, you know, Ren's *skull* separating them. So, the inevitable happened: the logs fell over.

"Told you so," they muttered under their breath, sour heat pooling beneath their skin. It had taken hours to put those logs together, and they didn't relish having to repeat the process once more. At least she hadn't broken anything that couldn't be fixed.

Yet.

Abandoning the mess she'd created in typical halfling fashion, without even a shred of shame, the halfling clomped over to the other side of the garden, where she promptly vanished from Ren's sight.

Smothering a curse between gritted teeth, Ren set down the fruits of today's foraging on the kitchen counter – an impressive assortment of mushrooms, sweet chestnuts, wild garlic and blackberries – and went to find a new vantage point. Dinner would have to be a matter for later. No way were they going to let this halfling roam around unsupervised.

Slinking across the floorboards like a shadow, Ren crept towards the living-room window, a half-moon opening along the cottage's front, framed in robin's-egg blue. They carefully nudged aside the thick veins of ivy their family had grown to serve as curtains; enough that only a single, narrow sunbeam spilled across the sparsely furnished space. Just because they'd noticed the halfling didn't mean the halfling needed to notice *them*. In fact, Ren would greatly prefer it if she didn't. Or, better yet, the halfling could just turn around and leave.

Sadly, things couldn't be so easy.

The halfling went right up to the front door and, after digging around in a vast array of bags and satchels that couldn't possibly mean anything good, produced a key.

A key! Not even Ren had a key, and their clan had been taking care of this place for decades!

Too bad, the indignation searing its way up Ren's throat would have to wait. The halfling had inserted the key into the lock and, discovering it unnecessary, had settled for simply turning the knob. A low creak then followed, unmistakable in its origin. If Ren was going to have any hope of keeping this halfling out of their house, they were going to have to act now.

"Oh, wow," the halfling said, near-breathless with wonder as she stepped into the entry hall, its exposed beam ceilings, each inlaid with loose swirls of living moss, unfurling overhead in a precise geometric pattern. "This place has held up really well. I was expecting some holes in the roof. Maybe some missing floorboards. But this—"

With teeth bared and arms raised, Ren leapt from the shadows and roared. It wasn't the fiercest of sounds – frankly, Ren had heard wolf cubs produce better – but it nonetheless had the intended effect. The halfling screamed, scrambling backwards without a second thought. Unfortunately, instead of racing out of the cottage like Ren had wanted, she slammed into the wall behind her at full-force, hard enough to send the beams overhead rattling and loose the carefully cultivated moss from its inlays.

Years of work, ruined in an instant.

"Stop! You're destroying it!" Ren shouted, dropping into a far less aggressive posture. It was one thing for the halfling to break the things they'd made. But the work of Ren's clan – well, that was something else entirely.

The halfling, however, wasn't listening. "Get out of my house!" she cried, kicking at a nearby cluster of moss. Perhaps she'd meant to launch it at Ren's face, but she only managed to send it fluttering weakly into the air.

"*Your* house?" Ren repeated, incredulous, their ears flattening with displeasure. "No. This is *my* house."

"Then why do I have a, uh…?" The halfling fumbled for something, temporarily lost in the eye-searingly yellow tangle of her skirts. "A key!" She raised it in a moment of triumph, holding it high for Ren to see.

They snorted, nostrils flaring around the halfling's heavily spiced scent, tantalizingly sweet even from a distance. "Is that supposed to mean something? Move your foot so I can try and salvage what you just broke."

The halfling didn't budge, which was hardly a surprise. She clearly had no concept of what now lay at her feet, the ruined tatters of moss scattered about her like bits of a desiccated corpse.

Ren knelt down anyway, well aware that doing so pushed them into range of the halfling's kick. But getting a boot to the face seemed a small price to pay if it meant scooping each green tuft into the safety of their palm.

Thankfully, the halfling's curiosity overshadowed her capacity for violence – at least for now. "What are you doing?" she asked, as if Ren hadn't already answered her question a second ago. Why couldn't halflings just *listen*?

They let out a harsh exhale, not even looking up as they continued to retrieve bits of moss. "All of this? Came from up there. My clan planted the spores years ago in the grooves lining each of the support beams. That's where they should've stayed, by the way; but apparently, destroying my mushroom farm wasn't enough for you."

Confusion streaked across the halfling's brow; and yet, there was something else, too, a glimmer in her eye that Ren might've called interest if they hadn't known better. Because, surely, no halfling would care one whit about goblin agricultural techniques.

Then again, maybe they would. If there was anything else as constant as the halfling penchant for running roughshod over everything, it was their love of food, made manifest in pantries so well stocked one would've thought these halflings were anticipating a several-centuries-long siege. But those didn't happen to halflings, "peaceful", "jovial" people that they were.

Obviously, whoever had popularized that belief hadn't found themselves on the wrong end of a halfling adventurer's sword. But, admittedly, neither had Ren, too young to have even constituted a spark in their mother's eye the last time a dark lord had plunged the Realm into chaos. Still, something dark simmered in their belly as they looked upon this particular halfling, her obnoxiously bright clothing as damning as her cluelessness. *Ugh.* Why couldn't she just *leave*?

"I'm talking about those logs you knocked over on your way in," Ren explained, even though she didn't deserve it. "But at least *that* I can fix. This"– they gestured around themself – "maybe not, and definitely not completely. This probably comes as a surprise to you, but cultivating edible moss isn't something you can do on a whim, especially like this."

The halfling's cheeks pinked. "Well, you shouldn't have been doing it here anyway," she declared with a huff, arms crossing over her chest. "This is my grandmother, Angelica Underburrow's, house. A house which she passed down to me, Pansy Underburrow. So, like I said, this is *my house*." She spoke the last two words emphatically, as if that would somehow render them true.

Ridiculous.

"If this is your grandmother's house, then why hasn't she lived here in over twenty years?" Ren asked, finally straightening back up.

The halfling – Pansy – scowled as she plucked a bit of moss from the front of her sweater. She gave it a quick sniff, then flicked it over to Ren. "Because she was old and needed help. That's why she moved back to town – to Haverow. Now, you have your moss; so, you can go back to … wherever it is you came from."

"I'm not going anywhere," Ren replied, standing as tall as they could manage. Thankfully, this put them at least an inch above Pansy. "Your grandmother left this place to rot. If not for my family, it would be exactly as you said: full of holes and missing pieces. Instead, it's thriving. Look at how much *life* there is now!"

Bellflower. Creeping thyme. Stonecrop. Selfheal. Impossible to name every plant that coiled along the walls or from in-between the floorboards. Then there were the animals: the fireflies that slept inside paper lanterns repurposed to serve as their nests; the mice with questionable taste that lived in an old, halfling-style armchair too soft for Ren's liking; and, of course, there was Pig, currently snoring downstairs, no doubt.

Somehow, none of this mattered to Pansy.

"This sort of mess belongs outside, you know." She scowled. "Not to mention, no one asked you to do anything in the first place."

Ren stared at her, incredulous. "What does asking have to do with any of it?"

"Oh, right. Yes. Of course. Silly me." Pansy bopped the heel of her palm against her temple. "I'm speaking to a goblin. You lot never ask; you simply take!"

"Better than letting go to waste what others could use!" Ren snapped back, teeth flashing as fire roared inside their chest. "My clan needed a place to live. This house was empty. Clearly, no one was using it; so, why shouldn't they?"

"Because. It's. Not. *Theirs*."

"Fine. So, a perfectly good home falls into disrepair such that no one can use it. You honestly think that's better?"

"I—" Pansy snapped her mouth shut, brow furrowing as she considered Ren's words. Whatever heat had ignited between them suddenly cooled, quelled by the need to think rather than simply feel. "Stealing is wrong," she declared at last, albeit without her earlier fervor.

Ren sighed. "At least you had enough sense to actually stop and think about it. Surprising for a halfling. Doesn't change the fact that you're *wrong*, which, for the record, is far less of a shock."

Fresh crimson streaked across the bridge of Pansy's nose. "Wrong or not, this is still my house, and I fully intend to live in it." As if to drive her point home, she slipped the vast assortment of bags from her shoulders and allowed them to fall to the floor with a resounding *thump*.

"What a coincidence," Ren remarked, their tone a touch too biting to be considered droll. "Because I was thinking the exact same thing."

Pansy's eyes bulged. "No! Absolutely not. You need to leave. Go be with your"– she gestured vaguely with one hand – "clan – or however you prefer to call it. I'm certain you'll be far more comfortable there anyway. This is clearly a *halfling* burrow, not a cave. Hardly suitable for a goblin like yourself."

Ren's chest constricted at the thought of returning to their clan. If only such a thing were possible. But duty bound them to this cottage, and here they would stay. How shameful it would be to return now, after only a day, rendering their word barely worth the breath that had fueled it.

Swallowing around the lump that had knotted in their throat, Ren said, "I'm quite comfortable here, actually. You'd be surprised how cave-like a so-called 'burrow' can be. But thank you for your concern."

Pansy huffed. "I'm trying to be nice here—"

"Oh, are you?" Ren cocked their head to the side, ears perking up in mock surprise. "I honestly couldn't tell. Because where I come from, we don't call someone who barges in unannounced, breaks things that aren't theirs and insults others 'nice'; we call them a—"

"Okay! Okay! I get it!" Pansy said, raising both hands in

surrender. "You're right. I haven't been very nice. But, in my defense, I didn't expect to find my grandmother's cottage already... *inhabited*." She ground out the word with something like a grimace, as if it physically pained her to acknowledge an otherwise readily apparent fact.

"If my presence is such a problem," Ren said, crossing their arms over their chest, "then feel free to go back to your village. That way you'll never have to see me again."

A strange expression took hold of Pansy at that, pinching her features together in a way Ren couldn't quite parse. It wasn't sadness or frustration or anything nearly so simple; but, rather, a current of something old and deep-seated, like a snarl of roots forced to grow around an obstacle.

"I can't do that," Pansy said, averting her gaze for the first time. "I need... I need to stay here."

There was a certainty to that statement, a level of conviction that Ren found admirable. But there was also desperation buzzing beneath that hard veneer, like a hive of frenzied hornets. Whatever had driven Pansy to this cottage, it would not be so easily dismissed; not even by an unwanted goblin like themself.

It was then that Pansy's expression brightened, understanding flashing in the hazel rings of her irises. "You understand that, right? That I *need* this cottage."

Her stare was back upon Ren, now with an added layer of expectation that hooked beneath their skin. They eyed her warily, uncertainty itching along their spine. "And? That doesn't change the fact that I need it too." *That my clan needs it.*

"Okay, but one of us can surely make better use of it than the other, no?"

"Of course," Ren answered quickly, so assured of their own need that they didn't think to consider where Pansy was going with this. What could possibly trump ensuring their clan survived the coming winter?

"So, that person should get the cottage. Easy. Problem solved."

Easy? The gall of this halfling ... "And how exactly are we going to determine that?" Ren asked, eyebrows arching. "You and I both know that words alone won't suffice here."

Then again, perhaps they were giving Pansy too much credit. She opened her mouth only to shut it again, whatever she'd meant to say lost beneath the press of her teeth. Ren nearly scoffed. Had Pansy seriously believed that they would simply take her at her word? Relinquish their clan's last and only lifeline because a *halfling* told them to?

Yes, answered Pansy's expression, the wide-eyed look of panic as she scrambled for another way forward. How self-centered she must be to think that her people's distrust of goblins hadn't sown similar seeds among the clans, too used to bearing the weight of their kin's sins that they no longer expected anything else. And yet, at the same time, she'd displayed a very real capacity for understanding. Instead of digging her heels in and continuing to speak about the cottage in terms Ren neither recognized nor cared for, Pansy had stepped beyond the bounds of her own culture and *listened*; something the monolithic halfling in Ren's mind would've never done. Maybe that was why they were still willing to hear her out.

"I've got it!" Pansy exclaimed, her expression sparking with yet another idea. "For now, we'll both live here. But if either one of us decides to move out, then that person forfeits their right to the cottage. Hard to make use of a home if you don't live in it, right?"

Ren blinked, wondering if they'd simply misheard. "I'm sorry, but did you just say you want to live *together?*"

"Well, it's not exactly my first choice," Pansy said with a shrug that was far too nonchalant given the circumstances. "But, like I said, I really need to live here, so I'll tolerate it. And just in case you get any bright ideas about forcing me out: no breaking each other's stuff. That's rule number one."

Ah. So, that was the halfling's real plan. She wanted to push Ren out, and judging from the grin on her face, she really thought she could manage it. A laughable thought. It would take more than some unpleasant behavior and halfling decor to convince Ren to turn their back on their clan.

"Fine," Ren agreed, their lips parting around a razor-edged smile; what Ren thought might be Pansy's first clue that she'd made a grave miscalculation. "But that rule extends to the cottage itself, too. We can only add to what's already there. Unless something is broken or needs to be repaired. In that case, we both need to decide on a solution together."

"Sounds fair to me!" Pansy chirped, then shoved a familiar hand, soft and sun-kissed, out towards Ren. "We have a deal then?"

A strange tremor curled in Ren's stomach as they stared down at the proffered palm. They'd touched it before, the memory of yesterday rising, unbidden, to the forefront of their mind, bringing with it a flash of remembered heat. So, why then, did an entirely similar prospect suddenly root them to the spot?

Probably just unease, they told themselves, reaching out to grip Pansy's hand before their hesitation could turn awkward.

Pansy, meanwhile, gave Ren's hand one quick, businesslike pump, then pulled away just as swiftly. Less than a second's worth of contact, and still it lingered, a tingling warmth that buzzed against Ren's skin, ever-insistent.

Did Pansy feel it too? they wondered, fingers flexing in a vain effort to chase the sensation away. It might've been just their imagination, but Ren swore that Pansy's fingers curled into the folds of her skirts a touch harder than before.

"Great," Pansy said, her voice coming out oddly strangled.

"I'm, uh, Pansy, by the way."

"I know. You already told me."

"Oh, right." Red bloomed high on Pansy's cheeks. "I forgot."

"Obviously." A beat. Then, grudgingly, "My name is Ren."

"Ren," Pansy confirmed with a nod. "I'll remember that. Now, with all that settled, I'm going to go ahead and take a look around. And don't you even *think* of throwing my stuff out behind my back while I'm gone. That, may I remind you, would be cheating."

"Don't flatter yourself," Ren said with a derisive snort. "As if I'd need to cheat to get *you* out." Then, with a sharp twist of their heel, they headed for the garden, pointedly leaving Pansy – and her plethora of bags – behind.

Granted, this didn't stop Pansy from calling out after them, the need to have the last word in all things evidently yet another universally halfling trait. "Don't forget to take off your shoes before coming back inside! Remember: dirt belongs *outside*, not in the house!"

We'll see about that, Ren thought with a smirk. Because now they had an idea – a very, very good idea – one that Pansy was all but guaranteed not to like.

3
Pansy

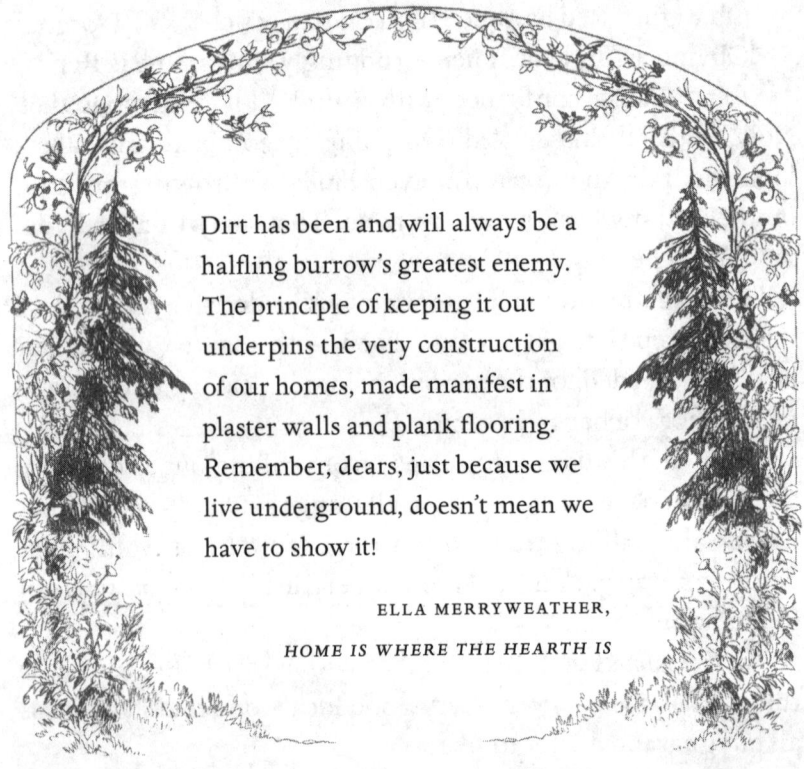

Dirt has been and will always be a halfling burrow's greatest enemy. The principle of keeping it out underpins the very construction of our homes, made manifest in plaster walls and plank flooring. Remember, dears, just because we live underground, doesn't mean we have to show it!

ELLA MERRYWEATHER,
HOME IS WHERE THE HEARTH IS

Although Pansy had been anything but serious when she'd made that quip about getting a new goblin housemate, it seemed the universe was determined to have the last laugh, even if it came entirely at her expense.

How to Lose a Goblin in Ten Days

To say that today hadn't gone according to plan would've been a tremendous understatement. Granted, Pansy's three-point "plan" relied on a generous interpretation of the word; its second step, lodged firmly between "acquire cottage" and "live happily ever after", little more than a long series of question marks. But even so, finding her grandmother's cottage – *her* cottage – beset by a longtime squatter didn't seem like the sort of situation any amount of foresight could've solved.

Though, perhaps said squatter wasn't quite so longtime as they would've liked her to believe. As Pansy wound her way through the cottage's expansive halls, she couldn't help but notice that most rooms were largely bare. With more plants than furnishings, the cottage seemed closer to an overgrown garden than an actual home. And while Pansy could believe that goblins didn't share her own people's propensity for decorating every last shred of available space, surely even they needed more than a tattered, halfling-style armchair and a handful of other equally worn pieces.

So, Ren lied to me. What a surprise. Pansy scowled, more frustrated with herself than anything else. Only a fool would take a smirking goblin's claim at face value, especially in matters of ownership. But she'd confront Ren about it later. Right now, there was still so much to explore.

Because unlike her parents' burrow in Haverow (and halfling burrows in general), the cottage wasn't confined to just a single level. Instead, it pushed deep into the earth, leading Pansy lower and lower via a series of wooden steps. There, the polished floorboards of upstairs gave way to rich, black dirt (necessitating a quick trip back up to retrieve her shoes), and the air, once bright and warm, was cooled and thickened with moisture. If Pansy hadn't known better, she'd have thought she'd just stepped into a cave. But this wasn't a cave; this was a *burrow* – just one that was a little rougher around the edges than most.

An expansion in progress! Yes, Pansy concluded with a satisfied nod, smiling at her own good thinking. Clearly, her grandmother – or perhaps whoever had owned the cottage before her – had simply not gotten around to putting in proper walls or floors. Once those were in place, there would be no question that this was a halfling burrow. But until then...

"I suppose a few carpets would go a long way," Pansy mused, surveying the space. "Maybe some nice tapestries, too – to cover the moss growing along the walls. And those icky mushrooms. But then again..." She tapped a finger against her chin, considering. "They are kind of useful, glowing like that. Who knows how dark it'd be down here otherwise."

Far too dark for any halfling to see; that was for sure. Even now, Pansy struggled to navigate the murky gloom, ever-pulsating with eerie bioluminescence. It was no wonder, then, that she eventually tripped, her foot catching on a bit of raised stonework, jutting just high enough to be a hazard.

She went down hard, landing in a graceless heap. The dirt, at least, was soft where she fell; though Pansy couldn't bring herself to feel grateful for it. The sting of indignity was too great to be soothed by such a small mercy.

Ignoring the twinge that had hooked into her ankle – a dull throb that was hardly worth any measure of concern – Pansy staggered to her feet. She dusted herself off, grimacing at the dampness that now marred her skirt in twin points by her knees. Hopefully, getting the stains out wouldn't take too much scrubbing.

Cursing her clumsiness, Pansy whirled around in search of her inanimate assailant. Her eyes landed on a small, stone circle, jutting out of otherwise unbroken earth; not quite a dais, but too large to be a mere steppingstone. It sat alone at the space's midpoint, its placement purposeful. But for what, Pansy couldn't say; unless it was simply there to trip the unaware.

Squatting down, she squinted closer at the flat stonework, her fingertips skimming across its surface. Strange swirls unfurled beneath the pads of her fingers, flowing into one another like the tide. They clung to the stone's edge, creating a circle within a circle. Indecipherable, yet familiar nonetheless.

"They're runes," she whispered, awe sweeping the breath from her lungs. She'd seen them before, stitched into her grandmother's favorite, magically warming blanket. Not these same runes – it wouldn't make much sense for a random stone to heat up – but similar enough that a thread of recollection, nestled somewhere deep in Pansy's brain, pulled taut.

"I wonder what they're for," she murmured, a question her own limited knowledge of magic would struggle to answer. That was the realm of elves and gnomes; not halflings, who "should know better than to muck about with that nonsense", as her mother had once put it. But perhaps there was a clue in her surroundings.

She glanced around, her eyes straining against the greenish half-light. However, apart from a couple of dusty old rugs, rolled up and shoved in a corner, there wasn't much to be found; this part of the cottage was just as empty as the last.

That being said, there *was* a stone archway embedded in the wall ahead of her, its surface decorated with an intricate pattern of drooping wolfsbane, identical to the plants growing along its base. But it led nowhere, its center revealing nothing but flat, unblemished rock. No seams or anything. Just another unfinished project.

"Add it to the list," Pansy grumbled.

Still, those runes did *something*. Was it too much to hope that they might help her with her current goblin predicament? Maybe. But that wasn't going to stop Pansy from noting them down on the small notepad she usually kept on hand. Just in case.

Had Ren already come across them? she wondered as she slipped the notepad back into her apron pocket, her shopping list now accompanied by a crude rendition of the runes at her feet. Better not to take any chances, she decided.

Seizing one of the old rugs she'd spotted earlier, Pansy dragged it over to where the stone was. She unfurled it, coughing as the motion loosed what must have been a couple of decades' worth of dust, and laid it out over the runes.

"There!" she said, smiling at her handiwork, the slight protrusion that remained easily dismissed as one of many wrinkles. "Totally hidden."

It was then that something solid brushed against her leg, quelling her triumph with a sudden deluge of ice-cold fear. Pansy jumped, letting out a high-pitched squeal that she hoped wouldn't make its way upstairs. Looking down, she found a familiar pig staring up at her, its head cocked to the side in confusion.

Pansy let out a breath, the tension unspooling from her shoulders. "Oh, it's just you, little thief." Bending down, she gave the creature a light scritch underneath the chin, which it received all too eagerly. "That wasn't a compliment, by the way," she added, when the pig pushed itself more squarely against her palm.

After a minute of petting, punctuated by ever-more-pleased-sounding snorts, Pansy finally withdrew her hand, much to the pig's dissatisfaction. When it realized it couldn't persuade

Pansy to resume her ministrations, it snuffled over to the rug and began pawing at it with one cloven hoof.

"No, no, no. Let's not do that," Pansy said, gently nudging the pig away with one hand. "It'll be our little secret, okay?"

Thankfully, the pig's listening skills seemed to have improved since their encounter in the forest. And though it did give her a dubious look, as if to say, *You're not fooling anyone*, before trotting off, at this point Pansy would take whatever she could get.

There was dirt on the floor – in the hallway and in the living room. A whole trail of it, too thick and uniform to have simply hitched a ride on someone's shoes. No, this looked deliberate, like someone had filled a sifter full of dirt and shaken it with every step, more heavy-handed than even the local baker, who always piled the powdered sugar a mile high. As for the culprit – well, that proved equally clear.

"Ren!" Pansy bellowed, loud enough to send whatever had been nestling in nearby fronds of bracken scampering away in terror.

"There's no need to yell," Ren said once she'd stomped her way into the kitchen, a narrow, galley-style room outfitted with dark green cabinetry and whitewashed paneling that had been nearly swallowed whole by the encroaching coil of some variety of plant life.

"*No need to—*" Pansy cut herself off with an aggrieved scoff, fury boiling red across her skin. "I have every reason to yell! *You*"– she jabbed an accusatory finger in their direction – "dumped a whole bunch of dirt in the house! After I told you not to!"

"I did," Ren agreed, not even so much as glancing her way

as they pulled a wicker basket towards them from across the counter.

Pansy blinked. "Is that really all you have to say for yourself?"

"What more are you expecting?" they asked, turning towards her at last. "We both agreed that we could only add to what's already here, and I added soil. I did nothing wrong."

Pansy would argue that the self-satisfied curl tugging at the corner of their mouth was proof enough that they had, in fact, done something wrong. But in that moment, she could only gape, her thoughts brought to a complete standstill by the sheer audacity of it all. In what world did *dirt* count as a worthwhile addition to any home?

Shaking her head, Pansy threw up her hands and said, "Fine. I'll just clean it up myself."

"Oh no you won't," Ren countered, their expression hardening. "No destroying each other's stuff, remember? Another part of our agreement."

"It's dirt! It's no one's '*stuff*'."

"Well, I'm telling you that it's mine. How else am I supposed to make this place more cave-like?"

"This is a halfling burrow! It's not supposed to be cave-like in any respect. If you want to live in a cave that badly, then just go home!"

Ren canted up their chin, obstinate to the end. "No."

"Well, I'm not living in a house full of dirt," Pansy declared, crossing her arms over her chest. "It's unsanitary."

"Good thing you can always leave," Ren replied with a shrug. "No one's forcing you to stay."

"Except it's *my* house! My grandmother wrote it into her will and everything! I can actually prove that, by the way; unlike your little story about your clan having lived here for years.

Because I looked around, and this place is practically empty! You *lied* to me, Ren."

"Ah. That." A pause, filled with the sounds of restless shuffling, of Ren turning back towards their basket and removing its contents, one by one; proof, in Pansy's mind, that she'd caught them red-handed. At last, Ren said, calm as ever, "I didn't lie to you. My clan has been using this cottage for decades now."

"Then where is all your stuff? And don't tell me that goblins don't use furniture because that's nonsense, and I won't believe it."

Ren let out a harsh breath, nostrils flaring as they cast a look up at the wooden beams overhead – seeking divine guidance or perhaps just patience. "Is there any point explaining it to you?" they asked, bitterness oozing from every syllable. "You've already come to the conclusion that I'm a liar, and I'd rather not waste my time beating my head against a rock that refuses to be moved."

Pansy stiffened, not sure whether to take Ren's comment as an insult. It probably was, all things considered – even if being called a "rock" was hardly the worst thing in the world. Still, Pansy wanted answers, not a crash course in goblin put-downs. She said, "I'm not so prideful that I can't admit when I'm wrong."

Ren scoffed. "You're a miracle among halflings, then. But – fine. I only became this cottage's Caretaker recently. Yesterday, in fact. This place used to be my aunt's responsibility, but she – she got sick. The clan needed someone else to shoulder the burden in her stead."

Seeing the way Ren's throat bobbed, how it snagged on the knot of emotion that had stoppered it, Pansy couldn't help but soften, the jagged memory of her own grandmother's recent illness still as sharp as ever. "I'm sorry," she said, the heat of annoyance evaporating from her skin as quickly as the early-morning dew in summer. "Is it serious?"

"Yes," Ren replied, a hoarse croak that spoke volumes. Far more than they'd wanted to convey, it seemed, because they immediately rushed to clear their throat. "As for the furniture, if I'd asked, my aunt would have left some things behind. But right now, she and the clan can make better use of whatever used to be here. So, I told them I'd be fine with only the necessities."

"And the absolute barest of them at that, given what I've seen..."

Ren shrugged. "Goblins have all learned to make do with little. I'm no exception."

Pansy paused, considering. "You called yourself the cottage's 'Caretaker'. That's an interesting choice of words."

"I'm sure you halflings would much rather call me a squatter," Ren snapped, their voice sharpening once again.

"Well, it wouldn't be inaccurate," Pansy shot back. "But my point is that 'Caretaker' is an awfully weighty word. Serious." Plus, there was something about Ren's explanation in general that had struck her as odd. Granted, it could've just been her imagination, but it almost seemed like they didn't actually want to be here. So, why stay?

Unless they had no other option...

"Because it *is* serious," Ren snarled, whirling around to face her once more. "This will probably be lost on you, but there's a beauty in living *with* the natural world instead of in spite of it. Do you even know how many trees were felled to build this cottage? How much earth was shifted? How many plants and animals were displaced?"

"I'm guessing a lot, judging from your tone."

"Yes. A lot," Ren said, their voice flattening with contempt. "That's why it's so important to make space for nature, to take only what is necessary and no more. Anyone who refuses to honor this truth is a fool, as blind as the snake that eats its own tail."

"All right," Pansy said, the word scraping across her tongue like an anchor. "But you don't seem very, um, happy? To be here, that is. I mean, you called it a 'burden' earlier, so . . ."

Ren blinked at her, their ears pricking up in what Pansy figured was an expression of surprise – but only for a beat. Soon, they were drooping once more, falling in time with the heavy sigh that escaped Ren's lips. "What I want doesn't matter."

"Of course it does!" Pansy protested, the words exploding out of her with more force than she'd intended. But that sort of weary resignation just didn't sit right with her – especially when it came at the cost of her own cottage. "What's the point of doing anything if it doesn't make you happy? Honestly, I—" She snapped her mouth shut, words too personal for someone who was still just a stranger crashing against the backs of her teeth. *I would still be back in Haverow if I hadn't put my own happiness first.*

"Fine," Ren said with something like a huff. "Then what I *want* is for you to stop bothering me." And with that, they turned on their heel yet again, seemingly convinced that the sight of their back would be enough to deter Pansy from making further conversation.

Unfortunately for Ren, the dirt crunching beneath Pansy's feet had been a declaration of war, one she fully intended to win. If being as irritating as possible was the way to do it, then she would dedicate herself to the task as wholly as a cleric committed themselves to prayer. From now on, she'd be the gnat buzzing in Ren's ear, utterly relentless, and if that alone didn't convince the goblin to leave – well, Pansy was certain she could come up with something else.

But for now, she stepped forward, wedging herself into the space over Ren's shoulder; not close enough to touch, but certainly well beyond polite boundaries. "What are you doing?" she asked, noting the way Ren stiffened in response. *Perfect.*

"Cooking. Obviously," they muttered, an odd tremor hooking into their voice as they ducked their head to the side, long hair drawing over their face like a veil. "And in the interest of pre-empting your next question, I'm making a warm chestnut and mushroom salad."

"What kind of mushrooms?" Pansy asked, curiosity, for the moment, overwhelming her desire to annoy as she peered at the tiny white buttons on Ren's cutting board. Although the mushrooms had been divested of their stems, Ren evidently hadn't gotten much further in their prep work, despite the knife in their hand.

In retrospect, the combination of "goblin" and "sharp object" should've sent alarm bells blaring in Pansy's head. Growing up in Haverow, there'd been no shortage of stories about goblins and other servants of the dark lords committing acts of violence against poor, unsuspecting halflings, the subject of Lillishire ever-present, even if not mentioned outright. And yet, standing here, Pansy felt no danger from Ren; not even when they whirled on her in a flash of sharp teeth and a sneer.

"Edible ones," they replied, upper lip curling. "Unlike those Bloodletters you stuffed into your basket the other day."

Masking the fresh rush of scarlet to her face with a huff, Pansy said, "Edible is hardly the sort of measure you want to use for a dish. As far as bars go, that one is practically on the floor."

"My cooking is fine." Ren scowled. "Besides, it's not like I'm making this for you or anything. There's no reason for you to have an opinion on the matter."

"Then why do you have enough ingredients for two servings?" Pansy asked, eyebrows arching as she pointed at the cutting board.

"I – I like having leftovers."

Pansy snorted. "That's about as believable as what I said yesterday about using those stupid Bloodletter Shrooms as decoration."

"Believe what you want," Ren said, turning back to their cutting board with an air of finality.

But, of course, things couldn't end there – and not just because Pansy had thoroughly committed herself to the cause of annoying Ren into submission. No, if there was one thing she simply couldn't abide, it was watching someone struggle in the kitchen. And Ren was struggling. Badly. For as much as their slices were perfectly even, each chunk of mushroom the same size as the last, they were slow – painfully, horribly slow. Like take-all-night kind of slow. Suddenly, it made sense why they'd started preparing dinner well before sundown.

"*Gods*," Pansy groaned. "This is painful to watch. Give me that."

Not even waiting for Ren to agree, she reached for the knife, pulling it free despite Ren's shouts of protest. Although Pansy would acknowledge, at least privately, that she'd risked cutting either one (or even both) of them with her impatience, in the end, it had worked out; so, what was the problem?

"Go get the other ingredients," Pansy said, quickly shooing Ren away with one hand before she began chopping up the mushrooms. In a matter of seconds, she'd accomplished what would have doubtless taken Ren at least an hour, given their earlier pace.

Honestly, this should have pleased Ren. Pansy had done them

a favor. But not even a mote of gratitude filtered through their venomous expression.

"You've ruined it!" they cried, jerking briefly against what Pansy assumed was the urge to wrestle their knife back before better sense prevailed.

"How am I ruining it?" She gestured to the chopped-up mushrooms. Although her knife-work was not as exacting as her mother's, it was still perfectly respectable. She might not have made the most even of cuts, especially compared to the couple Ren had managed to get through before she'd elected to put them (and her, quite frankly) out of their misery. But a bit of varying thickness never hurt anyone – so long as the pieces remained comfortably bite-sized, which they did.

Maybe Pansy's mother would disagree. *Presentation is just as important as taste*, she'd always say, chiding Pansy for every misshapen meatball, every cracked pie crust. But aesthetics alone wouldn't save a dry, under-seasoned chicken breast cooked within an inch of its life. Nor would it fill anyone's stomach come dinnertime when half the prep still wasn't done.

"You made it ugly," Ren groused, looking down at the fruits of her labor with unvarnished disgust.

Pansy rolled her eyes. "My gods, you're worse than my mother. Maybe *you* should be the one to go back to Haverow. You'll fit right in with that need for everything to look perfect."

They shot her a withering look. "I'd rather die, thanks."

"Well, I'd rather not. So, hurry up and bring me those ingredients. I already feel myself wasting away from hunger."

"You're ridiculous."

Still, for all their bluster and exaggerated sighs, Ren did as she'd asked, retrieving a number of items from a nearby cabinet and depositing them on the counter beside her. The only problem: aside from the mushrooms and chestnuts, Pansy recognized not a single one.

"What's all this?" she asked, squinting at the assortment of strange plants Ren had brought her. Where was the cooking oil? The cider vinegar? The standard assortment of seasonings she'd come to rely on in her everyday cooking?

"Ingredients," Ren said blandly. "For the salad."

"These aren't ingredients. They're just a bunch of weird plants! See?" She seized a tightly wrapped bundle of reed-like stems and thrust it out towards them. "How am I supposed to make a vinaigrette with a bunch of leaves?"

Ren blinked. "Do you not know what oilflute is?"

"No?"

At this point, Pansy assumed Ren would offer some kind of explanation. Evidently, she was just as knowledgeable about plants as she was about mushrooms, which was to say "not very". But Ren didn't say a thing. Instead, they laughed. And this wasn't just a giggle or a small chuckle. No, Ren full-on *howled* with laughter, to the point where they could no longer stand upright. Their body shook as they doubled over, hands clutching at their stomach, as if it ached from the strain.

"Stop laughing!" Pansy snapped, heat sparking in her anew. Unfortunately, her injured pride found their subsequent grin no more soothing.

Wiping the last bits of mirth from their eyes, Ren said, "I knew you halflings were an ignorant bunch, but to think that ignorance even extends to the one thing you can never seem to have enough of! The irony, it's – dare I say it? – delicious!"

"Excuse me?" Pansy demanded, an icy jolt now accompanying the fire licking its way up the sides of her face.

Ren's smile, however, only stretched wider. "You know, we

goblins joke that halflings must've uncovered the secret to time-travel magic, because you all seem to have more feast days than there are days on the calendar."

"Now, that's not true—"

"Isn't it?" Ren cocked their head to the side. "Could've fooled me with the state of your pantries, always stuffed to the brim. Though I suppose yours is rather lacking at the moment. How dreadful it must be to have nothing but 'weird', 'nasty' goblin ingredients at your disposal. *Gosh!* What will the neighbors think? Better go back to Haverton, where you can have a 'proper' kitchen with 'proper' ingredients like you so *justly* deserve."

"First of all, it's Have-*row*; not Haver-*ton*. Secondly, never once did I call your ingredients 'weird' or 'nasty' or any variation thereof – *nor* was I thinking it," Pansy quickly added when she saw Ren open their mouth in protest. "So, stop using your imagination to justify your cruelty towards me. And thirdly, I'm not leaving, so either show me how to use these ingredients properly or live with the consequences of whatever I make in the absence of proper instruction."

If she wasn't so furious, Pansy might have laughed at the wide-eyed look of shock Ren gave her, their lips parting uselessly, like a gasping fish out of water. Had they seriously expected her to turn and run because of a few mean words? Unfortunately for them, her time in Haverow had trained her to weather almost anything, her skin thickened beneath the brunt of a thousand tiny cuts. There, she'd already been "the other", the odd halfling girl too impatient, too *adventurous* for her own good, and every one of her many facets had, over time, been scrutinized into a flaw.

At least, Ren *knew* they were being cruel; getting her to leave was the point. But the halflings of Haverow would look upon Pansy's departure with nothing but confusion, wondering what could have possibly pushed her to leave their "perfect" village behind – as if the decades' worth of unvarnished criticism had been a kindness rather than a constant torment!

"Here," Ren said at last, grabbing a bowl from one of the cabinets and extending it towards her; the closest thing, it seemed, she'd be getting to an apology.

"What am I supposed to do with that?"

"You wanted to make a vinaigrette, right? Squeeze the oilflute in your hand over the bowl."

Pansy's expression turned dubious. "I don't see how a bunch of weeds are going to help with that, but okay." She did as instructed, eyes widening when a steady trickle of cloudy, milk-white fluid escaped from in-between her clenched fingers, pooling in a shallow puddle at the bottom of the bowl.

It wasn't anything like cooking oil in appearance, but in terms of consistency, the liquid the oilflute had produced was practically identical. Slick with a definite thickness, though not to the point where Pansy would call it viscous. Her curiosity piqued, she lifted her fingers, now glistening with an oily sheen, to her nose and gave them a sniff. A mild, savory aroma greeted her; far less pungent than what she'd expected. But what about the taste?

"Oh!" Pansy jerked away, her features fluttering like a pair of shutters, newly cast open. "It tastes almost like ... olive oil! That's incredible! The flavor's a bit milder, perhaps, but that shouldn't be too much of an issue. What about vinegar? I assume you have something for that too?"

Ren nodded and retrieved a jug from a narrow pantry, which proved just as sparse as the rest of the cottage.

"What's that?" Pansy asked as Ren set the jug down on the counter with a dull thump, enough to send the clear liquid inside sloshing.

"Vinegar," they replied, the corner of their mouth quirking up into a lopsided smirk that shouldn't have made them look nearly so handsome, especially after the cruelty they'd just lobbed from those same lips. "Made from sugarfern, which, I'm guessing, you've never heard of either."

"Well, it's a goblin ingredient, right? So it's no surprise I wouldn't be familiar with it." Pansy shrugged, her attempt at nonchalance thwarted by the visible tightness pulling along her shoulders.

"Which is exactly my point," Ren continued, their words heavy with emphasis. "You have no idea what you're doing. If you want to play around, go make mud pies outside like the children do. Don't waste valuable food on this nonsense of yours."

Pansy's lips peeled back around a grin that was all sharpness and teeth. "What? Afraid I'm going to do a better job than you? That my 'ugly' salad will taste better than whatever you were going to come up with?"

They snorted. "You're delusional."

Pansy cocked her head to the side. "Am I? Shall we make another bet then? If I'm really as 'delusional' as you say I am, this'll be an easy win for you."

A beat. "Fine. I'm listening."

"Right. So, if I manage to make a warm mushroom salad that's good – not just edible – with the ingredients you've laid out here, the kitchen becomes my exclusive domain. That means you leave it exactly as you found it every time you use it. No weird changes and definitely *no dirt*."

"And what if you don't?"

"Then I'll leave the kitchen to you and promise not to bother you from now on when you cook. Call it your safe haven."

"From annoying halflings?" Ren asked, arching a brow.

"From me," Pansy clarified. "If any other halflings choose to annoy you in there, that's on them."

Ren's eyes narrowed. "You better not be planning on siccing your friends on me."

Pansy barked out a laugh. "I don't think I could pay anyone in all of Halvenshire enough to come here for the sole purpose of pestering you." Except maybe Blossom. Though she suspected her best friend would help her for free.

"Hmm." Ren fell silent for a moment, considering. Then: "All right. I'll take that wager. But I'm staying here to supervise. I don't want you wasting food out of ignorance."

"I'm perfectly capable of figuring out flavor profiles myself," Pansy said with a huff.

Ren remained dubious, dismissing her words with a pointed roll of their eyes. Pansy might've found it insulting had their skepticism not ultimately been to her benefit. Unwilling to simply let her loose on the bounty they'd laid out before her, Ren insisted on explaining each of the ingredients, describing not just their flavors, but also how they were normally used.

Oilflute. Sugarfern. Beechmoss. Lichenberry. Pansy couldn't believe how many there were. What had once been nothing more than a tangle of strange weeds and foliage had unfurled into a fresh source of inspiration, seeding beneath her fingertips a desire to cook so great she could barely stand it. And not just because she wanted to win this latest bet.

To think that goblin cuisine, something she'd never given

much thought to until now, would awaken in her that same sense of wonder that had seized her the first time her mother had brought her into the kitchen as a young girl.

"This is going to taste *amazing*," Pansy said as she poured the mushrooms, now dressed in a mixture of vinegar, oilflute and lichenberry – the closest thing Ren had to a lemon – into a hot skillet alongside the peeled chestnuts. "Honestly, the smell is already making my mouth water, and the mushrooms haven't even started to brown yet."

"Whatever you say," Ren grumbled, their scowl now more pronounced than ever; no doubt because they agreed. Pansy had seen the way their nostrils had flared when the skillet let loose a cloud of savory steam, a tantalizing prelude to the symphony that would soon follow. Victory – or defeat, in Ren's case – would never taste better.

While the mushrooms continued simmering away, Pansy quickly chopped up some garlic and threw it into another bowl with some oilflute, vinegar and a yellow, tomato-like vegetable Ren had called ambervine. "This will be our dressing," Pansy explained as she mashed everything together, acutely aware of the way Ren seemed to be scrutinizing her every move – now, more so than ever.

"This is a lot of ingredients for one meal," Ren murmured, their eyebrows dragging low across their forehead.

"Is it? I think it's a pretty simple recipe, actually."

"I wouldn't have used most of these . . ."

"Then I'm glad I could give you some much-needed instruction." Pansy grinned.

Seeing that the liquid the mushrooms had released had finally cooked off, she tossed the finished dressing into the pan. A couple more stirs, enough to ensure that everything was properly coated, and she took the pan off the heat. "Now, to put everything together ... Ready to eat your words, Ren?"

"Just shut up and serve the food already," they snapped, arms snaking across their chest. "I can't believe you had the nerve to complain about *me* being slow . . ."

"*Ooh*. Is someone a sore loser?" Pansy teased, delighting in the hateful look Ren shot her way. "You should be grateful. After all, you still get a delicious meal out of this."

Granted, "delicious" turned out to be quite the understatement. Glorious was more like it. As the first bite crunched between Pansy's teeth, crisp lettuce marrying chewy mushrooms in a salty, sweet ceremony that was both familiar and new in equal parts, she found herself overcome with a sudden unshakable sense of certainty. *This* was what she'd been searching for.

"Wow," she murmured, lips parting around a swell of awe, bright and airy, like gossamer. "This tastes amazing."

Ren, meanwhile, said nothing. They didn't have to. The tip of their fork, resting against their lower lip, seemed caught between two competing impulses: the first, to keep the flavor, still clinging to the utensil's points, on their tongue; and the second, to prevent a second bite.

"So, it's my win, then?" Pansy asked, her expression overwhelmed by a near-face-splitting grin.

A curt nod, executed with something like a grimace, sealed her victory.

Make that one bet down. One more to go.

With her belly full and the day's exhaustion settling onto her bones like an especially rotund cat clambering onto its favorite armchair, Pansy decided it was time for bed.

The cottage, thankfully, was not without one. It sat at the center of the master bedroom – the only *real* bedroom, given the cottage's barely furnished state – an immense, towering structure of cast iron and ornate brass, polished to a near-blinding sheen. Though the craftsmanship was halfling in origin, with each whorl of brass fashioned into a budding bloom, it, like much of the cottage, had suffered a level of... call it encroachment. The four posts that would have once supported a canopy of fabric were draped in long trails of ivy, and instead of a down mattress there was a flat expanse of strange, spongy material.

Pressing a hand against it, Pansy conceded that it was not uncomfortable; though she did wonder whether her form would be forever etched into its surface once she'd laid upon it. An unnecessary concern, it turned out. The material sprang back into place the moment she removed her hand, leaving no evidence that she'd ever touched it.

Either way, this mattress, peculiar though it was, was preferable to sleeping on the floor, which Pansy had been a touch worried about during her initial tour of the cottage. Clearly the "necessities", as Ren had put it, included a bed – even if it didn't come with any sheets.

Thankfully, Pansy had plenty of those. She selected a set in soft, buttery yellow – one of her favorites by far – and spread them across the mattress with practiced ease. A horde of blankets, each woven from nearly a dozen different shades of yarn, soon followed, along with far more pillows than any one person could conceivably use, as demonstrated by the fact that most of them would migrate to the floor come morning. By the time she was finished, the bed looked almost exactly like the one she'd left behind in her parents' burrow. The ivy, of course, being the one key difference.

Pleased with her efforts, Pansy headed into the adjoining bathroom to finish getting ready for bed. She shivered as she crossed the threshold, the terracotta tiles cool against the soles of her feet, bare of socks for the first time since the start of the "dirt invasion". Thankfully, Ren had left the bathroom alone in that respect. Her slippers, hard-soled and warm, would protect her from the rest.

While she waited for the bath, a slate-gray tub crammed beneath the room's frosted window, Pansy organized her sizable collection of toiletries into the shallow cubbies that had been carved into the wall by the sink. Considering this was to be a permanent arrangement, she figured she might as well get things set up as she liked them. Certainly, before Ren had a chance to take over.

In a way, it was like a race. The goal? To infuse as much of herself into this cottage before Ren could do the same for themself. It reminded her of Pioneers of Plainsborough, a game she'd once played as a child, where each player sought to capture the most tiles on the wooden board in a bid to expand their respective "farms". Much to her peers' frustration (and her own delight), she'd taken to it like a duck to water, thoroughly sweeping the board every time she played. This situation with the cottage, she resolved, would be no different. She had already claimed the kitchen for herself, and now the master bed and bath too. A big win for the Pansy Dominion by anyone's standards, even with the added dirt.

And yet, somehow, Ren hadn't gotten the memo.

Pansy's eyes bulged as she padded back into the bedroom, the damp ends of her curls frizzing in the lingering steam. Because there was Ren, shoving aside her carefully manicured bedspread in favor of – you guessed it! – more moss.

"What are you doing?" she demanded, rushing over in a flurry of staccato slaps of slippers against hardwood; not even the shock of Ren's invasion could make her forget about her all-too-necessary footwear. "This is my bed!"

Ren paused just long enough to give her a withering, sidelong look, their long, pointed ears flattening against their skull in naked displeasure. "Just because you've thrown your stuff all over it doesn't make it yours." A point they punctuated by tossing one of Pansy's many pillows – a heavily embroidered sham with scalloped edges – at her face.

Pansy caught the pillow easily, setting it back onto the bed with a scowl. "We agreed not to destroy each other's things."

"How am I destroying anything? I'm just making some room."

Room. It was then that Pansy noticed Ren's clothing: a loose beige tunic that came down to their knees; far more like her own orange nightgown than the clothing she'd seen them wearing earlier. Her eyes widened anew, cold shock lancing through her nervous system.

"Oh, no. No, no, *no,*" she said, shaking her head again and again. "You're *not* sleeping here."

"Then where am I supposed to sleep exactly?" Ren asked, eyebrows arching. "This is the only bed in the entire house."

"I—" Pansy snapped her mouth shut. It was the only bed, wasn't it? But even so, did it really matter?

Definitely not, she decided after barely a second's worth of consideration. "Oh, I don't know. Maybe on the floor? Looks pretty cozy with all that dirt. Just like home, right?"

Ren scowled at her. "I'm not sleeping on the floor."

"If you put that moss . . . pad . . . thing"– she gestured towards the sheet of moss that had supplanted her pristine bedspread – "down, you can sleep on it instead."

"It's a blanket," they retorted, their tone as flat as the line of their mouth.

"Whatever," Pansy said with a shrug. "Call it what you want. All I know is that I'll be sleeping on the bed. *Alone*." And to prove it, she shoved the same blankets Ren had so rudely cast aside back into their rightful place. That sheet of moss be damned!

"Hey!" Ren shouted, barely managing to claw their mossy blanket into the safety of their arms before it fell to the floor.

"Oh, don't look at me like that," Pansy chided, once again the subject of the goblin's venomous stare. "It's just a bit of dirt. And you *love* dirt, don't you? That's why you covered the whole house in it, right?"

"You're acting like a child," they spat, yellow eyes blazing. "*No*. Worse than a child. At least a child knows how to share!"

"Maybe if there was someone worth sharing with, I would!"

"What if I just make you instead?"

Pansy's eyes widened as Ren reached down and grabbed a fistful of dirt. Slowly, they extended their hand, fingers still closed tightly around their devastating payload, until it hovered just over the bed.

"No," Pansy breathed, horror narrowing her throat. "You wouldn't dare."

"Wouldn't I?" Ren asked, the angle of their jaw brimming with triumph. "A little bit of dirt never bothered a goblin. But a halfling? Oh, I think that would bother them very, *very* much."

"But the floor . . ." Pansy protested.

"Is the floor," Ren explained slowly, as if speaking to an especially dim-witted child. "Would *you* like sleeping on the floor if there was a bed available? No? That's what I thought."

"Fine," Pansy said after a beat, masking her bruised ego with a dismissive huff. "But you need to stay on *your* half of the bed.

And to make sure that happens ..." She seized an armful of blankets and pillows, now jumbled in a haphazard mess, and dumped them into the middle of the bed. A bit of maneuvering later, and she'd fashioned them into a makeshift wall.

Ren spared it half a glance before letting out a derisive snort. "You really are careless in everything you do. That mess would fall over if you looked at it wrong."

"Then don't look at it," Pansy snapped, earning more mockery from Ren; this time in the form of an exaggerated roll of their eyes.

"Whatever makes you feel more secure," they said, finally returning the handful of dirt to the floor – something Pansy had never thought would fill her with any measure of relief. Dirt belonged outside; a fact she'd defend till her last breath. But with the sanctity of her bed hanging in the balance, what else could she choose?

"I'm just trying to ensure a certain degree of fairness," she insisted, hurriedly burrowing into the fluffy nest of bedding that comprised her side of the divide.

At least the bed's big, she thought, pulling the covers up to her chin. *Blanket wall or no. We probably won't even come near each other.*

And yet, something about the situation continued to speed her pulse, sending a strange flutter rooting deeper into her belly. For as much as this was nothing more than yet another installment in an ongoing string of unfortunate circumstances, there remained an undeniable sort of intimacy in the act of sharing a bed with someone. Sure, that someone was very much unwanted, but, given the state of Pansy's heart, that apparently didn't matter.

Each frenzied beat fed into the next, echoing so loudly in her own ears that it was a wonder Ren didn't hear it too. Sadly, no amount of deep breathing or calming mantras could assuage the static-like prickle that whispered across her skin. Every inch of her was alive, *buzzing*, suffused with an inescapable awareness of her surroundings – right down to the way the mattress dipped slightly beneath Ren's weight.

"Your sleeping arrangements are excessive," they grumbled, shifting beside her, each movement another jolt. If Pansy hadn't known better, she would have thought their behavior purposeful. A way to aggravate her further.

"Well, excuse me for preferring to stay warm," Pansy sneered over the tremor that ping-ponged through her chest, jittery and electric. "Now, *goodnight.*"

And with that, she rolled onto her side, as if turning her back on Ren might put them out of her mind just as swiftly. Their sharing a bed was out of necessity. Nothing more. And Pansy would remind herself of this fact as many times as it took; until the words became as second nature as the apathy that should have accompanied them.

4
Ren

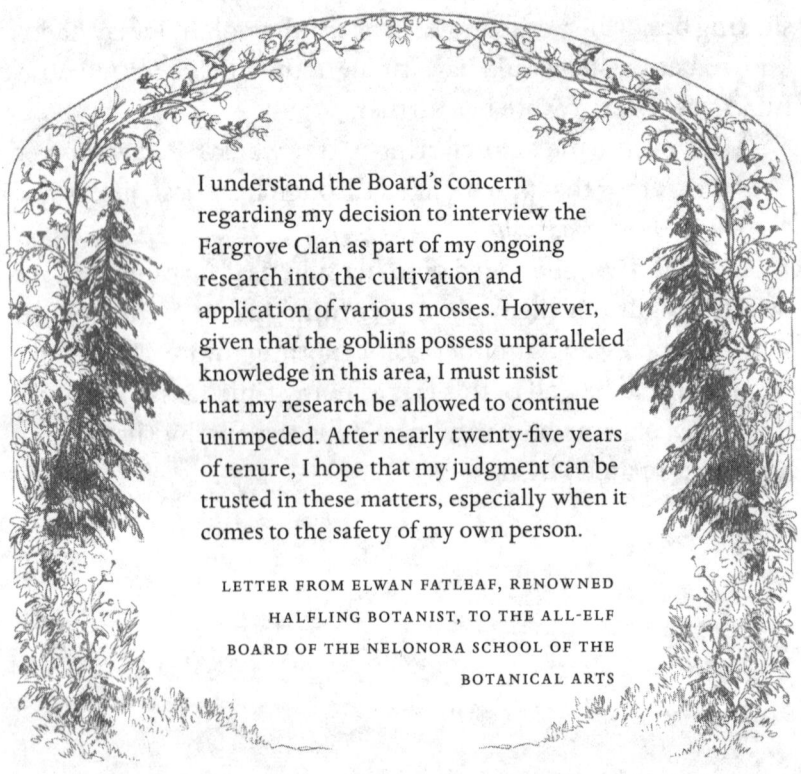

I understand the Board's concern regarding my decision to interview the Fargrove Clan as part of my ongoing research into the cultivation and application of various mosses. However, given that the goblins possess unparalleled knowledge in this area, I must insist that my research be allowed to continue unimpeded. After nearly twenty-five years of tenure, I hope that my judgment can be trusted in these matters, especially when it comes to the safety of my own person.

LETTER FROM ELWAN FATLEAF, RENOWNED HALFLING BOTANIST, TO THE ALL-ELF BOARD OF THE NELONORA SCHOOL OF THE BOTANICAL ARTS

Ren awoke with a start just in time to greet the floor face first. They landed without a scrap of grace, limbs flailing amid a tangle of unfamiliar bedding: not the moss blanket they remembered falling asleep under (as they did every night), but a loosely woven net of chunky, woolen fibers. Soft, warm, and undeniably *halfling*.

Ren forced themself upright, the motion as sudden as the snap of a well-oiled bear trap – and equally painful, it turned out. Their hip throbbed with the beginnings of a nasty bruise; soon to be mottled with sickly shades of chartreuse and aubergine. They half considered laying back down, let the dirt-dusted floorboards, still cool with the chill of night, soothe the hot swell of tender flesh, but the wool blanket knotted around their legs was too important for that. It could not – *would not* – be ignored.

"I told you to stay on your side of the bed!" said a familiar, high-pitched voice, rough with the barbs of broken sleep.

Oh, right. The halfling, Ren thought, recognition threading, at last, into understanding. *Pansy.*

While they'd been relegated to the floor, Pansy remained perched atop the bed, her quilt wrapped around her shoulders like a queen's mantle. She stared down at them, a halo of silver moonlight at her back. Beautiful, even with her sleep-mussed curls, spun into gleaming filaments, now more argent than copper.

How easy it would've been to lose themself in such a vision, but annoyance flared just as bright, and it *burned*.

Like a hot poker jabbed directly into Ren's sternum, reality reasserted itself. "Did you just shove me off the bed?" they asked, spitting the words with acid-laced heat, as much an outlet as a reminder. *Remember who this is: a halfling who would take this cottage from your clan for the sake of her own petty wants.*

"I didn't shove you," Pansy protested, with the sort of haughty vehemence that made it clear that *yes*, she had, in fact, done just that. "I simply . . . I *nudged* you. With my foot."

"So, you kicked me," Ren said flatly.

"Well, I wouldn't have had to if you'd just stayed to your side as agreed!"

"I did!"

"No, you didn't!" Pansy gestured at the misshapen wall of bedding that had once separated them, now partially collapsed, as if someone had unceremoniously yanked out part of its base. "And not only did you steal one of my blankets, you went ahead and shoved those icicles you have for toes against me!"

Ren flinched before they could stop themselves, the word "steal" cutting into their side like a knife. They sucked in a sharp breath around it, bracing, as if that could stop such a blade from sliding deeper. How long had it taken Pansy to accuse them of being a thief the previous afternoon? Five minutes? Less?

And yet, this time was different. This time, Pansy had *noticed*. Her expression softened, the knowledge that her comment wasn't – and could never be – a casual, throw-away thing unwinding the displeasure from her features.

Ren half-wanted to laugh, the ugly, mirthless kind that was as much bite as it was bark. This halfling had stabbed them *by accident*.

"I'm sorry," Pansy said after a beat, her gaze downcast. "I didn't mean it like that. Like – like before, you know?"

"I know." Their voice came out hoarse, flayed. "It's fine."

It wasn't fine. The knife remained, lodged between their ribs. So, why had they said it was fine? Shame flashed through Ren. Were they so unwilling to burden others with the weight of their own feelings that they'd carry the load for even a halfling? Apparently, yes.

One day you won't just bow beneath all that you've chosen to shoulder, their aunt had told them years ago, back when she'd still been the cottage's Caretaker, *you'll break*. Ren had ignored her; the melancholy that had gleamed in her eyes far too inconvenient to acknowledge. But had she been right? Even now, Ren didn't have an answer for that.

"Here," they said, holding out the blanket – *the stolen blanket*, their brain unhelpfully reminded them – as they moved to climb back onto the bed.

"Ew! No!" Pansy squealed, rushing to push them back. "Dust yourself off first! Or better yet, change into something clean. We agreed: no dirt on the bed!"

"I agreed to no such thing," Ren said and, to drive their point home, swiped their arm, still speckled with sediment, across the sheets.

Granted, it was *their* side of the bed; so, if anyone suffered as a result, it would only be them. But the distinction evidently mattered little to Pansy. She let out a banshee-like wail and flung herself at Ren, so desperate to shield her precious bed from a few specks of "nasty dirt" that she gave no thought to the possibility that she might crash to the floor herself.

Unfortunately, she did not go alone. With fingers knotted in the fabric of Ren's nightshirt, she pulled them right down with her, and in a staggering display of unfairness the universe decreed that Ren should be the one to break her fall.

Of course, this injustice was lost on Pansy, who shoved herself upright, using Ren's chest as leverage, and declared, breathless and haughty, "This is all your fault!"

"*My* fault?" Ren gaped at her, the sheer gall of her statement overwhelming the electric jolt of her touch. "You're the one who tried to push me!"

"Because you were trying to get dirt on the bed!"

"It was my side of the bed! What do you care?"

She huffed. "It's still gross."

"You're ridiculous," Ren grumbled. "Now, will you get off me already? I'm not a chair."

Somehow, the fact that Pansy remained seated atop them, her legs straddling their hips on either side, had managed to escape her notice until now. But feeling Ren shift pointedly beneath her, she jolted upright, eyes widening as a rush of scarlet overwhelmed her expression.

"I didn't — I wasn't," she stammered, each truncated phrase only driving the cherry-red stain deeper into her skin. "That wasn't on purpose!"

Ren snorted. As if they needed to be told *that*. Still, a strange current nonetheless prickled beneath their skin; the shock of her touch, perhaps, at last permitted to register. They hauled themself upright, fingers scrubbing uselessly at the wave of gooseflesh overtaking both arms, as if that alone could chase the sensation away.

It did not.

"I'm not an idiot, you know," Ren said, as much for their own benefit as Pansy's. "Anyway, here." Snatching up the blanket from where it had tumbled onto the floor, they gave it a good shake before extending it towards her.

Pansy jerked away with a grimace, hands flying up to shield herself from the blanket's apparent contamination. "Keep it," she said. "I have enough as it is."

"Oh, do you?" Ren arched a brow. "But what if someone could tell that there's a person under all that fabric?"

"Ha-*ha*. Very funny," Pansy replied, her voice flat with reproach. "But that's some pretty big talk for someone who spent half the night wrapped up in one of my blankets. You're welcome, by the way."

Ren flushed. "I'm not thanking you for something I didn't need."

"Funny. Those ice-cold feet of yours told a *very* different story," Pansy drawled, heaving the scattered pieces of her blanket wall back into position. To no one's surprise – let alone Ren's – she exercised no more care in the process than before, resulting in an equally unstable structure.

"My feet are fine!" Ren snapped, crossing their arms over their chest with a huff.

"Then they should have no problem staying on their half of the bed!" And with that, Pansy kicked the remaining dirt from her feet and flopped back onto her side, where she vanished once more beneath a crudely constructed fortress of wool and cotton.

"Whatever," Ren grumbled, too late to be anything other than an admission of defeat.

Pulling both their moss blanket and the one Pansy had relinquished against them – because as much as they'd avoided admitting it aloud, it *was* warm – Ren settled down onto their back, the mirrorsponge slab creasing in a precise reflection of their form. At that point, sleep should have claimed them. It was the middle of the night, and they were exhausted. And yet, somehow they found themself staring blankly at the ceiling, their pulse a dull, warm roar in their ears.

Earlier, Pansy's presence beside them had scarcely registered. If anything, it was ... comforting not to be alone, an imperfect echo of their sleeping arrangements back in the caves, where their clan slept at least three or four to one bedroll. But now, she plucked at the fringes of Ren's consciousness; each rustle of fabric, each measured exhale another anchor to the waking world.

Why couldn't Ren just forget about her and go to sleep?

It was that damnable blanket, they decided, fingers curling into its soft cords. No wonder the halfling weighed so heavily on their thoughts. Right now, Ren couldn't even take a breath without being reminded of her, the way she smelled of honey and spices. She'd *enveloped* them. Completely and absolutely. And, somehow, Ren couldn't bring themself to hate it; not in the way they should've.

As if this situation needed further complications . . .

And here I am collecting them as easily as a badger collects burs, Ren thought, forcing their eyes shut in the hope that their ever-spinning brain might finally take a hint.

Maybe it would have – eventually – if a sudden, explosive snort hadn't spurred them back into wakefulness. Ren's eyes snapped open, pupils flaring wide.

Had Pig decided to make her way upstairs? So far, Ren's companion had shown a distinct preference for the cottage's lower level. But the two of them had only been living here for a couple of days; hardly long enough to declare, with any sort of certainty, that Pig would never venture upstairs.

Ren's brow had only just started to furrow when the sound repeated, unleashed into the world with the same amount of violence as before. And they realized that it was coming from beside them, on the other side of the blanket wall.

Pansy was *snoring*.

Shaking their head, Ren settled back down and let out a long, drawn-out breath. "Maybe I'm a blanket thief, but at least I don't snore . . ."

5
Pansy

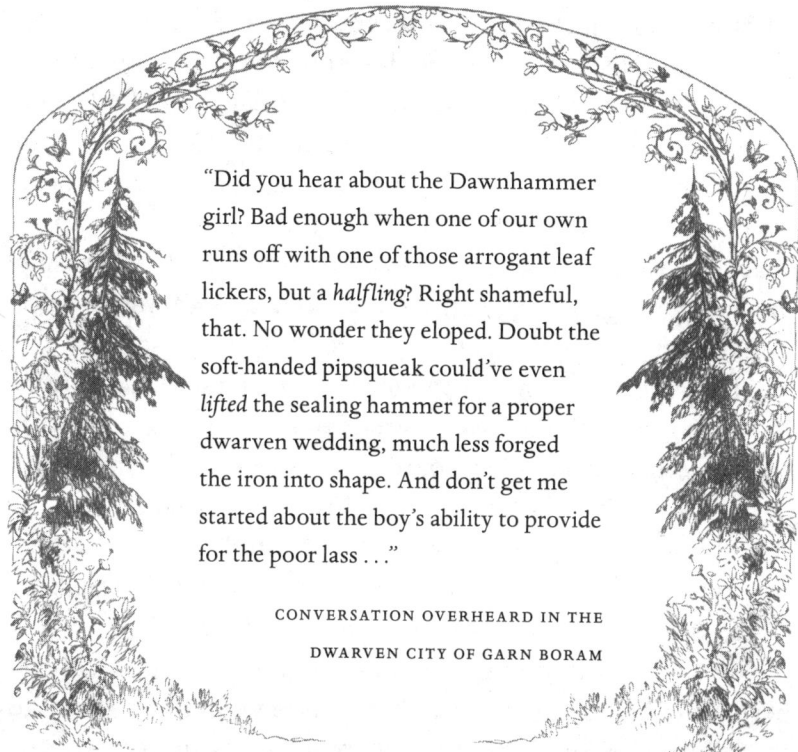

"Did you hear about the Dawnhammer girl? Bad enough when one of our own runs off with one of those arrogant leaf lickers, but a *halfling*? Right shameful, that. No wonder they eloped. Doubt the soft-handed pipsqueak could've even *lifted* the sealing hammer for a proper dwarven wedding, much less forged the iron into shape. And don't get me started about the boy's ability to provide for the poor lass . . ."

CONVERSATION OVERHEARD IN THE
DWARVEN CITY OF GARN BORAM

The walk back to Haverow – though longer than Pansy would've liked – was easier than expected. This time she wasn't weighed down by nearly half-a-dozen bags, all crammed to the hilt with too many "necessities" to be truly deserving of the name. Instead, she had only her wicker basket: empty for now, but certainly not for much longer. Pansy had a kitchen to stock, and stock it she would. She could hardly call the place her domain otherwise.

It was still early by the time she made it to the village proper, where the dusty, dirt roads of the rolling countryside transitioned to familiar mossy cobblestones. Even though the dawn mists had only just begun to disperse around beams of pale, yellow sunlight, the streets of Haverow were far from empty. Farmers, off to tend their fields while the weather was still cool, nodded politely at Pansy as she passed them by, as did many of her former neighbors, already tackling their day-to-day chores. No one, not even the trio of pram-pushing mothers who spent nearly every morning, from what Pansy could tell, discussing the latest village gossip, commented on her recent move – not until she made it to the village square.

There she found one of the local councilors, Mrs. Dorothy Millwood, squat and silver-haired, pinning a large, colorful poster to the village noticeboard.

"Returning home already?" Mrs. Millwood asked, her mouth stretching into a simpering imitation of a smile that didn't even so much as disturb the wrinkles around her eyes. "I'm not surprised that old cottage isn't all you cracked it up to be."

"Oh, no. I'm just doing some shopping," Pansy replied, lifting her basket for emphasis. She clamped down hard on the urge to be impolite, reaching for that too-pleasant mask Haverow always seemed to demand of her.

Mrs. Millwood's smile flattened along with her voice. "I see."

"The cottage is lovely, by the way," Pansy continued, unable to help herself. "Can you believe it's still in perfect condition?"

Mrs. Millwood sniffed, disapproval budding beneath her beak-like nose. "That's all well and good, but a young halfling like yourself shouldn't be so far from home. When I was your age, I didn't even *think* about leaving my parents' burrow until I was married! Speaking of—"

Oh no. This again. After she'd *just* gotten her own mother to drop the subject. "Councilor Millwood, I really—"

But it was too late. As far as Mrs. Millwood was concerned, Pansy hadn't said a peep. Her tirade continued unimpeded. "You should start thinking about settling down, Pansy. You're already nearly thirty and still without a partner. Surely you want to give your parents grandchildren sooner rather than later; while they're still hale and hearty—"

"Your concern, Councilor Millwood," Pansy began, raising her voice just enough to put a stop to the elderly halfling's rambling, "while appreciated, is entirely unnecessary. Thank you."

"Are you sure?" Mrs. Millwood pressed, her eyes widening with misplaced concern. "Your mother did mention that you were still looking. My nephew over in Oakton is around your age, and he really is quite strapping, very handy in the kitchen and in the fields—"

"I'm fine. *Really.*"

Mrs. Millwood frowned, her lips thinning. "Well, if you insist ... Though one can't help but wonder how you tolerate it, Pansy – being so alone all the time."

I'm not alone, Pansy thought to herself, her chest contracting around a flash of stubborn heat. *I have my parents and Blossom and – I guess Ren, too, technically. Though hopefully not for much longer ...*

She shuddered, remembering the way her bare feet had crunched in the dirt still strewn across the bedroom floor that morning, her slippers too small a target for her flailing, sleep-loose limbs. Yet like everything Ren had thrown her way thus far, it was nothing she couldn't handle. Mrs. Millwood, on the other hand ... that part was far less certain, especially if she started badgering Pansy about her nephew again.

Honestly, I'd rather marry Ren, and I don't even like *them,* she thought, suppressing a grimace at the prospect of having Mrs. Millwood for an in-law: the only thing more dreadful than taking a crotchety, perfectionist, moss-and-dirt-loving goblin for a spouse.

Granted, marrying Ren was an equally impossible proposition, as Pansy was quick to remind herself when the (absurd!) image of her and Ren exchanging vows beneath a white canopy sent an inexplicable rush of heat to her face.

Ridiculous. She scoffed, rapidly putting the goblin out of her mind as she turned her attention to the poster Mrs. Millwood had affixed to the noticeboard.

Bring the Annual Harvest Festival to Haverow! it declared in impressively large letters, meant to be read from all corners of the plaza. Unfortunately, the text that followed was not nearly so digestible; no doubt because Mrs. Millwood – or whoever had put together the poster – had insisted on turning a list of best practices to impress the Greater Halvenshire Festival Committee into a whole screed.

Amazing how something as beloved as the Harvest Festival could be rendered so joyless. Pansy made it approximately two lines before her eyes glazed over, and she gave up. *If this is what it takes to host the Harvest Festival, it's no wonder they haven't picked us in over twenty years. You'd need to fill the whole village with a wizard's simulacrums to even have a chance.*

Catching the direction of Pansy's gaze, Mrs. Millwood said sternly, "Ah, that reminds me. Pansy, I feel compelled to warn you that we won't be tolerating any funny business this year.

How to Lose a Goblin in Ten Days

Haverow *will* be hosting the Halvenshire Harvest Festival come autumn, and it's *very* important that all residents put their best foot forward – lest Halfend get the honor yet again." She shuddered, as if the prospect of attending the festival in a town barely even a few hours' ride away was a nightmarish proposition.

How fortunate for you that I'm no longer a resident, Pansy thought sourly. "I wouldn't dream of ruining Haverow's prospects on purpose, Councilor Millwood," she said, laying it on a bit thick, the words so choked with saccharine sweetness they were practically dripping with it.

"Not on purpose, no," Mrs. Millwood admitted. "And that's precisely the problem, Pansy. Everyone remembers what happened with your grandmother at the last festival – the way she attacked poor Fenwick when he was setting off the fireworks, thinking the noise was the necromancer come back to life or some such. All that adventuring never was good for the poor woman. And now that you've moved into that old cottage of hers, well ... people are beginning to wonder about you too. You always did ask far too many questions. Although curiosity is natural among children, you're a grown woman now. It's unbecoming. No one likes it when someone makes waves in an otherwise tranquil pond, and Haverow," she continued firmly, "is exceedingly tranquil. Far more so than Halfend, at any rate." She sniffed.

It took everything in Pansy's power not to gape at the woman. Surely, she couldn't be serious. Fury surged within Pansy, hot and bitter. It streamed into her ribcage, corroding muscle and bone alike. She wanted so badly to unleash it all on this woman, to spit in her face, and ask her, *How dare you?* But where would that leave her? Where would it leave *her parents*? Pansy had learned a long time ago that nothing was ever only about her. Everything she did, everything she said – it was all a mirror, one that reflected right back on the people around her.

I'm sorry, Grandma. Pansy forced a smile, her best one yet. By now, she had it down to an art, even if it left her cracking at the seams. "The Festival Committee will be coming around soon as part of the selection process, right? How about I bake some cookies for when they arrive? That way, they're sure to remember Haverow in the best possible way."

Mrs. Millwood paused, considering. "You are rather talented in the kitchen, even if the presentation can sometimes be a little unorthodox... Very well. But nothing – *adventurous.*" She said the word like a curse, her nose wrinkling.

"I wouldn't dream of it. Nothing but classic shortbread for our honored Committee, cut into perfect little squares."

And with that, Pansy turned on her heel and walked away, heading in the direction of the one place she knew she could safely detonate the bomb ticking down in her throat.

Blossom's Blossoms was, thankfully, not far. Decked in vibrant twists of purple wisteria, the two-story stone-and-mortar building sat on the other side of the square, down a narrow, tree-lined road always thick with the honeyed scent of fresh pastries, courtesy of the bakery next door.

On any other day, Pansy might stop in for a hot, buttered scone – a prospect that should have sent her empty stomach gurgling with approval – but the ember cradled on her tongue had turned forge-bright. Like a pot about to boil over, she shook with each step, every impolite word she'd bitten back during her conversation with Mrs. Millwood surging against her teeth in a blistering tide. One way or another, it was coming out.

How to Lose a Goblin in Ten Days

She barely made it into Blossom's store, her entrance marked as much by the thunderous slam of the door as the shop bell's delicate chime, before the last frayed vestiges of her self-control finally snapped. "I've been in town barely five minutes and I already want to scream!"

Blossom, who'd been in the process of removing thorns from a cluster of roses, looked up from her work, hands stilling mid-snip. "Should I get the cookies and tea ready?" she asked, her expression creasing sympathetically.

"Councilor Millwood accosted me in the village square."

Blossom immediately set the roses down and, with an emphatic nod, said, "Cookies and tea it is."

Whoever had ordered the bouquet, it seemed, would have to wait. Blossom's Blossoms had far more pressing matters to attend to this morning, the kind that necessitated flipping the shop sign back to *Closed* less than an hour after opening. The door's lock, however, remained untouched. No self-respecting Haverow halfling would do something so crass as to ignore a clearly posted sign.

The store now guarded against any unwanted interruptions, Blossom ushered Pansy upstairs to the flat she kept, in somewhat un-halfling fashion, above her shop. "It's more convenient that way," she'd said when questioned about the decision. And, somehow, that had been enough. The same people who couldn't bring themselves to extract their noses from Pansy's own business for more than one second had simply nodded along and let the matter drop.

At the time, it had enraged Pansy. Now, it frustrated her just as much, the memory stoking already-smoldering coals into new gouts of flame as she not-quite-stomped after Blossom, each footfall just heavy enough to send the frames filled with pressed flowers rattling against the plaster. In what way was any of this fair?

Of course, their situations weren't the same; not precisely. While Pansy had, up until very recently, lived with her parents, Blossom's parents had moved to Halfend a little over five years ago. Instead of joining them, she'd elected to remain in Haverow, a choice she'd been commended for. Not just because of the long-standing rivalry that existed between the two villages, which was serious enough that in any human town it would've surely culminated in a murder by now, but also because Haverow would've otherwise been left without a florist. Her decision had single-handedly kept the then-named Brimshine's Blooms open. So, what was a bit of oddness in the face of that?

But still. *Still.* The thought pulsed at the forefront of Pansy's mind, as gentle as the crash of a sledgehammer. Again, she found herself overcome with the urge to scream. It clawed up her throat, bit by bit, until her mouth was full of copper and salt.

"Why can't they just leave me alone?" Pansy asked, the words rushing out of her in one fell swoop; not a scream, but something equally charged with feeling.

"I know, I know," Blossom said gently, patting her on the shoulder. "Now, go sit while I put the kettle on and dig out those cookies."

Pansy did as instructed, flopping down into one of two cushioned chairs arranged on either side of Blossom's kitchen table. Her seat proved less comfortable than expected due to the honeycombed ball she found lodged beneath the embroidered cushion. One of Belladonna's toys, judging from the bell lodged at its center. Blossom really did spoil that cat rotten . . .

"She tried to set me up with her nephew in Oakton, you

know," Pansy said, tossing the ball onto the floor, where it landed with a too-cheery jingle.

"Councilor Millwood?" Blossom asked.

Pansy nodded.

"Oh. Well, is he handsome? The nephew, I mean."

Pansy shot her a wretched look – not that Blossom could see it. She was too busy clattering about the kitchen, her long, cornsilk-yellow braid swinging behind her as she moved from one cabinet to the next, searching for the box of cookies she'd stashed among a veritable avalanche of herbs. Doubtless, none of them were meant for cooking: elixirs and tinctures, more like. Blossom's other trade of choice.

"She wanted to make sure that I 'give my parents grandchildren before they fall into their graves'," Pansy said, her lips twisting in a scowl.

That got Blossom's attention. She looked over her shoulder, blue eyes gone wide with shock. "Councilor Millwood said that? Those words exactly?"

"Well, maybe not exactly," Pansy said after a beat, ducking her head slightly. "But the effect was the same, I assure you. To think, I finally got my own mother to drop the subject of my love life only for *Councilor Millwood* to take up the mantle in her stead! And she's also convinced that I'm going to sabotage Haverow's chances with the Festival Committee. Because of what happened last year with the fireworks."

Blossom's brow furrowed. "With your grandmother, you mean?" At Pansy's nod, the perfect bow of Blossom's mouth flattened into a straight-razor line. "*That old bitch.*"

Relief washed over Pansy, unraveling the tension that had knotted between her shoulder blades. It felt good to hear her feelings validated. Because sometimes even she couldn't help but doubt herself, picked apart by the most insidious question of all: *am I overreacting?*

Letting out a breath, Pansy sagged into her seat, one finger coming up to trace the tiny sunflowers that had been painted along the table's rounded edge. "I almost couldn't believe she'd said it, to be quite honest. But then she started going on and on about how my moving into my grandmother's old cottage was making people start to *wonder* about me." She spat the word, whetted into the same pointed barb the other residents of Haverow had lobbed her way more times than she could count, charging it with the collective weight of their judgment – and dismissal.

"How *is* the cottage?" Blossom asked, abruptly changing the subject as she pushed a plate of gingersnaps towards Pansy, a two-pronged approach to lifting her best friend's mood that soon turned into three when she returned a moment later with a steaming cup of tea. If only the cottage had been the happy topic she'd thought it was, rather than one newly tainted by frustration...

"*Ugh.* Honestly, it's a disaster, Blossom."

"Oh, no. Is it the roof? I know you were worried about that."

Pansy shook her head. "No. Worse. It's—" She snapped her mouth shut.

Even squirreled away upstairs, away from the shop proper, she couldn't shake the feeling of scrutiny that dogged her every step through town. Call it paranoia, but when it came to the subject of her new goblin housemate, the saying *better safe than sorry* immediately sprung to mind. The last thing Pansy needed was for this to become the latest bit of hot village gossip.

That being said, maybe she was being ridiculous. The shop was closed. No one would be coming in. And even if someone had taken it upon themselves to stand beneath Blossom's kitchen window, unless they actually *scaled* the side of the building, which would be far too much of a spectacle for any well-bred halfling, they wouldn't hear much of anything.

It all seemed perfectly safe. And yet, when Pansy opened her mouth again, the words came out as barely more than a whisper: "I found a goblin living there."

"*A goblin?*" Blossom repeated, far too loud for Pansy's comfort, her eyes blowing wide. If she'd been taking a sip of her tea, instead of simply cradling it in her palms opposite Pansy, she'd have surely spat it out.

"Shh! Not so loud!" Pansy hissed, fingers tightening along the table's edge. "And yes, I know I'm being paranoid, but considering the circumstances, can you really blame me?"

"I suppose not," Blossom conceded after a beat, the reproach unscrewing from her features. "Does that mean the goblin's still there? In the cottage?"

Pansy nodded, her lower lip catching briefly between her front teeth. "They refused to leave, and I couldn't really ... I mean, I wasn't going to *fight* them."

"Of course not," Blossom agreed. *Very sensible*, said her expression, now far more staid.

"So, we made a deal instead," Pansy explained. "For now, we'll live in the cottage together, and the first one to leave forfeits their claim."

Blossom's eyes widened. "Wait. If you're here, does that mean you've—"

"No! I'm just here to do some shopping. The note I left behind is very clear on that."

"And you think this goblin will honor that?"

In truth, Pansy had known the answer to this question

before Blossom had even opened her mouth. But still, she took a moment to consider – if only for appearances' sake.

"I wouldn't have agreed to this deal otherwise. Plus," Pansy added with a shrug, "it's not like they can lock me out. I'm the one with the key, after all."

Blossom's brow furrowed. "How long has this goblin been living in your grandmother's cottage exactly? I just don't understand how they can claim ownership when they don't even have a key to the place."

"That's what I said, but as far as they're concerned, the key is irrelevant. Although they only moved in recently, their aunt has supposedly lived in the cottage for several decades. Hence why the place is still in such good condition."

No sooner had the words left Pansy's mouth than a veil of confusion drew over her brow. She needed Ren out; not to defend their right to the cottage. In fact, as far as she was concerned, Ren had no right.

Blossom took a thoughtful sip of her tea. "You know, I'm abruptly reminded of the time I got up from my seat at the last Wilder Woods concert to get something to drink and returned only to find Danny Oldbough sitting in it."

"The solicitor?"

"Yes, well. He wasn't a solicitor then. This was about ten years ago, mind you. Anyway"– she waved a hand – "I asked him, quite politely, to go somewhere else, as it was my seat, which I'd arrived early to secure. He then started talking about some old halfling law called 'adverse possession'; how because I'd 'abandoned' my seat he was, therefore, entitled to it. But, being the magnanimous gentleman that he was, he would be more than willing to share – by having me sit on his lap."

Pansy made a low noise of disgust. "Gross."

"Obviously, I declined and watched the rest of the concert from a different, worse seat. But later I find out that this old law of his was stricken *centuries* ago. So, next time I saw him I gave him a bouquet full of poison ivy. As one does."

"A proportionate response, I think," Pansy declared with a nod. "Hopefully, he's become a better lawyer since then – for his clients' sakes, at least."

"Who knows." Blossom shrugged. "But all that to say, I guess I can see where your goblin's logic might be stemming from; not that that makes it any less flawed."

Her goblin?

Heat surged into Pansy's face. "Their name is Ren," she blurted out in a rush, seizing the first thing that came to mind in order to dispel the unfortunate implication nestled in Blossom's words, unintended though it probably was.

"So, you're on a first-name basis already, are you?" Blossom grinned, the perfectly manicured arches of her eyebrows soaring up towards her hairline.

Oh, gods. Not this again.

"It made sense to introduce ourselves," Pansy replied, stiffening in her seat anew. Her grip tightened on the table's edge, hard enough to turn her knuckles white.

"Oh, yes. It made *sense*. And here I thought my best friend would never have a crush on anyone! Admittedly, it being a goblin is a little ..." She winced. "But I can be open-minded! I mean, I just finished a book where the human heroine fell in love with a half-orc and thought it was very sweet."

Pansy groaned. "Blossom, it's not like that! Ren's a menace, and right now, all I care about is getting them out of my house before they manage to drive *me* insane. So, unless you have some suggestions on that front, you can keep your ridiculous romance novel plotlines to yourself!" She then snatched up a cookie and chomped into it with more force than was strictly necessary.

"Okay, okay!" Blossom said, throwing up her hands in surrender. "Are they really that bad?"

Pansy gave her a hard look. "They filled the house with dirt."

"Ah. Well, that's not very attractive, is it?"

"Not at all," Pansy agreed. "And the worst part is that I'm not even allowed to clean it up because of the terms of our stupid bet! We can only add, not subtract. *Ugh!*"

"That does seem like quite the pickle," Blossom said, nodding sagely. "Luckily for you, I *do* have something that can help you win this little wager of yours."

Pansy's eyes widened. "You do?"

"Mm-hmm. Give me a moment, I'll be right back."

Blossom swept out of the kitchen, returning a minute or so later with a small, black kitten cradled in her arms. "You remember how Bella had kittens a few months ago?" she asked. "Well, this little guy is your ticket to a goblin-free home."

"I don't understand . . ."

"Goblins *hate* cats. Or so I've heard. From reliable sources."

Pansy gave her a flat look. "Reliable sources? Really?"

"Yes. *The Definitive Guide on How to Lose a Goblin in Ten Days or Less.* Trust me, Pansy. This will work!"

The kitten, still tucked against Blossom's breast, its fur a dark void against the white lace of her blouse, followed up with a soft mew of endorsement. Immediately, Pansy felt something inside her crumble.

Her better judgment, no doubt . . .

"All right." Pansy sighed, mentally adding cat food to

her shopping list. "But that's absolutely not a real book, and you know it."

Blossom only grinned in response.

With a solid third of her basket now devoted to a ball of black fur, Pansy's haul from the grocer proved far more modest than she'd initially planned. Constrained to only the most basic of staples, the handful of ingredients she absolutely, positively could not do without, her more elaborate culinary creations would have to wait. A frustrating twist of fate. And yet, looking down at the kitten, now tucked into a perfect loaf atop the smallest bag of flour she could find, Pansy couldn't bring herself to acknowledge this fact with any real heat.

"You're lucky you're cute," she told the kitten, scritching him gently underneath the chin, where a single white stripe marred otherwise solid black. The kitten, pleased with this offering, began an appreciative purr, yellow eyes narrowing to contented slits.

As she crossed the town square for a second time, Pansy braced herself for another encounter with Mrs. Millwood, her shoulders pulling taut beneath the soft, pale yellow of her cardigan. *Why didn't I just take the long way around?*

Thankfully, while Mrs. Millwood's poster remained, plastered in full color for all to see, the woman herself did not. In her place stood a human man – tall even by his people's standards – clad in sweeping indigo silks dotted with golden thread like stars. He stuck out like a sore thumb, undoubtedly visible from all corners of town. And yet, he carried himself like a longtime resident, greeting everyone who passed him by name.

They all recognized him, too, of course. As did Pansy.

The wizard Agvaldir had a face that was impossible to forget, dedicated almost entirely to a full, brown beard that would doubtless stir envy in many a young dwarf. Supposedly this made him handsome in some circles – human ones, mostly – but Pansy couldn't see it. Nor could she see the kindly man the rest of Haverow loved so much. For the moment Agvaldir's gaze locked with hers from across the square, Pansy felt no comfort, no reassurance. There was only the icy plunge of fresh dread spearing her through.

"Hello, little lady," he said, his too-white smile stretching wider, all hunger and teeth. "Is there something I can do for you?"

The question dangled before her like a fishhook, exquisitely baited. Once upon a time, Pansy might've said "yes", stretched out her hand and allowed Agvaldir to sweep her away on an adventure without a second thought. Plenty of other halflings already had. She'd seen them over the years, off to quest beyond the dark swell of the horizon at Agvaldir's side, only to return months or years later, irrevocably changed. That is, if they returned at all.

But Agvaldir? Agvaldir never changed, and he always, *always* came back.

The man was as much a permanent fixture as the river that abutted Haverow to the west. Not even the oldest residents could remember a time without him, their earliest memories locked to the day he saved the village from a magical blight – now, almost a century ago. While those same elders had turned old and gray, Agvaldir had remained the same. He was as youthful as ever, instantly recognizable in a way normal people weren't; a consequence of his magic, no doubt.

Perhaps that was why he'd become such a blind spot, overwhelming familiarity truncating an otherwise obvious conclusion – especially when veiled in the barest sheen of plausible deniability. Agvaldir never advertised his true goal. He couched his words in allusions and implications, waiting until his target broached the subject first. Because if a halfling elected to become an adventurer of their own volition, well – he had no choice but to accompany them. At least *he'd* try to keep them safe, from orcs and witches and goblins and trolls, unlike anyone else willing to let a halfling join their party. He was Haverow's longstanding protector, the one who'd saved them from the Blight. *He cared.*

And so, the halflings lured in by his speeches, the indirect promises of glory and respect on a stage that had, heretofore, dismissed them by virtue of their short stature, were not victims, but, rather, selfish architects of their own misfortune. If only Agvaldir had been able to convince them of their folly, the other villagers often cried, somehow unaware that he was the one who had planted its seeds.

"I imagine you must've heard about the necromancer sweeping across the south," Agvaldir continued, his expression turning solemn, though the sharpness in his eye remained. "Much as it pains me to admit it, it'll be only a matter of time before her army of undead marches on the elven kingdom of Elhurian. Of course, that's still quite a long way from here, so there's no reason to be concerned. I'm certain my fellow wizards and I will find plenty of *brave heroes* willing to join us on our upcoming campaign to quash Evil's rising tide."

Heroes like Wolf Banefoot. *Like her grandmother.*

Pansy's chest simultaneously tightened and swelled. Evil certainly needed to be subdued. She wouldn't dare argue otherwise. But reality wasn't so simple. Just because wizards like Agvaldir only talked about saving innocents and preserving peace and prosperity, didn't mean there wasn't an ugly truth hiding underneath that golden sheen. Violence and suffering were just as real, as much a part of any campaign as the purported good, and to pretend otherwise was straight-up dishonesty. The Great War had changed Pansy's grandmother, just like it had changed so many others; and, unfortunately, that change had not been for the better.

Still, as much as Pansy would have liked to keep on walking, ignore Agvaldir and the unpleasantness roiling in her belly, right now, she needed him – albeit not in the way he was doubtless hoping. Her thoughts turned to the runes she'd discovered on the cottage's lower floor, currently hidden beneath a dust-choked rug. Curiosity, buoyed by the fleeting hope that the magic contained within them might prove useful somehow, curled inside Pansy's brain. Like an itch, it demanded to be scratched. And, as far as she knew, Agvaldir was the only one in the whole village who knew anything about magic.

"I'm sorry, but I'm no hero," Pansy said with well-practiced politeness and a shake of her head. "But I do have a question for you."

The wizard's smile thinned, but ultimately held. "What sort of question?"

"Do you recognize these runes?" Pansy asked, producing the notepad from her pocket for inspection.

Although she held the notepad well above her head, Agvaldir nonetheless insisted on squatting down until his face was nearly level with hers. Perhaps he thought he was being polite; though, surely, someone in Haverow would've disabused him of this notion by now, considering he'd been visiting for over one hundred years...

Then again, maybe not, Pansy realized. She couldn't

remember the last time anyone had openly disagreed with Agvaldir – if ever. The village elders certainly never had; he was their savior, after all, their memories of him elevated by childish wonder and simplicity. And if they saw fit to defer to him, so would everyone else. Such was the benefit of old age.

The wizard squinted at the runes for a moment, then asked, "Where did you find these?"

So, he does know something! Excitement sparked in Pansy's chest, obliterating the tar-like feeling that had previously congealed between her ribs. "I found them in the, uh, cellar of my grandmother's cottage." It wasn't quite a cellar, but what else was she supposed to call it?

"Interesting," Agvaldir murmured, a shadow of a thought flitting across his face, too quick for Pansy to parse.

"You know what they mean, then?" she asked, pressing closer in expectation.

Agvaldir shook his head, straightening back up to his full height and nearly taking Pansy with him when she rocketed up onto her toes on reflex. "I'm sorry, but no. In all my years, I've never chanced upon runes like this before."

Pansy's expression crumpled. "Not even in a book?"

"I'm afraid I can't offer anything of use to you."

There was something about the way Agvaldir's lips pursed behind his beard before he spoke that dug into Pansy's mind like a stubborn splinter. Surely, he wouldn't be so petty as to purposely mislead her all because she'd refused to engage with his usual tactics. However unnerving she might've found him, Agvaldir was still a hero by all accounts, a force of Good across the Realm. He'd pledged to help, not to hurt; and though Pansy couldn't say he'd never harmed anyone, she liked to think that those instances hadn't been intentional.

"That's too bad," she said, slipping the notepad back into her pocket. And then, because proper manners told her to (in a voice that sounded suspiciously like her mother's), she added, almost automatically, "Thank you for taking a look."

"Anytime," Agvaldir replied, lips parting around another too-bright flash of teeth.

Clamping down on the shiver that coiled near the base of her spine, Pansy spun away and headed for the other side of the village square as quickly as she could manage. Not quite scurrying, but close enough that the tempo of her steps matched the rapid-fire *thump-thump* of her own heartbeat.

It wasn't until she reached the edge of town that the tension knotting between her shoulder blades finally began to unwind. She let out a breath, her body sagging from the effort. "Well, that's the last time I ask him for anything," she muttered. "He's even more intimidating up close."

With a sleepy blink, the kitten let out another high-pitched mew. Agreement, if Pansy had ever heard it.

She smiled and gave him another scritch; this time, behind the ears. "Guess, I'm going to have to count on you. Don't let me down, okay?"

The kitten purred in response.

6
Ren

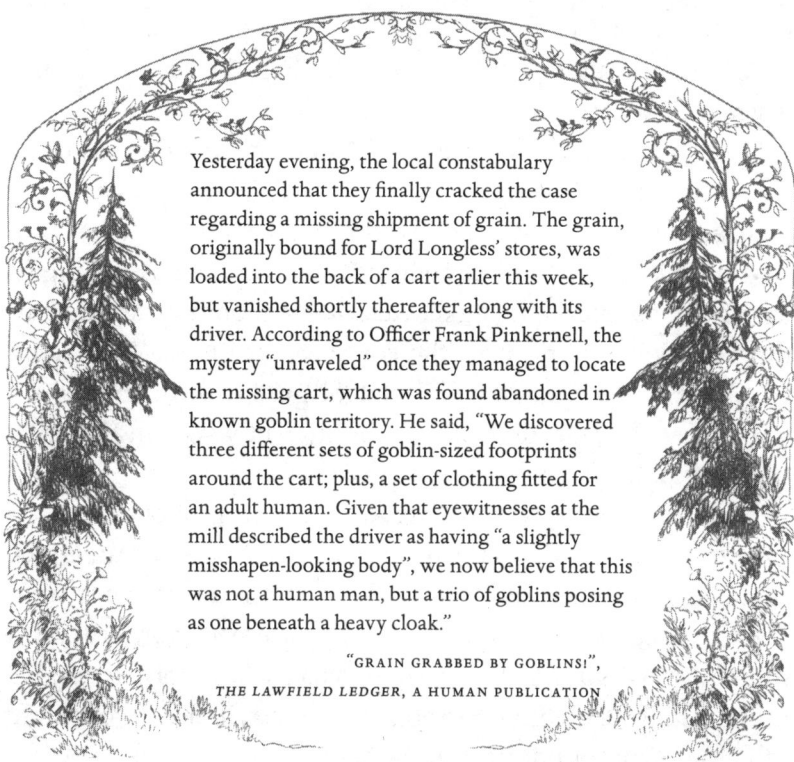

Yesterday evening, the local constabulary announced that they finally cracked the case regarding a missing shipment of grain. The grain, originally bound for Lord Longless' stores, was loaded into the back of a cart earlier this week, but vanished shortly thereafter along with its driver. According to Officer Frank Pinkernell, the mystery "unraveled" once they managed to locate the missing cart, which was found abandoned in known goblin territory. He said, "We discovered three different sets of goblin-sized footprints around the cart; plus, a set of clothing fitted for an adult human. Given that eyewitnesses at the mill described the driver as having "a slightly misshapen-looking body", we now believe that this was not a human man, but a trio of goblins posing as one beneath a heavy cloak."

"GRAIN GRABBED BY GOBLINS!",
THE LAWFIELD LEDGER, A HUMAN PUBLICATION

Ren awoke to an empty bed doused in yellow sunlight; not the thin rays of early morning, but a brilliant stream of unfettered daylight, soon to reach its pinnacle, turning what should've been a calm return to the bounds of wakefulness into a jarring crash.

They jolted upright, hands fisting the soft cords of their (still) borrowed blanket. How long had they been asleep? The thought surged to the forefront of their mind, perfectly in sync with the hard *thump* of their pulse. Suddenly, there was nothing beyond the number of hours wasted. Hours that should've been devoted to their responsibilities as Caretaker, instead frittered away on worthless sleep.

All because Pansy had kept Ren up half the night with her wretched snoring.

The ragged frenzy pulsating beneath Ren's breastbone abruptly stilled, coiling in on itself with a sour burn. They glanced over at Pansy's side of the bed, still delineated by a slightly misshapen wall of bedding, and frowned. Agreeing to this deal had been a mistake. Ren never should've let the halfling set even one *toe* over the cottage's threshold. That alone would've saved them a whole lot of grief; not to mention a good three-quarters of the headache currently swelling beneath their temples.

Unfortunately, it was too late to do anything about it – other than follow the terms of the deal. Honestly, it was just their luck that their particular halfling – "their" in the sense that they'd been saddled with her; nothing more – seemed more stubborn than most. Was it too much to hope that she'd simply absconded in the middle of the night? Probably. And yet, Ren allowed themself a moment to indulge the thought.

Only a moment, though. Once that tiny spark of hope had been extinguished, swift as an already fading ember, Ren turned their mind to more practical considerations – like where exactly Pansy had gone.

She didn't seem to be the early-riser type. No halfling did. They were the ones who sat warm and comfortable in their burrows, gorging themselves on the land's bounties without ever once thinking of the damage they'd left in their wake. Felled forests. Fallow earth. Slaughtering animals for meat. Theirs was an existence that had taken the concept of plenty and twisted it into excess. What else could explain the fact that they'd left an entire cottage to rot?

And if that wasn't proof enough, Ren need only turn to last night's dinner. How many ingredients had Pansy tossed into that single salad? Far more than Ren would have even *fantasized* about. Honestly, it bordered on obscene.

I should've stopped her, they thought, their stomach hollowing around the hot poker of shame that plunged into it. Because every bite of food they took for themself was another snatched out of the mouths of the people who needed it most. It was why they'd resolved to keep as little as possible from every harvest, such that the majority of the cottage's bounty went back to the caves of their clan. But Pansy had come along and promptly uprooted that plan, heedless of how carefully it had been seeded.

How very halfling of her . . .

Throwing aside their blankets, wool and moss alike, Ren launched themself out of bed, unwilling to waste any more time than they already had. They dressed quickly, pulling on a pair of straight-cut trousers and a loose-fitting shirt that had already been patched a half-dozen times thus far. No doubt, they should've retired the shirt by now – maybe even the trousers, too – but every time they held it in their hands they'd think, *One more use,* and slip it over their head. How they looked didn't matter. In fact, each disjointed patch of fabric was a badge of honor, tangible proof of what Ren had given up so that someone else in their clan could have more. Because as long their family was happy, Ren would be too.

They repeated these words to themself, more fiercely than ever, as they headed for the front door. There was no time for breakfast. The crops needed to be watered, the weeds pruned. And the clan's next shipment of ambervine and mudmoss needed to be harvested before the local wildlife beat Ren to it. A maze of old fishing nets and wire, no matter how elaborate, would only hold out for so long.

Thus far, there was no sign of Pansy. Unless the piece of paper stuck to the front door counted. Ren assumed it was her work. They squinted at it, struggling to make sense of the ink scrawled across its surface. A picture they might've been able to understand, but the strange script that popped up whenever Ren came too close to a halfling settlement, usually on a signpost or other wooden structures? Absolutely not.

Better leave this alone, they decided, and headed out into the glowing, noontime warmth.

Thankfully, the day's chores were swiftly accomplished. The sun hadn't even started on its downward crest towards the horizon by the time Ren finished loading their wagon with the fruits of their labor. Ambervine, elderberries, mudmoss, nettles and a small collection of slakegourd that had ripened ahead of schedule; all packaged into familiar wooden crates, each more banged-up than the last.

Blowing out a breath, Ren stepped back and admired their handiwork. Admittedly, they'd been hoping for a larger harvest, but the transition between Caretakers hadn't been entirely smooth this time around. A few ten-days of unmanaged responsibilities, while hardly a death sentence, had nonetheless left their mark.

Of course, Ren didn't blame their aunt. They couldn't. She was sick, her mind caught like sand in a sieve. How could she be expected to know that her grasp was slipping when she'd forgotten that there was anything to grip?

And yet, that didn't make Ren's concerns any less real; the unease that percolated in the pit of their stomach. Winter would arrive soon enough – always quicker than anyone thought – and so, too, would the floods. Last year had been bad, narrowing the cave system their clan inhabited to less than half of its usual footprint and stripping away valuable sources of moss and mushrooms in the process. Now, the clan had a group of dwarves to contend with, eager, as always, to drive out any "goblin pests" they stumbled upon, and Ren could only hope that the cottage was enough to make up that shortfall too.

They looked at the food they'd set aside for themself and frowned, considering. Should they keep less? Ren's initial knee-jerk response was, *Absolutely*. But, then again, they were no longer living alone. One mouth to feed had turned into two – three, if you counted Pig, who generally foraged for herself anyway. And though Pansy was certainly an adult who would manage just fine on her own, Ren's thoughts kept flitting back to that day they'd found her with a basket full of *deadly mushrooms* and ... yeah, no. Who knew what sort of "culinary delicacies" she'd scrounge out here unsupervised?

Ren would have to talk to her later about being more judicious in her use of ingredients, more *sparing*; but for now, the two-person share of the harvest would stay. They left it in the pantry, plain to see. So, if Pansy wanted to take from it, she could easily do so.

Perhaps Ren should've stuck around after that, to make sure she didn't immediately go wild in the kitchen upon her return, especially now that she'd been crowned its ruler (another bet

Ren never should have agreed to). But, surely, clearing out this much food in a single afternoon was beyond even her.

Confident in this conclusion, they called for Pig and headed back outside. Pig lumbered out a minute or so later, blinking the last bits of sleep from her eyes. Upon seeing the loaded wagon, she immediately perked up, the rose petals of her ears jutting up towards the sky. With a delighted squeal, she hurried to the wagon's front, where her harness waited, a tangle of tightly woven cords.

"All right, all right," Ren said with a smile as Pig stamped the ground impatiently, her head swiveling around so that she could deliver an all-too-pointed look. "I can only move so fast, you know."

Pig snorted. *A likely story*, she seemed to say, her stare narrowing with an uncanny perspicacity.

"I want to go back just as much as you do," Ren protested, securing the various straps in place. But did they really?

The first step in the direction of their clan's territory landed with a leaden *thump*, near-identical to the weight that dropped into their belly. They couldn't match Pig's exuberance, the way she'd bolted out of their grasp the very second they'd finished tying that final knot. Instead, they trailed behind her and the cart she was pulling, not so much stepping as dragging their feet, the lump of iron that had plummeted into their gut growing heavier and heavier and heavier still. A pressure matched only by the vice that had clamped around their heart. By the time the dense foliage parted around a familiar clearing, the cave mouth Ren had once considered their front door stretching open wide ahead of them, the crushing feeling had become all-consuming, thinning their breaths into the shallowest of gasps.

There it was. *Home*. One that both was and wasn't. Only a

handful of days had passed, and still it didn't feel real. Ren swallowed, emotion stoppering their throat like shards of broken glass. Even on the way down, it hurt; perhaps worse than if they'd simply allowed the feeling to sit. But the thought alone proved intolerable. Because how was Ren supposed to be the lifeline their clan needed them to be if all they could ever think about was themself?

Exactly, they thought, catching their lower lip with their teeth hard enough to taste blood. *This isn't about you. It's much more than that. It's—*

A group of children chose that moment to spill out into the clearing, interrupting Ren's thoughts with a cacophony of high-pitched shrieks and squeals. None of them had noticed Ren thus far, too consumed with their game of make-believe to pay even Pig any mind.

"I've got you now, vile wizard!" cried the tallest goblin, a boy of about nine who had taken to going by Dandy as of late; short for Dandelion. He brandished a rather impressive-looking stick, about as long as a short sword.

"Is that what you think?" retorted one of the other children – the apparent "wizard", who Ren knew as Robin. They raised their arms and waggled their fingers, as if preparing to cast a spell. "You always were a fool, Aconite. Look! You've walked straight into my trap! Minions, seize him!"

Following their "master's" command, the last two children, twin girls named Holly and Ivy, stepped out from behind Robin and started towards Dandy. Ivy leapt forward with a triumphant roar, raising her own stick high above her head in what was doubtless meant to be a display of ferocity, while Holly was more subdued, dragging herself along with obvious effort.

Noticing her lack of commitment to her role, Robin let out a long, frustrated groan. "Come on, Holly! You're supposed to be my halfling minion. At least *try* to play the part."

"I'm sick of being the smelly halfling!" Holly snapped, stamping her foot. "I want to be Aconite! You said I'd get a turn—"

"Yeah! Next time!" Dandy said, waving her off, stick still in hand.

"That's what you said before!"

Ren smiled, the tightness in their chest unraveling into a dull, deep-seated ache. It was no surprise that the children were playing this game again. They always were. Though a lesson was in order. As much as the older children seemed aware of the concept of "taking turns", it seemed they continued to struggle when it came to putting it into practice.

"All right. No fighting," Ren said, stepping out from the surrounding bushes and into the clearing proper.

Four heads swiveled towards them at once, and as the children's eyes widened with surprise – and, then, elation – the cause of their argument was swiftly forgotten.

"Ren's back! Ren's back!" they cheered in unison, crowding around Ren in a disorienting rush of flailing limbs and sticks.

"Did you bring us anything?" Robin asked, already peeling off to go peek into the wagon. Pig, aware that she was of less interest than her burdens, let out a decidedly unhappy snort, which went entirely ignored.

Ren chuckled. "Of course. I'd never come ho— *here* empty-handed."

Their mouth snapped shut, teeth fitting together with an audible *clack*. That was close. No matter what they did, that word – *home* – was always there, itching on the back of their tongue, ready to spring out the moment Ren let their guard down.

The cottage is your home now, they told themself, ignoring the way their insides curdled in response, the knowledge, deep down, that the cottage could never – *would never* – be their home. Even if they could get rid of that damned halfling.

Ren followed the children inside, trying their best to listen to four different stories at once as they all made their way down the gently sloping path, still shiny with moisture from the most recent rainfall. No matter how many times Ren chided the children, employing the ever-relevant phrase "one at a time", none of them was willing to take a backseat to the others. Instead, the competition for Ren's attention rapidly devolved into a display of who could shout the loudest, which, inside the Woodward Clan's sprawling network of caves, meant they were heard long before they arrived in the central cavern.

Homesickness or no, Ren would normally enjoy being welcomed back with all the excitement in the world. Except their echoing entrance had provided the more, shall we say, *eclectic* members of the clan with ample opportunity to stage an ambush.

Ren knew whose arms had grabbed them, lifting them up with startling ease, before the deep rumble of Thorn's voice confirmed it. "Couldn't stay away, could you?" asked their cousin, grinning over Ren's shoulder.

"Ugh. Put me down," Ren said, swatting the trunk-like mass of their cousin's forearm, left bare as always. "I have perfectly functional legs, you know."

"I haven't seen my favorite cousin in two whole days! Forgive me if I'm a little enthusiastic."

"*Over*-enthusiastic, more like," Ren replied with a roll of their eyes. Still, they couldn't help but smile.

Although Thorn was what more polite individuals would call an "acquired taste", known just as readily within the clan as the "weird one" as he was the "large one", Ren had spent more time in his company than not. From the moment Ren had joined the clan – the one bright thread amid the otherwise miserable tapestry of their early childhood – the two of them had been practically joined at the hip. Wherever one went, the other had been all but guaranteed to follow.

At least, until now.

Ren's heart squeezed around another swell of grief crashing against an otherwise quiet shore. They pulled Thorn into another hug the second he set them back down – a proper one this time, where everyone's feet remained firmly planted on the ground.

"I missed you too," Ren mumbled, their voice slightly muffled by the solid heft of Thorn's chest. Alas, the time when Ren had been able to tuck their face into Thorn's shoulder was long gone, buried beneath the most impressive growth spurt the clan had ever seen. "And don't you *dare* pick me up again. You already got your allotment for the day."

Thorn let out a scoff, his expression slackening into one of apparent innocence. "I wouldn't even *dream* of it."

"Uh-huh," Ren said, giving him a flat look.

Thorn shook his head, shoulders slumping as he threw up his hands. "Do you see how I'm being falsely accused?" he said, looking now towards the children, still clustered around them, his brown eyes creasing into an almost puppy-like plea.

"I dunno," said Dandy, crossing his arms. "You do pick up Ren a lot. Like, *a lot* a lot."

"It's 'cause he knows Ren doesn't like it," Robin explained. "Plus, Thorn's too dumb to come up with any new tricks."

"Hey! I have plenty of other tricks up my sleeve!" Thorn protested; not that it proved in any way convincing. Robin's stare, previously only dubious, turned pitying. Because what was a goblin without a vast and varied capacity for chaos?

"I wanna be picked up too . . ." Ivy mumbled, scuffing the toe of her boot against the mossy floor, a display of uncharacteristic shyness for a girl who'd been bellowing battle cries not even five minutes ago.

It all made sense less than a moment later, when Thorn hoisted her up with an exaggerated grunt of effort and the other children exploded into an absolute furor. How could she be so disloyal? they demanded, fists swinging as they stamped their feet. They were supposed to be *defending* Ren, not asking favors of the enemy! But by that point, Ivy was so lost in the delight of swooping through the air above Thorn's head that she either didn't hear them or, quite simply, didn't care.

"Again! Again!" she cried when Thorn finally set her back down, now huffing and puffing with the first hint of real exhaustion.

"Maybe later," he said, giving her hair a light ruffle. "But right now I've got to bring Ren down to the croplands. Nana's orders. We've got some *very* important business to take care of before they have to leave again."

"What sort of business?" Robin asked, their eyes bright with interest. They, along with Holly and Dandy, had quieted immediately at Thorn's statement. A new opportunity, perhaps, to be helpful to Ren – and, of course, to keep tagging along. *That* was the important part.

Realizing this, Ren turned towards them and said, with the utmost seriousness, "Business that absolutely can't wait. So, I need the four of you to help me out, okay? You see that wagon

I brought with me? All the food inside needs to be unloaded, and since I can't do it myself, some of the other adults are going to have to do it instead. Can you go find them and let them know?"

Dandy frowned. "Why can't we just unload it ourselves? We're plenty strong enough for that."

"Because I need you all to *supervise* them," Ren explained, seriously. "It's the most important job of all, and I can only trust the four of you to do it. Understand?"

Dandy, Robin, Holly and Ivy all nodded vigorously, practically glowing at the prospect of being put in charge, not just of something, but of *adults*.

Ren smiled. "I'm leaving this in your hands, then."

The children took off in a flurry of hoots and hollers and a marginally concerning, "Let's plant a stinkbomb in one of the crates!" Within seconds, they'd vanished from sight, ducking down one of the many branching tunnels, no doubt heading for the clan's living quarters. There, they'd find the requisite adults, not just for the task they'd been given, but for their other schemes as well.

Huffing out a breath, Thorn shook his head, his expression far graver than Ren had ever seen. "A moment of silence for the poor souls you've just sicced that bunch on," he said, pressing a hand over his heart in a common goblin expression of sympathy.

"Oh, come on," Ren said with a haphazard wave. "They're not *that* bad. They're cute!"

Another shake of Thorn's head. "You only say that because they actually listen to you. I have to chase them away from my toads no less than three times a day now – and I mean *actually* chase them. With a broom and everything!"

"Then maybe you shouldn't keep those toads. Ever think of that?" Ren grinned.

Thorn sighed. "Now you're sounding just like Nana."

The two of them found Nana waiting at the croplands, in the furthest of the three caverns, just like Thorn had said. She stood over the withered remains of a dying plant, both hands clasped around the gnarled end of her walking stick. Although her back had started to bow years ago – as much a product of her advanced age as the clan's ever-mounting burdens – it had somehow stooped lower in the days since Ren had last seen her. Now, she seemed to fold in on herself, crushed beneath a pall of exhaustion that lined the weathered map of her face in deep, inescapable shadow.

Never before had Ren seen such naked hopelessness etched into her features, the clan's de facto leader easily the most stoic of them all. But a few more steps, and it was plain to see why. The plant at her feet was not so much dying as already dead, brown and shriveled right down to the root. Its neighbors fared no better. In all these rows of mottled leaves and desiccated vines, not a single hint of green remained. A whole season's worth of crops – decimated.

But by what?

"Is it some sort of rot?" Ren asked, grimacing as their path cut through an especially tenacious stretch of sodden earth. It sucked at their boots like a starving animal, desperate for prey, rendering each step a struggle that could only be solved via brute force. Some level of damp was expected; this was a network of caves, after all. But by the time they finally reached Nana's side, Ren was practically panting for breath.

"I was hoping you could tell me," Nana said, turning towards them. Up close, her weariness became all the more apparent, unfurling across the whites of her eyes in jagged webs of sleepless red. "Hello, Ren. I'm sorry to drag you down here as soon as you arrived. But no one else has even come close to figuring out what went wrong here."

"It's all right, Nana," Ren said, forcing a smile. "You know I'm always willing to help. When did the ground turn like this?"

Nana let out a breath, her eyes fluttering shut. "We assume sometime in the night. But, given that this cavern's yields have been declining for months now, it's entirely possible that we're only just becoming aware of a long-standing problem."

"What about the other caverns?"

"Thankfully, unchanged – though who knows for how long." Nana's voice dropped as she said this, the words plummeting into the space between them with all the leaden weight of an anvil. It was all Ren could do to not allow themselves to be dragged down along with it.

Hopefully, this is just an isolated incident, they thought, squatting down so that they could get a better look at the dead plant and the surrounding soil.

The plant, itself, proved unremarkable – apart from being dead. No sign of pests or any sort of disease; nothing that would fell an otherwise normal Running Bean sprout. Ren prodded lightly at the black earth surrounding it, so choked with moisture it had turned into tar-like sludge, then frowned when foul-smelling water rushed to fill the depression their fingers had left behind. A strange, iridescent film undulated across the water's surface, ribbons of pink, blue and yellow cutting across otherwise murky brown. It might've been beautiful had Ren not immediately recognized what it was – and its origins.

Dwarves.

"The earth's been poisoned," they said, brushing their fingers off on their trousers as they straightened back up. "Run-off from a dwarven refinery. Adamantite, I assume. Nothing will grow here so long as it's in production – and, most likely, not for some time afterwards."

A clamor rippled through the small crowd that had gathered around Ren as they'd conducted their examination, other members of the clan eager to hear what had happened to the crops they'd been tending to. Now, realizing that this loss, like so many others, had come from beyond their borders, that worry turned to anger.

"So, it wasn't enough just to kick us out of our home?" demanded one of the goblins, exploding forward from the rest, her golden eyes bright with fury. "They had to poison what was left of it too?"

"Never ascribe to malice what can just as easily be attributed to disregard, Briar," Nana said with a tired sort of sagacity, the kind that flowed from years of choking down your own outrage, no matter how justified. All because it was *safer*. And Nana would know. She was the oldest goblin in the entire clan. At seventy-two years old, she'd reached an age almost unheard of among goblins. So, when she spoke, people tended to listen.

But not this time.

"No," Briar said, shaking her head. "I'm done with standing around and hoping that other people stop hurting us. It's time to stand up for ourselves and *make* them stop. We should go up there and tear down that refinery and—"

"Absolutely not." Nana's voice was firm, cleaved from the same stone as her expression. "There will be no sabotage of any kind."

"Maybe we could ask the dwarves to shut down the refinery, instead? Let them know that it's destroying the soil here," Thorn suggested with a half-hearted shrug. No doubt just a harried attempt at defusing the snarl of agitation already snaking through the rest of the crowd. Ren was certain he knew just as well as they did that any attempt to treat with the dwarves would only end with a hammer to the face. Although it had been years since the last dark lord rose and fell, the Realm's perception of goblins had not changed: they were evil, closer to vermin than to living, thinking beings, and any sort of mercy was wasted on them.

"No," Nana repeated, more forcefully this time. "No one will be doing anything to the dwarves – talking or otherwise."

"But we can't keep letting them get away with this!" Briar snapped, tightly balled fists trembling at her sides.

Nana's gaze sharpened, the gray of her irises glinting like polished steel. "And what do you think will happen after you set foot in their fortress, even if only to 'talk'? They'll come down here, and they'll do what they always do: scour us away with fire and iron until there's nothing left but ash and bone dust. We saw it happen to the Rivermud Clan thirty years ago, and I'll be *damned* if I'll allow the seeds of another such tragedy to be sown on my watch."

By some miracle, Ren managed not to flinch at the mention of the clan of their birth. They'd been only a small child at the time, barely out of diapers, and still the memory of that night remained, seared into their psyche with all the permanence of thickly roped scar tissue.

"I—" Briar faltered, her mouth devolving into a pale, thin line as two red blotches bloomed high on her cheekbones. Nana was right, and she knew it.

"What matters now," Nana continued, straightening up as

much as her aching back would allow, "is making up for what was lost. Do we still have enough seeds for that?"

Briar nodded. Although she'd conceded in their argument, her discontent persisted, made manifest in the subtle flexing of her jaw.

"Good. If what Ren says is correct – and they've never been wrong before in these matters, much like their late teacher – this cropland is useless to us now. We'll have to sow whatever seeds we have left elsewhere."

"Except the other caverns are already at capacity."

"What if we buy food instead?" hazarded another goblin from the crowd, who Ren recognized as Briar's younger brother, Bramble. "You know, from one of the villages near by. The gnomes will sell to us, right?"

"Only if you can pay them in coin, which we don't have," Briar scoffed.

Bramble let out a soft "Oh", his gaze dropping to the space between his feet, half-sunken into the soupy muck. "Then – what if I go get a job that pays in coin? I've heard that there's someone looking to hire goblins down in the south—"

"*No!*" The word exploded out of Ren before they even realized they were speaking, forceful enough to send them hurtling forward. Because there was only one kind of job that anyone hired goblins for, and every one of them knew it.

The dark lords, of course, knew it best of all.

"No," they repeated, softer, settling back onto their heels. "I'll plant the seeds myself. Above ground, by the cottage. I'll till new earth if I have to." Whatever it took to keep their family from becoming someone else's minions, forced to die for a cause no goblin could ever believe in. All because they felt they had no other choice.

"You don't have to do it all by yourself, Ren," Bramble said, his expression creasing with concern. "There are other fields above ground, other Caretakers."

But none of them were as skilled as Ren. This fact burned bright at the forefront of their mind, blinding them to all else. Because when it came to the good of the clan, only the best would do, and Ren – Ren *owed* it to them. Owed it in a way the other Caretakers didn't, the way any goblin who'd been born into the clan didn't.

"I'll make it work. Trust me," they insisted, the malformed debt that coiled in the pit of their stomach growing ever more ravenous, ready to take everything they could give and more. *It has to be me. It has to be.*

"I don't know..." Bramble glanced over at Nana, searching, as all the other goblins did, for guidance.

Her decision was almost immediate. "Give Ren the seeds. They'll be able to stretch them further while we gather more," she said, the finality in her words enough to finally loosen the tension pulsating across Ren's shoulders a much-needed fraction.

Unlike his sister, Bramble wasn't one to argue, especially not with someone like Nana. Still, when he returned a few minutes later with the seeds, tucked into a coarse drawstring pouch, he nonetheless passed them over with one last, half-mumbled, "I really don't mind going south, you know..."

"Okay," Ren acknowledged with a nod. "But you don't have to, so don't worry about it. Just focus on the mushroom walls and the other croplands for now." They gave Bramble's hand a reassuring squeeze and slipped the seed pouch into their pocket, where it settled, heavy as a stone.

"All right," Bramble said, letting out a soft puff of relief that quickly unspooled throughout his entire body. "Thank you, Ren."

Ren smiled, their outward confidence unshakable. Too bad their internal landscape was not so steadfast. For as much as their expression radiated certainty, matching every promise beat for beat, their knotted stomach told a very different story. Because, deep down, they knew that growing this much food in that little time on their own was a tall enough ask that it might as well have been impossible. And yet, they had to do it; not just try, but *succeed*.

Already, their thoughts spun in a disorienting cyclone, spurred onwards by their quickening pulse. Command after command swirled through their mind: *grow more, keep less, think of the clan in everything you do, be a blessing not a burden*. And then – *Pansy*.

Ren's breath hitched, caught on the pointed shard of their own mistake. All that food left behind – food their clan needed – devoted, instead, to a halfling who would never understand the true magnitude of this sacrifice. Or that it was even a sacrifice to begin with.

I need to get her out, Ren told themself; another reminder to follow the who-knows-how-many that had preceded it. *Get her out and fix everything she manages to break before then. Speaking of...*

"Thorn, do you have any more of that tonic of yours?" they asked.

Their cousin's face immediately split around a disconcertingly large grin. "You mean my *Juice*?"

Ren made a face. "Ugh. Yes. That." No way they were going to call it by that ridiculous name Thorn had come up with. It read as either juvenile or inappropriate – and distasteful either way. Which, considering the brain behind it, was probably the point.

Undaunted by Ren's disgust, Thorn gave a dramatic sweep of his arm and said, "Then follow me to my *atelier*, and we shall set you up with the *Juice* that you require."

Thorn's "atelier", as he liked to call it – a gnomish inflection he'd doubtless picked up from his last girlfriend – had been relegated to the furthest reaches of the clan's territory, down a series of winding tunnels, some of which narrowed to an almost uncomfortable degree. And that was for Ren, who, to be clear, was about sixty percent of Thorn's size. By the laws of physics, Thorn *should've* gotten stuck – or at least needed Ren to yank him through – but, somehow, he squeezed past even the tightest corners without issue.

When Ren asked him how he managed to do this, Thorn wiggled his arms and said, "I keep myself limber." As if that explained anything.

By now, Ren knew better than to push for more detail. They held their tongue and waited for Thorn to finish rolling aside the boulder he'd fashioned into a makeshift door; his latest attempt at keeping the children away from his beloved toads, no doubt. Speaking of...

"You got more of them," Ren observed, stepping inside at Thorn's behest. Their gaze immediately snapped to the two-dozen toads scattered about the circular space, all resting on carefully constructed beds of moss, dirt and leaves, as well as the occasional pile of (likely) dirty laundry.

"Course I did!" Thorn declared with a grin, chest swelling with pride. "I have to be ready when the next market comes around. I completely sold out of Juice last time, and each of my little beauties can only produce so much, you know. Honestly, I was real surprised by it. I didn't think that many people would be willing to open their minds to the beauty of traveling to a higher plane of existence."

In other words, get intoxicated off psychedelic toad secretions – which, for the record, was *not* what Ren was going to use them for. Recreational value aside, the secretions were also packed with nutrients: perfect for the growth paste Ren wanted to make.

"I'm sure Nana is thrilled," they drawled, the corner of their mouth twitching into a barely there smile.

Thorn winced. "Nana," he began, drawing out her name with guilty slowness, "doesn't know."

Ren sighed. "Of course she doesn't."

"It's not like the toads leave this place, anyway! No matter how hard the kids try to make off with them. Speaking of, do you think you could convince them to stop before you go? Like I said, they don't listen to me. And my excuse about 'getting in touch' with my Swamp Goblin heritage ran dry with Nana, like, ten toads ago."

Although Thorn had been born into the Woodward Clan, his parents had not. Why a pair of Swamp Goblins from the south had opted to settle among their cave-dwelling brethren, no one could say. But the clan had accepted them in much the same way they'd accepted Ren – completely and wholeheartedly.

Grimacing, Ren said, "Thorn, I think you're greatly overestimating my abilities."

"No, I'm not," Thorn replied, already hard at work rummaging through the chaos that inevitably unfurled across any space he claimed as his. "Now, where did I put it...? Oh! Found it!" He extracted a small amber bottle from an otherwise impenetrable sea of clutter with a triumphant flourish.

"That was quick," Ren said, eyebrows arching with genuine surprise. "Might be a new record."

"I've been trying to stay organized," Thorn explained with a nod, managing to sound utterly sincere even as he stepped across a series of rumpled-up shirts to present the bottle to Ren.

"Uh-huh," was all Ren said, their gaze flicking pointedly downward.

At least Thorn had the decency to look embarrassed at that, his olive-green skin darkening to a rusty red. "It was, uh, cleaner before you got here."

"I'm sure it was." In other words, *I don't believe you, but I'm polite enough not to say it outright.*

Though perhaps Ren should've, considering Thorn couldn't offer them the same courtesy when it came to letting unpleasant subjects lie.

"Hey, Ren?" he asked after a beat. "Are you sure you're okay with being the new Caretaker? You used to talk about wanting to find someone to settle down with. You know, start a family?"

Ren shrugged, somehow managing to exude nonchalance even as their muscles seized into a board-like stiffness. "We need a Caretaker, and I'm the one best suited to the role. It's pretty simple."

"Yeah, uh, that's not what I asked."

They blew out a breath, rolling the bottle between their palms. "Is it my first choice? No, of course not. But it's what needs to be done. As long as the clan's taken care of, that's good enough for me. Besides, living alone isn't so bad—"

Their brain, traitor that it was, took the opportunity to flash Pansy's face before their eyes; her delicate features, rendered in crystal-clear definition, enough to narrow their throat with a sudden, graceless jolt. And Thorn, far too observant for someone who lacked what most would consider common sense, jumped on this stumble with all the delight of a cat who'd just caught a mouse – or, perhaps, a fat dollop of cream.

"Oooh, you're hiding something," he said, grinning from one elongated ear to the other.

"No, I'm— *ugh*." Ren sank into themselves, arms folding over their chest as they silently cursed their ongoing inability to lie.

Ridiculous.

"Fine!" Ren sighed, the breath scraping through them like sandpaper. "I'm not living alone any more, okay? There's"– they grimaced, certain they were moments away from signing themself up for the biggest hit of regret they'd ever experienced – "someone else."

Thorn's ears pricked up immediately, wiggling with almost childlike delight. "Is it a girl? Oh, it's *definitely* a girl. I can see it written all over your face. What's her name? Is she pretty? What clan is she from?"

"She's a halfling."

"Okay," Thorn said, without missing a beat – a far cry from the shock Ren had expected. "That answers ... maybe one of my three questions. What about the rest?"

"Her name is Pansy."

"And? *Three* questions, Ren. Not two."

Ren gave him a weird look, their brow furrowing. "You can't seriously be asking me if she's pretty. She's a *halfling*."

Thorn shrugged. "Why wouldn't I? You know I don't discriminate based on someone's ancestry. It's what's inside that counts." He thumped his fist against his chest, as if to illustrate.

For a moment, Ren could only gape at their cousin. Then,

burying their face in their hands, they muttered, "Nature have mercy. You're absolutely ridiculous."

"Honestly, I'm surprised you're acting like this," Thorn said with a frown. "You were fine with me dating Towi."

"Because Towi is a *gnome*. Gnomes don't hate us like halflings do!"

"Yeah ..." Thorn sighed, his expression turning almost wistful. "They're too fixated on their machines for that. Which I guess is why Towi and I didn't work out. You know, 'cause I'm not a machine."

Ren rolled their eyes. "Even if Pansy *was* pretty, it doesn't matter because, like I already said, she's a halfling who hates goblins. And I, for the record, don't like her either."

"Then why is she living with you?"

"Because we have a deal." Then, realizing they'd neglected to add a necessary bit of context, added, "The cottage used to be her grandmother's, apparently."

"Ah."

"Anyway," Ren continued with a wave of their hand, "the only thing about Pansy that I care about is how to get her to leave."

"Well, you already know how to do that, don't you?" Thorn said, his lips parting around a downright devilish grin. "Halflings hate goblins. So make it as unrepentantly goblin as possible."

Ren scoffed. "I know *that*." The real question here was: how? So far, the dirt hadn't worked; though perhaps they just hadn't brought in enough of it. But even so, they could hardly keep banging away at the problem with a single hammer. Not if they expected results, at least.

As they dropped the bottle of toad secretions – *no*, they

weren't going to call it "Juice" like it was proper food – into their pocket, their fingers brushed against the pouch of seeds they'd stored there earlier, and the bud of an idea began to bloom at the forefront of their mind. Running Beans had gotten their name for a reason. Perhaps there was a way to "kill two birds with one stone", as the halflings liked to put it.

7
Pansy

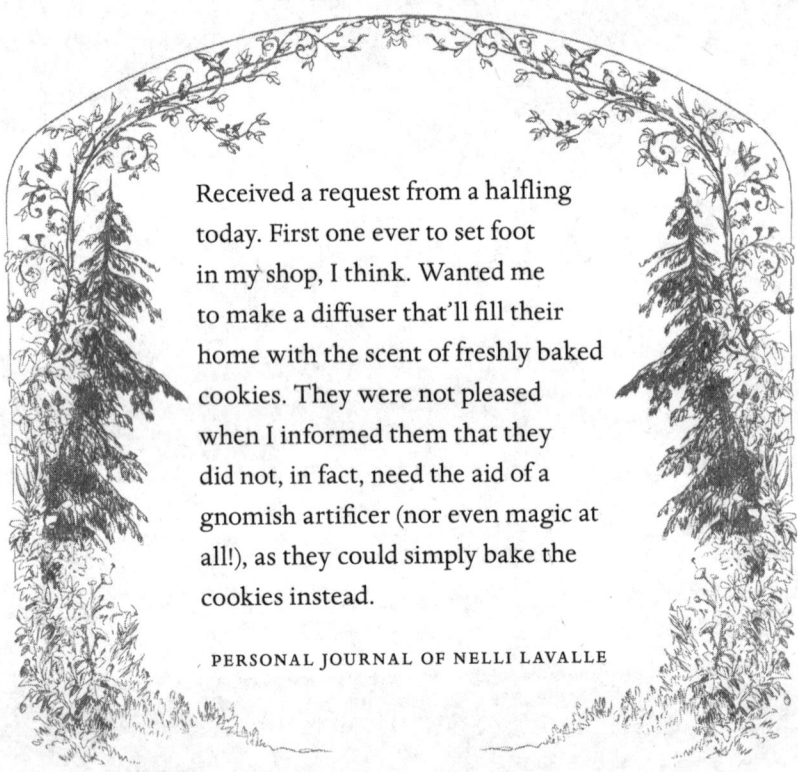

Received a request from a halfling today. First one ever to set foot in my shop, I think. Wanted me to make a diffuser that'll fill their home with the scent of freshly baked cookies. They were not pleased when I informed them that they did not, in fact, need the aid of a gnomish artificer (nor even magic at all!), as they could simply bake the cookies instead.

PERSONAL JOURNAL OF NELLI LAVALLE

In retrospect, Pansy should've left Haverow earlier in the day. Although the cottage wasn't exactly *far*, per se, it wasn't close either. By the time she rounded the last bend through the forest, dense foliage parting to reveal the cottage's thatched roof, gently sloping down to the mossy brick of its foundations, the sun had thinned to an impossible sliver. Once-golden light had turned hazy, purpling like a new bruise. Any longer and Pansy would have been forced to traverse this maze of trees in the dark, her precious kitten-shaped cargo in tow.

The thought registered with a barely repressed shudder. Already the details of her surroundings were fading, drowned in ever-lengthening shadow. Like a charcoal sketch beset by an errant palm, everything smudged together until only the murkiest of impressions remained. The path, at this point, was barely deserving of the name: a tract of dirt through the woods, studded with grass and the usual assortment of weeds. In the dark, she could veer from it and never know, wondering, all the while, as her surroundings got colder and darker and the howls of vicious, hungry beasts drew closer, why it was taking so long to get home.

That would certainly make things easy for Ren, wouldn't it? Pansy thought with a frown. If she got lost for ever in the woods, the cottage would go to them by default. How else were they supposed to interpret her leaving for Haverow one morning and then never coming back? Any reasonable person would assume she had simply given up. And even if Ren *had* managed to work out the truth, would that really change anything? It wasn't like they'd come looking for her...

Except... maybe they would? The memory of their first meeting surged to the forefront of her mind, frothing and foaming until she was completely awash with it. *You should go home before it gets dark*, they'd said; words that now echoed anew. Ren's concern, though certainly not born of any real affection, had nonetheless been entirely sincere. And it was only at this moment that Pansy understood: the inherent value they saw in all life – *all life*, including hers – could never be undone by something as petty as mere dislike.

The knowledge dragged over her like a warm tide, filling her chest with a strange, uncomfortable sort of certainty. Too light to be dread, but also too heavy for joy. A realization, half-formed, fluttered behind her eyelids, so close to revealing its truth. But what that truth was precisely, Pansy couldn't say. And perhaps that was for the best. A bell once struck couldn't be unrung, and Pansy's stomach told her, with a pointed, near-vicious twist, that this was one she ought to leave well enough alone.

"I'm going to need you to do your job, okay?" Pansy told the kitten, cleaving once again to her well-established plan and, more importantly, the semblance of security it offered.

The kitten, having napped most (read: all) of the way, roused with a comically large yawn. He blinked at her, each eye opening and closing independently of the other, and cocked his head to one side. His fur, still firmly in that too-fuzzy cotton-ball stage, stuck up in a way that only added to his confusion.

Pansy sighed. "You're really not inspiring much confidence, you know . . ."

"Confidence in what?" Ren's voice, sounding from somewhere to Pansy's left, arced through her like a lightning bolt.

She jumped, which, while not a problem in of itself, ultimately made for a rather difficult landing. Because landing, it turned out, was not so easily accomplished when one's legs could out-wobble gelatin. A mercy, then, that the cottage's old mailbox, a badly weathered thing that had probably seen more animal nests than letters over the years, sat within arm's reach.

Pansy caught it like her life depended on it. "Don't sneak up on me like that!" she snapped, her face flushing red with humiliation.

Still crouched amid several rows of freshly turned earth, Ren gave her a flat look, their eyes eerily luminescent in the waning half-light. "I'm literally working in the middle of the garden," they said, casting an arm out for emphasis. "How could I possibly sneak up on you like this?"

"It's dark." Pansy sniffed, scrabbling for some semblance of dignity – no matter how scant – as she hauled herself upright. Best not test the mailbox's structural integrity any more than she already had. "How can you expect me to see you when you didn't even turn the porch light on?"

Ren scoffed. "It's not *that* dark. Don't blame me because you're more easily startled than a newborn foal."

"I'm not—" The protest died in Pansy's throat, half-formed, culled by the scythe of Ren's arching brows.

"That's what I thought," Ren said after a beat, far more smug than they ought to have been – at least, according to Pansy's own bruised ego. Worse, their accompanying grin proved no less charming for it, and Pansy's heart, barely settled from its latest shock, threw itself into a new, even wilder set of acrobatics.

"What are you doing out here so late anyway?" she asked, if only to distract herself from the somersaults spinning inside her chest. It didn't work, but hey, at least she'd tried!

"Gardening. *Obviously.*"

"Yeah, I can see that, thanks," Pansy said, her tone bland. "What I meant is: isn't that something you're supposed to do during the day?"

"Maybe if you're a halfling who can't see in the dark," Ren replied with a snort. "Speaking of, didn't I already tell you not to wander around the forest this late? Do you *want* to get lost or are you just trying to annoy me?"

Okay. She definitely deserved that one. But even so, Pansy refused to give Ren the satisfaction of admitting it aloud.

"Whatever." She sniffed, waving away their less-than-kind concern with a haphazard flick of her hand. "It all turned out fine, didn't it?"

"Yeah, this time," Ren pointed out. "But, you know, if one night out here is enough to send you running back to your village at first light, maybe you should do yourself a favor and just stay there."

Plowlines of confusion streaked across Pansy's brow. "What are you talking about? I just went to pick up some groceries." She lifted the shopping basket to illustrate. "Didn't you read my note? I left it right by the door."

Something flitted across Ren's face at the mention of the note, a barely there flicker that vanished so swiftly Pansy was almost tempted to discount it as nothing but a figment of her imagination. "No," they said, shaking their head a touch too vigorously. "I didn't see a— *That's a cat.*" Their voice flattened with disbelief as their gaze snapped, at last, to Pansy's basket and the tiny kitten peeking out over its rim.

"Oh, yes!" Pansy said, her expression brightening with a mischievous twist. "My friend's cat had kittens, and she asked me if I wanted one. Of course, the second I saw this little guy's cute, fuzzy face I had to say yes. Don't you think he's adorable?" She thrust the basket towards Ren – kitten and all – and noted, with no small amount of delight, that they immediately recoiled, mouth thinning in what she suspected was barely restrained disgust, given the way their ears flattened in turn.

Maybe Blossom was onto something . . .

"Do you even know how to take care of a cat?" Ren asked, their eyes flicking back up to meet hers.

"My friend gave me a rundown of the basics," Pansy answered, curling her fingers into the soft fur beneath the kitten's chin once more. *Good boy! Keep doing what you're doing. We'll get Ren to leave in no time!*

"What about a name?" Ren asked.

"Huh?" Pansy looked up, her fingers briefly stilling until a plaintive meow kicked them back into action.

Ren rolled their eyes. "Did you give the kitten a name yet?"

"Not yet," Pansy replied with a shake of her head. "Why? Did you want to do the honors?" She grinned, wicked-bright.

"Absolutely not," Ren said with a derisive snort. "He's your cat. You take care of him."

Looking down at the still-purring kitten, now butting his head against the flat of Pansy's palm, she let out a thoughtful, "Hmm."

She'd never named anything before; anything other than a recipe, at least. But those were easy – especially when you followed the tried-and-true rule of "what it says on the tin". Unfortunately, that method wouldn't do her much good here. She could hardly name the kitten "Cat" or any variation thereof. Ren would almost certainly mock her for it if she did. Except, hadn't they named that pig of theirs "Pig"? Still, Pansy swore she could do better than that. She had to. Her pride demanded it!

"I'm sure something will come to me," she told the kitten as she headed for the door, more for her own benefit than his.

Pansy managed one step into the cottage before she jerked to a stop, her eyes widening as the smell hit her – dizzyingly sweet, like syrup drizzled over hot, sugar-powdered dough. She frowned, brow furrowing as she tried to place the source, a tall ask even after she'd cranked on the surrounding oil lamps, vestiges of halfling architecture jutting out from wild tangles of goblin-cultivated greenery.

Speaking of, there seemed to be more of it now. The moss

she'd accidentally dislodged upon her arrival had been returned to its proper place, nestled high above in intricate swirls. She guessed Ren had figured out a way to salvage it. If she wasn't so preoccupied with pinpointing the origin of the smell, still bearing down upon her with the warm weight of a loved one's embrace, she might've noted that they'd kicked up a fuss for nothing. But, as it was, there was nothing beyond the singular question currently burning a hole through her thoughts.

"What in the world is that smell?" she wondered aloud, her gaze sweeping across the entry hall again and again, always to no avail.

"The consequences of your own actions," Ren declared without missing a beat. Contrary to Pansy's expectations, they'd followed her inside. Now, they stood in the open doorway, hands on their hips, their chest puffed up in unabashed triumph.

Pansy blinked, the snag of her own confusion upending her thoughts as much as the sight of Ren's exultant grin. Wait – did they think she *disliked* the smell? How very wrong, but also – charming? It was the second time she'd used the word to describe Ren, and though it certainly *fit*, she couldn't help but wonder, somewhat distantly, whether she ought to be using it. Ren was a goblin – more specifically, a goblin she was actively trying to get rid of – and goblins weren't *supposed* to be charming. They were mean and cruel and, well, evil! Just like the dark lords who commanded them. And yet, the truth of this did nothing to quell the easy warmth seeping into her chest, buoying her up from the inside out.

She giggled, unable to stop herself. "The 'consequences of my own actions', huh? Then you better let me know exactly what I did, so I can do it again!"

"You – what? You *like* it?" Ren promptly deflated, their

expression splintering to pieces against the spearpoint of their own confusion.

"It smells good! So, what is it?"

"A paste. For the moss," Ren explained, almost grudgingly, as they pointed overhead.

"Interesting. I'd expect something like that to smell sour, not sweet." A beat. "Is it weird that it actually makes me want to bake something?" Pansy asked, a sheepish smile unfurling across her lips.

"You want to bake something?" Ren's ears perked up at that, revealing their interest despite an otherwise neutral expression.

"Mm-hmm. I'm thinking maybe some shortbread cookies." She needed to do a test batch anyway, the perils of an unfamiliar kitchen (and oven!) an already hard-learned lesson. The last thing she needed was for the cookies she'd promised Mrs. Millwood to go the same way as the cake she and Blossom had prepared for Blossom's mother's fortieth birthday several years ago – namely, hard and charcoal-like. No doubt, Pansy would never hear the end of it if they did.

"Any objections?" she asked, looking at Ren.

"I—" Ren's mouth opened then snapped shut as a bronze flush bloomed across the bridge of their nose. They looked away, long lashes dusting the curve of their cheekbones, and grumbled, "Do whatever you want."

"That's the plan," Pansy chirped, lowering the basket so that the kitten could hop out without plummeting the equivalent of several cat-sized stories.

Unfortunately, this didn't seem to make much of a difference. The kitten clambered over the basket's rim without any grace, somehow managing to trip over his own paws in the process. He tumbled out, landing in a fuzzy, flailing heap for all of half a second before he bounded upright, shook the dirt from his fur, and scampered off to explore parts heretofore unknown.

So much for "Don't worry if he spends the first couple of days hiding", Pansy thought with a laugh as the kitten tore across the living room, yowling all the way.

As much as she disliked the cottage's present lack of furniture – something she planned to rectify as soon as she was able – Pansy couldn't deny that, in this instance, it was probably for the best. In any appropriately furnished home, the kitten would've almost certainly crashed into something right out of the gate. For all that Blossom had insisted they were hardy little creatures, Pansy wasn't ready to put that to the test just yet.

Either way, she needn't have worried. The kitten abandoned his wild laps about the room soon enough, electing, instead, to bat at the ivy that framed a nearby window.

"Hey! You! Stop that!" Ren snapped, marching over to the kitten, now laid on his back, a single cord of ivy pinned between his front paws.

The kitten paused, yellow eyes nearly swallowed whole by the black of his pupils, focusing on Ren with an uncanny sort of awareness, as if he understood them. He didn't, of course. But it nonetheless made the kitten's decision to resume bunny-kicking his ivy prisoner less than a second later all the more hilarious – at least, from Pansy's perspective.

"Aw. Look at him go." She giggled. "How cute."

"He's not cute!" Ren snapped, whirling on her with a glare that could cut through glass. "He's a menace!"

"And what exactly do you want me to do about it?" Pansy asked, cocking a brow. "I can hardly stand there holding the ivy out of his reach all day. And even if I did, what's to stop him from setting his sights on any of the other plants growing around here?"

"Pansy."

"Oh, fine." She huffed. "Don't say I don't do anything nice for you."

And with that she scooped up the kitten, quick enough that surprise swept the ivy from his grasp, and deposited him in the one place guaranteed to annoy Ren just as much: the top of their head.

She grinned. "Better?"

"*Ugh.*" Shooting her one last festering look, Ren reached up to pluck the kitten from their scalp. However, unlike Pansy, they no longer had the luxury of surprise on their side, and so the kitten, unwilling to be manhandled a second time, sank his claws into Ren's dark hair and tender skin alike.

It took all of half a second for Ren to admit defeat, releasing their hold on the kitten with a hiss and a grimace.

"Get. Him. Off. Of. Me," Ren ground out between clenched teeth, every inch of them rigid as a board.

"But he seems so comfortable there! Plus, I thought you loved animals, Ren."

"Not when they're digging several tiny needles into my scalp!"

"You know," Pansy said, unmoved by the accusation searing through Ren's stare, "it's probably for the best that he's up there instead of on the ground. Cats apparently like to do their business in either dirt or sand. And who's to say he'll actually use a proper litter box when you've more or less advertised the entire house as a toilet."

"What?" Ren's eyes bulged. "You can't be serious."

"Oh, I am. Very much so. So, maybe you want to clean up

a bit? I wouldn't want to *destroy* anything of yours, given our agreement."

No sooner had the words left her mouth than Ren's stare narrowed. "You planned this," they said, their voice thick with the sour drag of someone realizing they had been outplayed.

Pansy shrugged. In truth, she couldn't take all the credit: Blossom had been the one to suggest she bring home the kitten. "Believe whatever you want," she said. "Either way, my point still stands, meaning I'd get to sweeping if I were you. It *was* a pretty long walk back from Haverow."

"This isn't over," Ren said with a scowl, jabbing a finger in Pansy's direction before stalking out of the room. No doubt they'd wanted to appear intimidating, their words as much a threat as the gesture that had accompanied them. But the kitten, still sprawled across the top of their head like a fuzzy black hat, had rendered such a thing an impossibility. Instead, they only managed to look ridiculous.

Make that another point for me, Pansy thought with a grin, riding high on her latest victory as she retreated into the kitchen.

For once, she was utterly untouchable. Ren had lost, and she had won, and all that damnable dirt was finally going to be swept away! Truly, nothing could ruin this for her, not even a finicky oven primed to burn her cookies to a crisp.

Only, Pansy didn't even get that far because she'd done it again: she'd forgotten the sugar.

The realization hit her partway through mixing her batter, well beyond the point of no return. Back when she'd lived in Haverow, this wouldn't have been much of an issue. She could just pop out to the grocer and be back within half an hour – or bother Blossom for a cup if the grocer was already closed. But out here in the forest, an hours-long walk from the village, the fact registered with stomach-plummeting devastation. Because no sugar meant no cookies, transforming the mixture sitting at the bottom of her metal bowl from a point of pride into a badge of shame. A waste.

Unless, she went back to Haverow anyway...

Maybe if I run, the grocer will still be open when I get there, Pansy thought to herself as she covered the bowl with a nearby lid. It was a silly thought, the kind that Ren would probably think of as halfling stupidity. But standing there, with her failure sitting on the counter before her, Pansy couldn't bring herself to discount it.

She strode out of the kitchen, her basket hanging off her arm yet again. The heat that had once stained her cheeks now sat beneath her breastbone, newly condensed into a far more determined flame.

Pansy nearly made it into the entry hall before Ren, now armed with a broom and exceedingly full dustbin, rounded the corner, with kitten still in tow, and said, "You can't possibly be thinking of going out this late."

"I forgot to pick up sugar," Pansy explained, tucking a stray curl bashfully behind one ear. "Since I already threw all the other dry ingredients together and melted the butter, it'd be a shame to let them go to waste."

"So, you're going to risk getting lost in the woods. Wow. What a well-thought-out plan you've got there," Ren said, their voice positively dripping with sarcasm.

Pansy flushed again, despite herself, and said, "I know it's not the best idea—"

"It's a *terrible* one."

"But I need that sugar. So, unless you know of some goblin alternative that you have on hand..."

Ren set down the broom and dustbin with a sigh. "I told you about sugarfern already, didn't I?"

Pansy thought for a moment. "That's what you said the vinegar was made from, right?"

They nodded. "You can also use it as a sweetener. Come on. I'll show you."

Ren led the way into the kitchen, with Pansy following close behind.

"Here," they said, handing over a single brownish-green frond. "Sugarfern."

Pansy turned over the frond in her hands, marveling at the way it scraped lightly against her skin. "It's like sandpaper!" she remarked.

"That's the sap. The leaves secrete it, and it eventually hardens into a sort of crystal; hence the rough texture, which becomes more pronounced once the leaves are dried like this."

Pansy frowned. "So, do I just throw it in like this or...?"

Ren let out a huff that might've been a laugh, given the way their eyes twinkled. "Grind it up first. You want it to be a fine powder before you use it. That's why we dry out the leaves."

"Got it. Say, do goblins bake? Like cookies and cakes? That sort of thing?"

"Does it matter?" Ren asked, cocking an eyebrow at her.

"Just curious," Pansy said, shrugging. "Also, I generally try to avoid preparing dishes that I know won't go over well. Waste of food and effort, that."

Something in Ren thawed at her words, their shoulders dropping as the stiff wall of their posture dipped into something far more malleable. "I already told you that you don't need to cook for me. But goblin desserts tend to be teas, or ices in the winter, usually sweetened with berries, sugarfern or some sort of nectar. And rose hip. That's my favorite," they added after a beat, their voice softening to the point where it seemed like they were divulging a closely held secret rather than a harmless fact.

Pansy was being trusted with something. And, somehow, that was enough to send her heart skipping a beat. Several beats, in fact. "You know, that does sound good. Maybe I'll try making it sometime." She cast a grin over her shoulder, only for Ren to immediately avert their gaze.

"Do whatever you want," they mumbled, cheeks darkening for the second time that evening.

"I guess it makes sense that goblin cuisine wouldn't really use milk and eggs," Pansy said as she continued to grind away at the sugarfern using a mortar and pestle. "They're not staples for you all in the same way they are for us. Wait—" Pansy's eyes widened. "You *do* eat milk and eggs, right?"

"I do. Some of us do – goblins, I mean. Where animals have been cared for well. No meat, though; never that."

Suddenly, all the stories of goblins stealing hens and cattle, often touted as proof that thievery constituted an inherent part of goblin culture, took on a decidedly different sheen. Because if the animals had been poorly cared for, was it truly theft or, rather, a rescue? From a goblin perspective, the answer was plain. Pansy remembered the way Ren had spoken about valuing life: how it should be nurtured, cared for, respected. Again, she thought of her grandmother's cottage, sitting out here in the woods, consigned to become a moldering tomb for old memories, until the goblins had saved that, too.

Pansy let out a breath of relief, shoulders slumping as she leaned over the counter. "Thank goodness you can eat them. These cookies would be a waste otherwise."

Ren cocked their head to the side, confused. "Why?" they

asked, wincing briefly as the kitten, disturbed by the motion, hopped down onto their shoulder, where he settled anew. "You could still just eat them yourself."

Pansy froze. They were absolutely right, so why had she gotten so stuck on the idea that the cookies needed to be shared with Ren too? She wanted to blame it on the sugarfern, the only reason the cookies were even on their way to baking instead of relegated to the bottom of a wastebasket. But the explanation, reasonable though it was, didn't quite land. Because Pansy knew, deep down, that this went beyond simple matters of politeness, the elaborate song-and-dance attached to every favor, given or received.

It's just pride, she told herself, willing the warmth building beneath her skin to recede. After the way Ren had criticized her cooking the night before at the outset, she wanted nothing more than to make them eat their words again and again; as many times as it took to instill within them the appropriate amount of regret. So, *of course*, she'd seize any and all such opportunities. And why shouldn't she?

Her heart still in her throat, she forced what she hoped would be a remotely convincing smile and said, "It's no fun cooking for just yourself. Food is meant to be shared!"

Ren made a thoughtful noise. "I suppose that's true enough..." Still, there was something about the way they said it – or perhaps it was their stare, turned unflinching in the time it had taken Pansy to become the subject of scrutiny – that made Pansy feel utterly transparent.

Thankfully, Ren said nothing further on the subject. Either they were simply being polite or their acuity was not nearly as devastating as Pansy had feared. This didn't stop her from sweating as she finished up her batter, every one of her senses so wrapped up in the sensation of Ren at her back that by the time she popped the cookies into the oven she felt utterly wrung out.

"How long before they're done?" Ren asked, suddenly far closer than Pansy remembered.

"Oh, uh, about ten minutes or so, depending on how the oven heats," she replied, blinking dumbly at the handful of paces that now separated them. Her brain, traitor that it was, couldn't think of anything beyond this unexpected proximity, how if she just stretched her arm out in front of her, her fingers would surely graze the front of Ren's shirt, undone at their throat.

What would they feel like underneath, she wondered before she could stop herself, the thought blooming across her mind in a warm haze. Soft or firm? It was impossible to tell from just a glance, considering all of Ren's clothing was so damn loose! Granted, it suited them, but how was Pansy supposed to see anything when— Wait. Why was she even thinking about this?

Heat surged into her face anew, tingling across the bridge of her nose all the way up to the tips of her ears. In no universe were she and Ren ever going to touch, let alone like *that*. It was a mystery that needed no contemplation and certainly no resolution. This, Pansy told herself with more vehemence than was probably needed, was the closest they were ever going to get and—

Her thoughts stuttered to a sudden, graceless stop as Ren's fingers grazed the curve of her cheek, still flushed a deep scarlet. They were touching her! As casually as they might a friend. But Pansy wasn't – they weren't. She wanted to open her mouth, ask Ren what they were doing, but all she managed was a choking sound, pulled from deep in her throat. And as the world narrowed to that single point on her face, where Ren's skin touched hers, her awareness never moved beyond that crackle of lightning, building beneath a barely there seam.

"You had some powdered sugarfern on your face," Ren explained, jerking away as if they'd been burned. They tucked their hand against their chest – protective or, perhaps, simply mistrustful – and looked off to the side, their head angled such that their hair drew over their expression like an impenetrable curtain. The only clue that remained was their ears, twitching frantically against the flat of their skull.

"Oh, um, th-thanks," Pansy somehow managed to squeak out, forcing her voice beyond the bubble of embarrassment that had lodged in her throat.

Still refusing to meet her gaze, Ren made a low sound of acknowledgment before turning on their heel and stalking out of the kitchen. In the half-second it took Pansy to realize what was going on, they'd already cleared the doorway and were halfway to slipping beyond her vision entirely.

"Wait!" she shouted after them, gripping the door jamb with both hands so she could lean beyond it. "What about the cookies? *Dinner?*"

"I'm not hungry!" Ren called back right before they darted around the next corner.

Pansy's brow furrowed. How could they not be hungry? Judging from the amount of work that had been done to the garden, they must have been out there nearly all day! Well, whatever, she thought to herself with a shrug. Ren was an adult. They could easily make themself something to eat if they got hungry later.

That didn't stop Pansy from putting aside a serving of creamy mushroom pasta from her own dinner. But that was only because making exactly one person's worth of this dish was downright impossible. In all her years of cooking, she hadn't managed it even once, and she was starting to suspect that the feat would forever remain beyond her.

As for the small plate of shortbread cookies, all far greener than she was used to but no less delicious for it – well, Pansy left those out too. Judging from the empty dishes she found the following morning, neatly arranged in the drying rack, it was safe to say her efforts had not gone unappreciated. Ren had eaten everything.

8
Ren

> He carries our voices to those we hold dear,
> To each of the four corners, both far and near.
> And in return, we need only share
> A handful of kernels, a price most fair.
>
> — GOBLIN SPOKEN-WORD POETRY,
> ATTRIBUTED TO THE GOBLIN BARD,
> KORBIN, TITLED "BLACKBIRD"

Idiot! Ren thought with the sort of viciousness that could only be reserved for oneself, as they stabbed the point of their trowel into the earth surrounding a tenacious weed. *Why did I touch her like that? I could've just told her about the powder on her face. Ugh!*

Behind them, the kitten, who Ren had already taken to calling "Mushroom" because he seemed to crop up everywhere, let out an impatient mew. Evidently, the glove they'd sacrificed in a bid to keep their newly planted Running Beans, already budding from the earth, from being subjected to a set of sharp kitten teeth had lost its luster. Now, Mushroom was padding over to Ren, belly expanding around another plaintive meow as he butted his head against their leg.

"Go inside and find Pansy if you want to play," they groused, nudging the kitten aside with the back of their hand. "She's the one who brought you here."

Mushroom, however, didn't seem to care much about this particular fact. He pushed his head up into Ren's palm, throat already rumbling with a full-blown purr.

Ren sighed. "You don't care that I'm busy at all, do you? No, definitely not. You're just like the halfling who adopted you. You just take, take, take. If not for you, I might've actually managed to drive her out. She *really* hated all that dirt."

Of course, said dirt was long gone by now, the floorboards returned to their original halfling- (and kitten-) friendly state. Still, Ren couldn't help but smile at the memory of Pansy's frustration. If only it had been allowed to grow to fruition...

An abrupt, near-deafening squawk yanked Ren out of their fantasies so swiftly it was a wonder they didn't tip right over, crouched as they were on the balls of their feet. By some miracle, they managed to catch themself, palm pressing flat against the soft earth as they whirled on the source of the offending sound.

A raven, it turned out, big and black, her feathers gleaming like an oil slick in the late-morning sunlight. She sat atop the stone fence that encircled the property, watching Ren for a moment before she fluttered down from her perch. Had

Mushroom not already vanished beneath the boughs of a nearby bush, the resultant gale that stirred beneath the raven's dizzying wingspan would've chased him off just as swiftly. That is, if it hadn't simply sent him flying.

"*Message for Ren from your favorite cousin, Thorn,*" squawked the raven in imitation of Thorn's voice. "*Just wanted to check in and see how things are going with the . . .*" The raven made a low clicking sound in the back of her throat. No doubt, Thorn had once again made some sort of gesture while dictating the message, forgetting, as always, that ravens, while excellent at repeating words, could only do just that. "*. . . the pretty lady. My atelier remains open to you should you wish to avail yourself of my, ahem, extensive knowledge of cross-cultural dating.*"

Extensive? Ren's face flared hot as indignation punched into their throat. Of course, this idiot would think himself an expert after having dated a single gnome, who, for the record, had been perfectly lovely, whip-smart and forthright in that very gnomish way that people of different ancestries often found culturally off-putting. Ren had liked Towi. But Pansy? Absolutely not.

"*On a less fun note, Nana wanted me to tell you that other croplands may also have been affected by the run-off. It's hard to say for certain right now, but the yields seem to be dropping. We're going to try a couple of purifying potions and see if that does the trick. But maybe you can take a look next time you come by? End message.*"

The angry heat that had suffused Ren's being faltered, drowned in an icy tide. Their stomach shriveled in on itself, their breakfast turning leaden in the hollow of their gut.

"Reply?" squawked the raven, now in a distinctly less-Thorn-like timbre.

"Yes, please," Ren said, swallowing the knot that had twisted in their throat. "Message for Thorn from Ren," they began, as messages sent via raven always did. "There is no 'pretty lady', much less any 'things' that could be happening with one. So, please do us both a favor and allow this subject to die the death it so deserves. Please tell Nana that the beans are growing well. I should be able to bring by the first harvest sometime in the next ten-day, at which point I'll plant another. Hopefully, by prioritizing a quick-growing crop we'll be able to make up for any decreased yields. End of message."

The raven clacked her beak a few times, as if to say, *Message received*. However, she didn't budge after that, her talons firmly planted in the shallow groove between two rows of budding Running Beans.

Ah, right. Ren dug around in their pocket for a moment until their fingers brushed against the handful of shelled peanuts they kept on-hand for moments like these. Scooping one out, they cracked it open with the tip of one claw and held it out to the waiting raven.

"For your service," they said. Then, deciding that the poor bird deserved a little bit extra – she'd had to deal with Thorn, after all – Ren reached back into their pocket and pulled out another two shells, which they split open just as deftly.

The raven gobbled down the proffered peanuts with a lightning swiftness, nearly snagging the fleshy part of Ren's palm between her beak in the process.

They chuckled. "It's like we don't feed you at all," they said, gently stroking the top of her head with the side of one finger. "You know, Thorn likes to keep peanuts in his pockets too. Feel free to help yourself to them once you return to him. I'm certain he won't mind."

A new gleam rising to her eye, the raven let out a throaty caw of thanks and turned around with a few not-quite-graceful hops. Realizing what was about to happen, Ren scooted backwards; this particular lesson was not one they were keen to re-learn, having already thoroughly committed it to memory in their youth. The raven's wings unfurled with an awe-inspiring flourish, a great black shadow stretching nearly as wide as Ren was tall. Two pumps, and she was in the air, soaring over the fence and into the forest beyond – thought not without nearly taking the head off a strange halfling making her way up the forest path.

Oh, mercy. No. Not another halfling. Ren nearly groaned as the halfling in question let out a high-pitched shriek, dropping to the ground like a stone. *What did I do to deserve this?* they wondered, looking up at the sky, cloudless and blue and far too cheery for the sort of day this was rapidly turning out to be.

"Sorry," the halfling said, smoothing out the few curls that had gotten loose from her thick, yellow braid, "that was just – that was a *very* big bird."

"Yes," Ren said flatly. "Ravens are large birds."

"Right. Um." The halfling coughed into her fist and, readjusting her grip on the colorful bouquet she carried – hydrangeas, roses and lilies dotted with sword fern and lemon leaf – approached the wrought-iron gate in front of her. "I'm Blossom," she said, forcing a smile that looked almost waxy in the light. "Pansy's friend. Is she home?"

Ren barely managed to choke down another groan. First, the kitten; now, another halfling. How many extra guests was Pansy planning on dragging into their home? "Their", of course, referred exclusively to Ren in this instance; because while Pansy did technically live at the cottage, this was an entirely temporary arrangement. She'd leave soon enough. Ren would make certain of it. Somehow.

But for now . . .

Ren jerked a thumb to the door and said, "She's inside."

"Oh, wonderful. Thank you." Taking Ren's answer as an invitation – which Ren supposed it was – Blossom eased aside the gate with one pale hand and headed up the cobbled path to the front door.

She was about to close her fingers around the heavy iron knocker, which had been fashioned into a wreath of aconite, when she paused, lips pursing as if evaluating a new flavor. Then, turning back towards Ren, she asked, "Your name is Ren, right?"

"Yes," Ren answered slowly, not entirely sure where this was going – and whether they were going to like it, given the glimmer in Blossom's blue eyes.

She smiled. "Pansy's told me a lot about you."

Ren nearly choked. "She – she has?" Nothing good, surely. Pansy didn't like them; much like they didn't like her. And still something stirred beneath their breast, sending a rush of warmth all the way up to the tips of their ears, which then gave a traitorous twitch.

"Oh, yes. You were all she could talk about when she came to visit. In fact, she told me that— Oh!"

Of all the times Mushroom could have picked to make his entrance, this proved to be the winning option. He sauntered out of the bush with a triumphant yowl, chest puffed high and mighty, as if he hadn't just made an expedient retreat. Evidently, he recognized Blossom – which made perfect sense: Pansy had said she'd gotten him from a friend – because he trotted over to her and pressed the full length of his body against her bare calf.

For some reason, Ren didn't like this. The heat in their chest turned sour, and they snapped, "Come here, Mushroom."

But Mushroom was a cat, and cats, as Ren was beginning to understand, did not do anything except on their own terms. And right now, Mushroom wanted to be with Blossom, so that's where he would stay, stuck to her leg like half-dried sap.

Traitor, Ren thought, even though it made no sense. Mushroom wasn't their cat. He was Pansy's. So why should Ren care who Mushroom cozied up to?

Blossom giggled and lifted the kitten into her arms with practiced ease. "Is that what Pansy named him? I'm glad. I was worried she was going to name him something uninspired like – oh, I don't know, 'Cat'."

"There's nothing wrong with that kind of name," Ren said, suddenly defensive on Pig's behalf. Sure, they hadn't been the one to name her. That had been the work of her previous ... owner, Ren supposed was the right term, icky though it was, and Pig had simply refused to take another even after Ren had liberated her from the slaughterhouse. "And not that it matters," they continued after a beat, feeling oddly unsettled by the whole thing, "but I'm the one who named him Mushroom."

Blossom's eyebrows, two delicate, perfectly manicured things, shot up high on her forehead. "*You* named him?"

Ren stiffened. "Is it so difficult to believe that a goblin could come up with a suitable name for a cat? Pansy certainly didn't have any bright ideas."

A line of knowing dragged across the corner of Blossom's mouth. "Oh, not at all," she chirped, her eyes once again sparkling with that same twinkling sheen.

Mischief, Ren concluded. That's what it was. They'd seen it in Mushroom's eyes too. Far too many times, in fact. Always right before he pounced on something that was *very much not* a toy.

"Just go on in," Ren said, gesturing towards the door. "I'm heading back inside anyway."

"Done with your weeding?" she asked, still far too pleasant for Ren's liking.

No. "For now," they answered. They would come out again later to finish the rest – when it was cooler. A believable enough excuse.

They started towards the door, and Mushroom, who'd seemed otherwise content to lounge in Blossom's arms, wiggled free, just barely managing to land on all fours. He then scurried over to Ren in a gratifying display of loyalty, for which he was rewarded with a firm scritch behind the ears.

Perhaps you're not a traitor, after all, Ren thought, heart swelling with unexpected fondness. Realizing that Blossom was watching them, they quickly swiped the feeling from their face.

"What are you waiting for?" they barked, embarrassment turning their voice rough. "I said go on in, didn't I?"

Blossom looked like she was trying very hard to stifle a laugh. She pressed one hand against her mouth and said, in a somewhat muffled voice, "I figured it'd be more polite to let you lead."

Rolling their eyes, Ren stepped up onto the stoop beside her and pushed down on the knob's latch. The door swung open easily, revealing the entry hall in all of its mossy glory – along with a few heavily patterned rugs and brightly colored knits that had *definitely* not been there when Ren had left that morning. They frowned, confusion weighing heavy and low on their brow.

"Ren, is that you?" Pansy asked, her voice echoing from the adjoining room.

"And Blossom!" Blossom noted cheerily as she strode through the doorway.

So much for wanting Ren to lead . . .

"Blossom?" Pansy's head popped out from around the corner, her expression already bright with anticipation. The second her eyes landed on her friend, dressed in a brilliant blue pinafore, her face turned downright *luminous*.

The sight speared through Ren, and for the briefest of moments they could almost believe that this look was meant for them.

But reality was ever so quick to reassert itself. Stuffing the mess of yarn she'd been in the process of knitting down into her apron pocket, Pansy rushed over to Blossom and swept her into her arms, leaving Ren to stand there alone, awkward and forgotten. It shouldn't have mattered. What did they care if their presence paled in comparison to Blossom's? Of course it did! Blossom was Pansy's friend, and Ren was . . . a nuisance, a thief, a *squatter*.

Each word was another coal plinking against the bottom of Ren's belly, still sloshing with acid from before. Their hands clenched at their sides, teeth gritting against the white-hot urge to scream. They swallowed it down, again and again, throat working around a feeling like tar, black and sticky and noxious.

"You've got more plants in here than I do in my entire shop," Blossom remarked, looking around now that she'd been released.

Pansy laughed, musical and bright, the opposite of the churning in Ren's gut. "Oh, you haven't even seen the half of it. But don't worry. Ren's assured me several times now that the cottage was designed for it. Plus"– she gave an easy shrug, not even so much as glancing Ren's way the entire time – "it's rather charming once you get used to it."

Charming. That's all this cottage was to her. Meanwhile, for

Ren, their clan, this cottage and its rich farmland were a lifeline! Somehow, she'd nearly made Ren forget this, distracting them with a full belly and a handful of not entirely unpleasant conversations. Were they so desperate for a reprieve from carrying the clan's future on their shoulders that a few plates left out on the counter for them was all it took to undo every last knot of their resolve?

"I brought you these." Blossom lifted up the bouquet. "But it seems like more plants are the absolute last thing you need."

"You know I always love your bouquets," Pansy assured her as she took the bundle of flowers, her fingers carefully running over the bit of twine holding it all together. "In fact, this'll look great in the sitting room. I spent most of the morning decorating it, adding some rugs, tapestries and paintings – that sort of thing. There's a bunch of stuff stored around the cottage. I assume they're my grandmother's old things. Anyway, sorry – I'm babbling. Have you already had breakfast?"

"I wouldn't survive the walk out here on an empty stomach," Blossom said with a laugh.

"Elevenses, then? *Ooh!* Ren has a whole assortment of goblin teas, if you'd like to try. They're actually quite good. I had one earlier with breakfast, and—"

"*You took my tea?*" The words burst out of Ren, violent as a lit barrel of spellpowder. Meanwhile, the tar-like feeling in their gut churned, condensing into something hotter, brighter: fury.

Pansy blinked at them, her lips parting around a soft "o" of surprise, as if she'd *forgotten* that they were still there. "Is that a problem?" she asked. "It was in the cupboard, and you'd told me how goblins often put sugarfern in tea, so I assumed—"

"That you needed it more? After all that I've already shared with you?"

The tea had been Ren's one and only indulgence, the one thing they'd allowed themself to keep in the overwhelming face of their clan's need. Now, the inherent selfishness of it all was plain to see. Because if a halfling needed it more than they did ...

Ren swallowed, unable to finish the thought, their throat squeezing around an unexpected clot of shame.

Pansy, meanwhile, had the decency to look somewhat ashamed as well – even if only for a moment. She came back at them quickly, her chin raised high in stubborn halfling defiance. "I've shared with you too! Remember who's been cooking all of your meals."

"With ingredients *I* grew!" Ren plunged headfirst into their own anger, desperate to scald away the miserable burn of their shortcomings. Because someone had to be the villain here, and it wasn't going to be them. Not for this.

Pansy sniffed. "I bought a fair number of them myself, actually. But, honestly, Ren. It's *just* tea."

"Then drink your own!" they snapped.

"I don't— I forgot to bring it with me," she admitted after a beat, her gaze dropping briefly to the floor.

For a moment, Ren could only stare at her, speechless. How was it possible that she looked more embarrassed by her own forgetfulness than by the fact that she'd simply assumed Ren had a limitless supply of tea?

"It's okay, Pansy," Blossom said, placing a gentle hand on Pansy's shoulder, swaddled as usual in a fluffy cardigan. "I don't need any tea. Water is fine."

"But it's not elevenses without tea," Pansy protested weakly. "It'd be like having steak for second breakfast!"

A *second* breakfast? Ren's head spun. Did halflings have

second dinner too? Second lunch? Was there two of everything? It seemed unreal, unthinkable. No goblin would dare engage in such wanton excess. But halflings clearly knew little else.

Disgust tore from Ren's throat, visceral and sharp, twisted as the thorns that wound around their thoughts, blotting out the truth. Greed, gluttony and selfishness – that's all halflings were. They didn't damage the land like the dwarves did, but that was almost certainly only because the vast majority of them never bothered to set foot beyond the bounds of their own villages. All they lacked was opportunity; Pansy was proof enough of that.

Upper lip peeling back to reveal the gleaming points of their canines, Ren said, with all the cold venom they could muster, "I'm not sure what I was thinking, expecting anything different from a *greedy, selfish halfling.*"

They spat the words, whetted to knife-point sharpness. And as Ren pushed past the two halflings into the welcoming darkness of the floor below, the last thing they saw was the barest quiver of Pansy's lower lip.

The blade had hit home.

The cottage's lower level, with all of its cool darkness and moist earth that smelled of home, proved far less comforting than Ren had expected. A current of unease prickled beneath their skin, insistent and relentless. No matter how studiously they dedicated themself to rearranging the contents of their potions cupboard, which, to be clear, was already plenty organized – immaculately so, even – the feeling continued to pick at them, whizzing through their thoughts like an especially irritating gnat.

Ren told themself it was just lingering fury; the fire

smoldering in their gut simply hadn't extinguished quite yet. However, the conclusion, plausible though it might've been in isolation, didn't stick, and that proved equally intolerable.

Letting out a snarl of frustration, Ren slammed the cupboard shut only to wince when the glass panes along the front gave a worrisome rattle. Okay. Clearly distractions weren't working and, at this rate, would probably end up doing more harm than good. Because Ren *liked* this cabinet, even if it looked like a rainbow had vomited all over it in that distinctly halfling sort of way. It was large, sturdy and altogether suitable for their purposes. Not to mention, the thought of having to secure a replacement sent a shudder roiling through them. The sheer inconvenience of it all! Not just finding an appropriate substitute, but also getting it down here, a task that would almost certainly require a full complement of featherflight talismans, which Ren didn't have. *Ugh*. And if that wasn't bad enough, the loss of the cabinet would mean one less thing of Ren's in a house that seemed to be rapidly skewing towards Pansy, given the sudden rug infestation.

That was it! Understanding unfurled across Ren's brow, smoothing out the wrinkles their frustration had carved. No wonder they felt so uneasy. They were meant to be pushing Pansy out, and apart from the dirt they'd ultimately been forced to clean up, all they'd done was plant some Running Beans in a garden she didn't seem to care about. Granted, they'd also applied some growth paste, but that had proved equally unsuccessful, much to Ren's consternation. Meanwhile, Pansy was throwing down rugs, putting up paintings and knitting who-knows-what. And Ren – Ren was hiding downstairs like a petulant child who'd just come off a tantrum. Truly the pinnacle of so-called goblin "craftiness", that.

Ignoring the slight twinge that hooked into their belly – the one that said, *No, you've rather missed the mark yet again* – Ren began to gather what they needed. First, several sheets of moss, all in various shapes and sizes; then, a squat section of log, perfectly proportioned to serve as a side table, its graying bark festooned with scraggly bits of lichen and flat whitecaps; and, lastly, an especially large red-and-white-spotted mushroom, its head bulbous and soft, hastily glazed with a Potion of Ever Endurance. While the moss had been easily procured from the cottage's lower level, the latter two items had necessitated a short trip into the forest, which Ren had undertaken at a near sprint – at least, in one direction.

The return journey would've doubtless proved equally quick had Pig been around to help, but for once she was nowhere to be found. Not even Ren's voice had been able to reach her. It was strange. Ren could've sworn they'd passed her on their way down, curled up on a patch of moss near the base of the stairs; Mushroom had been there, too, actually. But by the time Ren had set out in earnest, the two of them had vanished.

In the end, it didn't matter. Ren needn't have rushed. Pansy was well and truly occupied, having holed up in the kitchen with Blossom, where they spoke in low, hushed tones that Ren could've strained to hear, if they so cared. They didn't. Not really. The fact that they'd overheard Pansy complaining about "the kitten plan", as she called it, not having immediately driven them from the cottage, was nothing but pure chance.

Granted, they'd smiled at it, gratified to know that their own stubbornness had proved equally maddening. But when Blossom replied with a thoughtful, "It's so strange that the kitten seems so taken with Ren, though. Cats are usually excellent judges of character," Ren's smile promptly vanished.

Instead, there was only that same tightness in their throat from earlier, and not even the sight of the sitting room decked out in moss and wood and mushrooms, alongside the halfling rugs and hideous knitted pillows, could chase it away.

But maybe once Pansy saw it . . .

As luck would have it, when it came time for Blossom to leave, the two halflings took the long way around, bypassing the sitting room entirely. *Probably because I'm in here*, Ren thought with an oddly sour note.

From the entryway, Blossom asked, "Is it really okay if I take the rest of the cookies? They're so delicious I'd completely understand if you wanted to keep them for yourself."

Pansy laughed, and Ren nearly flinched, the memory of her trembling lip cracking across their consciousness. "You're acting like I can't just make another batch," she said, all warmth and openness. "I'm sure Ren will give me some more sugarfern if I—" Her jaw snapped shut with such force that even Ren could hear it.

"Oh, Pansy," Blossom said. "Do you want to spend the night with me in Haverow instead?"

"No. It's – it's fine. I don't really care what they think of me. I know I'm not selfish or greedy or . . ." She hesitated, wincing perhaps, around the word. ". . . or a glutton. Plus, I can't leave now. Ren will think they're winning if I do."

Yes, the bet. *That's* what was important. Unfortunately, no matter how fervently Ren attempted to remind themself of this fact, their thoughts slid right off it, down and down into the dark morass stoppering their throat.

Guilt. That's what it was. Like a thicket of bramble, it had ensnared Ren completely, tiny barbs digging deeper every time they tried to escape. But the truth, once acknowledged, could not be so easily discarded. It sat at the forefront of their mind, unmoved by the shifting of their thoughts.

You hurt her, it said, low and steady, as if fashioned from the earth itself. *Unwilling to suffer the sting of your own shame, you turned that blade outwards instead. Gave it a new target, one even less deserving of the blame than you.*

The admonishment registered with all the brutal clarity of a slap to the face, unflinching in its accuracy. As much as Ren wanted to deny it, they couldn't. Because Pansy, for all her faults, her annoying habits and occasional thoughtlessness, was not a monster or a villain. In fact, she wasn't even a bad person, merely flawed in the way all people were. And Ren – Ren, unfortunately, owed her an apology.

The realization sat heavy in their gut as they waited for Pansy and Blossom to finish exchanging their goodbyes – something that took far longer than it should have. By the time the front door finally clicked shut, Ren could've sworn an entire age had passed. They practically had to rouse themself, head jerking up as Pansy's footsteps began to pad down the hall once more, keeping closely to one side. The side *opposite* to Ren.

So, she means to avoid me, they thought, ribcage squeezing tight around their heart. *I shouldn't be surprised.*

Still, at the first sign of red hair, peeking around the corner in a familiar mess of curls, Ren called out to her. "I'm sorry about earlier," they said, the unfamiliar words rolling across their tongue like rocks. "You didn't deserve . . . I shouldn't have taken my frustrations out on you like that." *You're a person, not a punching bag.*

For a moment, Pansy said nothing. She didn't have to. Her expression alone spoke volumes, the tired lines framing her too-stiff mouth suggesting she'd rather swallow glass than have this conversation.

Eventually, she let out a sigh and said, "I know I'm not perfect, Ren. Far from it, in fact. I let my excitement get the better of me today, and for that I'm sorry. I shouldn't have taken your things without asking—"

"That's not—" Ren clamped their jaw shut, words too vulnerable for present company – or any company, really – itching across their tongue. At last, they managed a strangled, "You're allowed to drink my tea. I don't mind."

Pansy eyed them warily, her disbelief plain to see. "If you're certain... But I do want to point out that I'm trying very hard to leave the old prejudices of my village behind. I only wish you'd afford me the same courtesy. Why can't we just be 'Pansy and Ren' instead of monoliths of our respective heritages? It's rather exhausting being the be-all and end-all of halflings and goblins, don't you think?"

"It is," Ren agreed, their voice barely more than a low murmur.

"Also," Pansy continued, her expression softening around a small, self-deprecating smile, "I'm a very poor example of a halfling." Then, as if to underscore her point, she kicked off her slippers and padded into the room, letting out a tiny sigh of satisfaction as the bare soles of her feet dragged across the soft tunnel moss Ren had so painstakingly laid down.

Well, so much for that plan . . .

"You know, this is really quite nice," Pansy remarked as she settled into the old, halfling-style armchair, her toes pointedly curling into the bed of green beneath it. "Saves me the trouble of lugging some more rugs from Haverow. I've already cleared out the few that were put away here in storage."

"Of course I end up living with the only halfling who enjoys moss," Ren said with a sigh, their shoulders slumping a little in defeat. "Are you sure you wouldn't prefer a goblin cave, too?" As inconvenient as it was to see their plan so thoroughly foiled, they couldn't deny that the eccentricities that made Pansy a "poor example of a halfling", as she'd put it, were actually rather sweet. Hence why they found themself smiling despite it all – though only a little.

Pansy shrugged. "I've already embraced goblin ingredients, so why not goblin houseware, too? Speaking of, is that a real mushroom?" She pointed at it, positioned so that it could serve as an ottoman.

"No, it's dark goblin magic," Ren said, utterly deadpan.

Pansy paused for a moment, her eyes blowing wide. Then her expression collapsed, features flattening into an unhappy scowl. "You're making fun of me."

"Yes," Ren agreed. "It's obviously a real mushroom."

"Maybe to you. But I've never seen one that large. I— *Eek!*" Pansy scrambled out of the chair with a high-pitched squeal, nearly sending the log table spiraling onto the floor in her haste to escape . . . a trio of mice.

The snort that left Ren quickly devolved into a full-on laugh, the kind that left them folded in two, with their arms clutching their sides. Pansy, meanwhile, was not nearly so amused, given the sharp look she shot them. However, she didn't bother chastising Ren for it; no doubt she thought that a lost cause. She gestured towards Mushroom, who'd finally reappeared, settling atop the mushroom ottoman in a fitting display of his name. "Don't just go to sleep!" she cried. "Get them! You're a cat, aren't you?"

By the time Mushroom managed to open one sleepy eye, the mice were long gone, having vanished into the bowels of the cottage via some dark crevice. Not that it really mattered.

Mushroom only got up long enough to turn around and resettle – this time, with his butt facing Pansy.

"Ugh. You're really useless, aren't you? Cute, but ultimately useless." She sighed, shaking her head. "I guess I'll need to chase them out myself..."

"It's their home, you know," Ren said, having finally managed to snatch some semblance of composure amid their aching sides. "But you're right. They deserve better than an ugly old chair."

"It's not *ugly*," Pansy protested, seemingly offended on the chair's behalf. "Just because you hate color—"

"I don't actually."

"Any color other than brown, green or gray," Pansy amended with a pointed look in their direction.

"I like red too," Ren said before they could think better of it, their gaze drifting over to the curls framing either side of Pansy's face.

By some miracle, she didn't seem to make the connection. "Wow. Four entire colors," she scoffed. "What a feat."

Willing the heat to drain from their face, lest it ruin an otherwise clean getaway, Ren said, "But the chair *is* old. You have to admit that much."

"So, what did you have in mind then?"

"A new home," they replied. "Made of wood."

Pansy's brow furrowed. "Like a dollhouse for rats?"

"They're mice," Ren corrected. "And, I guess?" Honestly, they weren't quite sure what a doll would need a house for, but they certainly weren't about to ask Pansy for an explanation.

"Okay," she said with a nod. "Lead on, then – to wherever you, uh, keep your wood." A strange look came over her face as soon as the words left her mouth, pinching her features together beneath a pink haze.

"My wood," Ren repeated, eyebrows arching.

"Yes. For the, um, house," Pansy murmured, her face now the color of an overripe cherry. "The mouse house."

"Uh-huh."

"You know what?" Pansy declared, straightening up even though her cheeks were doubtless radiating enough heat to rival the sun. "I'm going to go get my knitting supplies from the kitchen. They'll need blankets and such, won't they? Something soft to sleep on. Yes." She nodded to herself once, then hurried out of the room, her breakneck pace no doubt meant to preclude any sort of response from Ren.

Still, they managed to call out after her, "I'll be out in the garden when you're ready." They could've pointed out that mice generally made their nests from shredded bits of whatever they could find, whether it be paper, fabric or straw, but that seemed unnecessary enough to verge upon cruel, and they'd already visited quite enough of that on Pansy for one day.

Once in the garden, Ren approached the small wooden shed that had likely been erected as a place to store firewood but now served as a repository for whatever useful bits of scrap they'd come across.

Crouching down, they began rummaging through the jumble of planks, sticks and iron sheets. It took a bit of time, but eventually they found some suitable pieces of wood, long and flat and seemingly structurally sound. They hauled them out, then went to retrieve their tools. Sharp though a goblin's claws could be, Ren had no desire to spend half the day scratching at the same seam again and again. Far easier to use a saw and get the job done in a single pass.

They'd managed to cut the wood into the requisite number of pieces and were in the process of arranging them into a house-like shape via carefully applied lines of stonesap, when Pansy finally reappeared.

"Oh!" she said, seemingly surprised by Ren's level of craftsmanship. "It looks just like our cottage, doesn't it? You just need to add a bit of moss across the top – to match the roof. Then cut a couple of windows; maybe paint them blue. I think that would look very nice!"

Ren's attention, however, had already hit a snag.

Our cottage? they wanted to say, a strange prickle skimming across their warming skin. Too bad that voicing the question meant acknowledging the sensation that had accompanied it, and Ren, for some reason or another, suspected they wouldn't like that part very much. So, they held their tongue, focusing instead on adding the finishing touches to the mouse house – including two windows, just like Pansy had suggested.

"Here," Pansy said once Ren had set their saw back down, thrusting a slightly misshapen square of orange and yellow yarn towards them. "A blanket."

Ren blinked. "It's small." *And ugly*, they thought, looking down at the strange snags and bulges that riddled the blanket's surface, courtesy of far too many uneven stitches to count. Evidently, Pansy's knifework wasn't the only thing that proved lacking.

"Well, it's for a family of mice. How big does it need to be?" As soon as the words left her lips, Pansy's expression shifted, worry dragging across her brow like a plowshare. "Wait. Should I have made it bigger? I can make another one. It shouldn't take me that long. I'm a really fast knitter!"

That's precisely the problem, Ren thought, impatience ever the enemy of a job well done. Still, they bit their tongue once more, murmuring a soft, "It's fine", as they pushed the blanket through the perfectly circular opening they'd carved into one side of the house. "See? It fits."

Pansy's shoulders dropped, her relief palpable. "Oh, good. I was worried for a second there. Admittedly, I got a little distracted..."

"Distracted?" Ren jerked their head towards her.

Her smile, which had already been rather sheepish, turned all the more so. "It's probably easier if I show you. Pig!" she called, turning towards the front door, which she'd left ajar. "Come out here and show Ren your new outfit!"

Outfit? Ren's brow barely had enough time to furrow before Pig was trotting over to them, pink snout raised high as she showed off the mess of color that had exploded over her body – more eye-searing than even the cabinet downstairs. How was it that Pig was strangely absent when Ren needed her, but the moment Pansy required a model for her latest knitting nightmare, Pig was right there, available and ready?

"What is *that*?" Ren asked, nose wrinkling as Pig gave an altogether unnecessary twirl, noticeably less graceful than usual, the clumsily woven knit straining and pulling as much as it slumped and dragged. *Land almighty*. Did she even use a pattern?

"A sweater!" Pansy chirped in response, her expression all brightness and light. "Doesn't it suit her? At first, I was only going to use blue and green yarn, but I figured a bit of orange would really make the whole thing pop!"

If by "pop", she meant visit serious harm upon Ren's eyeballs, then yes, it absolutely did that. The yarn was too bright, too pigmented, too – *halfling*. Not to mention it was all but certain to snag on every little thing when they went out foraging. As such, the sweater needed to go – ideally, straight into the bin. Truly, there was no salvaging this mess of errors.

And yet, when they came to deliver the news, Ren's tongue dropped against the bottom of their jaw like a stone. They stared at Pansy, enraptured by the sheer radiance of her joy. It had taken a hold of them, pinning them in place, as the sun did to the moon. Worse, the strange prickle from before was back – now with an added shot of heat, rendering it all the more potent as it swarmed across their nerves.

Ren swallowed, the words they'd wanted to say piling up in the back of their throat. "I-I suppose one sweater is fine," they murmured, ducking their head in shame at their own uselessness.

"Oh, I think it'll be a lot more than just one," Pansy said with a grin, already twining a bit of yellow thread around one needle.

And Ren, unfortunately, couldn't bring themself to say no.

9
Pansy

1. Roll Call
2. Halvenshire Harvest Festival Planning Session
   10:00 a.m. Emergency session to discuss potential challenges to Haverow's successful nomination ("the Pansy Underburrow situation")
3. Adjournment
   11:00 a.m. Tea and biscuits to be served

HAVEROW COUNCIL AGENDA, 14 HEARTHFIRE 768

It was amazing what a bit of decoration (along with the appropriate amount of furniture) could do to a living space. By the end of that ten-day, the cottage had finally started to take shape into a proper home, even with Ren's unique goblin flair. Though, if Pansy was being perfectly honest, she didn't mind the mushrooms or the moss or even the strange mobiles Ren had cobbled together from discarded feathers, pebbles and sticks, all arranged at precisely measured angles. It suited the cottage, with its strange mishmash of halfling and goblin sensibilities, which, at this point, seemed nigh on impossible to disentangle.

That being said, as much as she was learning to tolerate the more singular aspects of the cottage, Pansy couldn't say she'd come to accept it in its entirety. Not yet. Not when there were animals living in every nook and cranny, including a family of squirrels who had somehow collectively decided that her *hair* was the ideal place to store their bounty of nuts for the coming winter. While Ren had immediately burst out laughing at the sight of a handful of acorns dropping from an especially tangled nest of her curls, Pansy had been far less amused about the whole thing.

Granted, as her mind turned yet again to the sound of Ren's laughter – replaying the memory for the who-knows-how-many-th time, as she refused to keep count – Pansy couldn't help but smile. Her chest filled with what had quickly become an all-too-familiar warmth, and though she rushed to dismiss it, the sensation lingered nonetheless. Out of spite, she presumed. Because there was a part of her – a small but infuriatingly persistent part – that had become ... not *enamored* (she refused to stoop that low), but, perhaps, *fond* of Ren. In an entirely friendly sort of way, of course. Nothing more.

She liked that she could learn from them. When it came to developing her skills as a chef, the last ten-day had been more instructive than the past several years combined! Whatever rut she feared she'd fallen into was no more. Every recipe was fresh! Exciting! Never before had she felt so inspired.

And to think she owed it all to a goblin.

It felt weird to put it like that. Only a few short days ago she'd been furiously plotting how to get Ren to leave as soon as possible. But now – now, Pansy wasn't even sure she *wanted* Ren to leave. Which, ultimately, put her in a tricky position when it came to her parents.

She grimaced, remembering what she'd told her mother prior to moving out. That joke about getting a new goblin housemate had *not* aged well, to the point where it probably had about the same consistency as soured milk. *Ugh.* But that wasn't even the worst thing she'd said. No, that honor went entirely to that silly, thoughtless little promise she'd made about moving back at the first sign of any goblin.

Needless to say, she had not done that, even though finding a goblin already living in your new home was more than just a "sign". *A giant, flaming fireball of danger is what it is*, her mother would probably say. Right before she fainted from shock.

Best not to tell her about Ren, then, Pansy thought as she climbed the last few steps to her parents' front door. *No point turning an otherwise pleasant family dinner into absolute chaos.*

Unfortunately for her, chaos seemed to have made a point of finding her anyway.

Pansy should've known something was off the moment her mother didn't immediately sweep her into a bone-crushing hug after opening the door. She should've seen it in the tightness around her mouth, the way her smile thinned, never quite reaching her eyes.

"Hi, Mum," Pansy said with as much warmth as she could manage – anything to undo whatever strange snarl had come between them. "I missed you. Where's Dad?"

Her mother's smile tightened further. "Let's go sit in the front room."

Pansy frowned, confusion twisting across her brow. Never before had her mother made such a suggestion, not when it was just them. That sitting room was reserved exclusively for guests, a practice Pansy's grandmother had often derided as "unfathomably useless", much to her own daughter's (equally unfathomable) frustration.

It was a major point of contention between them. One of many, to put it frankly. Every time the subject came up, Pansy's grandmother would scoff and say, "What's the point of a sitting room where no one's allowed to sit? Waste of a perfectly good space, if you ask me." And like clockwork, Pansy's mother would snipe back, "Well, no one did!" and they'd be off to the races yet again, the same tired argument, regarding the merits of practicality versus propriety, unfurling between them with no end in sight.

All this to say, the chances of her mother changing her mind on the proper use of the front room were so small they might as well have been zero.

So, my parents invited someone else. Not a big deal, Pansy thought, with a nonchalance that didn't quite land, her stomach curdling around a solid chunk of ice. This wouldn't have been the first time her parents had invited someone without telling her. The neighbors, Mr. Sweetbriar and Mr. Sourbloom, had shown up at the dinner table more times than she could count, and that was fine! She *liked* Mr. Sweetbriar and Mr. Sourbloom – and not just because they always made sure to sneak her a piece of homemade taffy. So, why was she so damn *anxious*?

The answer, of course, was waiting for her on the sofa.

"Hello, Pansy," said Mrs. Millwood, her tone so icy it was a wonder the cup of tea she'd raised to her lips hadn't instantly frozen over. "Is there something you wish to tell us?"

Pansy blinked, her mind unable to process anything beyond

the shrill klaxon the councilor's presence had set off in her ears. She barely even noticed Blossom, positioned on one of the adjoining armchairs, and not just because her friend seemed halfway to vanishing into the swell of its cushions. In that moment, there was naught but a single question, propelled to the forefront of her mind by the cold, slick slide of dread up her spine: *why in good Harvest's name would her parents invite* her?

"I don't—" She glanced at her mother, then her father, hoping that her wide-eyed look of panic-slash-surprise would coax out something in the way of an answer. It did not.

While her father, ever-reluctant to draw attention in these sorts of situations, only looked away in response, his lips nearly lost beneath the impressive heft of his mustache, Pansy's mother was not nearly so silent.

She shook her head, a look of what could only be described as complete and utter betrayal slicing across her expression. "You promised me," she said. "You *promised* me."

Pansy's heart leapt into her throat, narrowly dodging the lance that speared into her chest. Had her mother found out? But how? No one other than Blossom had come around the cottage and—

"No," Pansy whispered, the word echoing in the breathless hollow of her chest. Blossom wouldn't. She couldn't have. But there she was, sitting on the other side of her room, her fingers twisting in the fabric draped across her lap, *fidgeting*.

"Gods!" her mother exclaimed, blinking rapidly against the shine that had crept into her stare. "You could've been *hurt*, Pansy! What were you thinking?"

She knew. They all knew. Everyone in this room knew exactly who Pansy had been living with all this time. And yet, she couldn't bring herself to admit it out loud. Every time she tried, the words caught in her throat, clogging it until she relented and swallowed them back down.

In the end, all she could do was play dumb, force a smile more brittle than glass and ask, "Why would I have gotten hurt?"

Her mother's reply was instant: "Because you've been living with a goblin!"

The truth cracked through the air like the tail of a whip, unleashing a sudden, shocking stillness that stole even the breath from Pansy's lungs. Her mind went blank, the fake smile tumbling from her lips. Any chance of denying her mother's accusation had been dashed to pieces, splintered apart like her expression.

"So, you don't deny it, then?" Mrs. Millwood said, unsettlingly sedate. Her teacup clinked against its saucer as she set both down on the low wooden table in front of her. It took everything in Pansy not to flinch.

Seeing her friend at the mercy of her least-favorite councilor seemed to set something off in Blossom. She straightened in her seat, hands no longer tangled in the weave of her own skirts but, rather, curled around the cushioned armrests at her sides. "Look at yourselves! The way you're behaving over a plate of *cookies*."

"Cookies"– Mrs. Millwood's eyes flashed – "made with an ingredient that only goblins are known to cultivate. Was this what you were planning on feeding the judges?" she asked, now whirling on Pansy, her voice having taken on a shrill edge. "You'd shame the entire village just to satisfy your own damnable curiosity!"

"That's not – I wasn't *planning* on doing anything with those cookies," Pansy protested, weaker than she would have liked. She didn't know what it was about Mrs. Millwood or any of the other village elders, but every time she found herself face-to-face with one of them, locked in yet another argument about all the ways she'd been found lacking, Pansy struggled to find her voice.

Perhaps it was the fear of reprisal that knotted her tongue, the fear of making things more difficult for her parents than they already were. It wasn't their fault they'd gotten a *curious* daughter – though many would certainly point at her grandmother and say, with that lamentable shake of their head, "It's true that the apple doesn't fall far from the tree." To them, she was just another branch of the Underburrow family tree gone rotten.

Our family used to be on the village council, you know, her mother's voice, pulled from some ancient, half-forgotten memory, whispered in her ear. *It would be nice if we could go back to those days.*

If only Pansy hadn't rendered such a thing an impossibility.

"Whatever your plans might be," Mrs. Millwood continued, giving a haphazard wave of her hand, as if sweeping trash into a dustbin, "your cookies nonetheless found their way here, to our village, where they waited, ready to be passed around like an *infection.*"

Pansy jerked back, her cheeks coloring. "My cookies are delicious and perfectly sanitary, thank you. With all due respect, Mrs. Millwood, I think you're blowing this very much out of proportion. All I did was share some cookies with Blossom—"

"Which she then shared with your parents," Mrs. Millwood interjected.

"Because I thought they might enjoy them!" Blossom threw up her arms with a huff. "Was that really so wrong of me?"

Yes! Pansy wanted to shout at her. *If not for you, none of this would be happening!*

A gross oversimplification – and an entirely unfair one to

boot. But Pansy could barely keep her head above the rising tide of her own fury, and so the thought registered as dimly as sunlight at the bottom of an ocean trench.

"We want nothing that comes at the cost of our daughter's safety," Pansy's mother declared, her hands, clasped tightly at her front, flaring white around the knuckles.

"You know we love your regular cooking, Pans," her father added after a beat – the first sign of his voice thus far. No doubt he thought he was softening the blow. In truth, his words did just the opposite.

Pansy exploded. "There's nothing wrong with using sugarfern!" she snapped, her skin now the same shade of red as her curls. "And so what if a goblin is the one who gave it to me? I'm the one who asked them for help!"

Mrs. Millwood recoiled with a high-pitched gasp, one hand coming up to clutch at some invisible strand of pearls. "You *asked*?" She spoke as if such a thing were unthinkable, the greatest of sins. Certainly not something any *true* halfling would even consider, let alone actually carry out. And Pansy had done both.

She wanted to scream, to cry, to do whatever it took to get people to finally *see* her. The real her. Not this paper stand-in defined by a cluster of insurmountable flaws. Pansy looked at her parents, pleading. If they spoke up for her, maybe it would be easier to add her voice to the chorus; not just to defend herself, but also Ren, whose shortcomings, much like her own, didn't merit this level of disdain.

Unfortunately, only silence rose to meet her.

The councilor turned towards Pansy's parents – first, her father and then her mother – and said, with far too much vitriol, "I've said it before, and I will say it again: it was a mistake to give Angelica such latitude with your daughter. You should never have allowed her to fill Pansy's head with those ridiculous stories. It's little wonder she is off cavorting with goblins. Soon, she'll be acting just like them!" She shuddered.

"If you find me so objectionable," Pansy said, the words sweeping through her like a frigid gale, "then maybe I shouldn't come back to Haverow at all from now on."

"Yes," Mrs. Millwood agreed, before anyone else could even open their mouth to interject. "I think that would be for the best, given your continued disregard for our village's standing. We have no use for such selfish behavior here."

It took all of half a second for the room to erupt into a flurry of objections, shouted by Blossom and Pansy's parents alike. Perhaps Pansy should've stuck around, listened to the way they rallied to her defense. These were the people closest to her; their words should have shattered the wall of ice that had enveloped her heart. And yet, the chill remained, undaunted.

So, she left, stormed out of her parents' burrow without a word, barely hearing the shouts that unfurled in her wake. She felt cold, hollow. Her eyes burned, but no tears came. How strange, that. Shouldn't she be crying in a moment like this?

Maybe it was because this moment had been a long time coming, the wound left behind not so much a fresh cut as a peeling scab. Pansy had known for years that she didn't belong in Haverow. Wasn't that why she'd left in the first place? This town, with its rigid ways and ideas, would never change for someone like her. Not unless she *made* it.

Though who was she kidding? She'd barely mounted much of a defense back there. Her voice had been such a fragile, timid thing, forming only the easiest of words, which, unfortunately, also proved the least necessary. The core of what she'd wanted hadn't even so much as strayed from the prison of her chest.

There, it continued to pulse, a single white-hot ember amid the hollow void of her defeat, a monument to her own uselessness.

Even so, Pansy wanted to try. Her gaze landed on the same Harvest Festival poster she'd seen during her last trip into town, her feet having carried her to the village square. Was there anything more halfling than the Harvest Festival? she wondered, an idea slowly solidifying at the front of her mind.

If I enter and win the Crop Competition, she thought, a single ray of hope cutting through the lightless black clinging to her insides, *then maybe that'll prove that I still belong here, that I'm as much a halfling as anyone else in town. I can't change, but maybe Haverow can.*

It was a nice thought, so who could blame Pansy for immediately clinging to it with all her might?

Yet if she was going to do this, the first thing she needed to do was get some seeds. She thought of Ren, but quickly dismissed the idea. Although they almost certainly had plenty of seeds, chances were their collection consisted entirely of "goblin" plants. And seeing how a bit of sugarfern had prompted certain individuals to completely lose their minds, Pansy suspected that her plan would be better served by more... *familiar* vegetables.

Blossom probably has some seeds in her shop, Pansy thought. *And it's not like she ever locks up when she goes out.*

Granted, going in and taking some of Blossom's seeds without asking wasn't exactly a very "friendly" thing to do. But, well, Blossom *owed* her, and Pansy was determined to collect.

10
Ren

If you should ever lose your way,
Look to the land to guide you home.
From the moss on trees to the rush
   of a stream,
So long as you look and listen,
You will never be lost.

GOBLIN SONG OF UNKNOWN ATTRIBUTION, SAID TO HAVE BEEN WRITTEN BY A MOTHER WHOSE CHILD HAS JUST LEFT HOME TO FIGHT IN A WAR, TITLED "THE WAY HOME"

As far as Ren was concerned, Pansy had a death wish. Or, to put it less dramatically, a get-horrifically-lost-in-the-dark wish.

When she'd told them she was heading back to her village to have dinner with her parents, Ren had immediately posed two questions: "Are you crazy?" and, "Are you trying to get lost?" Dinner, after all, implied returning home well after dark, which, again, Ren had warned her *not* to do several times – all to no avail, it seemed.

"I should just let her get lost," Ren grumbled, tapping their foot impatiently against the dirt path. It had been about an hour since they'd come all the way out here to the forest's edge, saddled with a heavy lantern they had no use for, and Ren was starting to wonder if they, too, had completely lost their mind.

"I should be at home, tending to the garden. Instead, I'm out here playing *babysitter*," they scoffed. "And to think she told me to butt out when I told her she was acting like a fool! Can you believe that, Mushroom? The gall of it . . ."

Mushroom, who'd made himself quite comfortable in the depths of Ren's hood, let out something between a squeak and a yawn and snuggled closer. Although it still wasn't quite fall yet, the weather had reached that stage where nighttime brought with it an undeniable chill, one that Ren's cloak staved off for the most part. For both of them.

"Why am I out here, then?" Ren blinked, their gaze dropping to their feet as a rush of warmth spread across their face. "Well, it would be poor form to win our wager by default, right? Not to mention, as Caretaker, I have a whole ecosystem to watch over here. It wouldn't do to let the predators around here develop a taste for halfling meat."

"*Mrrmp*," said Mushroom, simple and to the point.

Ren's head swiveled back around. "What's that's supposed to mean?" they demanded, eyes narrowing. "Did Pig teach you that? Barely a few months old and you've already learned to talk back? Nature preserve me . . ." They sighed.

At least their wait might soon be over. Someone was coming towards them, a dark, halfling-sized shape cresting over the last gently rolling hill. Actually, who were they kidding? It was definitely Pansy. Who else would be daft enough to enter the forest at this hour?

"Finally!" Ren groaned, dragging themself towards her. "You made me wait long enough."

"R-Ren?" Pansy squeaked, jerking back slightly in surprise. She did, however, manage to remain completely upright this time, a definite improvement over her usual flailing.

They rolled their eyes. "Who else would it be? You know any other goblins willing to drop everything on your behalf?"

"My—" Pansy frowned. "I didn't ask you to come all this way."

"No, you asked me to sit around and do nothing while you got horribly lost – as if I could tolerate such a thing." Crossing their arms, Ren let out what was supposed to be an especially put-upon huff, meant to prune back the vulnerability that flourished at the heart of their words. But with every last mote of accompanying heat lost to the reddening tips of Ren's ears, the performance fell flat. So obviously manufactured that even Pansy had doubtless noticed.

Except, maybe she hadn't. Because there was no laughter, no teasing; none of the things Ren had braced themself against. Instead, Pansy's expression crumpled, as quick and sudden as the side of a mountain after a heavy rainfall. Her features twisted and pulled, fighting a losing battle against the emotion creeping up her throat in a blood-red flush.

"Am I really such a burden? Someone who only serves to make the lives of the people around me worse?" she asked, her voice cracking as she wiped ineffectually at the tears gathering at the corners of her eyes. "I mean, I must be, considering a goblin and a halfling are in agreement. First Councilor Millwood; now you."

Ren froze. This was *not* how they'd expected things to go. When it came to the matter of her ill-advised nighttime jaunts, Pansy was supposed to wave Ren off or, ideally, admit they were right. Instead, Ren had struck a nerve – and an especially sensitive one at that.

Probably because I'm not the first one to hit it today. Just their luck. Now, they were every bit the "cruel, mean goblin" that showed up in far too many halfling bedtime stories – always as the villain, of course. Normally, such a thing wouldn't bother Ren – halflings could think what they wanted – but knowing that Pansy had been hurt to this extent – well, it just didn't sit right with them.

Letting out a breath, Ren steeled themself for what had to come next. "I'm sorry," they said. "That's not what I was trying to imply."

"Yes it was." Pansy sniffed, a petulant edge to her scowl.

"No, it wasn't. I just—" Ren clamped their jaw shut, exhaling forcefully through their nose as they grappled with the ongoing challenge of translating their feelings into words. "This forest is dangerous at night, and I wanted you to recognize that."

She blinked at them, her lashes gleaming with tiny pearls of moisture. "Were you actually worried about me?"

"Why does this surprise you? Haven't I already shown plenty of concern for your safety?"

"Well, you're always so ... gruff about it. Maybe, if you worded it more nicely ..."

"Fine."

"And delivered it better, too."

Ren gave her a sharp look, eyebrows arching in a way that clearly said, *Don't push your luck*. Still, they relented. "I'll keep that in mind for the future. Now, who's this Councilor Millwood you were talking about?"

"A miserable busybody who spends so much time with her nose crammed into other people's business it's a wonder she even manages to come up for air." Pansy sniffled, wiping again at her eyes, this time with slightly more success. Mostly because she'd stopped crying. "If she was just another overly concerned old woman, she'd be easier to ignore. But she sits on the village council, so you can say she's one of our leaders. Anyway"– she waved a hand, as if trying to soften the blow of what followed – "she kicked me out of town."

Ren's brow furrowed. "What do you mean she kicked you out?"

"Exactly what I said. Look, can we start walking? It's a little chilly just standing here. And *please*," Pansy begged, "don't tell me I should've worn a jacket."

"Well, you should have," Ren said to Pansy's audible dismay as they fell into step beside her, lantern held high to illuminate the path ahead. "I'd offer you my cloak, but I'm afraid it's already spoken for."

Right on cue, Mushroom poked his head out of Ren's hood, earning a wet hiccup of a laugh from Pansy.

"I guess the rumor I heard about goblins hating cats was massively overblown," she said, dabbing weakly at her eyes. "So much for getting you out in ten days."

"Ten days? You could at least have given me more credit than that," Ren groused through a smile.

Pansy only shrugged, as if to say, *Maybe*.

"You know," Ren said after a long pause, filled with only the sound of dirt crunching beneath their heels, "if you want to talk about what happened – even if it's just to complain – I'm willing to listen."

Pansy gaped at them, her eyes near-perfect mirrors of the full moon overhead. "You want to hear me *complain?*"

Now it was Ren's turn to shrug. Another *maybe* to follow the first.

"Honestly, there's not much to say," Pansy said once she'd managed to wind her jaw back up. "Councilor Millwood found out that I've been living with a goblin and promptly hit the roof. Called me selfish – an infection even, like I'm going to poison the village with my wild ideas of using goblin ingredients." She snorted, kicking at a stray pebble with the toe of her boot.

"But that wasn't even the worst part," she continued, her tone turning mournful. "My parents *agreed* with her. Sure, they protested when she told me to stay away from Haverow. But not because they thought what I was doing was fine or anything. No, they just want me to come back home – like they always have – completely ignoring the fact that the village hasn't been home for me for a long time. To be honest, maybe it never was." She sighed.

"You feel like you don't fit in," Ren said soberly.

Pansy nodded. "Yeah. I'm too"– she waved a hand – "different. *Weird.* Too much like my grandmother, I guess. Because I'm curious and ask questions and want to *see* things beyond the familiar and the usual."

"I take it your grandmother wasn't very popular either?"

"Well, she spent most of her life outside of Haverow. She was an adventurer, you see," Pansy said, her expression creasing apologetically. Evidently, she knew as well as Ren did what that implied, the bloody history shared between their two peoples, of wars fought in other people's names rather than their own.

"Given how much your village seems to hate goblins, I would've thought that this would make her rather popular," Ren said, blunt as always. No point tiptoeing around something they were both acutely aware of, especially if the goal was to have an honest conversation.

"I never said my village made a lot of sense," Pansy replied with another shrug, easier than the last. "She did the exact same things as the local wizard. And yet he gets all the praise while she just gets criticized."

"Why?"

"Because she was a halfling," she said simply, as if that was all the explanation needed.

"So, you're expected to stay in the village?" Ren asked, trying their best to understand. "And do what?"

"Have a family, live quietly, don't cause trouble. Be boring, I guess. Obviously, I wasn't very good at it," she added with the tiniest curl of amusement.

"Is that why you came out here? To escape boredom?"

Pansy thought about it for a moment. "I think it was more that I wanted to find a place where I could be myself. It was exhausting being judged every time I expressed any interest in things that weren't appropriately "halfling", or behaved in ways that others found "unbecoming". What about you? I know you said you became the Caretaker of the cottage, but was that something you chose or . . . ?"

"I volunteered," Ren replied, stiffening imperceptibly against the tension winding down their spine. "I was the best option the clan had. I've always been good at foraging up here away from our caves. Plus, I know the most about botany in general. It made sense for me to take over the garden."

"So, you weren't . . . I don't know . . ."

"Forced out? No." Ren snorted. "Exile is something reserved for criminals."

Pansy went quiet, one knuckle pressing hard against her lips. "What about living with a halfling? Is that something your clan would consider criminal?"

Ren laughed, which, in retrospect, was likely a touch cruel, given the circumstances. However, what else could they do in the face of such sheer ludicrousness? "Ill-advised and stupid, yes; but not criminal. Honestly, they'd probably wonder if I'd bumped my head on something, or fallen under some sort of spell."

"But if you told them that you were doing so willingly, while in possession of all your faculties?"

"They'd question me, no doubt. But, at the end of the day, my clan trusts me." Granted, they probably wouldn't be too pleased if Ren brought Pansy onto clan territory. But Ren figured it was better not to mention that.

"They really wouldn't kick you out?" Pansy asked, her brow creasing with disbelief.

Ren blew out a breath and said, with the utmost seriousness, "Pansy, if being weird was all it took, then my cousin Thorn would've been thrown out of the clan years ago. He collects *toads*. I say 'collects', but sometimes he steals them."

"Toads? What kind of toads?" She cocked her head to the side, the grooves in her forehead softening beneath the press of her – ill-advised – curiosity.

Knowing her, she'll probably want to add Thorn's "Juice", or whatever he's currently calling it, to her next dish. Better change the subject . . . "What's that?" they asked, gesturing to the small packet peeking out from Pansy's pocket.

"Oh, I . . ." Pansy ducked her head, her expression turning sheepish. "You have to promise not to laugh."

"I never laugh," Ren declared, with all the deadpan stoicism of a wizened old goblin.

This pulled another chuckle out of Pansy; this one, thankfully, less wet than the last. "Okay, well, I was thinking of planting something and entering the annual Harvest Festival's Crop Competition. And, um, winning. As a way of proving I'm not a terrible halfling." She blushed and quickly added, "I know it's a stupid idea, but I—"

"It's not stupid."

Pansy blinked, and then her eyes widened. No doubt she thought she'd simply misheard.

So, for the sake of absolute clarity, Ren repeated themself: "It's not a stupid idea."

"You're only saying that because you don't know how terrible I am at gardening," Pansy murmured. Still, she was smiling, a familiar dimple wedged into her cheek, so that must count for something.

In fact, it counted for a lot, given the way Ren's heart thumped hard against their breastbone, bringing with it a wave of warmth so fierce it rendered their cloak largely unnecessary. Hence why they pulled it higher, dipping their chin beneath its heavy folds. They gave an awkward-sounding cough and said, "It's a good thing my thumb's green enough for the both of us, then."

"Oh, you say that now," Pansy replied, shaking her head. "But you have no idea just how limited my capacity for gardening is."

Ren arched an eyebrow. "I saw you knock over an entire mushroom farm and nearly kill several decades' worth of painstakingly cultivated moss. I think I'm well aware of your destructive capabilities."

Pansy laughed. "Okay, point taken. That being said..." She

trailed off, catching her lower lip between her teeth in a fit of hesitation. "You actually want to help me with this?"

Faced with the sight of Pansy gazing at them through her lashes, Ren's insides gave a discomfiting squirm. *No*, they wanted to say, desperate to clamp down on the jittery, storm-like buzz blooming in their belly, a mirror to the flush spreading across their cheeks. But their mouth went dry the second their lips moved to form the word, leaving their tongue, rendered heavy and useless, to flop soundlessly against their soft palate. One swallow turned into two, until, finally, Ren had no choice but to concede.

"I'll help you if you ask me to," they said, oddly hoarse. Not a lie, but, rather, a too convenient truth, used to obfuscate instead of reveal.

"Okay," Pansy said, with a decisive sort of finality, "I'm asking, then."

How strange that a handful of words could send Ren's heart soaring, the rush of giddy pleasure so overwhelming, they couldn't keep it from showing on their face. It swept across their lips in a broad arc, flashing teeth without a hint of restraint. "Let's go win this competition."

Pansy made a half-strangled sound low in her throat and quickly jerked her gaze away. Wide-eyed and red in the face, she said nothing for several beats, seemingly devoting all of her attention to the simple act of putting one foot in front of the other. "Y-yeah," she said at last, releasing a shaky, knotted breath.

Ren stared at her, confusion twisting across their brow. Wait – did she *like* them? No. Certainly not. It was too complicated a possibility to consider. They gave a quick shake of their head, their pulse fluttering hot and quick beneath their skin. The thought, however, would not be so easily dislodged.

But what if she does? Ren wondered, despite themself, the possibility worming deeper still. What would it mean for them?

Nothing, came the reply, almost instantly. *Absolutely nothing.* Because Ren didn't like her like that, and they never would. Sure, they were helping her out with this festival thing, but that was hardly proof of any romantic desire on their part. In fact, it confirmed just the opposite! Because if Pansy won, she'd have no reason to stick around. She'd have all the acceptance she'd ever need back in the village, where she belonged, away from Ren – which, for the record, was exactly what they wanted. It would be better for both of them.

"What kinds of seeds do you have?" they asked, ignoring the way their chest tightened at the thought of Pansy's departure.

"Oh, uh, flowers mostly," Pansy replied, digging out a few sachets to illustrate. "With the festival so soon, I figured they were a safe bet."

"I thought it was a crop competition."

"I mean, edible flowers *technically* are crops too, right? But yes," she admitted with a sigh, shoulders slumping, "I'd have to enter the flower division, which is . . . smaller." *And less prestigious*, came the implication.

Ren thought for a moment. "You want to enter the main division, right?"

"Well, yes. Assuming it was feasible. But it's not, so there's no real point thinking about it."

"It's only not feasible if you're planning on planting the seeds today."

"But . . . I am," Pansy said, her brow furrowing. "So, unless you've got some goblin magic that'll let you turn back time—"

"No. I've got something better." They grinned. "An established garden. How does a pumpkin sound?"

Pansy gaped at them. "You have a pumpkin? *Where?*"

"In a plot a little way away from the cottage, near the back fence," Ren replied. "Admittedly, I've – I don't want to say *neglected* it. It's still doing fine on all counts. But I've had to prioritize the other, faster-growing crops, so that part of the garden might be a little overgrown in comparison." They grimaced.

"Why faster-growing crops?" Pansy asked, cocking her head to the side.

"I like being prepared for the winter," was all Ren said. Again, not a lie, but not the entire truth either. And that's exactly how it would have to be. Because it was one thing for Ren to involve themself with Pansy; that was a choice they were free to make. The clan, however, was a completely separate thing. Their needs superseded Ren's own. And what they needed was to be protected.

Plus, Ren added almost mournfully in the privacy of their own head, *it's not like she'd understand. Plenty is all she's ever known. It'd be foolish of me to expect otherwise.*

If Pansy sensed there was more to the story, she gave no indication of it. With a definite skip now to her step, she grinned at Ren and said, "Shall we go see this pumpkin, then?"

11
Pansy

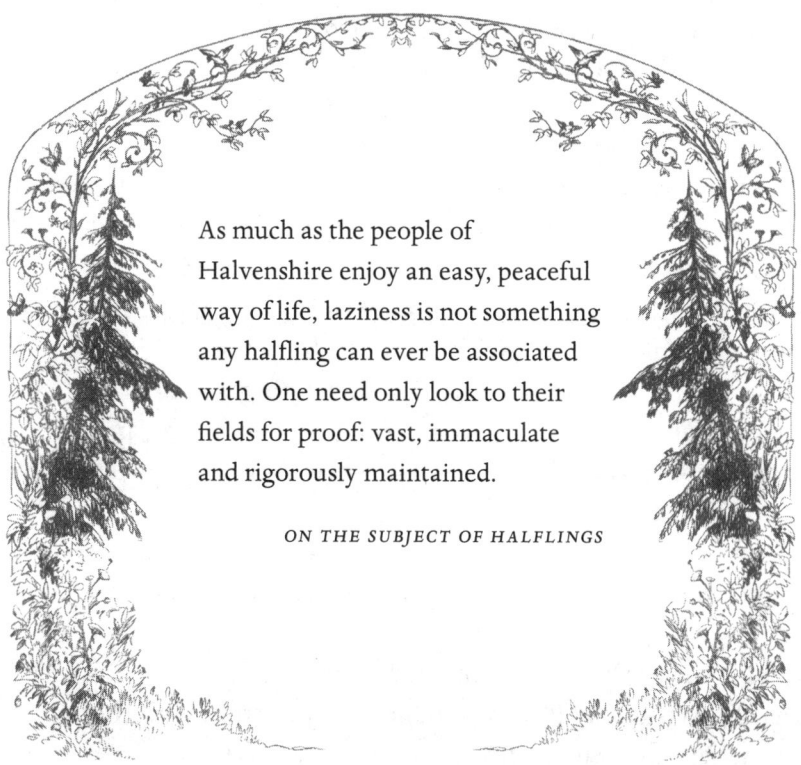

> As much as the people of Halvenshire enjoy an easy, peaceful way of life, laziness is not something any halfling can ever be associated with. One need only look to their fields for proof: vast, immaculate and rigorously maintained.
>
> ON THE SUBJECT OF HALFLINGS

"A *little* overgrown?" Pansy repeated, staring at the tangle of vines that spilled across the plot of earth Ren had assured her was their aunt's pumpkin patch. "Ren, if there's a pumpkin under all this, I certainly can't see it. And *no*, it's not because of the dark."

"In my defense," Ren said, stiffening against the assault on their pride, "Running Beans grow absurdly fast."

"No kidding. When did you even plant these?" she asked, squatting down so that she could slide a hand beneath a trio of long, flat shells, each about as broad as her thumb. From this vantage point, they reminded her of sugarsnap peas, though who knew how the inside might surprise her.

"Near the start of the last ten-day," Ren answered.

Pansy whirled around, eyes bulging. "*That fast?* Wow. You weren't kidding about it being absurd."

"It's why we plant so much of it." No sooner had the words left Ren's mouth than they were snapping it shut, a wide-eyed look of horror slicing across their face in a jagged arc.

It was as if they'd revealed something they shouldn't have – though what, Pansy couldn't say. To her ears, their statement sounded utterly innocuous, an interesting bit of trivia that would serve her well if goblin agriculture ever came up during one of the quizzes held every Fifthsday at the village pub.

Still, as laughable as that particular prospect seemed, it was probably best to reassure Ren that their *Secret Goblin Gardening Techniques* would remain entirely between them. "Don't worry," Pansy said, patting Ren gently on the boot, the only thing she could currently reach, crouched down as she was. "I think the halflings back in Haverow are perfectly content with their own varieties of green bean."

Ren gave her an odd look, confusion digging a deep wedge between their thick brows. "What? That's not what I—Never mind." They shook their head. "Anyway, as you can see, we'll need to clean this up first if we want to get at the pumpkins underneath. Sorry."

"Oh, there's no need to apologize," Pansy assured them with

a smile. "How were you supposed to know that I was going come up with such a crazy plan?" She laughed.

And yet, despite her easy attitude, the guilt spreading across Ren's face, saturating their features like an ink blot on parchment, persisted. Their mouth twisted, revealing a pained grimace. "Maybe I didn't know exactly," they said, "but I did plant these beans in the hope that you'd find them a nuisance. Of course, I had other reasons, too."

"But you mostly wanted to annoy me?"

They nodded. "Like how you wanted to annoy me when you brought home Mushroom."

"And look how well that turned out." Pansy chuckled, nodding towards Mushroom, still snoozing away inside Ren's hood. "You even gave him a name and everything."

"I'd say it turned out about as well as the Running Beans," Ren replied, the corners of their mouth quirking up ever so slightly.

"Definitely a cautionary tale against taking rumors and stereotypes at face value. Granted, I can't bring myself to regret adopting Mushroom. He's very cute."

"He is," Ren agreed, their expression softening as they reached over to give Mushroom a gentle scritch.

The sight struck Pansy like a lightning bolt to the chest. She quickly jerked her gaze away, her breathing stuttering as a rush of heat surged into her cheeks. By some miracle, she managed to keep her voice steady when she spoke next, asking, with what might've been a touch too much enthusiasm, "What do these beans taste like, anyway?"

Ren shrugged, their gaze still fixed on the sleeping kitten. "Like Running Beans. We usually steam them before dusting them with rock salt."

"In the shell?"

"Yes, but you can also peel them beforehand if you want to throw them into a soup or a stew."

As always, food proved to be the perfect distraction. Pansy let out a soft "ooh", her face brightening as her focus shifted away from the strange current that had hooked beneath her skin. "Gosh, I don't even know what I want to make first," she said, tapping one finger thoughtfully against her chin. "Maybe this one tomato-based stew I really love. It's perfect for autumn, and these beans would fit right in."

"I don't know . . ." Ren mumbled, shifting awkwardly from one foot to the other, their expression equally restless.

"Don't worry!" Pansy chirped, flashing them an exuberant grin. "It's completely vegetarian, so you can enjoy it too!"

"That's not what I— *Ugh.*" They gave a frustrated little stamp of their foot, their hands balling into fists at their side. It wasn't until Ren let out a steadying breath that they finally started to unclench. "*Fine*," they grumbled. "I guess I can spare a little bit. But only a little!"

Abruptly, Pansy found herself yanked back in time to the day of Blossom's visit, self-consciousness crashing over her in a familiar storm of white-hot pinpricks. She ducked her head, ashamed of the ease with which she'd once again helped herself to Ren's garden.

No wonder Ren thought her gluttonous, her thoughtlessness somehow always running parallel to her love of food. Sure, she cooked primarily for others rather than herself, but Ren didn't know that. Not really. So, what else could they reach for but the "selfish, greedy halfling" they and who-knows-how-many other goblins had constructed over the years, a monolith to rival the "evil thief" Pansy's own people had built in turn?

Except, perhaps, Ren was beginning to understand her. They

could have just as easily lashed out like before, snarled a few heated insults and stormed off in a huff. Instead, they had opted to meet her halfway, offering compromise in the place of an unbending line. The fact that Pansy even recognized this was, maybe, proof that she, too, was beginning to understand them just the same.

Of course, with Ren it wasn't exactly crystal clear, her understanding of them more like a cobbled-together patchwork than a complete tapestry. Because even when they *did* open up to her, Pansy couldn't shake the feeling that they were always holding something back, drip-feeding her the truth in tiny, frustrating little increments.

As much as it grated on her, Pansy knew that trust wasn't something she could force. She'd simply have to wait. Wait and hope that she could show Ren she was someone worth trusting.

"No, no. It's okay," she said quickly, waving a hand in front of her. "If you already have plans for the beans, I can figure something else out. I've made quite a dent in your pantry as it is. In fact, how about we plant the rest of these seeds I have? I think there are a few different vegetables in here. As much as I tried to be realistic about the whole thing, I couldn't stop myself from dreaming."

Ren blinked, seemingly taken aback by her suggestion. "You want to help me plant more seeds?"

"Yes. Absolutely. Honestly, I wish I could plant them on my own, but, as I've already said, I don't know that much about gardening, and I'd hate to ruin anything you've already put work into. This garden is your space, after all."

For a long moment, Ren seemed at a loss for words. Several times they opened their mouth only to shut it a second later, until, finally, they said, in a soft, barely there murmur, "Most of the food I grow here, I grow for my clan. It's why the role of Caretaker is so important."

Understanding dawned on Pansy like a sunbeam piercing a storm cloud. *No wonder Ren was so upset with me*, she thought, her nerves sizzling beneath a fresh swell of acid-like shame. *I might as well have plucked the food right out of their clan's mouths!*

"I'm so sorry, Ren," she said, almost breathless with sincerity as she shot up onto her feet. "I didn't know. I— Of course, I understand why you didn't tell me, but I do wish you had. I truly just wanted to"– she made a helpless motion with her hands – "share with you. But I managed to do just the opposite."

"It's all right," Ren said, shifting awkwardly. "I realize now that you didn't mean any harm. But . . ." They trailed off, their jaw working. "Do you really want to plant all those seeds, knowing that the end results will just go to my clan?"

Admittedly, it hurt, the way they looked at her then, like they were terrified she was going to take it all back. Still, Pansy swallowed past the sting, forced her biggest, brightest smile and said, "Ren, knowing all that makes me want to plant those seeds *even more*."

"Oh." Ren looked down at their feet, their expression suddenly – maddeningly! – unreadable. The only hint Pansy received as to what they were thinking was the slight upwards twitch of their ears, which she hoped was a good thing. She *thought* it was, but . . . well, she wouldn't put it past herself to engage in a bit of wishful thinking.

"Really, don't worry about me," Pansy continued, probably babbling at this point – not that she could bring herself to care. "From now on I'll just go to Haverow for my groceries, okay? I still have some coin left over from my last catering job."

They gave her a sidelong look. "I'm not saying this to be rude, but weren't you banned from town?"

It was only by some miracle that Pansy managed not to flinch. She gave an easy wave of her hand, determined to appear unbothered even though the laugh that tore free of her throat sounded hollow to even her own ears. "Oh, don't worry about that. Surely Councilor Millwood wouldn't go so far as to post guards by the gates."

No, far more likely she'd just instruct the rest of the village to shun her, and knowing just how desperately most of Haverow clung to the words of their council, they probably would. The fact dropped into the pit of Pansy's stomach with a nauseating churn, the kind that persisted even after the worst of the feeling had passed, a low-grade rumble of unease that settled into her joints like lead.

Don't think about it, she told herself, scrunching her eyes shut as the world gave a queasy wobble. *Just focus on winning the competition. Everything will work out once you manage that.*

"Are you all right?" Ren asked, suddenly far closer than she remembered, their hand hovering so near the crook of her elbow that she swore she could feel the heat of their palm against her skin. Obviously, they merely meant to steady her should she begin to topple over; and yet, the prospect of them touching her – a rarity, provided Ren was still conscious – was enough to send a giddy jolt lancing through her from head to toe.

Not to mention leave her terribly tongue-tied . . .

"I, uh . . ." she stammered, blinking dumbly at the scant distance now separating them. Ren's face filled her vision, drowning out everything else until there was nothing but the soft curve of their jaw and the maddening fullness of their mouth.

The sounds of the surrounding forest faded, leaving only the gentle rustle of the wind as it carded through the trees. Here under the stars and clear night sky, they might as well have been the only two people in the world. Pansy swallowed, her mouth abruptly dry. How easy it would be to tip forward, all under the guise of "losing her balance", and press her lips to Ren's. They wouldn't even know it had been on purpose and— Oh *goodness*, what was she thinking?

Pansy jerked away, her arms pressing flat against her sides. Now was not the time to be taking chances!

"Maybe we should leave this for tomorrow," Ren said with a frown.

"I'm fine. *Really*," Pansy assured them through the vice-grip of her own jittery pulse. "Otherwise, I'll just wake up tomorrow and find that you did all the work while I was asleep."

Ren gave a sudden jolt at that; proof, Pansy would argue, that her accusation had landed right on the mark. They huffed, crossing their arms over their chest. "I just don't like procrastinating when I know something needs to get done."

"Hence why you let this part of the garden turn into a veritable *bean jungle*."

"If you're going to complain about it, then you can do us both a favor and make yourself useful. Start harvesting the beans, including the vines. I'll go bring over some crates to load them into."

A few minutes without Ren turned out to be exactly what Pansy needed to get her heart rate back under control, not to mention her *thoughts*.

You're acting insane. Stop it, she told herself, squeezing down hard on the garden shears Ren had brought over earlier.

The first vine snapped off with a violent *schnick*, followed by a second, and then a third. By the time Ren finally made their way back over, one beat-up crate slung under each arm, Pansy had amassed quite the pile.

"Not bad," they said, setting one of the crates down beside her. Miraculously, it stayed in one piece – a true feat, given the worrying groan it emitted upon touching the earth.

Pansy grinned. "I told you I'm good at destroying plants."

"Not destroying – *harvesting*. You don't need to be so forceful. That's not a dagger in your hands, you know. Be more methodical, careful. It's not a race."

"Yeah, yeah," Pansy said, waving them off. She was about to ask if they needed to use the shears too when Ren extended their claws with a quick flex of their fingers and promptly pinched off a vine between them. "Why even bother with the shears if you can just do that?" she asked, watching them repeat the motion.

"Because some plants have thorns or leave behind a sticky residue," they replied, not even so much as glancing her way as they continued to make steady work of the beans before them.

Right. Of course. In retrospect, that had been an awfully stupid question on her part. She ducked her head, focusing on the task at hand as heat scoured her cheeks. A few seconds passed in silence, punctuated only by the soft *snip* of her shears, until her brain, no doubt sensing the opportunity to add salt to her latest wound, piped up with some not-so-well-meaning advice.

You know what you should've done, it began, sage as always, *was ask Ren to give you a demonstration.*

On how to use the shears? Pansy nearly snorted aloud. *Just because they already think I'm an idiot doesn't mean I need to go out of my way to prove it.*

See, her brain declared, with all the tired, head-shaking

resignation of a disappointed parent, *this is your problem. You lack vision, Pansy – at least when it comes to matters of romance.*

Oh, gods. This wasn't her; this was *Blossom*. Blossom had somehow found a way into her head, and now Pansy was never going to hear the end of it!

Hey! I'm on your side, the tiny Blossom-inside-her-head insisted, pouting in the same way the real Blossom did whenever Pansy didn't immediately put her advice into practice. *Look. If you'd asked Ren for a demonstration they would've had to guide you, and you know what that means.*

Pansy could practically hear the eyebrow waggle.

Touching! Not-Blossom declared with a triumphant flourish. *Their hand over yours. So romantic. Like something right out of a novel.*

Which makes it just as realistic, Pansy thought with a roll of her eyes. *Far more likely Ren just gives me a flat, unimpressed look and tells me to figure it out for myself.*

Well, maybe if you batted your eyes at them a little . . .

Absolutely not. The thought alone was enough to send Pansy cringing, any attempt she made at flirting all but guaranteed to end in disaster. If she was lucky, she'd end up looking like she'd gotten something caught in her eye.

Flirting was Blossom's thing for a reason. Unlike Pansy, she'd gotten plenty of practice over the years, her list of romantic partners as long as Pansy's was short (or, rather, non-existent). And Pansy refused to embarrass herself around Ren more than she already had – and in new ways to boot! Besides, she had a competition to focus on. Thankfully, not-Blossom seemed to understand this, though she didn't vanish without offering one last disgruntled huff.

No longer fighting for space among her own thoughts,

Pansy devoted herself entirely to the task of trimming back the Running Beans. It wasn't easy. With each snip, more vines appeared, like a verdant hydra armed with edible seedpods instead of razor-sharp spines. She smiled, thinking of her grandmother's stories about fighting monsters, and imagined herself an adventurer of the garden lands.

By the time Pansy and Ren had managed to beat back the worst of it, reducing the "bean jungle" to a "bean thicket", a dull pain had taken root behind her eyeballs. Dehydration, she assumed, from both sweating and crying, but nothing she couldn't push through. The slightly sharper throb near the base of her spine, however, was far less tolerable.

She rose with a soft grunt, her back popping as she stretched her arms high above her head. *That's better*, she thought, the pain receding into a low burn. *Now, let's get a good look at that pumpkin.*

There ended up being four of them, bright orange spots against the dark earth. Based on Professor Fatleaf's description of the Bloodletter Shroom, now forever seared into the fabric of Pansy's mind, none were yet overripe. Unfortunately, on the matter of size . . .

"Oh, they're a little, uh, small, don't you think?" Pansy said, tilting her head to the side in an effort to provide the pumpkins with the most flattering angle possible. Not that it made much difference.

"Hmm." Now, Ren was cocking their head to the side too, lips pursing as they assessed the fruits of their garden with a more critical eye. "How big are the crops that are entered into the competition usually?"

"Oh, as big as possible! I think the biggest one I ever saw was a pumpkin about this size." Pansy stretched her hands apart, stopping only once they were slightly wider than she was.

"Did it win?"

"I assume so," she said with a shrug. "It was easily the biggest vegetable there. Though they do grade on other things. Like color and smell; things of that nature. Whatever makes a crop appealing."

"You assume so," Ren repeated, their brow furrowing. "Does that mean you don't know for sure?"

"Well, no." Pansy looked away, one hand rubbing absent-mindedly at her biceps, where a familiar bitter chill had started to stretch beneath her skin. "My family had to leave early that year. My grandma ... It wasn't a good day for her, let's just put it that way."

"I understand." Ren's voice was soft, as comforting as the warm press of a palm against her shoulder. Of course, they hadn't actually touched her. This was Ren. They didn't seem to *do* touch. At least, not with her. Not even to catch her when it seemed like she might fall. That moment when they'd dusted the sugarfern from her cheek had been a one-off, an aberration, never to be repeated.

In a way, it was somewhat ironic. Pansy had gotten so upset that first night, when she'd woken up to the sensation of Ren's cold feet wedging between her calves. And now, only a ten-day later, she found herself *wishing* that Ren would hurry up and reach for her already!

What would they even say to that? she wondered, smothering a would-be laugh in her throat as an image of Ren, red and sputtering, surfaced from the well of her thoughts. If that were the result, then perhaps asking them directly might be worth it.

But – no. She couldn't do that. The real outcome was bound to be far less amusing. Rejection was never funny.

Pansy's stomach tightened at the prospect, bringing with it

the sour burn of bile, working its way up her throat. She pressed a hand against her lips, willing the swell of acid to recede. But a single glance at Ren set loose a new flood, filling her mouth with the bitter taste of the impossible.

"I'm going to go get something to drink," she said quickly, already turning on her heel. "Do you want me to bring something back for you?"

If not for the slight shake of their head, Pansy would have assumed Ren hadn't heard her. Their gaze remained fixed on the pumpkins, lips pursing as concentration pulled hard at their brow. The lamp flickered, casting the slim lines of their form in gold and shadow, a burnished halo amid the black of night.

In the dark, goblins were supposed to be terrifying, a flash of claws and equally sharp teeth. And yet, looking at Ren now, all Pansy could think, with a breathless sort of helplessness, was, *Gods, they're gorgeous.*

Then came the crash of reality, churning through her anew, a harsh, stinging reminder that what she wanted could never be – so, best not to want at all.

She hurried away, her steps shaky and weak. The cottage closed around her with a welcome coolness, a balm to soothe the ache blooming across her chest. She filled a glass with water, then downed it in seconds. Each gulp hit the bottom of her stomach like oil on a fire, sending the burn shooting ever-higher until even her eyeballs had become wreathed in flame.

She groaned, pressing the heel of her palm into one eye socket. Her head ached – now worse than before – and she felt so *miserable*, so pitiful and small. Why did her heart always want the least possible of things? Maybe with Haverow, she could win the competition at the Harvest Festival and convince her fellow halflings that she ought to have a place at their sides. But with Ren? Ha! Think again.

Irony – or, perhaps, shameful desperation – pushed her to lie down not in her bed, where it made sense, but on the dirt floor of the room Ren had filled with vials, alembics and other potion-making implements, all nearly identical to the ones Blossom kept in the flat above her shop. The space, which had once troubled Pansy, the oft-cited dangers of goblin magic rising as swiftly and naturally as the tide, had somehow become a comfort instead. From the cool earth beneath her cheek to the clean-sharp scent of herbs she couldn't name, it all swept around her like an embrace, bringing forth a singular thought: *This room reminds me of Ren.*

She smiled, closed her eyes, and exhaled.

Pansy had meant to close her eyes only for a moment, just long enough to drag the pain in her skull to something close to bearable. But the next thing she knew, Ren was shaking her awake, peering down at her with a look of unvarnished concern.

"Are you all right?" they asked, watching as she pushed herself up onto her knees, their palm an impossibly hot brand against her shoulder blades. "You were gone a long time, so I came in to check on you."

"I'm fine," Pansy mumbled, her voice thick with sleep. Her mind felt slow, sluggish, unable to move past the question of *Is this really happening?* Because Ren was *so* close, their hand still resting against her upper back. They were touching her, something she'd thought an impossibility. And yet . . .

"I told you we should've left the garden for tomorrow," Ren said with a shake of their head. They released a frustrated-sounding breath and rose to their feet, their hand falling back to their side – away from her.

Pansy nearly keened at the loss, her shoulder suddenly unbearably cold. Thankfully, the pitiful whine died before it could slip out, strangled into silence by the last remaining vestiges of her pride. "I just have a bit of a headache," she said, trying not to wince at how weak the words sounded, the vice that had kept her from making a fool of herself still notched around her throat.

"A bit of a headache, huh? Wait there a moment."

Their expression settling into an inscrutable mask of concentration, Ren began rummaging through a nearby cabinet, its paint chipped and fading. Even in the eerie half-light that pervaded the cottage's lower level, pale shades of green and blue waning and waxing like the rise and fall of a breath, the halfling-style motifs that swept along the cabinet's exterior were plain to see. Perhaps it had once belonged to Pansy's grandmother. Though, by now, Ren had thoroughly made it theirs, stuffing shelves that may once have have displayed plates and bowls as colorful as the patterns imprinted onto the surrounding wood with grasses, flowers and other plants. It was a merging of both goblin and halfling sensibilities – a long-running theme within these walls, it seemed. And looking at it, Pansy couldn't help but feel a spark of hope flare bright in her chest.

"Found it," Ren declared after a few seconds of searching, coming away with a fistful of tiny pale blue flowers.

To Pansy's eye, the flowers looked like nothing more than a ragged tangle of weeds, something that would rapidly find itself beset by the point of a trowel. But what did she know? She wasn't a gardener, let alone anything like an herbalist. She was a baker, a chef. So, she kept quiet, watching as Ren moved to the workbench positioned against the far wall.

There, Ren began to fiddle with the complex network of glasswork and tubes sprawled across the workbench's pitted surface. They worked quickly, their hands barely more than a blur. A bit of bubbling and a long puff of steam later, they turned around, their fingers coiled around a long, narrow-necked vial.

"Here," they said, holding it out to her. "Drink this. It'll help."

Pansy stared at the vial. The liquid inside was crystal clear, tinted greenish blue in the surrounding light. "What is it?" she asked, carefully taking the glass tube between her fingers. To her great surprise, it felt cool rather than hot, as the steam had suggested.

"An old goblin remedy. You should feel better almost immediately."

"Okay," Pansy said and swiftly knocked back the vial's contents, an action that would have doubtless left Mrs. Millwood screeching in horror – and probably her parents, too, for that matter.

She giggled, the thought, for once, filling her with delight rather than hopeless, aching dread. Though, to be fair, that could also just be Ren's remedy, now settling into her stomach with all the gentleness of a lover's kiss. It washed over her in a cool, tingling wave, scrubbing away every ache and worry as easily as chalk on a board.

"Oh, wow," Pansy murmured, one hand coming up to press lightly against her temple. It didn't even so much as twinge. "You weren't kidding about it being quick."

"Cold Flower is a natural anesthetic," Ren explained, showing her the crushed-up remnants of the tiny blue flowers, still soaking inside an alembic. "It's usually brewed into a tea, like I just did for you. But our healers will often pack it into their poultices too, as a way to provide comfort alongside the healing."

Pansy's brow furrowed. "A tea? But the liquid inside the vial was cold."

Ren shrugged. "It's called Cold Flower, isn't it? No matter how long or hot you boil it for, the resulting tea will always go cold the second you take it off the flame."

"Huh. What an interesting plant. You know, Blossom would probably love to see it." No sooner had the words left Pansy's mouth than she snapped it shut, shame tinged with the dulled remnants of her earlier anger flaring hot across the bridge of her nose.

For a moment, Ren watched her, their eyes seemingly tracking everything from the slight thinning of her lips to the tight set of her jaw. Then, they said, "I take it something happened with Blossom?"

Pansy sighed. "That obvious, huh? Yeah. Remember those cookies I gave her? Well, she decided to share them with my parents. Normally, this would be fine except the cookies had sugarfern in them, which I guess prompted my parents to get Councilor Millwood involved – or maybe she just happened to see them. I'm not exactly sure. But, either way, someone figured out why those cookies were greener than usual. And you know what happened after that."

A beat. "I take it you blamed Blossom for this?"

Hearing it now, her logic sounded so obviously flawed – and, truthfully, it had been. Maybe she'd even known it at the time, but anger and hurt had always blinded her the worst of all. She swallowed, regret a hard lump in her throat, and nodded. It was a quick jerk of her head, all shame and remorse, and finished with her gaze pointed towards her feet.

"I just felt so betrayed," Pansy said, her voice strained, whisper-thin. "All I could think about was the fact that if she hadn't given my parents those cookies, none of this would have happened. I would be have been able to have dinner with my parents like normal, and come back here and live my life how I wanted. So, I told myself that she owed me, and that's why it was okay for me to go to her shop and take some of her seeds."

"Ah. So that's where all those packets came from."

"Yeah." Pansy sighed, her lips twisting into a mirthless smile. "Maybe Councilor Millwood was right about me. I'm a terrible halfling."

"Because you stole from your friend?"

She nodded. "Among other things."

"You know," Ren said after a brief moment of silence, "a goblin only takes something if they feel it's being wasted or misused. Like this house, for example, or even my gardening tools."

"You *took* those?" Pansy asked, mouth agape.

Ren shrugged. "Only because their previous owner preferred swinging them at any animal who made the mistake of stepping into his garden. Nature forbid anything so much as *breathe* on that man's prized tulips, which, for the record, I also took."

"Was he misusing them too?"

"On a more conceptual level, yes. But I admit I was mostly being petty with that one. In any case," Ren continued, with a haphazard flick of their wrist, "the point I'm trying to make is that taking something that would otherwise languish in someone else's hands isn't necessarily wrong – at least, from a goblin's perspective."

"So, I'm turning into a goblin, then, am I?" Pansy asked with a soft huff of a laugh. "Great. Councilor Millwood will *love* that."

"Well, I do. So, who cares what that busybody thinks? Her opinions are shit, anyway."

Pansy's heart didn't so much as skip a beat as fly right off the rails. It zigged then zagged, soared then plummeted, the pattern it stamped into her breastbone about as coherent as the jumble of words careening across her consciousness. Ren loved that? About *her*? Even just repeating the words sent a fresh surge of lightning arcing through her already frenzied pulse.

Calm, Pansy. Calm, she told herself, muscles tightening against her own tittering nerves, the rush of heat across her skin. Saying that they loved something about her wasn't the same as saying they loved her; the gap between those two sentences was wide enough to accommodate even a behemoth's impressive girth. *Don't get ahead of yourself.*

Except, she already had. Now all she could do was damage-control.

A few deep breaths later and her pulse had settled into something far more manageable, the buzz beneath her skin no longer a few bolts shy of launching her into the stratosphere. "I didn't know you could swear," she mumbled finally.

Ren rolled their eyes. "Of course I can swear. In fact, if you'd like, I can do it right to Councilor Millwood's face."

"Oh, gods." Pansy choked and quickly shook her head. "No. Don't do that. That would be a *terrible* idea. Hilarious. But also terrible."

"Suit yourself," they said with a shrug. "But the offer remains open if you should change your mind."

"Thank you, Ren. I – I appreciate you trying to make me feel better about this whole mess, my own shortcomings as a friend included."

"You know, when a goblin hurts a friend, a gift usually goes a long way to making amends."

Pansy made a thoughtful sound, her mind turning yet again to the Cold Flower Ren had shown her earlier. "That's actually a very good idea."

"Yes, I know," Ren said, their lips peeling back into self-satisfied smirk. "I'm full of them."

Pansy scoffed. "No one likes a person with a big head." The fact that she'd said this with a smile had undoubtedly lessened the impact of her words, as evidenced by the nonchalance with which Ren received them – namely, another shrug.

Still, they were absolutely correct: a gift *would* help her apologize to Blossom, and in the realm of "Gifts for Blossom" the Cold Flower was pretty much perfect. But would it be all right for her even to ask Ren for some? She'd already asked them for so much, to the point where it seemed wrong to impose on them yet again. Pansy hesitated, her lower lip catching between her teeth, bringing with it the taste of copper and salt. Her uncertainty painted in blood across her tongue.

"You can ask, you know," Ren said, their voice cutting through the silence that had settled between them. "I won't assume the worst. I didn't say it earlier, but I've never considered you to be a burden, Pansy."

"I really do think that Blossom would be interested in that Cold Flower you just showed me," Pansy began, her cheeks heating anew. "Do you think, perhaps, that you could spare some? Or I could pay you for it? I'm not really sure what's the best way to do this." Did goblins even use coin? she wondered. Maybe. They had their own markets, after all.

"Unfortunately," Ren said, slowly enunciating the word in a way that made Pansy's stomach drop, "that was the last of my Cold Flower. But there are several merchants who sell it at the Goblin Market. I can take you to them next time the market opens."

Relief swept through Pansy's body, erasing all traces of the sinking feeling from before. "When does it open?" she asked.

"No idea," they replied, easy as could be. "It's not exactly on a precise schedule. But I'll keep an eye out for the signs."

Well, that was ... Not exactly disappointing, but inconvenient, perhaps?

The feeling must have shown on Pansy's face because Ren continued after a beat, "For what it's worth, I don't think we'll be waiting long. It's about time for it to come around again. On that note, I think I have a solution to your other problem, too."

Pansy blinked. "What other problem."

"The pumpkin," they replied, rolling their eyes. "Or did you already give up on winning that competition of yours?"

"Of course not!"

"Good," Ren said, giving a nod of approval. "So, a pumpkin will continue to grow as long as you leave it on the vine. But that takes time, and it sounds like we're a bit short on that."

Pansy frowned. "I thought you said you had a solution. It sounds to me like you're just telling me winning is impossible."

"Nothing's impossible with a little bit of goblin ..." They paused, a wicked grin slicing across their face. "... ingenuity."

"Magic?" Pansy asked, eyes widening. Should she be worried about this? Her stomach tightened, the prospect of getting involved with goblin magic plunging her back into that dark well of distrust that decades' worth of oft-parroted stereotype had excavated around her heart. But so much of what she'd been told about goblins had already been proved wrong, so why not this too?

Ren shook their head. "No. Just a growth potion. Think of it like a fertilizer. An especially powerful fertilizer."

Oh. Well, if they put it *that* way. The tension pulsating across Pansy's shoulders abruptly unraveled, released along with the breath that had knotted beneath her diaphragm. "That sounds fine," she agreed. Surely, everyone entering the competition would have used *some* type of fertilizer.

"Great." They grinned. "Just leave everything to me."

12

Ren

"Even the tallest tree was once a sprout."

But with a trick of the light, both shadows can be just as long.

GOBLIN RESPONSE TO AN OFT-USED ELVEN PROVERB

Ren looked down at the skull resting in the palm of their hand and frowned. For any goblin, it would've been the perfect gift. Bird skulls were notoriously fragile, and this one was almost entirely intact, the only flaw being a small, barely noticeable chip near the left orbital bone. A truly lucky find! The only problem was Ren didn't want to give it to a goblin. They wanted to give it to Pansy.

Funny how quickly things had changed. A month ago, their thoughts had been consumed with plot after plot, so determined to emerge the victor when it came to the deal the two of them had struck that Ren had even gone so far as to help her with her little competition – or at least, that's how they'd justified it to themself at the time. But now that the Harvest Festival was fast approaching – the pumpkin Pansy meant to enter grown fat and round off a steady supply of growth potions – Ren discovered that their conviction was not nearly so resolute as it had once been.

Somehow, the (very real) prospect of Pansy winning – *and then leaving* – sent a cold shock skittering beneath their skin. Dread, probably; though it didn't make any sense. Ren ought to want this: the cottage rendered theirs and theirs alone. It would be better for the clan, they'd reasoned, back when the first rumble of unease had roiled through them, as much a precursor to disaster as the suffocating stillness that followed a predator through the woods. Except that wasn't true either.

For all of Pansy's faults, in particular her self-described "uselessness" in the garden, she always tried. Yes, she worked slowly, planting one row for every three of Ren's and weeding even more slowly than that; but she *tried*. This was the flip side to so-called "halfling stubbornness": sheer perseverance. And every time she went out into the garden and tended to the seeds they'd planted together – exactly as she'd said she would – the wall Ren had built around their heart crumbled a little more.

Now, it was nothing but a pile of rubble, and Ren – Ren *liked* her. Against their better judgment, of course, but they did. And more than that, they wanted her to stay – or, at least, come back to visit. Now, if only they could tell her that without, well, actually having to say it. The mere attempt alone would surely kill them, and what good would that do?

Hence the bird skull. A gift.

But would she even like it? Ren wondered, brow furrowing as they lifted up their prize to the light. They'd done a good job of cleaning it; they always did. And the Diamondback Potion had added a subtle luster to the delicate bone on top of strengthening it. Ren could imagine the skull as part of a necklace or, perhaps, a brooch; something to cinch a cloak shut against the wind. It'd look good either way. The envy of goblins everywhere. And yet, it was also completely unlike anything Pansy owned.

Whether this was a good or a bad thing, Ren didn't know. But as they looked from the skull to the various decorations Pansy had filled the living room with over the past several tendays, from the colorful, crudely knitted doilies stacked atop the log-side table to the painted glass baubles that dripped from the ceiling on near-invisible wires, Ren started to suspect that it was most likely the latter.

"What are you doing?"

The sound of Pansy's voice, coming up from behind them, nearly sent Ren shooting right up into the rafters. They fumbled with the skull for a moment, miraculously managing to keep their grip on it, before shoving it into their pocket. Couching themself in their best attempt at nonchalance, they turned around and said, "I thought you were outside."

"I was," Pansy said, with a knowing sort of slowness as a familiar dimple dug into her left cheek, "until approximately thirty seconds ago. The pumpkin is looking splendid, by the way. But what are *you* doing?"

"I'm ..." Ren floundered, their gaze darting around the

room, frantic as an animal scrabbling for purchase atop rain-slick stone. "I'm looking at your books!"

The words slipped out before Ren could stop them, their mouth thick with the cold slide of panic. It took everything in them not to grimace, knowing that they'd only managed to secure their own downfall. The first excuse that came to mind rarely was the best – or even good, for that matter. So why had they seized on this one without a second thought?

Ren braced themself for the inevitable *Why are you looking at my books if you can't read?* A question for which they'd have no answer. And yet, the question didn't come.

Instead, Pansy hurried over to Ren and the bookshelf situated behind them, her expression a scintillating beacon of delight. "Which books?" she asked, not so much gesturing as flailing. "Was it this one? *Ooh*, it should be! This one's the best! All the Wolf Banefoot books are good, mind you. But he goes up against a dragon in this one! Hard to get more exciting than that, don't you think?"

"I ... suppose," Ren answered haltingly, their eyes flicking over to the book in question, bound in a dark green leather that had been embossed with a scale-like pattern; an attempt to mimic dragonhide, no doubt.

"Have you started reading any of them?" Pansy asked, undaunted in her enthusiasm. Did she really not know?

"No, I—" Ren cut themself off with an aggrieved sigh, their fingers closing around the skull, still hidden in their pocket. They couldn't lie to her. Not about this – or, well, anything, it seemed. "I can't read."

For once, Pansy's expression was inscrutable. She blinked. "What?"

"I can't read," Ren repeated, hating the way their face started to burn at the admission. They had no reason to be ashamed. Goblins didn't use paper. Never had. Why would they, when it would simply molder in their underground homes, damp and dark as they were? And still, when they told Pansy all this, it wasn't to inform, but to *justify*, as if their inability to read was a fault for which they needed to apologize.

They couldn't even blame Pansy for it. Her tone was entirely neutral when she nodded her head, then asked, "What do you do if you want to communicate with someone far away? I assume you don't send letters because, you know, paper." She laughed.

"We use ravens," Ren explained, the tension pulling across their limbs unwinding just a fraction. "They'll repeat any message, provided it's not too long."

"Really?" Her eyes widened. "That's amazing! I had no idea ravens could speak. But what about when you want to record something like a story? Surely, even the shortest ones are too long for a raven to repeat."

Ren snorted out a laugh, the gentle curve of their mouth softening the otherwise harsh sound. "Do halflings not have storytellers?"

It was now Pansy's turn to flush. She ducked her head, tucking a stray curl behind one rounded ear as she looked up at Ren through lowered lashes. "When I was younger, my grandmother would read these books out loud to me at bedtime, but I suspect that's not quite what you're talking about. She was rather good, though; she did voices and everything."

"Voices?" Ren arched an eyebrow.

"Yes. For all the different characters. It was"– Pansy's blush deepened – "very entertaining. As a child."

"Then perhaps a goblin storyteller is not too different from your grandmother. Every story they tell they tell from memory – and with more than just a few voices to help bring the tale to life." Grinning, they waggled their fingers in what was apparently a universal sign, given the way Pansy's eyes immediately widened.

"Like ... with magic?" she asked, her voice a barely restrained whisper.

"Or a variety of illusory potions."

"Wow," Pansy breathed, her expression going slack, as if entranced. "Do you think, maybe – that is, if it's all right; I wouldn't want to impose ..."

Ren pressed their lips together, smothering a laugh. Honestly, it was almost cute, the way she'd twisted herself into knots over a simple request. As if Ren could ever tell her no; that much had been an impossibility, even from the start. "There's usually a storyteller at the Goblin Market."

"Which will be ... ?"

"Soon."

"Ugh!" Pansy deflated, all of her bright-eyed hope and excitement whizzing out of her in an instant, replaced instead by a petulant scowl. "That's what you said three ten-days ago."

Ren shrugged again. "I have about as much control over the market as I do the weather. Complaining to me won't change anything."

"I know, I know," Pansy grumbled. The scowl, however, didn't budge. "I'm just – impatient, I suppose."

"You 'suppose'?" Ren repeated, eyebrows arching.

"Stop! You know what I mean," she said, laughing as she gave their arm a playful shove.

It had been barely more than a second of contact – and not even skin-to-skin at that – yet still Ren felt as if their entire world had been upended. They sucked in a sharp breath, their throat constricting in time with their awareness, now narrowed to single, hand-shaped point atop their biceps.

Touch me again, they wanted to say. *Lighter. Softer. Lower.* But they couldn't. Their mouth was too dry, their tongue too heavy. All they could do was swallow thickly, their fingers curling around the spot Pansy had touched, still pulsing with lingering heat, perfectly replicated in the flush that spread across their cheeks.

"If you're interested in my books," Pansy began, a hopeful gleam rising to her eye, "what if I read one of them to you? Like how my grandmother used to do for me. There won't be any magic, and I certainly don't have any potions. But so long as you promise not to laugh, I can at least try to do the voices."

In truth, Ren hadn't been interested in her books at all. They'd been nothing more than an excuse, hastily cobbled together – and rather poorly at that. But the warmth that suffused their being at Pansy's suggestion was entirely genuine. They *wanted* to listen to her, to learn more about her interests. The fact that those interests involved a halfling hero was ... unfortunate, to say the least; no doubt this Wolf Banefoot, like the rest of his ilk, had skewered plenty of goblins on his road to fame. But Ren had weathered worse in the name of affection, including several-dozen hallucinogenic toads.

"I think I'd like that very much," they said, their voice soft for fear of it turning into a hoarse croak.

"And you promise not to laugh?" Pansy asked, fixing them with her most serious look.

"I promise."

For what it was worth, Ren kept their word; at least, until the eponymous hero of *Wolf Banefoot and the Remarkable Raiment* confronted the story's villain, a cruel human lord who'd taxed a halfling village into abject poverty. Pansy, true to her word, had done the voices. However, for some reason, she'd decided that the human lord ought to have a haughty, nasally way of speaking, which – fair. But she accomplished this by pinching her nostrils shut! How was Ren supposed to keep a straight face when she did that?

"You promised not to laugh!" Pansy huffed, indignant. Crossing her arms over her chest, she allowed the book to fall into her lap, where it remained, propped open against her thighs, sitting cross-legged as she was on the floor.

"It was funny!" Ren protested, palms turning upward into a sort of half-shrug that Pansy clearly didn't appreciate, given the way she huffed a second time, her gaze pointedly turning away from them.

"I'm not reading to you any more," she declared, chin jutting high despite the red tinge that had risen to her cheeks. "You'll just forever have to wonder how the story ends."

"Oh, I will, will I?" Scooting closer, Ren scooped the book out of her lap with a devious grin, ignoring the offended gasp that pulled from deep in Pansy's throat. Granted, in her position, they'd have gasped too – albeit, for entirely different reasons.

Though they'd been sitting beside her the entire time, Ren had been careful not to get too close, the narrow gap between the two of them as much a lifeline as it was a curse. Now, that sliver of space was gone, swallowed by the joint seam of their thighs, where every inch seemed to spark with the charged air of an approaching summer storm.

It took everything in Ren not to react to it, the heat of Pansy's proximity, new and wonderful and horribly distracting. Grateful that their hands didn't tremble as they raised the book high, a perfect imitation of how Pansy had looked only moments before, Ren began to read.

Or, well, "read". They hadn't miraculously developed that skill in the half-hour Pansy had spent reading aloud to them. The text on the page still looked like indecipherable scribbles, lines of meaningless black flowing together into a never-ending stream. But the story had tugged at a familiar thread in the recesses of Ren's mind, reminding them of a different tale. A goblin one, in fact, about a kind-hearted trickster named Aconite, who, like the hero in Pansy's novel, had sought to free his people from tyranny.

Granted, the version Ren was familiar with featured significantly more necromancy, a natural consequence of casting a dark lord as the story's villain. But the similarities were so striking that more than once Ren forgot which tale they were meant to be recounting, and Aconite's name slipped out instead.

The first time, Pansy had kept quiet, allowing Ren to narrate the beginning of the story's climax, where the hero, masquerading as a famous tailor, presented the cruel lord with a "robe" that was just as non-existent as the "rare, elven material" it was purportedly made of. However, the second time Aconite's name slipped out in place of Wolf Banefoot's, she stopped Ren mid-sentence with a light touch to their forearm, so quick they might've thought it their imagination if not for the lingering heat that bloomed in its place.

"Who's Aconite?" she asked. "You keep saying his name instead. Also, I don't remember the cruel lord secretly being a necromancer – or the villagers' employer, for that matter."

Ren winced. Another slip-up to join the first. "He's ... a goblin hero," they explained after a beat of deliberation. Better to call Aconite that when introducing him to someone otherwise unfamiliar with the legend. Trickster could be such a loaded word, especially to a halfling's ears.

"Who tricked a paranoid necromancer into wearing nothing under the guise of it being a Robe of Invulnerability?"

"It's hard to boss your employees around when everything is on display," Ren said with a shrug.

Pansy laughed. "Hard to tax people too, I imagine."

"Is that how Wolf Banefoot's story ends?"

"Oh, yes. The cruel human lord, thinking he'd be the center of attention at the king's court, eagerly donned his new 'outfit' on a visit to the palace. He wasn't entirely wrong. The moment he stepped into the Receiving Hall, all eyes were on him – just not for the reason he had in mind. You see, greeting one's king in, well, nothing"– she giggled – "is generally considered poor form, and the king in question was not known for having a sense of humor. The cruel lord, therefore, found himself on a one-way trip to the palace dungeons, but not before being stripped of his title and lands, which were granted to the halflings instead."

Ren grinned. "A happy ending, then."

"Of course!" Pansy said, her chest swelling with pride. "Wolf Banefoot always wins."

"As does Aconite. By stripping the necromancer of the fear he'd cultivated, Aconite was able to give the goblin workers the confidence they needed to advocate for themselves. For better pay. Better treatment."

"You know," Pansy began, her expression turning thoughtful, "it's really interesting how close the stories are. Instead of a vain lord wanting to be the best-dressed noble at court, you have a paranoid necromancer afraid of death, which, in retrospect, is a bit ironic, isn't it?"

"Not as ironic as halflings stealing a goblin story," Ren teased, lips parting around a gleaming flash of teeth.

An affronted noise tore free of Pansy's throat. "You know, I'd really like to say something else," she said, straightening up as far as she could, which, as always, put her a tiny bit short of Ren – much to their intractable delight. "But given our circumstances, I've decided that it's probably best to keep it to myself. So, instead, I'll just say that you're entirely wrong."

Ren's eyebrows shot up into their hairline. "Oh, I'm wrong, am I? And how do you know this exactly?"

"In the same way that I knew that you weren't really reading that book. Still, it was cute of you to try." She smiled, her expression softening until the hazel of her irises had turned almost molten, amusement twinkling around its edges in a burnished eclipse.

Ren's throat tightened, their breath stuttering in time with their pulse, fluttering high just beneath their jawbone. They coughed, masking the all-too-familiar tide of warmth dragging through them with another attempt at nonchalance. If it worked, Ren didn't know. They couldn't bring themself to look at Pansy, afraid that a single glance was all it would take to turn this low simmer into an inferno.

"So, why didn't you say something sooner?" they asked, picking at a loose bit of rug by their knee. "You obviously knew that I was getting the story wrong."

She shrugged. "I was curious, and your story was entertaining. I wanted to see where you'd go with it. That being said," she continued, her expression darkening, "it was rather unfair of you to laugh at the voice I did for the lord when you went on to do the same exact thing."

In truth, that had been a bit of a peace offering, an apology not so much in words but in action.

"Isn't imitation supposed to be the most sincere form of

flattery?" they hazarded, putting on their best wide-eyed display of innocence.

Pansy, however, wasn't falling for it. "Ha-*ha*," she said flatly. "You're far too cheeky for your own good, you know."

"It sounds like you just called me clever." Ren grinned.

She scoffed, but the dimple in her cheek told the real story. And this was where the consequences of looking at Pansy reared its head. Because, in that moment, Ren realized, with startling, abject certainty, that they'd do anything for that dimple.

"I have something for you," they blurted out, their fingers reflexively closing around the skull in their pocket.

Pansy's eyes widened. "A gift?" she asked. "What for? Don't tell me today is some sort of goblin gift-giving holiday."

A month or so ago, Ren might've said something along the lines of, *Even if it was, what makes you think you'd be on my list of people to give things to?* No doubt they'd have bitten out each word, forming the sounds with more teeth than lips. But now, they only shook their head, certain that if they opened their mouth to reply, their voice would come out as nothing but a hoarse quiver.

Slowly, Ren withdrew the gift from their pocket, their heart racing for an altogether different reason. *Please let her like it*, they thought, a silent plea cast out to whatever higher power might be listening – goblin or otherwise. Because once they'd extended their hand, the skull plainly visible against the seat of their palm, where it sat like a hunk of lead, there was nothing left to do but wait for Pansy's response.

Blinking, she looked down at the tiny offering, painstakingly polished and preserved, and ... didn't smile. Granted, she didn't frown either; not exactly, which Ren supposed was a good thing. Instead, her lips pursed, considering.

At last, after what had probably only been a handful of seconds but had registered as the slow drag of an eternity, she cracked a lopsided smile and said, "And here I thought I only had to worry about Mushroom bringing me dead things."

The response hit Ren like a slap, stinging across their cheek. They flinched, both hands closing around the skull as they drew it into the safety of their chest, where Pansy could no longer see it. Their breath shuddered out of them, shallow and jagged. This was a mistake. They should never have even considered it. *Land almighty*, what had they even been *thinking*?

The hurt must've shown on their face, etched into the dark hollows of their cheeks and the knotted crease of the brows, because Pansy was *there*, closer than ever before, one hand flying to Ren's shoulder while the other reached for the bone-white trail of their knuckles.

"I'm sorry," she said quickly, her voice thick with guilt. "That wasn't meant to be a dig at you. It was just a joke. A bad one. Obviously, one I'll never repeat. I'll treasure anything you give me."

"So you say," Ren grumbled, the sting not quite entirely soothed.

"I mean it," Pansy insisted, giving Ren's hand a tender squeeze. "You clearly put a lot of care into cleaning and preserving that skull. It couldn't have been an easy task, given how delicate it looks. I'd love to show your hard work off to everyone – assuming you'd still like to give the skull to me."

Of course they did! How could she possibly think otherwise? Again, Ren's throat narrowed, closing around all the words they couldn't bring themself to express. So, they just shrugged, helpless, and held out the skull once more, their gaze pinned to the rug beneath them.

If Pansy noticed the way Ren's hand trembled as her fingers brushed against their palm, she said nothing, scooping up the skull with such gentleness that an observer might've thought Ren had offered her their heart instead. "Thank you," she said, her voice full of warmth as she cradled the skull against her breast.

A prickling heat skittered across Ren's cheekbones, and they ducked their head down further, vanishing beneath the dark veil of their hair. "It's nothing," they mumbled, a blatant lie. "Just something I found outside. We goblins hate seeing anything go to waste, including leftover bones and skins. Death is still a part of the natural cycle, even if we don't eat meat."

"Well, I love it just the same," Pansy assured them, her weight shifting closer still. Granted, that last bit might've just been Ren's imagination, their feverish pulse heightening every sensation to an outlandish degree. A barely there brush became a pointed drag, another jolt to the chest that sent the cycle rolling anew.

In a way, it was like getting caught in a stretch of hungry quicksand. The harder Ren struggled against it, the quicker it swallowed them down.

But maybe, in the end, they didn't want to escape. Because as Pansy held up the skull to her collarbone, wondering aloud if it'd look good as a necklace, Ren found that being on the other end of that smile was the only place they wanted to be.

13
Pansy

Grab the tankards, crack the casks,
Got no place for tiny flasks!
Streams of ale and golden mead,
What more does a halfling need?

"ALL A HALFLING NEEDS",
TRADITIONAL HALFLING FOLK SONG

It was the night before the Harvest Festival, and for Pansy sleep seemed as distant a prospect as the nearly full moon suspended beyond the trees outside her bedroom window.

She lay on her back, staring sightlessly into the silver-tinged gloom that surrounded her. There was just so much that could go wrong tomorrow, a dozen different possibilities already crowding inside her skull, with plenty more on the way.

What if the pumpkin didn't work? she wondered, turning over onto her side. What would she do then? It had been hard enough staying away from Haverow these past few ten-days, but the thought of never being able to return, not even to visit – that was unthinkable. Intolerable, really.

As much joy as living in her grandmother's old cottage had brought her – a fact she owed largely to Ren, as living alone would never have suited her – at the end of the day, Pansy missed the people she'd grown up with. She missed her parents, her neighbors; Blossom, especially. Mrs. Millwood she could still do without, but one unpleasant old woman too set in her ways paled in comparison to all the good Pansy had left behind.

She let out a breath, hoping that it might unravel – or, at least, loosen – the knot that had formed in her belly. Unfortunately, it accomplished neither. Frustrated, Pansy rolled over again, now onto her other side, such that a familiar wall of blankets filled her vision.

In light of Ren's heat-seeking toes, she'd given the wall some additional mass, reinforcing it against any would-be incursion from her goblin bedmate, whose unwillingness to retreat had turned the Battle for the Master Bedroom into an eternal stalemate. So far, the blanket wall had held fast, though Pansy suspected forcing an additional blanket on Ren had helped too. She smiled, remembering how vehemently Ren had protested against it; their moss blanket was quite sufficient, thank you! But, of course, she'd found them wrapped in it the following morning, swaddled as tightly as a pig-in-a-blanket.

A quick glance over the top of the wall proved that nothing

had changed on that front. But as Pansy settled back down, Ren's sleeping form vanishing once more from sight, she found herself beset with a pang of longing. It would be easy to discount it as mere envy: Ren's ability to drop into unconsciousness the moment their head hit the pillow was especially desirable, given Pansy's present insomnia. But it wasn't that.

Pansy's lashes fluttered against her cheek as she brushed her fingers, tentative and light, over the blanket wall. With her ears full of Ren's steady breaths, slow and even, she could almost imagine it was them beneath her palm instead. What would that be like? she wondered, her own breathing slowing to match theirs.

Her imagination rushed to provide her with an answer, transforming the warm weight of her blankets into the sensation of Ren's arms slipping around her, pulling her close. She sank into the feeling, her limbs going slack. A brief indulgence wouldn't hurt anyone; not when it only existed within the confines of her own mind.

But then she was waking up, squinting into the too-bright rays of morning with an unfamiliar pressure curled around her waist, too warm and too heavy to just be a tangle of bedding. Her vision focused, and she realized why. It wasn't just a bunch of blankets, tossed around in the night; it was Ren's arm.

Once again, the wall had fallen in the night. Only this time, it had come apart completely, and in its ruins lay Pansy and Ren, entangled in one another, with a sleeping Mushroom stretched out over their heads, like a fuzzy, black crown.

"You're awake," Ren's voice rumbled from beside her, their eyes sliding open with the ease of someone who hadn't been asleep for quite some time. So, why they hadn't bothered shifting away?

The question swirled in Pansy's mind, going round and round in a storm. She barely managed to squeak out a soft "Good morning" as her heart leapt into her throat, buoyed by a surge of heat that swept across her face in a red-hot stain.

"I didn't want to wake Mushroom," Ren explained, as if reading her mind, a bronze flush, less virulent than Pansy's own, stretching across the bridge of their nose in turn. "I remember you were looking for him before bed last night. He was probably just on another adventure with Pig, but I figured seeing him would put your mind at ease."

"Right. Of course." Pansy nearly choked, acutely aware of Ren's arm, still draped across her hip.

And there it remained for several long moments, not even so much as twitching as Pansy's pulse thrummed beneath it, all the blood in her body seemingly pooling in that one spot. Then, Ren finally shifted, sending a gust of too-cool air across the space their arm had previously occupied, and asked, "Shouldn't you head for the festival soon?"

The festival. Right. She'd nearly forgotten.

"You should come with me," she blurted, the leaden knot of tension that had been building in the pit of her stomach unraveling all at once.

Ren froze, their dark eyebrows flying into the rumpled mess of their hairline. "I don't think that's a good idea," they said. "Look, I'll help you load up the pumpkin into the wagon, but—"

"It's your pumpkin too!" Pansy protested. "You should be there when it wins."

They watched her for a moment, then sighed, their features collapsing into a softer, less guarded expression. "I don't know, Pansy..."

Admittedly, Pansy hadn't realized it back when she'd first come up with this plan, but every time she'd fantasized about winning first prize at the Halvenshire Crop Competition, Ren had been right there with her. It hadn't even been a conscious decision on her part. They had simply been there, as naturally as her parents or Blossom. For Ren to not be by her side . . .

The possibility curdled in the pit of her stomach, sour like spoiled milk. Pansy couldn't stand it. She *wouldn't*.

"I really want you there with me, Ren," she said, earnest in a way she'd never been before; maybe even a little bit desperate, if she was being honest. The request scraped out of her, leaving her insides feeling strangely raw; or perhaps *exposed* was a better way to describe it. Because, in that moment, she'd allowed herself to be vulnerable, bringing all that she'd left unsaid that much closer to the surface. Surely, Ren could see it, looking at her the way they were now, their face only a handful of breaths away.

But for too long, Ren said nothing, their expression as still as the breath caught in Pansy's throat. And then she saw it: the slightest twitch of their ear – a sign that had taken her multiple ten-days to understand but one she could now read as easily as the spark of interest in another halfling's eyes.

"You'll do it?" she asked, not even waiting for Ren to put it into words, her lips stretching around a grin so wide it nearly hurt.

They blinked at her, seemingly taken aback by the certainty in her voice. "How did you—"

"Your ear." She gestured towards it. "It twitches when you're interested in something, I think."

Their cheeks darkening anew, Ren clapped a hand over the offending appendage, as if that might erase the secrets it had already so thoroughly divulged. "I can't believe you noticed that," they grumbled.

"I'm very observant," Pansy declared sagely.

Letting out a soft huff of laughter, Ren allowed their hand to drop back down against the mattress. "Fine. I'll go with you. But I'm telling you, it's a bad idea. If a bit of sugarfern is all it takes for everyone to lose their minds, how do you think a full-on goblin will fare?"

"It's okay. No one will be able to think anything bad about you once they see our enormous pumpkin. The easiest way to a halfling's heart is through their stomach, you know."

Ren snorted. "Is that why you've been so insistent on feeding me all this time?"

Somehow, the statement proved just as shocking to Ren as it did to Pansy. They stared at her with wide eyes, lips parted around a tiny *oh*. Then they began to stammer, the flush from before deepening to a ruddy, orange-tinted brick. "I didn't – that wasn't – *it was a joke.*"

"R-right," Pansy agreed, her own face feeling equally as hot. "A joke. Of course." She laughed weakly.

Ren quickly rolled away from her, kicking away the blankets they'd (once again) snatched from Pansy's half of the bed. "If I'm going with you, I should go get ready," they said, pointedly keeping their back facing her as they moved about the room. No doubt, they meant to hide their blush. However, the tips of their ears had been lost to that same bright flood and remained as visible as ever, poking out from in-between their sleep-tangled locks.

It was cute. Almost painfully so. As she continued to watch Ren dig through their wardrobe, every outfit seemingly ill-suited for the day's events, a rush of fondness squeezed around Pansy's heart. And she knew that whatever awaited her in Haverow, she could face it easily so long as she had Ren at her side.

They didn't encounter much in the way of obstacles on the way to Haverow, and even less once inside the village. Granted, it was still early. Most people would be either in their homes, preparing dishes for tonight's feast, or down in the nearby meadow, working on the festival grounds themselves. The few people they *did* encounter in the street barely spared them a passing glance; Ren, out of not unfounded caution, had opted to wear their cloak with the hood up, disguising the most telling of their goblin features, at least for a casual observer.

Thankfully, Pansy had been right about the guards – namely, the lack thereof. Evidently, Mrs. Millwood hadn't completely lost her sense of proportionality, which was heartening to see. Or perhaps she'd just been so swamped with preparations for the festival that Pansy (and any and all chaos associated with her presence) had simply slipped her mind. Honestly, Pansy was betting on the latter.

It was plain to see that Mrs. Millwood and the rest of the council had spared no expense in outfitting the town for the day's festivities. Banners in harvest gold, orange and red unfurled overhead in scintillating streams, strung from one iron lamp post to the next, each inundated with wheatsheaves and garlands of strawflower, copper beech and sunflowers. Blossom's handiwork, no doubt.

Pansy's chest clenched at the thought of her friend, who she hadn't seen since that disastrous afternoon in her parents' burrow. It had been easy to lose herself in caring for Ren's garden, carrying water from the cottage's nearby stream, picking beans and ambervine, encouraging pests away from the garden with netting and offers of a new, alternative home. She had replaced the deep-seated sting of regret with the marvel of new growth. But as the day of the Harvest Festival had drawn closer and closer, the weight of her damaged relationship with Blossom had borne down with oppressive force. Now, as she navigated the familiar cobblestone streets of Haverow, all choked with her best friend's blooms, she couldn't think of anything else.

And not just her relationship with Blossom. Her parents had been there too, their silence in that moment when their words would have mattered most even more deafening. No doubt they would be at the festival, too; they all would. Perhaps, if she kept to where the crowds were thickest, she could avoid them. But was that really what she wanted?

No. Of course not. Her heart clenched, choking the breath from her lungs. Running away would be easier. So much easier, she realized, as her eyes snapped to her parents' burrow, fast approaching on the left. However, she had come here to fix things, and that meant facing her fears head-on. All of them.

Ren's hand found her elbow as her apprehension stretched taut beneath her skin, their touch almost tentative. "You don't have to see them if you don't want to."

Pansy shook her head. "I'll likely see them at the festival anyway. It's"– she swallowed, her fingers finding Ren's and giving them a grateful squeeze – "better to do this now. Rip off the bandage, you know?"

Ren's brow furrowed. "You shouldn't *rip off* a bandage," they said, sounding moderately horrified by the idea.

She waved a hand. "It's an old halfling saying."

"It sounds barbaric."

"*Be nice,*" Pansy chided.

"I am nice!" Ren protested, their free hand sweeping out in a dramatic arc. They looked at Pig, lagging slightly behind them, her muscles straining against the weight of the cart, now heavy with their pumpkin. "Aren't I being nice, Pig?" A snort. "See? She agrees!"

"If you say so . . ."

A few more steps, each punctuated by the sharp *clack* of the wagon's wheels against the dark cobbles, and they'd arrived. Pansy put one hand on the wooden gate, ready to push it aside, but found herself unable to put the necessary force behind the movement. It was as if every last scrap of strength had left her, evaporating without a trace.

"Pansy?" Ren was once again at her side, their fingers an anchor on her elbow.

"Sorry, I'm—" *Tired,* she'd wanted to say. But the lie caught in her throat, filling her mouth with bitter salt.

Silence stretched between them, heavy and thick. At last, Ren asked, "Do you want me to come with you?"

"I've already demanded so much of you," Pansy mumbled, her cheeks darkening beneath the hot brand of her shame.

The corner of Ren's mouth twitched. "That's not what I asked."

Of course it wasn't. That was the point. Pansy looked down at her feet, her teeth catching on her lower lip. "I can't promise my parents won't say something insensitive," she said at last, her gaze darting up to meet theirs.

"Good thing I have plenty of experience dealing with thoughtless comments from halflings."

No doubt Ren had meant the comment as a joke. They were

smiling, for Harvest's sake! But the memories of those early days had taken on a razor sharpness, whetted on a grindstone of constant shame. Now, they cut across Pansy's mind like a filleting knife, slicing open parts already tender to the touch.

She must have winced because Ren's smile dropped all too swiftly, their touch on her elbow ever more insistent. "I'm sorry. I didn't mean it like that. I—" They faltered, lips pressing together hard.

"It's okay." Pansy smiled weakly. "What's one halfling burrow when you've already wandered through a whole halfling village, right?" The laugh that followed proved even weaker – and to Pansy's own ears, at that.

"No, that's not it at all," they said, shaking their head. "Pansy, I – I'd like to meet your parents."

She blinked. "But – *why?*" she asked, incredulous, prompting Ren to let out a short, half-aborted noise of frustration.

"Just let me go with you," they insisted. "I came all this way, didn't I? I hate doing things halfway."

This time, the snort of laughter that pulled from Pansy's throat was entirely genuine. Warmth swelled beneath her breastbone, as comforting as the press of Ren's palm. "All right," she agreed. "But let me go in first to ... prepare them."

"Yes, I wouldn't want to *frighten* anyone. That being said, I *am* curious. Who do you think can scream louder – you or your parents? I think my ears are still ringing from the squeal you let out your first day at the cottage."

"I'm going inside!" Pansy all but shouted as she shoved aside the gate.

In stark contrast to her earlier attempt, this motion had too much force behind it. The gate's hinges, well oiled as always, shifted with barely a whisper, but the gate itself hit the adjoining fence with a splintering *crack* that seemed to echo down the empty, burrow-lined street.

It was no wonder then that Pansy's mother appeared in the window a moment later, hazel eyes narrowed. She spotted Pansy immediately, already halfway up the pebbled garden path. In fact, her daughter was probably the only thing she *did* see, given how quickly she rushed to the door, ripping it open before Pansy could even so much as lift a hand up to knock.

"Oh, blessed Harvest, you're finally home!" her mother cried, sweeping her up into a bone-crushing hug. Then, turning her head to the side, she called back into the burrow, "Borage! Pansy's home!"

"Mum, I'm—"

"Pansy, you have no idea how *worried* we were," her mother said, cupping her face with both hands, unerringly gentle even as she ran roughshod over the conversation. "Every day, your father and I have thought about going into the woods to find you, but the forest is so *large* and *dark*, and I barely even remember where your grandmother's cottage is these days. Plus, with your father's awful sense of direction, it was far more likely we'd just get ourselves horribly lost, as Councilor Millwood and Agvaldir so kindly pointed out to us when we were at our least rational."

Pansy's heart sank at the mention of the elderly councilor and the wizard. "So, you just waited here," she said flatly, her voice icier than a winter's gale. "Waited and hoped I'd come back."

"Of course we hoped," said Pansy's father, appearing in the doorway behind her mother. His face was moderately flushed. So, either he'd raced over from the far end of the burrow or – and this was the option Pansy herself was betting on – he'd swiped a taste of her mother's famous apple crumble, fresh out of the oven judging from the smell, the moment she'd left to go peer out the window. He'd never been much good at hiding guilt, and he *loved* his wife's apple crumble.

"Pansy, sweetheart," her mother began, gently stroking the curve of Pansy's cheekbone with her thumb, "we're so sorry about what happened the last time you were here. We were afraid that something could happen to you. You know, all your father and I want is for you to be safe and happy—"

"Then there's someone I want you to meet," Pansy said, the words coming out strong despite anxiety roiling in her belly.

It was then that her mother finally noticed Ren, still standing by the wagon, their attempt at a casual posture undone by the pronounced line of tension running through them from head to toe. Although their hood was still in place, it was no match for this level of scrutiny.

Pansy's mother tensed. "You brought a goblin? *Here?*" she hissed, her voice thinned not by anger but by fear, etched in sharp lines across her face. She glanced around – searching, it seemed, for the invading horde of goblins and orcs that Ren's presence surely heralded.

"Is this the one you've been living with?" asked her father, managing to sound almost calm. The pallor of his lips, however, told the true story. He was just as afraid as her mother was.

"Yes. Their name is Ren, and they're the kindest, most gentle person I've ever met. I need you both to remember that, okay?" She gave her parents a hard look, hoping to impress upon both of them the seriousness of this moment to her, *the importance*. Her fingers found the bird skull, now suspended on a leather cord around her throat, and gave it a barely there squeeze.

Caught by the motion, her mother's gaze snapped to the necklace, and something in her expression softened. "All right," she agreed, finally releasing Pansy. "We'll meet them."

"And we'll be nice," her father added with a smile.

Pansy let out a breath, the snarl of tension between her shoulder blades finally unspooling. She smiled. "Then you should probably take down Grandma's old dagger from the mantelpiece."

"Oh!" Pansy's mother said, one hand flying to her mouth, as if she'd forgotten the dagger even existed. "That's probably a good idea. Honestly, I've been wanting to take that thing down for years, anyway. I never liked it. I was just waiting until I had something to replace it with. The sitting room would look so *empty* otherwise."

Pansy didn't bother challenging her on this. She knew her mother's relationship with her own mother had always been . . . complicated, for lack of a better word. Full of conflicting emotions, knotted together in the most perplexing of ways. Obviously, they hadn't gotten any easier to sort through in the eight months since Angelica Underburrow had passed. In fact, the task had likely only grown more difficult.

So Pansy simply said, "I'll go get Ren."

There were tea and cookies waiting for them when Pansy and Ren made their way into the sitting room. So far, a much better reception than the last time she'd been here. Granted, the fact that Mrs. Millwood wasn't perched on one of the sofas helped tremendously. Then again, her reaction in this instance might prove rather entertaining. Here was the goblin she'd lost her mind about only a few ten-days ago, sipping barley tea from an "obnoxiously halfling" – as Ren would no doubt put it – floral-printed cup. The irony of it all was downright exquisite.

Though not as exquisite as the butter biscuits her mother had set out on an equally "obnoxiously halfling" plate, rimmed with delicately painted florals and vines. A sentiment Ren seemed to agree with, considering the speed with which they'd devoured their first biscuit. Now, they looked at the ones remaining on the plate, their stare full of longing as they sucked the last sweet crumbs from their fingertips.

"You can have another one, you know," Pansy assured them with a soft chuff of laughter. "Honestly, I'm sure my mother will love it if you help yourself to as many as you want."

Hearing this, Pansy's mother, sitting primly in one of the adjoining armchairs, to the point where her back had become an unbreakable rod, jolted out of her otherwise guarded posture. "Do you like them?" she asked hesitantly, her gaze focusing on Ren with an uncommon intensity – one Pansy recognized. Although she and her mother were dissimilar in many ways, the quickest way to both of their hearts was an open appreciation for their cooking. Which, come to think of it, Ren had done with her, too.

"They're delicious," Ren said around a mouthful of biscuit. Normally, the lack of manners inherent in speaking with one's mouth full would've prompted a frown or some other form of silent disapproval from Pansy's mother, but evidently all could be forgiven by simply reaching for another serving.

"Wow!" Pansy said, eyes widening in mock surprise. "From the way you're wolfing down those biscuits, I'm starting to think that you prefer them to mine." She paused, a devilish gleam rising to her eye. "Well, do you?"

"Uh ..." Ren paused mid-chew, eyes widening to near-perfect circles as a handful of crumbs dropped from their slackening jaw.

"Don't say anything! It's a trap!" Pansy's father laughed.

"He's right. I'm only teasing." Pansy gave Ren's thigh a gentle pat. "Enjoy the biscuits."

"That being said," Pansy's mother said after a beat, her tone bordering on sly, "if you *do* prefer mine, that's perfectly fine too. I have plenty of food to go around. Oh!" She popped out of her chair. "You should try my apple crumble!"

"What?" Pansy's father said, aghast. "You told me it's for the festival!"

"It is." Her mother sniffed. "Besides, you have no right to complain, *sir*. I know you swiped some earlier while my back was turned."

Pansy laughed. So, she'd been right on that front. Her father, meanwhile, flushed anew, until his face was as red as his thieving hands. "It's okay, Mum. We're going to the festival later, so we can have some then."

"And fight the entirety of Halvenshire for a slice? I think not. You'll take your portion in advance. And if you *do* manage to get another slice at the festival, well . . ." Her mother shrugged, already on her way towards the kitchen. "Call it the privilege of being family."

Family. One that now included Ren. Because when her mother returned, she did so with two plates, each laden with crumble – though one proved a touch more generous than the other. That serving, which would normally be given to Pansy, was instead passed into Ren's waiting hands. It had taken nearly three decades, but Pansy's position had been finally usurped, and as far as she was concerned, it couldn't have gone to anyone more deserving.

Pansy had nearly finished polishing off her plate – Ren, for the record, had already beaten her there – when her mother straightened up in her seat, eyes widening around the abrupt spark of an idea. "Borage, darling," she said, turning to Pansy's father, "do you think we should give Ren the dagger? The one that was on the mantelpiece?"

Feeling Ren stiffen on the sofa beside her, Pansy pressed a hand against their shoulder and explained, "It was my grandmother's. She won it during her time as an adventurer and brought it home with her."

"And I should have it because . . .?" Ren's voice had gone flat; no longer pleasantly neutral, but cautiously so.

"We think it was originally a goblin dagger," Pansy said quickly, her heart thumping hard against her chest. She wanted to scream! Things had been going *so well*. Ren had been enjoying themself, their ears pricked high for all to see. Now, they sat hunched over, knuckles blazing white around the plate in their lap, their ears gone flat against their skull.

"We understand that you're not the original owner," Pansy's mother rushed out, her expression creasing with worry. "In fact, it's unlikely you're even related. I just thought that . . . well, a goblin dagger might be more at home with a goblin, instead of decorating a halfling burrow."

"Can I see it?" Ren asked.

Following a quick, pointed gesture from Pansy's mother, her father scrambled out of his seat, returning a minute or so later with the needle-like dagger, tucked inside a mossy sheath, its hilt, plain and unadorned, gleaming in the light. He held it out to Ren, who took it after another pause, the motion almost grudging.

"As a general rule, we goblins don't like to fight," they said. "We believe that violence isn't a first resort, but a last. Unfortunately, there are people in this world who disagree. And, sometimes, when a goblin who has been stripped of absolutely everything cries out for help, it's only those people who are willing to answer."

"Dark lords," Pansy murmured in understanding.

Ren nodded.

"I've often thought," Pansy's mother said, once the silence had stretched beyond the bounds of what was comfortable, "that a wizard is, in many ways, not too different from a dark lord. All they do is take advantage of another kind of desperation: the desire to be seen, respected, treated as an equal. I'd say they treat us like children, but we're far too expendable for that. *We* die so that *their* children may live. It's—" She swallowed, her expression tightening. "I don't understand why we tolerate it. But perhaps I've already answered my own question: desperation."

"It's a powerful motivator," Ren said, their voice soft.

"Yes, it is," Pansy's mother agreed.

Setting the weapon down beside them, Ren said, "Thank you for the dagger. I will treat it like the gift that it is."

"Oh. I— you're welcome. Though I sincerely hope you never have cause to use it."

Ren's expression was grim. "As do I."

A weight settled into the pit of Pansy's stomach at Ren's words. They felt . . . foreboding, ominous, a precursor to some disaster she couldn't quite make the shape of – or, rather, simply didn't want to. Desperate to chase the sensation away, she hopped to her feet and began clearing the empty plates.

"Don't bother," her mother said, quickly moving to wave her off. "I'll take care of the dishes myself."

"Too late," Pansy replied, her hands already full of floral dishware.

"Should I help?" Ren asked, shifting forward in their seat, as if to rise.

"No," Pansy and her mother barked in unison, sending Ren sliding obediently back into the sofa.

"And *you*," her mother continued, leveling an almost accusatory finger at her daughter, "are a guest. You shouldn't be cleaning up anything."

"Oh, well," Pansy said with a shrug, already on her way out of the room. "Next time, then." As if she wouldn't do the same exact thing . . .

Her mother, of course, was acutely aware of this fact. She said as much, chasing after Pansy into the kitchen, where she finally managed to haul her daughter away from the sink before she could fill it with water.

"*Mum*," Pansy huffed. "It won't kill me to wash some dishes."

"I know, I know. But you're my baby. Fully grown and out of the burrow, which leaves only so many ways for me to take care of you; so, forgive me if I'm a little protective." Her mother smiled, a touch wan.

She'd missed her, Pansy suddenly understood. Granted, she'd said as much. But Pansy's absence had cut deeper than she'd realized.

Taking her mother's hand in hers, Pansy said, "I want to come visit, Mum. Leaving Haverow, meeting Ren – none of that changes the fact that I love you and Dad. *That's* why I promised to come by for dinner every ten-day. Not because I felt obligated, but because I wanted to. It just . . ." She sucked in a deep breath, lips thinning. "It just really hurt me that you and Dad turned something I'd been looking forward to into something so – *so awful*."

Her mother's expression crumbled. Shoulders slumping, she looked towards the floor. "I – I know, sweetheart. I was just so *worried* about you. I saw the way you'd left home, and somehow all I could think about was my own mother – your grandmother – and how she'd left home too."

"Mum . . ."

"I try not to talk about it, especially not to you." She swallowed, blinking hard against the moisture glazing her eyes. "A parent shouldn't burden their child with such things. But . . . It was hard for me, growing up with a mother who was never there, even when she wasn't off on an adventure. Her mind was always . . . well, you saw some of it. Your father and I couldn't hide everything from you, no matter how hard we tried."

"I know. I remember," Pansy said, and she did. She remembered the screams in the night, the sounds of her grandmother waking up from yet another nightmare; the vacant, unseeing looks throughout the day; the names of lost friends and allies that she would call to in moments of distress, moments when her grandmother seemed to have been transported somewhere else entirely, sometimes even mid-sentence. And, of course, Pansy remembered what had happened at last year's Harvest Festival – though, doubtless, everyone did.

"When you were born," her mother said, a whisper of old happiness curling at the corner of her mouth, "the moment the midwife placed you in my arms, small and precious beyond words, all I could think about was how I needed to protect you from all the horrors of this world. I would be the mother my own mother never was. I would be there, every day, a shield around your happiness. And somehow, along the way, I let my own fears get the better of me, and instead I became the sword that cut it down. I'm sorry, Pansy."

"Thanks, Mum," Pansy said softly, pulling her into a hug. "I forgive you. Just promise me you'll never invite Councilor Millwood over again when I'm around."

Her mother laughed and swiped lightly at her eyes. "I promise. But Pansy . . ." She pulled away, her expression serious. "I need you to answer me honestly. Does Ren make you happy?"

Pansy didn't even need to think about it. The answer sprang to her lips immediately: "Happier than anything in the world."

"Good. That's all that matters to me. Though, I suspected as much," she added, smiling in that knowing, all-too-motherly sort of way. "A mother always knows when her baby's in love. Does Ren know? Have you told them? Honestly, you should at this point, considering you've already brought them to meet your parents. It's a little out of order, don't you think?"

Pansy flushed. "*Mum!*"

Thankfully, it had gotten late enough that she could plead needing to head down to the festival, thereby sparing herself any further embarrassment at the hands of her mother. But just to be sure, Pansy more or less rushed Ren out the door, the festival once again serving as the perfect excuse. Who knew what else her mother might say if given the chance? Pansy certainly didn't want to find out, her face still burning from earlier.

"They're nice," Ren said as they made their way down the garden path, the dagger now strapped to their hip. "Your father was surprisingly interested in foraging. He started asking me all kinds of questions while you were in the kitchen."

"It went better than I expected," Pansy agreed.

Ren cocked an eyebrow. "You expected the worst."

She shrugged. "It's not like I didn't have good reason to. But I think, in the end, the only thing my parents care about is my happiness. And I'm . . . I'm happy now – with you."

Ren's eyes widened, a brief beat of surprise before their features softened into something tender and warm. They smiled and said, "I'm happy too." And Pansy knew immediately, her heart soaring higher than ever before, that they meant it.

Now, if only the rest of Haverow could see them the way her parents had.

14
Ren

"Dark lords are just wizards who refuse to wear color."

UNKNOWN

Ren heard the festival long before they saw it. Music and laughter tumbled over the hills, rising on the wind like the twinkling of a chime, building and building until it overwhelmed all else.

Pansy had warned them on the walk over from the cottage

that halfling parties could get "a little wild", as she'd put it – especially once they brought out the casks of ale. But nothing could prepare Ren for the sight that unfurled ahead of them, sweeping across an enormous meadow dotted with tiny yellow wildflowers.

The festival was a veritable maze of stalls and tents, all packed so closely together in a haze of colorful streamers that one would've thought space came at a premium. In truth, it did. Despite the meadow's impressive size, it was barely enough to contain the full breadth of the festival. Every single scrap of free space had been put to use, plugged with tables, chairs, decorations and, of course, food. So much food.

Although Ren had been prepared for it, the sight nonetheless registered like a kick to the chest. Not even the clan's stores at their fullest could match the sheer scale and variety on display; and here the halflings were about to devour it all in only a day.

Granted, there were a lot of them. Ren had never seen so many halflings in one place. It made sense; Pansy had said that this festival was for all of Halvenshire, which, as Ren understood it, included at least six other villages, several of which were quite a bit larger than Haverow. So, the amount of food made *sense*, especially for something like a festival. Ren was just... envious, they supposed.

In a way, it had been easier, hiding behind the ill-fitting veil of unkind stereotype, to discount the feeling congealing between their ribs like blackened tar as mere contempt, rather than the complex tangle of want mixed with fear. Because as much as Ren wished they could give their clan the ability to celebrate like this, they were only one goblin, and no amount of hard work would change that. This fact was inalienable, situated well beyond the bounds of their control, and still it felt like a personal failure, one they needed to atone for.

"Are you okay?" Pansy asked, her face, creased with concern, abruptly jutting into Ren's line of sight.

"Fine," Ren lied. Now was not the time to bog either of them down with Ren's personal baggage. Nature knew that Pansy had already brought along plenty, and today her burdens were as much Ren's as they were hers. Unfortunately, Pansy proved, yet again, far too perceptive for her own good, and so Ren added an all-too-believable "I'm just a little nervous," if only to erase the line of discontent that had etched itself into one corner of her mouth.

"It'll be okay," Pansy assured them, her lips stretching into a smile. "I'm right here with you. See?" As if to underline her point, she slipped her hand into Ren's, fingers twining together until they were nigh on inseparable.

Ren blinked, the shock of her touch momentarily overwhelming the rush of heat that sparked against their palm. "Are you sure—"

"More sure than I've ever been in my life." Pansy grinned and, with one last squeeze, pulled them down into the festival proper.

Immediately, everything stilled. In her exuberance, Pansy had sent Ren's hood flying. Now, it lay flat around their shoulders, leaving their face, their ears, the long strands of their hair, for once untangled to the best of their ability – everything about them that was innately, unmistakably *goblin* – plain to see.

As all eyes turned towards them, Ren fought against the urge to retreat knotting tight in the pit of their stomach. "Pansy . . ." they started to say, their voice barely managing to squeeze past the unease narrowing their throat. *Perhaps this wasn't such a good idea.*

But Pansy's grip on their hand only tightened. She held her

chin high, marching headlong into a crowd that was about as welcoming as the roiling sea, thick with salt and scorn.

That's right, Ren realized, eyes widening. It wasn't Ren the other halflings were looking at; it was Pansy.

Barely hushed whispers rose from the crowd, piling up and up until they'd amassed into a deafening roar.

"Is that the Underburrow girl? What is she *wearing*? Is that a skull?"

"Some disgusting goblin trinket, no doubt. I always knew that girl wasn't right."

"You know what they say: 'the apple never falls far from the tree'. And I'm sad to say that this tree is *rotten*. What happened last year with the grandmother was bad enough, but this is on another level completely."

"Truly. We should be lucky if that goblin doesn't immediately make off with everything that isn't nailed down."

"And to think I was told my fears were unfounded when I said that moving the festival from Halfend to Haverow was a mistake . . ."

"The Committee really should have made barring the Underburrow girl a condition for hosting."

"Gosh, I hope my own little ones don't turn out like that. How terrible her parents must feel."

The deluge of cruelty was endless; each comment meted out as casually as a polite greeting, as if the serrated edge that flashed in the noontime sun wasn't poised to cut right down to the bone. Ren struggled to wrap their head around it. These people knew Pansy. They were her neighbors, people she'd grown up alongside. And somehow, in this moment, none of that seemed to matter. She was an outsider, someone who didn't belong – and everyone was going to make sure she knew it.

Ren wanted to say something, the desire to flee overwhelmed by another, fiercer urge. Already, the words had gathered on their tongue, as painful to contain as a fiery coal. A few more moments and they'd burn right through. But the fear of making things worse forced Ren to hold on, to lock their jaw and pin the words in all their ardency behind a wall of teeth. They looked at Pansy, the question – *Should I?* – gleaming bright across their eyes, unspoken yet heard all the same.

She shook her head and closed her free hand around the skull still resting against her collarbone, framed with delicate lace from the collar of her blouse. "It's okay. We'll make them eat their words soon enough. They have no idea they're looking at the next winners of the Halvenshire Crop Competition." She grinned.

Something in Ren's chest softened, unleashing a tide that was equal parts love and sadness. *I'm not the one who needs comfort right now*, they wanted to say, but found themself struck by the strange sensation of looking into a mirror.

Words they'd discounted at the time floated back to the surface from whatever recess they'd been crammed into: *You'd set yourself on fire if it meant keeping someone else warm.* That's what Thorn had said the day Ren had volunteered to be the cottage's next Caretaker. Funny how it was only now that Ren understood them.

They gave Pansy's hand a squeeze. "Let's go show everyone what we can do."

Apart from the fact that they'd nearly missed the cut-off, as noted by the middle-aged halfling tasked with minding the booth, entering the pumpkin in the competition turned out to be surprisingly straightforward. There was, apparently, no rule against goblins entering the competition: an egregious oversight for a people so staunchly against them, but not one the halfling who dutifully registered their entry cared to interrogate – especially not after they laid eyes on the pumpkin itself.

"My word!" they declared, pushing up their spectacles with the pad of their forefinger. "That's the biggest pumpkin I've ever seen! Even if you *were* late, I feel like I'd have to let you in just so the judges could take a gander at this beauty. How did you get it to grow so large?"

"Love and sunlight," Pansy replied, cutting in before Ren could so much as open their mouth. In retrospect, this was smart of her. Even if a goblin growth potion was, in Ren's view, no different from whatever fertilizer halflings were partial to these days, chances were the entirety of Halvenshire would see things rather differently.

The bespectacled halfling gave a slow, knowing smile. "All right then. Keep your secrets. In the meantime, try not to wander off too far. I can't imagine it'll take too long to determine this year's winner." They winked.

As the pumpkin was carted away, Pansy nudged Ren with the point of her elbow. "Did you hear that?" she said, grinning. "Biggest pumpkin they've ever seen!"

"I was honestly more focused on the fact that they seemed unbothered by my presence."

"Oh. Well," Pansy shifted awkwardly beside them. "I think that their interest in vegetables didn't leave room for much else. But to be completely fair, our pumpkin *is* very impressive. One might call it the king of all pumpkins – or, perhaps, the Pump-*king*."

Ren snorted. "You're terrible," they said, smiling even as they rolled their eyes.

"I disagree. In fact, I think I'm rather clever."

"Perhaps your genius is simply beyond me," Ren replied with a shrug, the curl at the corner of their mouth deepening.

"Maybe it is – *ooh*! You're making fun of me again! Well, I'll have you know that—" She reared back, ready to give as good as she'd gotten, falling into the familiar comfort of their usual back-and-forth, when a voice, unerringly smooth in its tenor, promptly knocked the air from her lungs.

"Miss Underburrow," said a startlingly tall human man – a wizard, Ren presumed, given his ridiculous, gem-studded staff and equally ridiculous colourful robes, shimmering like silken velvet in the sunlight. "How good to see you. Was that your pumpkin I just saw Horace carting away?"

"Hello, Agvaldir," Pansy said, pinning her mouth into a thin-lipped smile as she turned around to face him. The last time Ren had seen her this unenthusiastic was when they'd had to prune the garden of parasitic slugs. "Ren and I decided to enter the competition together this year."

At the mention of Ren, Agvaldir's eyes briefly flicked over them, lingering just long enough to drop a note of barely concealed distaste into the oil-slick brightness of his too-white smile. "I wondered if we might have a moment to talk in private about the matter you raised with me the last time our paths crossed in town."

Pansy's brow furrowed. "What matter? Oh! The thing I showed you from my notebook. Never mind about that," she said, waving her hands about as if to sweep aside the subject. "Please consider the issue resolved. I'm so sorry for having troubled you about it in the first place. It really wasn't that serious."

"Resolved?" It was now Agvaldir's turn to look confused, his thick brows pinching low across his deep-set eyes. "Miss Underburrow, the fact that this goblin is still following you is very much proof that this matter is *not* resolved."

Ren jerked their head towards Pansy, every inch of them abruptly pulling taut. "What's he talking about, Pansy?"

"It's nothing," Pansy replied, too quick to be reassuring. Already, her expression seemed to be straining at the seams, her eyes too wide, her mouth too tight. Whatever truth coiled behind that mask of manufactured politeness, it wasn't anything good – especially not for Ren, given that a wizard was involved.

Their stomach gave a violent twist at that, cold dread seeping through every pore. Ren saw the way Agvaldir looked at them. To him, they were nothing more than a nuisance, an insect that needed to be squashed. And Ren knew, with heart-stopping certainty, that this wizard, like any other, could do just that. With but a flick of his wrist or a half-mumbled spell, Ren would cease to exist, gone the same way as who-knows-how-many goblins before them. For as far as this man was concerned, all goblins were the same, agents of Evil just like the dark lords and necromancers he'd sworn to fight. Never before had he thought to question this belief, so secure in his conviction as a force of Good that the horror inherent in exterminating entire peoples registered only as a mild inconvenience.

This was who Pansy had gone to for aid.

To get rid of me? Ren thought, throat narrowing like a vice. Because if their being here was proof that this "matter" wasn't resolved, then . . .

"Miss Underburrow," Agvaldir said, more forcefully this time, "I really think we should discuss this in private. The implications of—"

Pansy, however, was already turning away, her grip on Ren tightening just beyond the point of comfortable. "I think they're going to announce the results soon," she said, in a tone utterly devoid of excitement. "Let's go over to the main stage. That's where they always do it."

Without waiting for an answer, much less any sort of agreement, she dragged Ren off into the maze of stalls and streamers, where the air was thick with the smell of hot pies and candied apples. Unfortunately, these mouthwatering treats passed in as much of a blur as the various handmade crafts on display, from fluffy wool scarves to painted wooden figurines. Pansy had set a pace in between a brisk walk and a jog. Hardly appropriate for such cramped surroundings, especially with most attendees proceeding at a more leisurely gait. Perhaps, if she was excited, it would make sense. But Pansy wasn't excited. She was—

She's scared, Ren realized, a fresh spike of fear surging up their spine. *She knows she did something bad, and she's afraid I'll find out.*

"What did you ask of him?" they demanded, yanking their hand away as they jerked to a sudden stop along the fringes of the crowd clustered around the nearby stage.

"I didn't ask anything of him!" Pansy protested, looking almost hurt by the accusation. *The gall.* "All I did was ask him a question."

"Like: *How do I get rid of a goblin?*" they sneered, ears flattening against their skull.

Pansy flinched; it was as much an answer as the flush that crept across her cheeks, staining her skin a mottled, ruddy red. "That's not— I didn't ask *that*."

"Then what? What are you so afraid I'll find out about?"

"It's no—"

"Don't tell me it's nothing!" Ren snapped, eyes flashing. "I was there, Pansy. I saw the way you reacted when that wizard started talking! You know something."

"I don't know anything! I just – *ugh*! I just don't like him, okay? I'm probably the only halfling in all of Haverow who doesn't. But every time I look at him, all I can think about is the fact that he's the one who recruited my grandmother to fight in the Great War against the last dark lord. Maybe that's petty of me. My grandmother was her own person; she made her own choices. But still. *Still*." She looked away, the bone-white of her jaw flexing hard beneath reddened skin.

It took half a second for Ren to deflate, all their anger, their righteous indignation, smothered beneath a sudden avalanche of understanding. Now, the heat that had pooled beneath their skin burned in a different way – sour, shameful.

"I'm sorry," they mumbled after a beat, their gaze pinned between their feet. "I saw that he was a wizard, and I— Never mind." They shook their head. "For what it's worth, I think you have good reason to dislike him. He took advantage of your grandmother, saw her only as a tool to be used rather than another living being. And when she was no longer useful to him, he discarded her without a second thought. That's not something a good person would do."

Pansy blinked, surprised. "You agree with me?"

"Absolutely. We can be in the I-don't-like-Agvaldir club together."

"Shh! Not so loud!" she said through a smile. "He's very popular around here, you know."

Of course he is. "Well, halflings *do* tend to have terrible taste," Ren pointed out.

"Hey!" Pansy gave them a light shove on the arm. "I have great taste! I'm here with you, aren't I?"

Ren's eyes widened. Now, *that*, they hadn't expected. "I . . . y-yes," they stammered, their face going hot.

In truth, they should've continued to press her for an answer to their initial question, still hanging between them, unaddressed. If there was any sort of possibility that they might wake up one day and find a wizard-shaped problem on their doorstep, Ren wanted to know about it ahead of time.

And yet, standing there, caught in the radiance of Pansy's smile, now fully realized, they couldn't bring themself to raise even the first syllable to their lips. Surrounded by music and laughter, the smell of spiced wine and sweet mead, it seemed wrong, ruining this otherwise golden moment. Plus, did it really matter what she'd asked Agvaldir? Pansy didn't even like the man! Surely, there was no danger here – a conclusion Ren rushed to reassure themself of all the more when Pansy reached out and took their hand in hers yet again.

"You know, Ren," she began, a weighty quiver creeping into her voice, "I—"

"Are you the one who grew that really large pumpkin?" asked a youthful-looking halfling, the thick crop of dark facial hair growing along his jaw doing little to mask the overall softness of his features.

If he realized he'd butted into their conversation at an inopportune moment – which, to be fair, the ale-slick tankard he clutched in one hand might've precluded – he gave no indication.

Either way, whatever Pansy meant to say she promptly swallowed back down, replacing it instead with a too-stiff smile and an overly bright, "Ren here did most of the work, actually."

"Ren? The goblin, you mean?" The halfling looked at them, his eyes going wide.

Immediately, Ren braced themselves for some variety of derision – or, at the very least, a vaguely thoughtless comment. But the halfling cocked his head to the side, let out a soft, "Huh", and promptly began questioning them about their technique.

"What sort of fertilizer did you use?" he asked, pressing in close enough that Ren nearly took a step back out of reflex. There was an intensity to his stare – no, an *enthusiasm* – that seemed ill-advised given the comments Pansy had been forced to endure on the way in.

Did he not care that he was talking to a goblin? Ren wondered, blinking in surprise. No matter how drunk he might've been – which, in retrospect, might've been far less than they'd initially presumed – engaging with the "enemy" was, surely, a line every Halvenshire halfling knew not to cross.

But, then again, Pansy had certainly crossed it. Her parents, too. Perhaps this "line" wasn't so much a hard rule as a vague guideline – and an oft-disregarded one at that.

"I think that sort of thing counts as a trade secret," Pansy said, her tone still registering as friendly even as she angled herself into the space between Ren and the halfling. A silent request that, thankfully, did not go unheard.

"*Come on*," he pleaded with a pout that only served to undermine his beard further as he moved back a few paces. "I promise I won't tell!"

"But you'll use it in next year's competition, won't you?" she countered, eyebrows arching.

Of course he would. The small quirk at the corner of his mouth said as much. He shrugged. "Can't blame a man for trying. Anything for a large squash, yeah?"

"Actually," Ren said, interjecting at last, their voice softened by their lingering hesitance, "I don't mind telling you – though you'll probably have trouble finding most of the ingredients. They're—"

A sudden swell of music, trumpets and drums punching through the festival din with a near-manic fervor drowned out the rest of their answer. They didn't bother trying a second time. By that point, the dark-haired halfling's attention had swiveled away, resting instead on center stage and the other halfling that now occupied it.

"Hell-*ooo*, Halvenshire!" declared the halfling, nothing short of bombastic in his delivery, from the volume of his voice to the breadth of his motions. "I certainly hope you're all enjoying this year's Harvest Festival!"

The cheer that rose from the crowd, punctuated by a handful of startled shrieks thanks to a too-swiftly-lifted tankard of ale sloshing everywhere, indicated that yes, everyone was enjoying themselves rather well actually.

The halfling on stage let out a chuckle. "Looks like *someone* has already gotten too deep in their tankard," he said to another rousing chorus of cheers – and a few more slops of jostled ale. "But never fear, the moment we've all been waiting for is here! That's right. It's time to announce the winner of this year's Crop Competition!"

"Oh, gods," Pansy breathed, gripping Ren ever-tighter – now with both hands. "Do you think it'll be us? I sure hope it's us . . ."

Looking at Pansy, the way she watched the halfling on stage flick open the folded piece of paper he'd been handed with a tremendous flourish, seemingly unable to tear her eyes away, not even for a moment, Ren couldn't help but smile. "And you were so certain of our victory earlier." They chuckled.

"That was different!" Pansy protested, still clutching Ren's hand tightly in hers. "Oh, please, please, *please* let us win. I mean, we should, right? Horace said it themself! The biggest pumpkin they'd ever seen! Not to mention that other halfling seemed pretty impressed too. He was even asking you for tips!"

Ren gave her hand a steadying pat. "I know, darling."

Pansy's head jerked towards them, the halfling on stage somehow forgotten as her voice caught in her throat. "Dar—?" she started to ask, repeating the first syllable of a word Ren couldn't rightly say they'd meant to use but had slipped out all the same; nor could they bring themself to regret it, seeing the rush of color that surged into her cheeks thereafter.

Yes, they imagined themself saying, doubling down with a grin just a fraction shy of a smirk. *Darling.*

No doubt that would've swept the very last of Pansy's breath away. Too bad the halfling on stage had started to speak again, and against these words Ren had no hope of winning.

"I'm pleased to announce the winners of this year's annual Halvenshire Crop Competition – and yes, you heard me correctly: that's *winners*, plural, because we have two. Let's give a big congratulations to Pansy Underburrow and Ren Woodward!"

If there were any cheers or even polite clapping from the other attendees, Ren couldn't say. They heard nothing beyond the high-pitched squeal Pansy let out, practically jumping up and down with excitement at the news. But more than that, if there were any sounds of disapproval at what came next, Ren didn't hear those either – because Pansy had thrown her arms around their neck and with one last cry of delight, pressed her mouth against theirs, firmly and without restraint.

In that moment, there was nothing beyond the warmth of her lips, the softness of her body as it curled around them. Everything else had fallen away, the world contracting to that single, brilliant point where intelligent thought ceased to exist. Ren's mind had turned in on itself, caught in an endless litany of *Pansy is kissing me! Pansy is kissing me!* – uttered with all the devoted fervency of a fresh-faced acolyte's prayers. And, in a way, perhaps that's what it was, because what was a prayer if not a wish, and Ren would give anything, *everything*, to stay like this for ever.

But eventually Pansy pulled away, her face flushed in the same way Ren's own doubtless mirrored. She smiled, shyly, the wet gleam on her lower lip as beautiful as a diamond's shine.

Nature's mercy. Ren wanted to kiss her again. Their lips tingled with desire, goading them on. But before they could bend their head, angling their chin so they could kiss her all the more thoroughly – their audience be damned! – a voice Ren had rapidly come to *loathe* rang out across the surrounding area.

"I'm afraid I'm going to have to step in here," said Agvaldir, striding onto the stage with an elderly halfling woman trailing not too far behind, forced to take three quick steps for every one of his.

"Oh no," whispered Pansy, every ounce of her earlier elation sweeping out of her on that one breath as her expression fell to pieces. "It's Councilor Millwood."

The miserable, old busybody? Ren nearly asked, in a voice rough with want and frustration, only to think better of it at the last possible moment.

"It has come to my attention," said Agvaldir, enunciating each word with pointed precision, as if the air itself could be flayed apart by his voice, "that the winning entry was cultivated using ... unorthodox methods, which Miss Underburrow went out of her way to obfuscate during the registration process."

"A deplorable act of deceit – one no doubt owing to her recent choice of company," declared Mrs. Millwood, who having finally caught up with Agvaldir, took her place on the stage beside him, her hands clasped gravely at her front.

"What are you talking about?" Pansy demanded, striding forward. "We grew that pumpkin fairly! Just like everyone else who entered!"

"You used magic!" Mrs. Millwood jabbed an accusatory finger towards her. "And magic, may I remind you, not only contravenes the rules established for this competition but also runs contrary to the whole spirit of it!"

"Granted," cut in Agvaldir, his tone infuriatingly staid, "it's rather insulting to equate something as crude as a goblin growth potion to proper magic—"

"It's not magic!" Ren snapped, now stepping forward as well, their anger a sizzling ember in their throat. "The potion I made is no different from any sort of halfling fertilizer!"

"So, you admit it then?" said Mrs. Millwood, her chin lifting a touch higher. She stared down her nose at them, her lips pressing together in a hard, unflinching line. "Very well. It seems we have no choice. Miss Underburrow and her"– she sniffed – "*companion* are hereby disqualified. Their entry is null and void."

"You can't do that!" Pansy cried, the first crack splitting through her voice. "Just because you're upset that Ren and I won fair and square—"

Mrs. Millwood's eyes flashed. "You did *not* win 'fair and square'. To think that your perception of honesty and truth would become so swiftly skewed."

"Councilor," Agvaldir said, calm as ever as he placed a heavy hand on Mrs. Millwood's shoulder, "is it not in Haverow's way to extend a helping hand to those that need it the most? I cannot imagine a more deserving person than one of your own who has so tragically lost her way." His gaze rested meaningfully on Pansy at that, his blue eyes strangely cold in contrast to the apparent warmth of his words. "It's as I've always said to those who join me on my campaigns: no matter how far one may go, there is always a road home."

"I – I haven't lost my way," Pansy protested, her throat working around each word as if they were shards of splintered glass. She looked about her, searching, it seemed, for some shred of support among the slew of familiar faces.

At last, she caught sight of her parents, standing off to one side, their expressions frozen in wide-eyed looks of horror. *Say something*, pleaded her gaze, already awash in a watery film.

But her parents said nothing. Instead, they looked away, fear and shame drawing tight over their features.

Something snapped in Pansy then. Ren saw it in her face, the dark jolt that sliced across it, twisting her mouth into a sneer. Ren wanted nothing more than to gather her into their arms and tell her that they were there for her, that they'd always be. Too bad it wasn't their support she needed right now.

Teeth bared, Pansy whirled on Agvaldir and snarled, "Well, you can take your 'helping hand' and shove it!" Where exactly he could do so was an answer readily deduced, given the rude gesture with which she capped off her statement.

"My word!" cried Mrs. Millwood aghast, clutching one hand to her breast, as if that alone could shame Pansy into immediately apologizing.

"Let's go get our pumpkin," Pansy bit out, already starting towards where they'd dropped it off. "It's not like anyone here deserves it."

She walked quickly, each footfall landing more heavily than the last. Her hands, knotted into trembling fists at her side, pulsed with the same tension that wound along her jaw, locking it tight. Sheer stubbornness had turned her into a paradox, simultaneously as strong as iron forged in the hottest of flames and as fragile as wafer-thin glass.

"Hey, it'll be okay," Ren said, touching a gentle hand to her shoulder once they'd managed to catch up. "We'll go home and turn that pumpkin into that stew you mentioned before, the one that's perfect for autumn. Then we'll sit down together and enjoy it – just the two of us. Does that sound good?"

To Ren, it absolutely did – but whether Pansy agreed, who could say? She certainly wasn't giving any indication one way or another, her lips an unflinching, pale line across the mottled planes of her face.

"Or we could do something else," Ren continued, the fear of having said the wrong thing congealing in the pit of their stomach like a hunk of ice.

Still, Pansy said nothing. She only walked, her gaze fixed firmly ahead, as unchanging as the seam of her mouth.

It wasn't until Blossom appeared on the path ahead of them, her face damp and flushed with exertion, that something finally changed. Pansy flinched, as the sound of her name, cried from Blossom's mouth, registered with all the force of a punch to the gut.

All Pansy managed was a weak, "I can't do this," uttered in the thinnest of whispers, before she turned on her heel and ran.

This time, Ren let her go. And when Blossom moved to follow her, they put a hand out to stop her and shook their head. "Don't."

Blossom seemed almost offended by the suggestion, the knots plaguing her brow oscillating between annoyance and genuine confusion. "I just wanted to apologize," she explained, stiffening beneath the weight of Ren's stare. "I'd planned to drop off a letter, once all this"– she waved a hand around her – "craziness was over. But then I heard that Pansy was here, and so I thought to try to catch her in person instead. I ran all the way from where they're setting up tonight's feast." A beat. "Did – did something happen?"

Part of Ren wanted to laugh, mirthless and sharp. *Did something happen?* The question sounded even more stupid the second time around. But Blossom hadn't been there; she hadn't seen. In fact, she'd barely even gotten a glimpse of Pansy herself, and from a distance at that.

So Ren forced themself to nod, to tuck away the part of themself that had been left jagged and sharp, for they were as much a blade as they were Pansy's shield. And they said, "Give her time."

Ren caught up with Pansy a little way outside town, just far enough that Haverow's burrows could almost be discounted as nothing more than distant hills.

She sat in the middle of the road, curled in on herself, her knees tucked against her forehead so tightly it was a wonder she could even so much as sway in the breeze. But Pansy wasn't a statue, stock-still and made of stone. Her shoulders heaved around every sob, tearing through her like a saw-toothed blade through bark, while the rest of her shuddered with the desperate gasps that followed, made only to fill her lungs with enough air to repeat the cycle anew.

Ren said nothing as they knelt down beside her. As far as they were concerned, it wasn't necessary. The hand they brought up to rest lightly against her scalp, smoothing out her hair with tender strokes, said everything that needed to be said.

"That feels nice," Pansy mumbled at last, her voice clotted with snot and tears.

"Nana – my clan's leader, I guess you could say – used to do it for me whenever I couldn't fall asleep," Ren explained, their voice as gentle as their touch. "I always found it rather soothing."

Pansy let out a honking sort of laugh. "Trying to put me down for a nap?"

They shook their head. "Just trying to help you feel better. Even if only in some small way."

"Yeah," Pansy said after a beat, the word riding away on a wistful exhale. "I know."

"Is it helping?"

She sniffled, shrugged. "A little. It's just—" Her voice cracked, emotion once again flooding the splintered web today's events had left behind.

Seeing the way her lips trembled, spasming around the mere shape of the words she wanted to say, Ren took it upon themself to finish them for her. "Today didn't go as you hoped."

She nodded. "I knew my plan was stupid. Deep down, I knew it. And don't look at me like that," she chided as Ren opened their mouth to protest. "It *was* stupid. Stupid in the way children's dreams are, or hoping for the impossible to come to pass."

"There's nothing wrong with dreaming," Ren said gently. "Or hoping that things could one day be different."

"Then why does it hurt so much?"

"Because it matters," was all Ren said, the hand stroking the top of Pansy's head an ever-enduring constant.

"Did I ask for too much?" she wondered aloud, her nails digging half-moon crescents into the skin of her upper arms, left bare by the puffy sleeves of her blouse. "All I wanted was for them to see me for who I am – to look beyond the differences, my apparent flaws, and see all the good that's in there too. Just once! It's all I've *ever* wanted, and they couldn't even give me that."

As Pansy's forehead dropped once more to her knees, Ren shifted closer, the bright seed she'd planted in their heart reaching out for her with gleaming tendrils. It ached, seeing her like this. But there were some wounds not even Ren could shield her from. All they could do was soothe the resultant sting.

Dropping their hand to her shoulders, Ren pulled Pansy into their chest and, with lips grazing the crown of her head, said, "I see you, Pansy."

She choked, her shoulders shuddering with the force of another sob. "I wanted them to see you too, Ren," she whispered. "To see you the way I see you – all your kindness, your wit, your determination. I should've . . . I should've told them. Maybe they wouldn't have listened, but at least I'd have said it, you know?"

"You told your parents. That's what matters most to me."

Ren didn't know how long they held her there, sat in the middle of the road with nothing around them but the breeze and birdsong. Certainly long enough that Pig, still hitched to the wagon, trotted over to investigate. She dug her snout into their lower back, a gesture fueled as much by concern as by impatience. Figuring that Pansy wouldn't appreciate the feeling of a cold, slightly damp nose pressing into any part of her, Ren shooed Pig away with a half-muttered admonishment, unwilling to relinquish their hold on Pansy until her sobs quieted into wet, shaky hiccups.

Eventually, they did, and soon Pansy's breathing trended towards something that could be called even. Swiping at her cheeks with the back of her hand, she raised her head with an embarrassed-sounding sniffle. "Do you like pumpkin pie, Ren?"

"Do I—" Ren started to repeat, their eyes briefly widening in surprise before understanding dawned upon them. They smiled. "I love it."

15
Pansy

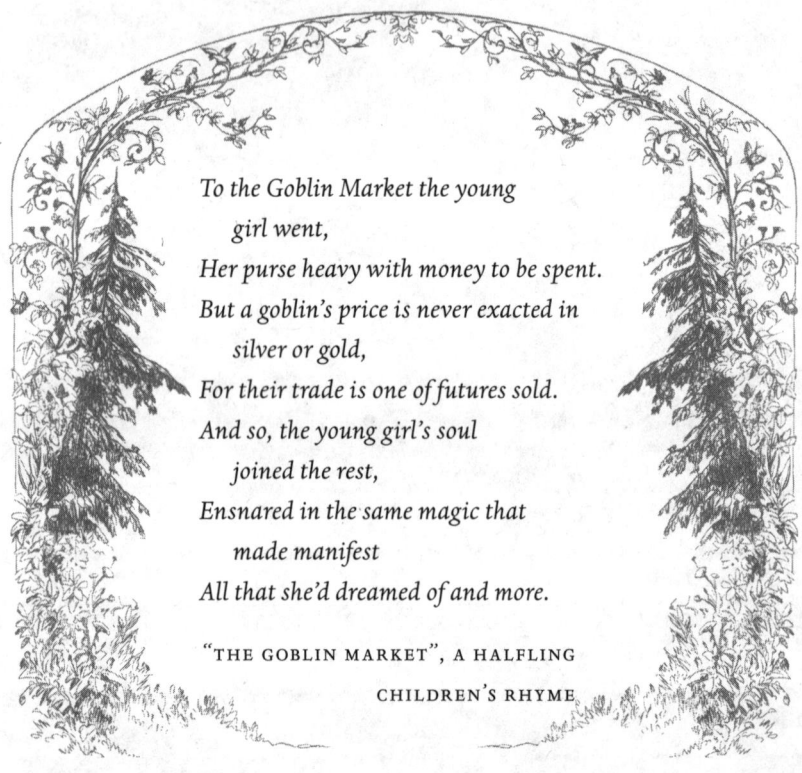

To the Goblin Market the young
   girl went,
Her purse heavy with money to be spent.
But a goblin's price is never exacted in
   silver or gold,
For their trade is one of futures sold.
And so, the young girl's soul
   joined the rest,
Ensnared in the same magic that
   made manifest
All that she'd dreamed of and more.

"THE GOBLIN MARKET", A HALFLING CHILDREN'S RHYME

For once, the comforts of the kitchen did little to ease the miserable knot Pansy's insides had wound themselves into. Even with Ren by her side, encouraging her with soft words and gentle touches, the day's disappointment remained an ever-present specter, haunting her at every turn. Nothing could slip beyond the chill of its grasp; things that had once brought her joy suddenly turned bitter as ash. And the cottage, now infused with the smell of warm stew and freshly baked pumpkin pie, proved the most intolerable of all.

So, Pansy made her excuses, mumbling something about needing some air as she shoved herself away from the table, where her dinner sat largely untouched. No doubt Ren would think it a waste, but the fact that she'd even managed a handful of bites was already a miracle in itself. Gods knew the weight in her belly had left little room for anything else.

Ren, for their part, said nothing about the wasted food – much to Pansy's relief. Instead, they only asked, "Do you want me to come with you?"

The answer to that was "no". For as much as Ren had lent a touch of brightness to an otherwise miserable day, their presence had nonetheless become a blade that cut both ways. Every time Pansy remembered the kiss they'd shared at the Harvest Festival, the memory of Agvaldir was hot on its heels, all too ready to send her soaring heart plummeting back to earth. Whatever had bloomed between Ren and her, it was a fragile, half-cracked thing, hamstrung by a secret barely deserving of the name.

Pansy would insist that she hadn't done anything wrong. Not really. But still, her stomach turned, its meager contents frothing like the sea in a storm at the mere *thought* of telling Ren the truth. Because now that Haverow had well and truly rejected her, they were all she had left. She couldn't risk damaging that. Not now; not ever. Maybe, if having feelings for one another was enough, she'd feel differently. But they were a halfling and a goblin, and at this point even the world itself seemed determined to keep them apart.

"I'll just be a moment," Pansy assured Ren, her lips stretching around a too-stiff smile.

No doubt Ren wanted to accompany her anyway, judging from the concern that slashed across their brow. Still, they did as she asked, settling back into their seat as she headed for the front door.

Pansy stepped out into the garden alone, the cool night air barely registering amid the sour heat that roiled beneath her skin. It was strange being out here without Ren. For one, the garden was far darker than she was used to; the lanterns Ren had arranged for her benefit still unlit. Had Pansy planned on doing something other than plopping down on the front stoop and stewing in her own misery, trapped in an unending loop of *just-tell-them-but-I-can't*, she might have gone to the trouble of lighting them herself. But, as it was, she saw no real point. Just a lot of wasted effort and burnt-down wicks.

It wasn't like she couldn't see. The garden remained discernible enough for her purposes, familiar shapes cast now in gold and silver, the warmth of the cottage meeting the cool glow of the moon.

The forest beyond, however, was a different story.

Pansy had barely settled onto the stoop, her skirts folded neatly underneath her, when a sharp snap, like that of a twig crunching underfoot, rang out from the black mass of the nearby treeline. Her breath snagged in her throat, eyes flying wide as her head jerked in the direction the noise had come from.

In truth, it shouldn't have been nearly so startling. The forest was full of sounds, from the rustle of leaves to the low groan of shifting bark.

And yet, there was something different about this. A chill had come over Pansy, washing down her limbs in streams of gooseflesh. She squinted into the murky void, eyes straining to make sense of what little she could actually perceive, a jumble of barely there outlines that slowly coalesced into a handful of bushes, some trees. So far, nothing unusual or out of the ordinary.

Then one of the shapes shifted, retreating deeper into the thicket; what Pansy had once thought to be merely a tree turned out to be anything but.

"Ren?" she squeaked out, unable to keep herself from hoping, even though it made no sense. If that had been a person – rather than some strange, terrifying monster of the forest – they were much too tall to be a goblin or even a halfling. "Ren, is that you?"

"Pansy?"

Pansy's heart kicked into her gorge. Ren's voice had come from behind her. She turned and found them standing in the doorway, their forehead knotted with thick ropes of confusion.

"What's wrong?" they asked, frowning at the sight of her expression, wide-eyed and devoid of color.

"I—" Pansy glanced back to the forest's edge. *Did I just imagine it?* "I thought I saw someone . . . In the trees over there."

"Stay here," Ren said, yanking on their shoes, which they'd left on one side of the doorway. "I'll go take a look."

"I'll come with you," Pansy said, already shooting up from the stoop. If someone *was* out there, there was no way she was going to let Ren face them alone.

For a moment, it seemed like Ren was going to argue with her. But one look at the hard set of her jaw, and whatever fight had been building inside them promptly fizzled out. "Fine," they said. "But stay behind me."

Together, they approached the black tangle of the forest, each step speeding Pansy's already frantic pulse. She shivered as they pushed beyond the treeline, branches unfurling overhead like thick veins of ink. Unable to help herself, she gripped a fistful of Ren's tunic, flushing when they cast a quizzical look over their shoulder.

"I can't see," she mumbled by way of explanation, ducking her burning face beneath a veil of red curls.

"Then stay close," Ren replied, their vision once again trained on the forest floor, searching for footprints, no doubt – or, perhaps, some other clue, one that sat equally beyond Pansy's present reach.

"Do you see anything?" she asked, half-hoping the answer was no, if only because the alternative proved far more frightening.

Ren shook their head. "No footprints. Just some scattered leaves, a few animal droppings. You're certain this is where you saw them?"

"Positive."

"Hmm. Then perhaps— *Oh!*"

Oh, gods. They'd found something, hadn't they? It hadn't been her imagination. Someone had been out there, watching her, watching the cottage.

Pansy swallowed, her throat narrowing in what had now become an all too familiar sensation. "What have you found?" she asked, her words nearly upended by the quivering warble that had hooked into her voice.

"Nothing frightening," Ren assured her, gently disentangling her hand from their tunic. "Whatever you saw, it was probably just an animal. Perfectly normal for the forest." They smiled.

"I know *that*," Pansy protested, her face heating anew. "It just . . . it was tall. It didn't really look like an animal . . ."

Ren shrugged. "Well, I'm not seeing any evidence of anything else having passed through here, and as far as I know, this forest isn't home to any sort of horrifying monster."

"'As far as you know', huh? That isn't exactly a reassuring qualifier..."

"Pansy, I've been roaming these woods since the day I took my first steps. So, take the good news for what it is and *come look.*"

They were right about one thing, at least: it *was* good news – even if it made Pansy look like a fool. But she supposed that was par for the course at this point, a thought that registered with an undeniably sour note alongside the heat pooling in her cheeks.

With Ren tugging insistently on her arm, she had no choice but to follow. Pansy's brow furrowed as they led her to what otherwise looked to be a perfectly normal bush. It was only once they'd pushed aside one of its boughs, revealing a cluster of tiny blue flowers, each sporting five finely tipped petals, that she understood.

"They're like little stars," she murmured, squatting down beside Ren so that she could take a closer look. She wasn't sure if it was a trick of the moonlight, seeping through the dense canopy overhead in narrow beams of silver, but the flowers seemed to glow amid the surrounding darkness.

"Goblins call this particular flower Wayfinder," Ren explained, their eyes equally bright. "It blooms only on nights that the Goblin Market is open."

Pansy's eyes widened. "Does that mean...?"

They grinned. "Want to go?"

Absolutely, Pansy wanted to say. However, when she opened her mouth to reply, the words simply wouldn't come.

Because what was the point? Today had shown that Haverow

would never accept Ren. In fact, they'd probably never accept Pansy either. Could she really believe that Ren's clan would prove any different? Sure, they wouldn't kick out a goblin for the high crime of being "weird", but that meant nothing when the person in question wasn't even a goblin to begin with.

Pansy remembered the things Ren had said to her in the beginning, all the times they'd mistaken her desire to help – or just to belong, really – for halfling selfishness and gluttony. She didn't hold it against them. How could she, when she was far from innocent herself? Still, the thought of hearing those same words again, from the people Ren considered family, no less – well, it certainly put a damper on the excitement that had swelled in her breast.

And, again, what was the point? Why weather all this pain, this hurt, for a relationship that was already doomed? Because Ren had made their stance on Agvaldir clear. Seeking his aid was a betrayal, one that no number of explanations or apologies could overcome. It was unfair, decidedly so.

Things were different then, she wanted to scream, the words bubbling like acid in her chest. *If I'd known you then as I know you now, I never would have gone to Agvaldir for help!*

But her mouth stayed shut, lips pinned together as tightly as the gates of a castle under siege. Better to stay silent, she decided. Stay silent and hope that Agvaldir stayed away, that the shape in the forest was truly just her imagination and not a prelude to the disaster she feared was taking shape on the horizon. If that happened, then ... then maybe her future with Ren wouldn't be nearly so bleak.

"Pansy?" Ren asked, their voice yanking her back to reality with all the suddenness of a fall from a great height.

"Oh! Yes. Sorry," she said, the color dusting her cheeks

darkening a fraction more. "I-I'd love to go. I was just thinking, that's all."

"Thinking," Ren repeated, their voice oddly toneless.

"About things," Pansy continued, elaborating with an equally vague gesture.

Cocking their head to the side, Ren watched her for a moment in silence. Then, mumbling a soft "I'll be right back," they disappeared into the darkness of the forest. A minute or so later, they returned, carrying some sort of twig, still flush with feather-like leaves. Plump red berries dripped from in-between the sheaf of green, bright as a cascade of rubies.

"Here," Ren said, holding it out to her. "It's a rowan sprig. It'll protect you from any wayward charms or spells while we're at the market."

"Oh, that's not what I—" Pansy snapped her mouth shut, realizing the boon she'd been given. Even so, she couldn't help but ask, turning over the twig in her hands, "Is it really okay for me to go?"

"To the market?" Ren blinked at her. "It should be fine. Everyone there knows me, so they'll probably at least give you a chance."

Probably. Not the most encouraging of words, but Pansy supposed it could be worse. "Would bringing along some pie help?" she asked. "I mean, everyone loves pie, right?"

Ren considered her proposal for several moments. "That's actually a good idea," they said at last. "The market runs off a barter system rather than the currency you're probably used to, so you'd need to bring something along to trade anyway."

"What sort of things are usually for sale?" Pansy asked, unable to deny her burgeoning curiosity.

They smiled at her, the curve of their lips just shy of a smirk.

"You'll see for yourself soon enough. Far be it from me to spoil the surprise."

The way to the Goblin Market was long and dark, even with a path of tiny luminescent blooms to map every step.

It took two stumbles, one of which nearly sent the pie flying from her basket, for Ren to reach for her hand again. "It's only going to get darker from here on out," they said, their eyes two gleaming points in the tarnished gloom. "Stay close."

It did indeed get darker – something Pansy hadn't thought possible until Ren pulled her through the gaping maw of a hollowed-out tree. There, the trail plunged downwards, winding deep into the bowels of the earth, where the occasional Wayfinder, still studding their path, served as the only source of light.

But faint and flickering, these tiny blooms could only illuminate so much, like the stars overhead on a moonless night. Thank the gods she had Ren to guide her, their hand an anchor amid the warm, weightless black. Without them, she'd have doubtless walked right into solid earth the moment the tunnel veered to one side, which at this point seemed to be happening every few paces or so.

"It's just a little further," Ren said with a reassuring squeeze. "See the light ahead?"

What light? Pansy almost wanted to laugh. *I can't see anything!*

But Ren was right. The gloom, stubborn though it was, had started to disperse, chased away by a purplish glow that, while still faint, grew brighter with each step they took in its direction. Soon, Pansy could even see again. Not perfectly, mind you, but well enough that she didn't need to rely on Ren any more. Still, she made no move to remove her hand from theirs – and, for the record, neither did they.

So, when the two of them finally stepped out into some sort of vestibule, its walls more tree root than dirt, they did so hand in hand. This proved quite the shock to the goblin positioned on the far side of the room, where the roots had formed something like an archway, edged with delicate, drooping boughs of wisteria and iron lanterns bearing purple flames.

"Ren?" the goblin intoned, his eyes going wide. Judging from the dagger strapped to his hip, a perfect mirror of the one Ren carried, he seemed to be some sort of guard, presumably there to keep out undesirables.

Undesirables like her, Pansy realized, her chest constricting as the goblin's gaze narrowed on her, his fingers already inching towards the hilt of his dagger.

"Halflings aren't allowed in here," he said quickly, before Ren had even had a chance to say hello.

"She's with me," Ren replied, their chin held high.

The guard scoffed. "Yeah, I can see that. But why?"

"Because . . ." Ren hesitated, their brow creasing as their lips thinned, seemingly unsure of how to answer.

The question, though deceptively plain in its wording, was not nearly so simple at its core. *What is she to you?* the goblin might as well have asked, the very thing Pansy herself had wondered yet feared to know, her heart once again kicking against her ribs. She awaited Ren's answer with bated breath, her insides churning with every shift in their expression.

At last, Ren said, unflinching and determined, "Because she's special to me."

The goblin let out a snort, the same words that had sent warmth snaking down Pansy's limbs pulling nothing but derision from him. "Then let her be special to you somewhere else. We all know that halflings ruin everything they touch. Nothing in those heads of theirs besides *me, me, me*. No doubt this one didn't even think of how it'd make you look when she begged you to bring her here."

"I'm the one who offered," Ren corrected, their posture winding a touch more rigid.

Another snort. "Sure you did."

As Pansy moved to adjust her basket on her arm, the pie proving surprisingly heavy, an idea occurred to her. "What if I trade you a slice of pumpkin pie?" she ventured, peeling back the embroidered cloth covering the top of the basket. "I baked it fresh this afternoon."

"Are you trying to bribe me?" the goblin asked, eyebrows arching high beneath his shaggy hairline.

Pansy's eyes widened. Aghast, she shook her head with as much vigor as she could muster. "No! Of course not! I just thought . . . Ren said that when goblins want something, they trade for it, so I—"

"Thought you'd give me a slice of pie in exchange for letting you in," the goblin finished for her, the corner of his mouth twitching ever so slightly.

Well, amused is better than offended, Pansy thought, though it failed to keep her cheeks from burning.

Seeing an opportunity to cut in, Ren said, "It's very good pie. Pansy's an excellent chef."

"Hmm." The goblin cocked his head to the side, eyes trained on the pie sitting in Pansy's basket. "Well, it does look good. And I guess she can pass for a gnome if she covers up those ridiculous ears of hers . . ."

"Then it's settled," Ren declared, their tone unusually

clipped. "Pansy, give him a slice. We'll call it a token of 'new friendship'."

For a moment, the goblin seemed like he was going to offer further protest. But as Pansy passed a slice, neatly balanced on a paper napkin, into his outstretched hand, whatever additional arguments might have been building on his tongue promptly vanished. Granted, that didn't stop him from offering one last quip, formed around a rather large bite of pie: "If I get in trouble for this, I'm blaming you, Ren!"

"Don't talk with your mouth full," Ren snapped, already breezing past him with Pansy in tow.

Evidently, the goblin's comment about her ears had struck a nerve, though Pansy herself wasn't offended in the least. Her ears were perfectly attractive by halfling standards. Still, there was something about that whole exchange that left her feeling ... off, as if the world beneath her feet had been knocked slightly off its axis, and the sensation of tucking the rounded shell of her ear beneath several curls only made it register that much more sharply.

"Oh, blessed Nature," the goblin guard gasped, clutching at his chest with equal melodrama, "that girl's turning Ren into a halfling!"

Pansy snorted, the words *I didn't realize having table manners turned you into a halfling* itching to be let loose. And they might have, had the sight of the Goblin Market, stretching across the massive cavern that lay beyond the archway in an eclectic mix of cobbled-together stalls and patchwork tents, not swept the very breath from her lungs.

Even just the cavern itself was something to behold, flush with greenery across its many levels, the roots coiling along its walls not just roots but seemingly entire trees, with branches as lush and full as those that crowned the ones in the forest proper. Had Pansy not known for certain that they were still underground, she might have thought this just another glade, illuminated by gently swaying lanterns and thick beds of Wayfinder flowers.

"Wow," she breathed, her eyes wide with wonder, the goblin at the entrance all but forgotten. "This is amazing."

"Is it everything you imagined it to be?" Ren asked with a grin.

In truth, she wasn't sure what she had imagined. Maybe the stalls packed with mushrooms and moss, the herbalists stirring their cauldrons in order to add yet another tincture to the walls of glass bottles behind them. But certainly not the bulbous tents that seemed almost alive, rising and falling with each puff of sweet-smelling, not-quite-floral smoke that wheezed out from underneath their flaps, nor the merchants hawking strange, singing crystals in every color of the rainbow and then some.

Equally unexpected was the diversity of the market's attendees. Although there were plenty of goblins, as the name suggested, the bustling crowd was far from homogenous. A group of trolls, their shaggy pelts thick with scrub moss and other high-altitude growth, sat around a nearby campfire, slowly roasting some variety of beast until its skin crackled and gleamed. They paid no mind to the tall, spindly limbed woman circling them like a shadow, her form oscillating between youth and old age with every step.

Had she come for their dinner? Pansy wondered. Admittedly, the woman would not have been the only one, lured in by the rich aroma of fat rendered in a honey glaze. A cat-like creature, its coat black as night save for its white belly, had already settled onto its hindlegs beside the largest of the trolls, watching the spit turn with hungry eyes. However, it seemed the woman had a different prize in mind.

She darted in without warning, her pale skin a bone-white blur against the fire's flickering shadows. A quick snip of her shears, and she retreated once more; now, with a few sprigs of green clutched in her palm, each a perfect match for the trolls' new bald spots. Not that they seemed to care – or even notice, really.

A witch, then. Collecting ingredients for a spell, no doubt. And though Pansy had insisted the rowan branch Ren had offered her was unnecessary, she suddenly found herself acutely grateful for its presence, pressing her palm over its shape in her pocket. Who knew what else she might encounter this night?

Pansy let out a startled shout as a kite trailing the bleached-white remains of some sort of serpent swooped low overhead, narrowly missing the top of her head before cresting upwards to join its equally macabre brethren in a cackle of clattering bones. How they managed to stay airborne in a cavern seemingly devoid of even the faintest breeze Pansy didn't know. Goblin magic, she assumed.

"Are you okay?" Ren asked, her shrieks, for once, eliciting concern rather than amusement.

"Fine," Pansy said, resisting the urge to tuck her hair behind her ears as heat bloomed across her cheeks. She'd covered them for a reason; one rendered all the more salient now that half the market's eyes were on her – though, thankfully, only for a moment. Her "disguise" was evidently working. "I just didn't expect . . . that."

"Do children in your village not play with kites?"

"Kites? Yes. Skeleton kites? Absolutely not. Though . . ." Pansy cocked her head to the side, surveying the kites circling overhead anew. "I suppose the bones add an interesting dimension to the whole thing. It's almost like the skeletons themselves are moving." A beat. "Is it bad that my first thought was that you could pull off a great prank with one of these?"

Ren grinned, all feral, bright-eyed delight. "Councilor Millwood won't know what hit her."

She laughed. "It's like you read my mind. Anything else we can add to her night of terror?"

"Well . . ."

Kites, it turned out, weren't the only thing goblins had outfitted with a skeletal twist, ever-determined to find a use for anything and everything. Pansy should've known as much after passing more than a handful of shops selling nothing but bones, all cleaned and polished to perfection. Even so, the sight of several skeleton marionettes, dancing along to the cheery jig that spilled from a strange, box-like contraption, gave her quite the shock.

"Wait . . . How are they . . . ? No one's moving them!" Pansy gasped.

"Modified featherflight talismans, I assume. Am I right?" Ren asked, turning towards the especially slight goblin operating the box's crank.

"Yep!" chirped the goblin in-between ragged breaths. Evidently, keeping the contraption running took a significant amount of effort on her part. "Course, it's nothing compared to some of the artifices the gnomes put out, but, well, it gets the job done."

"I think it's amazing," Pansy blurted out. "The fact that you managed to get them all to move in sync with the music! Honestly, it makes me want to dance myself. Speaking of . . ." She turned to Ren expectantly.

They blinked at her. "Wait. You want to dance? Here? *With me?*"

She chuckled. "Who else? Unless some other charming goblin would like to step in . . ."

The goblin working the crank barely had enough time to blush before Ren snatched up Pansy's hands. "Fine," they said, pulling her nearly flush against them. "But I'm a terrible dancer."

"It's okay," Pansy assured them, her skin already warming beneath their touch. "I fully expect to get upstaged by the marionettes anyway."

And they did. Badly. Ren's movements were stiff, uncertain. They spent so much time thinking about what to do next that they completely divorced themself from the actual beat; not even the marionettes, with their loud, percussion-like clacks, could get them back on track. And still, Pansy had never had more fun in her life.

She grinned the whole time, giggling as the furrow between Ren's brow deepened with each mistimed step. Perhaps it would have been easier if she'd led; it would certainly have saved her feet from being trodden upon more than a few times. Yet Pansy liked the way Ren's hand fitted against the curve of her waist, the way they drew her towards them with every movement, as if that alone was all that mattered.

Granted, she couldn't deny that some dancing lessons were in order. No way the two of them would be able to keep up with the rest of Haverow at the Flower Dance come spring, at this rate.

Except, there wasn't going to be a Flower Dance. Not for them.

How quickly reality rushed to reassert itself, sweeping through her with a baleful chill that not even the warmth of Ren's hands could thaw. She faltered, stumbling for the first time, her stomach plummeting into the space between her feet.

Ren, taking this as a criticism of their dancing abilities, pulled back with a huff. "I warned you," they grumbled.

"No, it's not that," Pansy said, almost breathless in her haste. "I was just thinking about the future. About Haverow."

"Ah."

She winced. "Sorry. I didn't mean to bring down the mood. Come on. Let's keep exploring. What about that storyteller you told me about? Do you know where they might be?"

Ren shook their head. "We'll just have to take a look around and see if we can spot them."

Given the sheer breadth of the market, Pansy assumed this would be something easier said than done. However, not even ten minutes later, Ren led her to a small makeshift stage – what was really a very large, worn-down stump – upon which an elaborately dressed goblin stood, hunched over a gnarled walking stick.

"How did you know where to go?" Pansy asked, careful to keep her voice low, so as to not interrupt the storyteller's performance.

Ren gestured to the veritable sea of goblin children currently clustered around the stump-turned-stage, their eyes wide in rapt attention. "It's easy," they replied. "Just follow the children. They always seem to know where there's fun to be had."

"And let me guess, there's nothing more fun than listening to stories about a certain goblin trickster named Aconite?"

"You know it," they said, their lips parting around a grin. "Now, shh. She's getting to the best part."

Smothering a laugh behind one hand, Pansy did as instructed, turning her attention to the storyteller, whose voice swelled in anticipation of the coming climax. Although the two of them had arrived well into the story's course, following it proved surprisingly easy. Not because the plot was especially simple or anything like that, but, rather, Pansy already *knew* this story. Knew it in the same way Ren had known the Wolf Banefoot halfling story she'd read to them that one afternoon.

It was strange, hearing a tale that was so familiar yet also not, with goblins in the place of halflings and a dwarven dam threatening to flood a series of caves instead of a valley dotted with halfling villages. Every time Pansy tried to lose herself in the storyteller's performance, to allow herself to be awed by the flashpowders and the scented smokes, the way they brought to life what had otherwise only existed in her imagination, another thread of recognition served to pull her right out.

"I recognize this story," Pansy said once the storyteller had taken her leave in a cacophony of clinking beads. "There's a Wolf Banefoot one just like it. He sabotages the construction of a dwarven dam to save a bunch of halfling villages that would otherwise have been flooded."

She half-expected Ren to make another wry comment about halflings helping themselves to every good goblin idea, but they were surprisingly quiet, their brow furrowing, as if lost in thought. At last, they said, uttering words she never could have predicted, "What if both stories are true? As much as goblins and halflings proclaim to hate one another, we do often end up living rather close to each other. So, it's entirely believable that a dam like the one in this particular story could flood two sets of homes at once, one underground and one ... slightly less underground, I suppose."

"That's a fair point," Pansy said, now thinking too. "And you're right: at the end of the day, what really is the difference between a burrow and a cave?"

"Humidity," Ren answered with a smile. "No way we could

grow our moss and mushrooms half as well in a burrow like your parents'."

"Some of us do have cheese cellars, you know," she pointed out, not unkindly. "Not only are they much cooler, they're also rather damp."

"Great," Ren drawled. "So, we goblins can go live in a halfling cheese cellar. Wonderful. I'm certain my clan will be positively jumping for joy at the suggestion."

"All right, all right," Pansy said with a laugh. "I'm just saying that all these differences we've made such a big deal about over the years, maybe they're not actually that significant? Take Wolf Banefoot and Aconite, for example; if they were able to be this ragtag goblin and halfling duo, why can't the rest of us find common ground too?"

Ren was quiet for a moment, then they said, "I'm actually suggesting something far more radical – at least, when it comes to Aconite and Wolf Banefoot. I've been thinking about it since you read that first story to me. What if . . .? What if they're the same person?"

Pansy's eyes widened. "You mean he's both halfling *and* goblin? Is that even possible?"

"Children of mixed heritage have been born within the clans. Though, as far I know, none of them have had a halfling parent."

"I suppose that makes sense," Pansy admitted after a beat, her face coloring as an image of a child bearing a mixture of her and Ren's features sprang to mind. "But why conclude that Wolf Banefoot and Aconite are the same person, instead of two close friends working together?"

"The halfling and goblin versions of these stories aren't just similar – they're practically identical, especially when it comes to the hero himself. If this was actually a case of two different people working together, I feel like there'd be more differences. Subtle ones, to show a change in perspective. Because no two people are going to think alike, no matter how aligned their goals might be. Also," they added, their lips parting around a long, slow smile, "the names are too on-the-nose for any other possibility. Aconite? Wolfsbane? It's all the same plant."

Pansy's eyes widened. "Really? Oh, gosh. You're absolutely right! I can't believe I didn't notice that."

They shrugged. "In your defense, you're not the one who enjoys gardening."

"Hey! It's growing on me. That being said, there's one thing I'm still getting snagged on." She tapped a finger against her chin. "What about the stories where Wolf Banefoot fights against other goblins? Because if he is a goblin – or part-goblin, rather – why would he fight against his own people?"

"To free them," Ren replied, seemingly surprised that this conclusion hadn't occurred to Pansy. "No goblin should have to serve under a dark master."

"Oh." Pansy ducked her head, her face heating in an all too familiar way. "The Wolf Banefoot stories never talk about that, so I didn't realize – sorry." She chewed on her lip.

"It's okay," Ren said with a shrug too stiff to convey the nonchalance they were doubtless going for. "But I do wish the assumption that goblins want to fight on the side of Evil wasn't so ingrained; this idea that it's 'natural' for us, so we shouldn't be upset or disappointed when a loved one does end up falling into a dark lord's service. If it was, I wouldn't be working so hard to keep members of my clan from making that sacrifice."

Pansy's breath caught in her throat, her eyes going wide. If things were truly so dire ... Something hardened inside her chest, the fires of her determination solidified. "I'll go back to Haverow, talk to my parents. Blossom, too. Maybe we can get more seeds or convince some of the younger residents to open up their own pantries. No halfling likes seeing anyone go hungry – not even goblins."

Ren sighed, their shoulders already slumping in defeat. "As nice as that sounds, Pansy, I don't really know how much good it'll do. They didn't want to listen to you earlier at the festival. What makes you think this time will be any different?"

"Because this time I'll *make* them listen," she replied, hands balling into fists at her sides. Whatever future she and Ren had, it couldn't be cobbled together from hopes and dreams alone. This time, she wouldn't run, not even to spare her own feelings. Plus, if Ren was right – if Wolf Banefoot and Aconite were the same person – then that was proof enough that what she wanted with Ren was possible, and that alone was worth fighting for.

Ren watched her for a moment, seemingly searching for cracks in the armor she'd forged from her own resolve, then said, "Thank you. I'm sorry if I sounded ungrateful. I've spent so long trying to shoulder every burden on my own that I've forgotten how to accept help from others. Even now, it feels like a failure on my part, relying on someone else."

"It's not a failure," Pansy assured them. "That's why we have friends, family"– *partners*, her brain unhelpfully supplied – "to share the load. No one will think less of you for it. I certainly don't."

Ren let out another breath, their shoulders dropping another fraction – this time from relief rather than hopelessness. "You're right. My clan's been saying the same thing for years. Maybe it's about time I started listening."

I think we're past the point of "maybes", Pansy was about to say, when a heavy stone plunked down into the ground beside her, sending a flurry of damp earth spraying halfway up her skirt. Letting out a yelp, she jumped right into Ren's waiting arms, their foresight nothing short of blessed. Without them, she would surely have a whole lot more mud on her person.

"Sorry!" called out a voice from somewhere higher up. Turning, Pansy found the largest goblin she'd ever seen peeking over the edge of a nearby slope with an embarrassed grimace twisting across his lips.

A goblin, it turned out, Ren recognized. "Please, no," they groaned, casting a pleading look up at the ceiling.

Unfortunately for them, their prayer went unanswered. As if summoned, the goblin's gaze swiveled to focus on Ren instead. "Ren!" bellowed the goblin, his expression parting around such unadulterated glee, Pansy might have found it sweet had he not just single-handedly ruined her skirt. "I'll be down in a second!"

"We need to run," Ren whispered in Pansy's ear, their arms still keeping her upright. "Quickly. Before he catches up."

"Why? Who is he?" she asked, unable to tear her eyes away from the goblin's mad dash towards them, punctuated by several shouts of surprise, a half-collapsed tent, and the distinct sound of glassware breaking.

Grim-faced and full of distress, Ren only said, "My cousin, Thorn."

"The weird one?" Pansy managed to ask before every last mote of air was forced from her lungs, the world devolving into a strange, indecipherable blur as she found herself swept up alongside Ren into a great, near-bone-crushing hug. Not even the most impassioned of halfling grandmothers could hold a candle to the sheer power of this display.

"We can't ... breathe," Ren managed to choke out after a

handful of seconds without reprieve, prompting their assailant to relax his grip at last.

"Oh, sorry," said Thorn, setting the two of them back down. "I got a little over-excited there." Then, turning to Pansy, who was in the process of smoothing out the front of her mud-spattered skirt, now freshly rumpled at that, he added, "I'm Thorn, by the way."

"Pansy," she said, flashing him a small, slightly nervous smile as she folded her hands primly across her front. Her skirt, unfortunately, proved a lost cause.

"I know." Thorn grinned. "Ren's told me all about you."

Pansy's eyes widened. "They have?" she asked, darting a look at Ren, who studiously managed to avoid her gaze.

"Mm-hmm. Sorry about the wayward stone, by the way. I promise I wasn't aiming for you – or anyone else. I entered tonight's moss-put competition, and, well, obviously I ended up with a slippery one." He grinned sheepishly.

Pansy blinked. "Moss . . . put?"

"It's a goblin sport," Ren explained, though not before they shot their cousin one last dirty look. "The goal is to throw a moss-covered rock as far as possible. Sometimes, the moss is sticky; sometimes, it's slippery; sometimes, it's dry and springy. Depends on the variety. You never know what you're going to get until the rock is in your hand."

Pansy looked at the slope and then back down at the rock, still embedded in the earth. "Is this far?" she asked, gesturing towards it.

"I believe Thorn was supposed to throw it in the *opposite* direction."

"You caught me there," he said with a chuckle, lifting a hand to scratch at the back of his head. "Hey, uh . . ." He darted a worried look behind him, where the swell of discontent left in his wake was growing louder by the second. "Why don't we go up to my stall and talk there? I need to be getting back anyway. Bad for business to be closed for too long."

"Stall?" Pansy perked up at this new information. "What do you sell?"

Toads. The answer was toads – or, rather, their secretions? Pansy wasn't entirely sure, only because Thorn kept calling it "Juice", which was about as illuminating as the moon this deep underground, and every time she opened her mouth to pursue some sort of clarification Ren cut her off with a withering, sidelong look. Whatever Thorn was peddling, they didn't approve of it in the least.

"Why? Is it dangerous or something?" Pansy asked, ignoring the way Ren's eyes widened, as if the question, perfectly harmless in all respects, had been formulated as a personal affront.

Thorn laughed. "Dangerous? Maybe if you drink too much. But even then, it'll just knock you flat on your arse for a few hours while the ceiling spins and swirls. Which, I suppose, could be rather terrifying if you're a first-timer," he added after a beat, looking thoughtful.

"Exactly," Ren said emphatically, eyes flashing. "As such, neither of us will be purchasing anything today."

"What about a free sample?" Thorn asked with a grin. "You can use it to make more of that plant paste of yours."

Pansy perked up at that. "Plant paste?"

Ren let out a snort. "You don't even like gardening," they pointed out, arms crossing over their chest.

Now it was Pansy's turn to look affronted. Crossing her arms as well, she canted up her chin for an extra dose of defiance and said, perhaps a touch too whiny to have the impact she'd hoped for, "I told you it was growing on me!"

They rolled their eyes, clearly gearing up for some sort of smarmy retort. However, the deep rumble of Thorn's laughter swept it from their lips before they could properly loose it.

"You both argue like an old married couple," Thorn said, his grin, which already seemed to occupy the majority of his sturdy face, somehow stretching larger. Two fangs, unsurprisingly larger than his cousin's own – even with the rightmost one sporting a rather pronounced chip – peeked out over his lower lip in what proved to be a universal goblin trait.

"Don't be ridiculous," Ren scoffed, but the flush that had stretched across the bridge of their nose told the true story. "And just in case you're trying to distract me," they added, fixing Thorn with a particularly potent glare, "I'm going to remind you *again* that we don't need any of your 'Juice'. The garden is doing quite well, thank you."

"But, *Ren*," Thorn all but whined, lips budding into an exaggerated pout, "who comes all the way out to the market without buying anything? You even made poor Pansy haul along stuff to trade, judging from that basket of hers, which, by the way," he added with a flash of teeth that was all charm, "smells *amazing*."

"I thought you said your 'Juice' was free," Ren said, flatly, brows arching.

"Well, I—"

"Would you like some pumpkin pie, Thorn?" Pansy asked, pre-empting whatever silly argument was building between Ren and their cousin. She once again pulled aside the cloth covering her basket, revealing the pie nestled within, now one slice short. "I baked it this afternoon."

Ren shot her a sharp look. "I *said* we're not purchasing anything."

Pansy waved them off. "I'm not offering it as a trade. Just a gift."

Thorn gave a slightly bashful-sounding cough. "I wouldn't want to turn down such a generous offer. That'd be downright rude. But, say, Pansy, do you happen to know any other pretty halfling ladies who might be looking for a *strapping, young goblin*?" He gave a pronounced flex of his biceps as he said this, drawing a low groan from Ren, who clearly had been anticipating a moment like this – and dreading it.

Pansy giggled and passed him a slice of pie. "I only have one friend right now who isn't already married. Her name is Blossom, and she runs the local flower—" Her eyes snapped open wide. "The Cold Flower! I almost forgot!"

"Is that what you came here for?" Thorn asked, his words half-muffled by the pie openly rolling around in his mouth. "The herbalist set up near Nana had some in stock last I checked, but you might want to hurry. Cold Flower always sells out fast."

Ren's head jerked up at the mention of Nana – their clan's leader, from what Pansy remembered. "Your Nana's here?" she asked.

"Of course. You know she loves making Union Crowns, and it's not like anyone within the clan is going to need one. Not yet, at least," Thorn amended after a beat, his gaze resting meaningfully on Ren in a way Pansy didn't quite understand.

She wanted to ask what a "Union Crown" was, but Ren had already slipped their hand into hers once more. "Let's go," they said. "Nana's pretty much always set up in the same spot."

They found her atop one of the cavern's slopes, manning a stall that wasn't so much a stall as a simple, worn-down table, its pitted surface almost completely obscured by a mountain of blooms, all woven into multicolored crowns. Nana stood behind her wares, leaning heavily against a gnarled branch repurposed as a walking stick. Her deeply lined face, drooping slightly with age, brightened as Ren pulled into view. Unfortunately, the moment her gaze shifted, landing on the rounded shell of Pansy's ear, newly revealed by the jostling crowd they'd had to squeeze through, her smile fell. And so did Pansy's stomach.

Oh no, she thought, dread clawing its way up her throat as Ren continued to drag her towards the elderly goblin. *She already hates me.*

"Hi, Nana," Ren said, a touch of hesitation edging into their voice. No doubt they had noticed the change in their leader's expression just as keenly. They gestured towards Pansy, their lips stretching into a wide smile, marred, much like their words, by ever-encroaching stiffness. "This is Pansy, the halfling who's been living with me at the cottage – and helping me in the garden."

Nana's features seemed to soften at that, a current of curiosity unwinding the tight guard of less-than-flattering expectations. "Has she now?"

"Yes," Pansy said with a nod, forcing a smile. "After Ren told me how important the garden is to your clan, I had to help. To be fair, I'm not exactly much of a gardener. The kitchen is more my area of expertise."

"Pansy's been a great help," Ren insisted, with more force than she had anticipated. Then, shifting gears, they nodded to an adjoining stall: a tent, really, fashioned in the shape of an enormous red mushroom. "That's the herbalist Thorn was talking about. Wait here. It's probably easier if I do the trading."

A single glance at the herbalist in question, plainly visible through the tent's flap, told Pansy precisely why. Even with several stalls' worth of space between them, the goblin herbalist watched her with the intensity of a halfling shopkeeper beset by a gaggle of rowdy schoolchildren. His eyes narrowed, betraying every ounce of his distrust, his hatred, virulent and cold.

It was like being doused in several buckets full of ice water. Pansy jerked her gaze away, fingers tightening around the woven handle of her basket, its scratchy fibers scraping against the soft flesh of her palm. She said nothing, simply nodding as she strained against the dark pull in her chest. Wordlessly, she held out the basket. She refused to take advantage of Ren's generosity more than she already had.

"Ah. I think a herbalist will be more interested in trading for a growth potion," they said, gently nudging the basket back towards her. Every word had been spoken with the utmost kindness, and, somehow, that made the moment all the more painful.

Pansy's ribs squeezed in on themselves, sharp points digging into the most tender parts of her. She swallowed and nodded, blinking rapidly against the wet sting blooming across her eyes. *It's just one goblin*, she told herself, each word ringing more hollow than the last. *He's probably not even part of Ren's clan, anyway. So, who cares what he thinks?*

She shouldn't have taken the herbalist's behavior to heart. None of it had anything to do with her as a person. But, maybe, the fact that her own village had so thoroughly rejected her not even twenty-four hours prior had left her feeling especially vulnerable. Because even though Ren had certainly weathered worse on her behalf, at least they still had their clan on their side.

"You can't make everyone like you," Nana said after a beat, a near-perfect echo of words she'd heard long ago. "You're just setting yourself up for disappointment if you try."

Pansy huffed out a breathy whisper of a laugh, one that ended up coming out slightly wet, despite her best efforts. "I know. My own grandmother told me the same thing once."

"She must've been a smart woman then."

"That she was." A wave of wistfulness swept through Pansy as the words left her lips, a softer, lighter complement to the darkness still clotting in the narrow recesses of her ribcage. "I miss her a lot. But it's only because she's gone now that I got the chance to meet Ren, so the feeling . . . it's strange."

Nana watched her for a moment, oddly silent, her features arranged into that same inscrutable mask that Ren sometimes wore. Perhaps it was a clan thing, or maybe simply a goblin one. Ren's ears *did* tend to be the most expressive part of them.

At last, Nana said, "You like Ren a lot, don't you?"

"I do," Pansy confirmed with a nod. "They're . . . they're special to me. More special than they probably know, in fact." As she spoke, her hand drifted up to the skull, ever-present at her throat. No sooner had her fingers curled around it than she found herself smiling, warmth buoying her up from the inside.

Because Ren *liked* her. The necklace was proof of that. Yes, perhaps liking alone wasn't enough, their circumstances being what they were. But Ren had trusted her enough to bring her here, and Pansy – Pansy wanted to show them that that *meant* something to her, something that words alone couldn't express. A halfling might have cooked something or taken care of the washing or done some other practical chore that conveyed care and closeness, but a goblin, Pansy had come to realize, often gave gifts, small tokens that seemed to say, *I saw this and thought of you.*

"I'd like to trade for one of these crowns," Pansy said abruptly. "Do you like pumpkin pie? I baked it fresh this afternoon!"

Nana blinked at her. "What could you possibly want with one of these?"

"I want to give one to Ren. To show them just how important they are to me."

The old goblin let out a soft chuckle at that, her wrinkles growing more pronounced as her lips stretched into a small but genuine smile. "I don't think they'll have much doubt about that if you do."

"Perfect! So, does a slice of pie work? Honestly, I can give you the whole thing if you feel that'd be more fair. Granted, a couple of slices are already missing."

"Oh, no, no," Nana said, waving off her offer with one hand. "I don't sell these crowns. The happiness they bring is more than enough payment for me."

"Are you sure?" Pansy pressed. "I mean, I feel similarly when I see someone enjoy my cooking."

"Take it, Nana," Thorn said, suddenly appearing at Pansy's side. This time, his entrance was heralded by neither frenzied shouting nor shattered objects, rendering it all the more unexpected. "If you don't eat it, I will."

"Thorn!" Pansy jumped, the shock kicking hard against her ribcage. "I thought you had a stand to tend to."

Thorn shrugged. "I sensed something interesting was happening, and apparently I was right." He grinned, his gaze pointedly dropping to the crown Nana had retrieved from her pile.

"I think Ren will like this one," she said, passing one made of rust-colored hydrangeas, yellow begonia and oak leaves into Pansy's hands. "And don't worry about me. I'm too old for sweets these days. You can go ahead and give the pie to Thorn. I've no doubt he'll enjoy it enough for both of us."

"Don't mind if I do!" Thorn declared, already moving to liberate the remaining slices from Pansy's basket.

Months ago, this might have offended Pansy, registering as nothing more than another example of "rude" goblins understanding nothing of manners. Now, she found Thorn's enthusiasm – and the gusto with which he wolfed down each slice – somewhat endearing.

And maybe, on some level, so did Ren, now returned, given the way their mouth twitched before they said, "You're going to turn *into* a pumpkin pie at this rate."

Thorn retorted with something that might've been "No, I won't", but had otherwise been rendered unintelligible due to an imbalance in the ratio of pie to mouth-space.

Turning to Pansy, Ren held up a surprisingly scant bundle of what she assumed was Cold Flower. "The herbalist was a jerk. Demanded two vials of growth potion in exchange for this pittance, but I managed to get his remaining stock in the end." They grinned, the flash of triumph across their face hitting Pansy like a bolt to the chest.

All the more certain that this was something she wanted to do, she thrust the crown out towards Ren. "Here," she said, barely able to stay still as every inch of her buzzed with anticipation. "This is for you."

Ren blinked at the flower crown now occupying the space between them, seemingly stunned by the fact that Pansy had offered them a gift. "Are you sure?" they asked after a long beat, looking over at her with eyes full of uncertainty, but also hope.

"Of course I'm sure, silly," Pansy said with a soft laugh. "Why wouldn't I be? You're special to me too, Ren, and I want you to know it."

Ren was kissing her before she even knew it, lips crashing against hers with such desperate want that it almost hurt. She let out a gasp, largely muffled by the all-consuming heat of Ren's mouth. The ground lurched beneath her, sending her scrabbling for purchase against Ren's back, fingers twisting in the loose fabric of their tunic. They were tipping her back, she realized, arms sweeping around her waist with surprising strength. Someone, somewhere, let out a hooting cheer; Thorn, probably, Pansy guessed, the thought hardly more than a distant bubble as she sank into the depths of Ren, their warmth, their smell, the way they seemed to fit against her perfectly. In that moment, there was nothing beyond them.

When Ren finally pulled away, a handful of heartbeats or an eon later, Pansy nearly whined at the loss, her grip on their shoulders turning all the more desperate, insistent. But they weren't alone, even less so now than before. And Pansy quickly shoved aside the heat building in the very depths of her belly in favor of *some* semblance of decorum. That wasn't to say it was easy – especially once she caught sight of Ren, breathing heavily beside her, their lips dark and wet and gleaming.

Gods, they looked positively *wrecked*.

Thankfully, Thorn was there to douse the fire that flared back to life inside her, clapping two large hands on either of their shoulders as he said, "So, are we thinking about a summer wedding, then?"

"Wedding?" Pansy repeated breathlessly, the word dragging her right back to the cold, hard earth without mercy.

"Oh, yeah!" Thorn grinned. "I've always wanted to go to a halfling wedding. I hear they're *wild*!"

He might have said something more – about goblin weddings or summer weddings or some other sort of wedding – but Pansy was no longer listening. Her head swam, lost in the panicked thrum of her own pulse. Had she just accidentally proposed? It was just supposed to be a gift!

It's called a "Union Crown", dummy. Of course it's a proposal, sneered a voice from the back of her mind, a reminder that instantly left her feeling foolish. Because Thorn *had* called it that. How could she have missed it?

But is it really so bad that you did? asked another voice, kinder and gentler than the one that had preceded it.

No, Pansy supposed not. But her error had already made itself known, and Ren was looking at her with something like betrayal – or, hopefully, just disappointment – skittering across their features.

"We need to talk," they said, grabbing her by the hand and yanking her away from the growing crowd, now swelling with a different sort of hooting, led, unsurprisingly, by Thorn.

There might have been some words shouted, too; something along the lines of "We'll see you in the morning! The whole clan can't wait to celebrate!" But Pansy, for better or worse, was no longer listening.

"Talk" turned out to be a rather generous way of putting it, given the two of them ended up sitting largely in silence once they reached their destination, another cavern, significantly smaller than the first, located several offshoots away.

They were closer to the surface now, as evidenced by the night sky, glimpsed beyond a massive tear in the cavern's ceiling. Water dribbled through it, sliding down thick sheets of moss and cascading vines before dropping, at last, into a large, impossibly blue pond, its waters turned reflective in the light of the full moon.

"So . . ." Ren said at last, their gaze fixed on the nearby waterline lapping gently at moss-covered banks. The word hung between them, as impossible to ignore as a barrel loaded to the brim with spellpowder. "You didn't know what that garland meant, did you?"

"No," Pansy admitted, after a beat spent worrying her lower lip.

Ren blew out a bitter-sounding huff. "Right." Reaching up, they grabbed the crown, still perched atop their head, the oranges and reds of its flowers contrasting beautifully with their dark hair.

"Wait," Pansy said, before they could start to remove it.

Their eyes snapped to her, confusion and hope – that same damnable hope! – streaking across their brow. If the hesitation steadily clotting in Pansy's throat had planned to seize her, it had already missed its chance. No way could she back down now.

Swallowing, she curled her fingers into the fabric of her skirt, uncaring of the new creases she dragged across its surface. It was already wrinkled beyond belief anyway; not to mention covered in mud. "Do you . . .? Are you sure you actually want to marry me?" she asked. "I mean, Thorn's right. Halfling weddings can get pretty crazy." She huffed out a small laugh, only to cringe at how flat it sounded, even to her own ears.

"Pansy," Ren said, their tone nothing short of serious, and when she turned, she found them watching her with an intensity not even the sun itself could hope to match. "No one else has made me feel the way you do. My day is better simply because you're in it. And when I think about the future, I can't imagine sharing the rest of my life with any other person. So, yes, I'm absolutely certain I want to marry you."

"Ren, I—" Pansy choked, the font of emotion welling up inside her less of a steady stream and more like an erupting geyser. Dozens of words rose to her lips, each more inadequate than the last. Honestly, how could she hope to encapsulate all *this* – the rush of warmth, buzzing just beneath her skin; the way her chest felt like it was primed to burst – in a handful of syllables? It was impossible!

And still, she had to try.

"I want …" she started to say, in halting, half-strangled speech. "I want to wake up beside you every day, with no more blanket walls to separate us. I want to help you in the garden, even if I'm bad at it and, yeah, kind of don't like it, because what I like most is being with you. I want to see you smile every time I cook your favorite foods, and I want you to tell me when you don't like something, so I don't make it for you again. I want—" It was then that the sob welling up in her throat finally got loose, tearing through her so fiercely her entire being shook from it.

Ren's eyes widened. "What? Why are you crying?" They reached for her, panic sweeping through their voice like an arc of lightning tearing across the sky.

"I'm …" Pansy sniffled, her lips parting around a sodden laugh that to Ren's ears, no doubt, sounded like a sob. "I'm just so happy! I was worried you wouldn't want to be with me. Because – because of what happened at the festival."

For a moment, they could only gape at her. "The – the festival? I couldn't care less about what happened at the damn festival."

"But Agvaldir—"

"Well, I'm not talking about marrying him, am I? I love *you*,

Pansy. And, from the sound of it, it seems like you feel similarly about me."

"I-I do," she said, rushing the words out so quickly she nearly tripped over them. "I love you too, Ren."

"Then smile!" said Ren, sounding as exasperated as they were perplexed. "Don't cry! What in the world is wrong with you? Who cries when they're happy?"

Pansy laughed again, louder this time. "Well, I do, and you better get used to it," she said, swiping at the dampness clinging to her cheeks. "Because I'm *definitely* going to cry at our wedding."

Huffing out a breath, Ren shook their head. "Honestly ... What am I going to do with you?"

"Kiss me until I can't think straight?" Pansy suggested, a hopeful lilt rising to the corner of her mouth.

Ren snorted. "You're incorrigible," they muttered, but they were already shifting towards her, one leg sweeping over her hips. "At least this time I don't have to worry about you causing a scene in public."

"Me?" Pansy asked, aghast, even as she let Ren ease her down onto the soft bed of moss beneath her. "You were just as much a part of that as I was!"

"Because you drive me crazy," Ren breathed, each word misting hot against her lips. "I look at you, and suddenly it's like the rest of the world doesn't exist."

Pansy fully expected them to kiss her then. By that point, they practically had her *aching* for it. But, instead, they dipped their head towards her neck, peppering the skin there with quick, butterfly-soft kisses.

"*Ah!* Ren," she whined, arching up into them, "don't tease. I'm getting moss stains all over my clothes for this."

"Shall I play the part of the hero, then?" Ren intoned, their voice turning husky, seemingly dropping a whole octave as their fingers skimmed up her side, each point of contact another charged spark between them. "And divest you of your clothes?"

"Yes," Pansy said, her voice hitching as Ren's fingers, needing no further encouragement, slipped beneath the hem of her skirt to trace the white-hot outline of her thigh. "I think I'd like that very much."

16
Ren

So begins the longest absence
On a bed of nascent roots.
Where death and life intertwine,
These seeds shall turn to shoots.

"THE RETURN TO EARTH",
A GOBLIN POEM TRADITIONALLY
RECITED AT FUNERALS

The door to the cottage was open when they returned the following morning – early, because the ground was apparently too hard for overly sensitive halfling spines, even with a blanket of plush moss and a makeshift pillow in the form of Ren's arm. Except, the door wasn't open, Ren realized with a frigid, heart-seizing jolt, the kind that locked every joint into place. No, it had been knocked clear off its hinges.

Pansy saw it too, less than a second later, lying flat across the entryway, a once unremarkable slab of wood now cracked and splintered, all fanning out from a single, central point. Her breath catching in her throat, she stuttered to a sudden stop beside Ren, fingers tightening reflexively around their biceps.

"What happened?" she asked, voice breathless and thin. "The door . . . *The garden!* It's all ruined!"

Multiple ten-days of hard work destroyed overnight. What had once been a flourishing garden, thick with Running Beans, slakegourd and more, had become a grave of disturbed earth and broken roots. Salvageable, perhaps – assuming the culprit hadn't salted the ground out of spite – but not for the current season.

As Ren's gaze swept over the damage, familiar in the worst possible way, the smell of ash and ruin tickled at their nostrils, dredged up from a memory they wished they could forget, of the day they'd lost the clan of their birth. One deep breath, then another, and all they could smell was the fading sweetness of the flower crown still perched atop their head. At last, they said, in a tremulous croak, "Dwarves."

Pansy's brow furrowed, the confusion that streaked across it an unknown privilege. "Why would dwarves break into our home?"

Ren's voice was flat and toneless. "Because I live here."

Before Pansy could open her mouth to unleash the torrent of questions no doubt churning behind her teeth, a familiar face popped out from behind the doorway.

"Pansy!" Blossom exclaimed, relief and worry tugging at her

features in equal measure. She rushed over to them, careful not to trip over the fallen door on her way out. "Thank goodness you're all right – that you're both all right," she amended after a beat, her gaze flicking briefly over to Ren.

"What's going on?" Pansy asked, her grip on Ren's arm tightening as she pressed herself more firmly into their side. "Ren said it might be dwarves?"

"It's Agvaldir," Blossom replied, pulling a horrified sound from deep in Pansy's throat. "He came to town with a small party of men, humans and a dwarf. Said he was going to 'free you' from Ren's 'goblin magic' or something." She spat the words, upper lip curling in disgust. "We tried to stop him, but he wouldn't listen."

"We?" Ren asked.

"I and some of the other townsfolk. They're all downstairs, including your parents."

Pansy blinked. "My parents are here?" She sounded incredulous, as if her friend had instead suggested that Wolf Banefoot himself was waiting for her.

Blossom nodded. "Unfortunately, none of us are sure what to do. We're not fighters. Not to mention, Agvaldir is a wizard, and the men he has with him . . ." She trailed off, the words left unsaid, yet echoing just the same: *They're all bigger than us.*

Well, it wouldn't be the first time a goblin had stood up to someone more than twice their size, Ren thought, their fingers finding the hilt of their dagger, still sheathed at their side. The steel felt strangely warm against their skin, reassuring. It was there if they should need it, though Ren sincerely hoped they wouldn't.

"I'm going downstairs," they declared, slipping their arm out of Pansy's grasp. No need to drag her into danger too.

Of course, she was quick to rush headlong into it herself. "I'm going with you," she declared in a tremulous voice, her chin canting up at an all-too-familiar defiant angle. *Don't try to stop me*, it said. *You'll just waste your breath.*

So Ren didn't bother, knowing their efforts would be for naught.

Somehow, the inside of the cottage was worse than the outside. Floorboards had been ripped up, revealing the subfloor and joists underneath, while the rugs that had once covered them, both moss and knit alike, lay in tatters in nearly every corner. Furniture sat upended and, in some cases, broken in two. Pillows and blankets had been ripped apart, blanketing everything in a hail of torn fibers and stuffing. Hours of knitwork on Pansy's part, gone; just like the moss inlays Ren had worked so hard to save. This time there was no salvaging any of it.

Ruin had come for the cottage, stretching across every square inch. It had gathered up everything the two of them had come to treasure and crushed it without a second thought. Now, instead of joy and comfort, Ren saw only wretchedness. And amid that dark, churning sea, one particular loss stood out: the small house Pansy and Ren had constructed for the mice. Someone had thrown it against one of the bookshelves, dashing it to pieces along with anything vaguely fragile in its path, including all of Pansy's glass baubles.

The mice, at least, seemed to have escaped unharmed, from what Ren could see. A small mercy, desperately needed at the heart of all this grief. For once, the cottage was unbearably still, free of the usual buzz of insects and the soft scuffle of small mammals underfoot. There was only the distant groan of something deeper down, as if the cottage itself was crying out for help.

Hopefully that meant Mushroom and Pig had gotten out

safely too, the pillows they'd napped on during the laziest hours of the afternoon tossed aside like trash.

"Mushroom! Pig!" Pansy called out, frantic. "Where are you?"

"Somewhere far away, I hope," Ren said, their stomach plummeting when neither one made a miraculous appearance.

Pansy let out a choked sound, hands flying to her mouth. "How could someone do this?" she asked, her eyes shining wetly in the muted morning light, dampened both by cloud cover and the pall of loss that had drawn over their home.

"Because they hate us," Ren said simply, the words cresting over their tongue like hot bile. "To them, goblins are nothing but pests, taking up space they believe should be theirs. Everything we do is wrong; our existence, in of itself, is already a problem. They don't understand us, and they never will. You wouldn't try to understand a fly or a mosquito, would you?"

"But you're not a fly or a mosquito!" Pansy protested, her voice cracking. "You're a *person*, Ren."

"And that's precisely what sets you apart from them."

Heat, protective and fierce, bloomed inside Ren's chest as they headed for the stairs, ignoring the crunch of ruined plants beneath their heels. They didn't even need to think, their pupils flaring wide against the approaching gloom.

Unfortunately, this part of the cottage hadn't been spared either. Whole chunks had been carved from the walls and floor only to be dumped elsewhere in a spray of dirt, rock and frayed moss. Although the anxious knot rising in their gorge screamed at them to make a left at the upcoming junction, desperate to ascertain the status of their potion room, Ren ignored it. Instead, they turned right, following the low groan of shifting ground, echoing ever louder.

At last, they reached the source: the hallway that went

nowhere, the archway at its end as impassable as ever, filled with solid stone. Dozens of halflings, enough to leave the reasonably wide space feeling cramped, turned to stare at them, their eyes, bright with fear, shining in the gleam of far too many lamps.

Ren flinched, the sudden transition from dark to light stinging their over-wide pupils. As they raised one hand to shield their aching eyes, vision bleached white and useless, Pansy took the opportunity to push past them, taking to the new light source like a moth to a flame.

No. Don't, Ren started to say, lips parting around the first of only two syllables, but Pansy was already speaking.

"Agvaldir!" she shouted into the cavernous hall, loud enough that Ren could feel the reverberation against their skin. "What do you think you're doing?"

"Exactly what you asked me to do, Miss Underburrow," Agvaldir said, so devastatingly smug that even with their eyes pinched shut Ren knew that he was smirking.

"I didn't ask you to do any of this!" Pansy snapped, her voice a bright spot of heat at Ren's front. "And why would I? You broke into my house, destroyed my things—"

"Ah." Agvaldir clicked his tongue. "To think you would forget our conversation about those runes of yours so swiftly. Perhaps I should be hurt. I'm only here for your sake, you know."

It was then that Ren finally managed to crack open an eye, the lanterns still bright but not painfully so. "What's he talking about, Pansy?" they asked, seeing the way she'd gone stiff, her jaw flaring stark white beneath an angry, mottled flush. *Just like at the Harvest Festival . . .*

She ignored them. "I didn't ask for this," she repeated, now with the slightest tremor.

Agvaldir smiled, placid as ever, his face devoid of even a shred of kindness. His entourage was no better. Four men stood at his back, dressed in hard leather and steel. Three were human; the last was a dwarf, and though he stood a full two heads shorter than his compatriots, he easily outmatched them all in sheer breadth. His muscles flexed as he hefted his war hammer over his shoulder, perfectly shaped to crack open a door.

Or a goblin skull, Ren thought, stomach souring as the dwarf's eyes swiveled to them with razor-tipped sharpness.

Swallowing, they forced themself to look at Pansy instead, the dwarf's bearded face dancing in front of their eyes like a hazy, sun-spotted after-image. "*Pansy*," they said, more forcefully this time, an edge of something like hysteria scraping across their fraying vocal cords. "What's he talking about?"

For a moment, it seemed like she was going to respond – how she *should've* responded the last time Ren had asked her this question. Then, her gaze dropped; not to her feet, but to a point on the ground further in, near where Agvaldir himself stood, so tall his buoyant hair nearly flattened against the ceiling. Her mouth snapped shut.

Ignoring the way their stomach churned, Ren followed the direction of Pansy's stare and found a rug, old and dusty and balled up to one side. But it wasn't the rug that was important; it was what it had once covered: a small raised platform, barely wider than a stepping stone. Although it was difficult to see from their present angle, it looked like something had been carved into the smooth, gray surface. But as to what exactly, Ren couldn't say.

Agvaldir shrugged, infuriatingly casual as he passed his staff from one hand to the other. "A bit clumsy, hiding them underneath a dirty old rug, but I suppose I can't complain. You did manage to keep that unwanted houseguest of yours away while I made my preparations."

"I didn't—" Pansy choked, her hands trembling at her sides.

"Then why ask me about the runes?" he intoned, head cocking to the side in a display of mock innocence. "You were so desperate when you came up to me in the town square that day. You were practically *begging me*, asking if I was certain that I didn't know what these runes meant, if I didn't have any books. You *asked*, Pansy. You *wanted* my help. And more than that, you wanted that goblin *gone*." He grinned, lips peeling back with a serpent's grace, needle-bright and slick with venom.

Ren wanted it all to be a lie. Every last word. But as they looked to Pansy, saw the recognition twisting across her features like the final throes of a dying animal, they knew that it wasn't.

Acid burned up Ren's throat, sliding across their tongue in a fetid tide. They staggered backwards, their legs unsteady beneath them. "Why?" they demanded, hating the way their voice cracked. "Why did you bring him here? Why didn't you *warn* me? I could've – I could've saved the garden! My clan—" They choked, their horror a noose around their throat, tightening with the weight of every new realization.

She could've told them. *She should have*. Ren had trusted her with so much; so why hadn't she trusted them in turn?

Pansy whipped around. Her cheeks had gone shockingly pale, as if every last mote of color had been sucked from her flesh. "Ren, I promise you, I didn't ask him for any of this. Yes, I asked him about the runes, but that was different. That was before—"

"Before what?" Ren snarled, uncaring of the way their bared fangs made the surrounding halflings gasp. They all saw a monster when they looked at Ren anyway, so why not give them one?

"Before I fell in love with you," Pansy whispered, glancing

up at them through her lashes, a move Ren had once found so undeniably charming, but that now only sent a web of ice fanning across their guts.

Agvaldir barked out a laugh, his expression all disgust and disbelief. "You love a *goblin*?" he asked, only to finish with a resounding snort. "My gods, Miss Underburrow, you should be grateful that I arrived here when I did. To think that you could fall under a goblin's spell so swiftly. Never fear, they'll be the unwanted pest you first saw them as soon enough."

"Ren's not a pest!" Pansy shouted, whirling back around. Rage had splattered a fresh coat of red across her face, rendered all the more stark by her preceding pallor. "Ren's—"

Not wanting to hear whatever was meant to follow – their heart too fragile, too unsteady, like a cold glass dumped in boiling water – Ren ripped the flower crown from their head and threw it to the floor. "I never should have trusted you," they hissed, fixing Pansy with the iciest glare they could manage.

Her words catching in her throat, Pansy stared at them with wide eyes. "Are you . . .? You can't seriously be blaming me for this. All I did was ask him if he recognized the runes. Yes, I probably should've told you about them too, but I was afraid—"

"And you think I wasn't? I'm a goblin, Pansy; he's a wizard! I have every right to be afraid. Plus, you know what sort of person he is. What did you think would happen?"

"Not this!" Pansy snapped, her hands fisting at her sides. "The cottage is my home too, Ren. I don't understand how you could possibly think that I would ever want to see it torn apart like this."

"But you'll survive, won't you? You can just go back to Haverow and weather out the winter there. But *my clan*—"

"Don't you put that on me, Ren," she said, biting out the

words with surprising swiftness. "You know all I've ever wanted to do was help."

"Well, at this point, I think we'd all be better off without your help!"

Pansy flinched, and Ren distantly wondered if they'd gone too far. Was it really reasonable to expect that Pansy should've foreseen all of this? But the ice in their chest had started to burn, and their own hurt eclipsed this thought not even a second later, answering their question with an emphatic, *Yes*.

"Fine," Pansy said after a beat, her words coming out brittle and strained. "If I truly am such a terrible person, then maybe you should just be rid of me and go. In fact, that's *exactly* what you should do. Far be it from me to subject you to any further consequences of my apparent stupidity!" Her voice dipped at this point, plunging straight into a vat of venom that splattered over the parts of Ren already left aching and raw.

"No need to tell me twice," they snapped and spun away from her, doing exactly as she'd suggested even though the motion tugged at something deep in the pit of their stomach.

If Pansy called for them on their way out – regret setting in, as always, the moment reality reasserted itself – Ren couldn't say. They'd already stopped listening.

17
Pansy

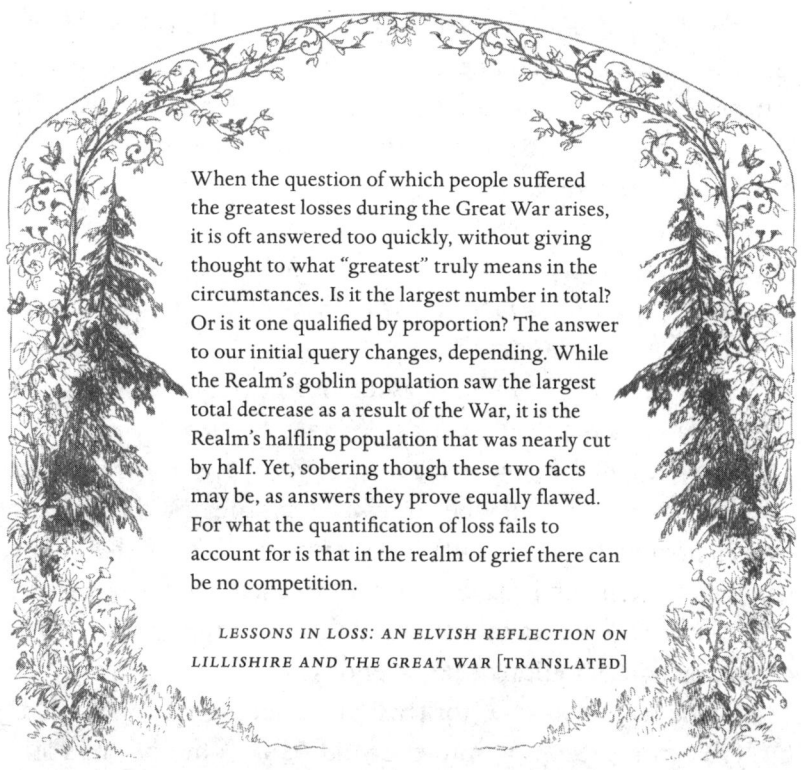

When the question of which people suffered the greatest losses during the Great War arises, it is oft answered too quickly, without giving thought to what "greatest" truly means in the circumstances. Is it the largest number in total? Or is it one qualified by proportion? The answer to our initial query changes, depending. While the Realm's goblin population saw the largest total decrease as a result of the War, it is the Realm's halfling population that was nearly cut by half. Yet, sobering though these two facts may be, as answers they prove equally flawed. For what the quantification of loss fails to account for is that in the realm of grief there can be no competition.

LESSONS IN LOSS: AN ELVISH REFLECTION ON LILLISHIRE AND THE GREAT WAR [TRANSLATED]

Standing there, staring into the dull black of the empty tunnel, Ren's retreating form already long gone, swallowed by darkness as cold and desolate as the regret clotting in her throat, Pansy swore she was about to shatter. Her happiness already had.

To think that only a few short hours ago it had felt so assured, as enduring as the sun's ever-cycling path across the sky. But now she realized that it too was nothing but a fragile, precious thing. The moment she'd slackened her grip, it had slipped through her fingers, more fleeting than a hot breath in winter. Worst of all, she only had herself to blame.

"It's all right, Pansy," her mother said, pulling free of the crowd. "You can come home, live with us." Her hand touched Pansy's elbow, familiar but not in the way Pansy wanted; the skin was too soft, too plush, the callouses she remembered nowhere to be found.

Jerking her arm away, Pansy said, in a voice like broken glass, "I don't want to come back to the village! I want to live here! With Ren!" *I didn't mean what I said. I was just ...*

Angry. Stupidly angry.

"Is the spell still in effect?" asked one of the other villagers, sending all heads turning back to Agvaldir – *the wretched man.*

"It's not a spell!" Pansy snapped, practically spitting the words as she whipped around, viper-quick. "Ren's the best thing that's ever happened to me. My life is better not in spite of them, but *because* of them. And maybe none of you will ever understand why, but surely you can understand that I'm happy! If you truly care about me, shouldn't that be enough?"

No one had an answer for that, not even her mum and dad. Only Blossom, stepping into the void Pansy's mother had left behind, managed a soft, "Of course it's enough." But her voice was a solitary one, too soft on its own to pierce through the wall of unease the rest of Haverow formed beyond.

So, Pansy continued, riding the wave of heat cresting through her chest, equal parts impassioned and vicious. "You know, Ren didn't even *want* to live here at first. All those vegetables out front, the ones Agvaldir and his men destroyed? *That* was the reason Ren stayed. Because they knew without the extra food they were growing here, their clan wouldn't survive the coming winter!"

It shouldn't have been a revelation; just like it shouldn't have been a revelation for Pansy when Ren had first told her. Still, her words drew more than a few startled gasps, and when she paused to take a breath, the wide-eyed stares she found waiting for her proved that she'd struck a chord. As she'd suspected, the concept of someone going hungry was so anathema to halflings, and not even the oldest of prejudices could hold up against it.

Picking up the discarded flower crown, Pansy hugged it close and said, "We halflings like to talk about how family is the most important thing for us. How we'd do *anything* for our families. But from what I've seen, the person who's embodied that value best isn't a halfling. They're a goblin."

"Pansy, perhaps that's a little unfair . . ." her mother started to say, but Pansy wasn't listening.

"I left Haverow because I constantly felt like I didn't belong. I was the puzzle piece left in the box, the one doomed to never quite truly fit. Because everything I did was wrong. Who I *was* was wrong. I was told this again and again. Maybe not in those exact words, but the message was just the same: *Stop asking questions. Stop looking for more. Why can't you just be content at home like the rest of us?* She parroted the comments, their sharp edges excruciatingly familiar. "And then there was Ren, who by all accounts was supposed to hate me. I was a halfling and they were a goblin; what other end could our story possibly have? Except, Ren accepted me when my own people wouldn't, and I understood, for the first time, what caring for one's family is *supposed* to be like. Funny how it wasn't a halfling who taught me that lesson."

Pansy's words seemed to reverberate in the ensuing silence, so thick one could surely cut it with a knife. And through it rumbled a current of shame, snaking through the crowd in a flurry of downcast stares and flushed faces. They'd heard her. For once, they'd truly *heard* her.

One beat. Then another. And, finally, Agvaldir broke the silence, letting out a derisive scoff. "You have no idea what you've found, do you?" he asked. "This old cottage isn't just a burrow – it's a *barrow*, a tomb. It took some time to figure out, of course. Ten-day upon ten-day spent cooped up in the lowest floors of the capital's library, puzzling out those strange runes of yours. But, as always, I uncovered the answer: they're a lock."

"A lock for what?" asked a voice, unpleasantly familiar. *Mrs. Millwood.* No surprise she was here, positioned near the back, closest to Agvaldir, her short, slightly hunched form swallowed by his ever-lengthening shadow. Although she'd doubtless taken comfort in his presence, she now turned a wary eye to the runes at his feet. *A lock is there for a reason*, Pansy could imagine her saying. *A magical one all the more so.*

"To keep out would-be grave robbers, I imagine. If I'm correct – and I usually am," Agvaldir added with a too-sharp flash of teeth, "the person entombed here, on the other side of this stone door, is none other than Wolf Banefoot, a person I believe we're all familiar with."

As titters of excitement ripped through the crowd, washing away the weight of Pansy's words as quickly as a sudden springtime flood, a cold pall settled over her shoulders. For the first time, she hated Wolf Banefoot, resented him for the mere act of existing. She'd been so close to turning the tide, to ripping off the yoke of the past, with all of its hurt and preconceptions.

And all Agvaldir had needed to do was spout off about *Wolf Banefoot*, and suddenly it was like Pansy hadn't said a word!

But wait . . .

The fire building inside her stilled, the flame retreating to a dulled coal. Because Wolf Banefoot wasn't just Wolf Banefoot any more; he was also Aconite, the goblin folk hero.

Immediately, all the cottage's strange idiosyncrasies made sense, understanding crashing over her in a wave. Pansy seized it, hope swelling inside her anew. If her experience wasn't enough to sway the other halflings off their well-trodden path, then perhaps a beloved hero could give her a much-needed hand.

"You're certain this cottage used to belong to Wolf Banefoot?" she asked, stepping closer. The crowd parted around her, allowing her passage.

Agvaldir, no doubt thinking she meant to challenge him, turned his nose up at her. "Of course I'm certain," he snapped, bristling. "Halflings have never produced a finer warrior than Banefoot. It's fitting that his gravesite would be honored thusly. Proof that halfling wit and fortitude can accomplish great things. Granted, sometimes a bit of *guidance* is required to turn these particular energies in the right direction."

Pansy ignored the implied insult. "Then haven't you noticed something strange about this cottage?" she asked, still striding towards him, one deliberate step at a time. "Doesn't it seem like two types of homes in one? A halfling burrow and a goblin cave?"

"The work of that little goblin *friend* of yours, no doubt," he sneered, upper lip peeling away from his too-white teeth.

Pansy shook her head. "Oh, no. Ren and their clan did surprisingly little to the place, actually. This is entirely Wolf Banefoot's original design. I'm sure Grandma suspected this. She read me those stories. She *wanted* me to have the cottage."

Agvaldir scoffed. "Ridiculous. What halfling would design such a home?"

"I certainly wouldn't," murmured someone in the crowd.

"Me neither," concurred another halfling. "It's far too dark down here. Not to mention *dank*."

Pansy, however, remained undeterred. She pressed on. "Maybe not a halfling," she agreed, inclining her head. "But what about someone with both halfling *and* goblin ancestry?"

In truth, she half-expected Agvaldir to laugh at her – and not just him, but a good portion of the room as well. From their perspective, what she was suggesting was downright unthinkable. However, there was no laughter, only a current of disgust. And Agvaldir was its herald.

He recoiled, the corners of his mouth pinching down, souring his sneer into something far more judgmental. "Don't be disgusting," he spat, knuckles flaring white along his gnarled staff. "That's like suggesting a goblin would rut with a human." Some of Agvaldir's men laughed.

"I'm not being disgusting," Pansy countered, now so close that she had to crane her neck to meet Agvaldir's gaze. "Whatever your opinion might be, it doesn't change the fact that Wolf Banefoot and Aconite, as the goblins call him, are one and the same."

"How do you know this?" asked one of the halflings, a beacon of genuine curiosity amid a dark sea of rejection.

Pansy smiled. At least there was one person willing to listen. "It actually becomes pretty self-evident once you start comparing the stories about Aconite with the ones we know about Wolf Banefoot. They're practically identical."

"So, the goblins have stolen our stories along with our livestock. There's nothing novel about that," Mrs. Millwood said with a scoff, her pinched face a brand across Pansy's vision.

Heat flashed through Pansy, peaking in twin points across her cheekbones. "They didn't *steal* anything! Those stories belong to them just as much as they do to us. Think about it! Halflings and goblins have always lived near each other. Is it really such a ridiculous proposition that something other than ire might bloom between our two communities? Why do we treat mutual hatred like a foregone conclusion? The reality is we halflings have more in common with goblins than we do humans, orcs, elves or even dwarves! When the larger peoples wage war, it's not them who die out on the fields of battle. *It's us.*"

Silence echoed in the wake of her words, so all-encompassing that one could surely hear a pin drop. And though no one dared speak, the crowd nonetheless rippled with uncertainty, disquiet bubbling across their expressions. They understood what war did to people, what it did to their community, their loved ones. Yet as inescapable as war's shadow was, its source had always proved far more nebulous, impossible to grasp. Until now.

"What a gross oversimplification." Agvaldir tutted. "The safety of the Realm isn't resting solely on the backs of halflings, I can assure you."

"Then why are you constantly in Haverow trying to recruit? And why do *you* allow it?" she asked, now turning to Mrs. Millwood. "You know deep down that's exactly what he's doing. His excuses about protecting the adventurers that join up with him are paper-thin, at best; plausible deniability in the absolute barest sense. So, I have to ask, if people like my grandmother are such an embarrassment, such a *blight*, then why do you allow wizards like Agvaldir to continue making them? When a child breaks every single one of their toys, you don't just give them another one! And make no mistake, that's all we are to him: toys, to be used and discarded at his pleasure."

Mrs. Millwood went pale at that, her bloodless lips moving soundlessly, like a fish plucked from a pond. Unsurprisingly, she didn't have an answer. Until now, she'd probably never even thought of it like that, too blinded by her own childhood worship of the wizard who'd once saved her village.

"Men like him care about us just as much as a dark lord cares for the goblins pinned beneath their thumb," Pansy continued, seizing her newfound momentum. "So, why have we turned our anger against the people least deserving of it? We should be banding together, finding strength in the common ground we share. I promise, unity between halflings and goblins is possible. Just look at this cottage!"

A snort came from behind her. *Agvaldir*.

"I don't have time for this," he growled, his kindly veneer worn as thin as his patience. Raising his staff as high as he could manage without jabbing one end into the ceiling, he called upon his magic, now rising around him in a crackling swell.

Within seconds, the runes at his feet began to glow.

"Stop!" Pansy cried, shoving herself into the sliver of space between Agvaldir and the tiny dais. She didn't care that the air there was thick with magic, wild and hungry. It lashed at her outstretched arms, scouring painful welts into whatever skin it could find. In that moment, all that mattered was keeping Agvaldir away from those runes.

Her efforts were not appreciated in the least. Agvaldir let out a snarl of frustration, pausing his spell just long enough to press one enormous palm against the flat of her collarbone and shove her aside.

Pansy did not stumble so much as fly backwards, a strangled cry tearing from her throat as she landed in a heap several paces away. Perhaps Agvaldir had forgotten that she was less than half his size when he'd pushed her; or maybe he simply didn't care. Either way, Pansy's head throbbed where it had cracked against the ground. And though it had thankfully been a patch of soft earth rather than hard stone or rock, her vision nonetheless swam as she pushed herself up onto dirt-caked elbows.

Everything around her seemed to have slowed, her awareness stretching like hot caramel on a spoon. Somewhere, her mother screamed. Her father too, actually. They were both moving towards her now, with Blossom not far behind, pushing their way through a shell-shocked crowd, a horde of moon-bright eyes fixed only on her, unblinking.

"Mum ... Dad ..." Pansy mumbled, eyes scrunching shut against the nauseating lurch of the world tilting on its axis.

Except, it wasn't her mother who slipped an arm around Pansy's shoulders, supporting her as she gave a worrying wobble. No, the hair was the wrong color: dark, instead of red. And the face was more defined, with a nose Pansy had always thought was so cute.

"Ren ..." She sighed, reaching for them. "You came back."

18
Ren

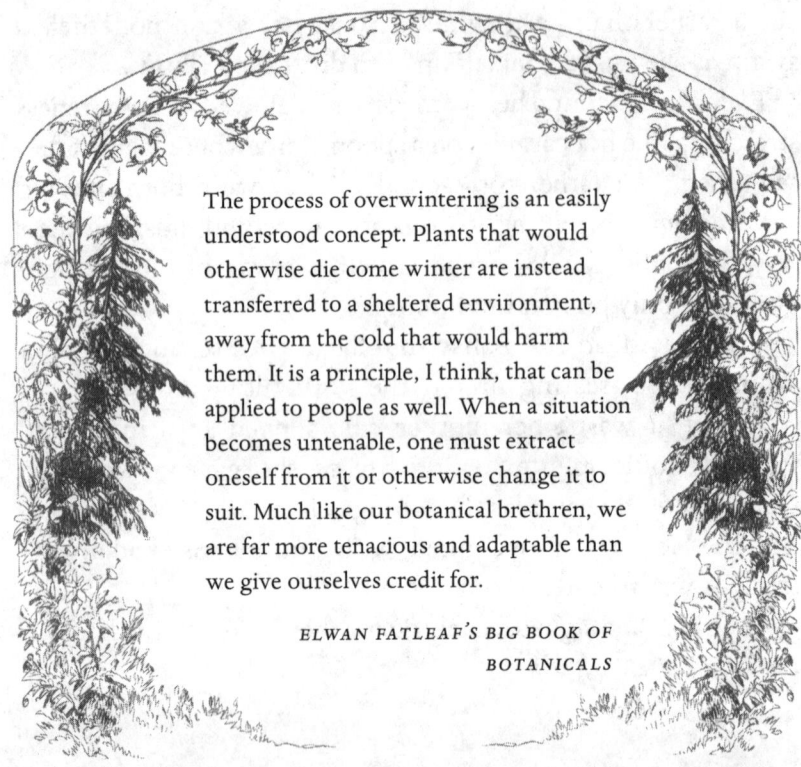

The process of overwintering is an easily understood concept. Plants that would otherwise die come winter are instead transferred to a sheltered environment, away from the cold that would harm them. It is a principle, I think, that can be applied to people as well. When a situation becomes untenable, one must extract oneself from it or otherwise change it to suit. Much like our botanical brethren, we are far more tenacious and adaptable than we give ourselves credit for.

ELWAN FATLEAF'S BIG BOOK OF
BOTANICALS

"Of course I came back. How could I not, after all the things you said – the way you defended me, my clan?" Ren said, barely contained fury scraping across their vocal cords, roughening words that should've been sweet.

Unfortunately, not even all the self-control in the world could dampen the sight of Pansy lying flat on her back in the dirt, tossed aside as casually as a piece of trash. In fact, staying here, with her, rather than barreling towards Agvaldir in a flurry of claws and teeth, had already stretched Ren's restraint to its absolute limit.

Even now, they strained against the impulse to fly at the wizard, the sneer twisting across his face stoking the fire burning in Ren's gut like an iron poker. If not for Pansy, sagging into their grasp with all the relief of coming home, they might've actually given in.

"You heard all that?" she asked, hazel eyes widening. "I thought you'd left."

"Not for very long," Ren admitted, helping her up onto her feet, which she managed with only a slight wobble. "I realized about halfway up the stairs that it was wrong to blame you for all this. As much as I wish you'd told me the truth, you couldn't have known what Agvaldir was planning. Also," they added after a beat, "in the context of our bet, conceding to you is one thing, but admitting defeat to that miserable wizard over there? That's something I simply can't tolerate."

"I tried to get him to leave, but . . ."

"It's okay. Leave it to me." Ren then turned to Pansy's parents, who had finally finished wiggling their way through the crowd, with Blossom barely more than a step behind, and asked, "Can I leave her with you?"

"Of course!" all three of them declared in unison, with Pansy's mother barking out an additional, "I'm her *mother!*" as if the question itself had been an insult.

With Pansy safely entrusted into her family's care, Ren turned their attention back towards Agvaldir, his presence still congealing around them like a stubborn, suffocating clot. He needed to be dealt with; Ren knew that much. They'd seen how a single parasite could choke the life out of an otherwise healthy plant if left unchecked, and Agvaldir was exactly that: a parasite, one that needed to be cut out by any means necessary, no matter how distasteful.

Quickly bridging the distance between Agvaldir and themself, Ren slid their dagger free of its sheath and leveled its needle-sharp point at the wizard, now only a handful of paces away. They ignored the cacophony of startled gasps that unfurled at their back and said, "I think it's time for you to go."

Agvaldir didn't even so much as flinch, the blade before him seemingly about as terrifying as a limp noodle. Instead, he looked vindicated, his arms sweeping wide in a grand gesture as he addressed the roiling, pale-faced crowd.

"See!" he declared, almost gleefully. "This is exactly why you can't trust a goblin. Perhaps they can disguise it for a time, as Miss Underburrow demonstrated for us with her impassioned speech, but a goblin will always revert to their evil nature when push comes to shove." His stare hardened. *"Always."*

Part of Ren wanted to retreat, to tuck the dagger back in its sheath. But the heat that flashed through them in that moment was as much anger as it was shame. Because violence hadn't been a first or even a second resort here; it was the absolute last, and Ren had only barely reached for it. They were still talking, the blade in their hand just adding emphasis – at least for now.

Their insides twisted as the very real possibility that they'd have to actually use it dropped into the pit of their stomach like an anvil. Ren hated violence; they hadn't lied when they'd said as much while visiting the Underburrows at their home. But for Pansy, they'd do anything. Even this.

Agvaldir cast a look back over his shoulder, making

eye-contact not with the dwarf, who would've undoubtedly jumped at the opportunity to reduce Ren to a fine paste, even without the promise of fresh territory to claim, but with one of the humans, a blond, heavily-stubbled man, who seemed more interested in toying with his dagger than whatever was going on in front of him.

"Take care of this," Agvaldir said, jerking his chin towards Ren.

The blond man gave one last flip of his knife and, with a heavy sigh, shoved himself off the wall he'd been leaning against. "Really making me work for my cut this time, huh, boss? Staking out the place last night wasn't enough to pay my dues?"

"Not when you nearly got caught," grumbled Agvaldir.

"Wait. That was you in the woods?" Pansy blurted, her eyes flying wide.

The blond man grinned.

Quick as a lightning bolt, he darted towards Ren, the dagger's serrated edge flashing bright in the oppressive glow of the surrounding lanterns. Miraculously, Ren managed to catch it with their own blade, though the force of the blow sent even their teeth rattling. They clenched their jaw, steeling themself against the truth coiling in their belly, sour and cold. This wasn't even a contest, so wildly were they outmatched. A single glance at the man's bored expression proved as much, as did the strike that came thereafter, even stronger than the first.

Ren's arms gave out almost immediately, their entire being reverberating with the harsh *clang* of steel against steel. They only just managed to flatten themself against the earth as their guard broke, sending the man's blade sweeping through empty air instead of their side. Unfortunately, there was no time to catch their breath.

Realizing that Ren wasn't going to go down easy, the man came at them more seriously, his features rearranging themselves into a hard, expressionless mask. Ren threw themself from one dodge to the next, the world narrowing to nothing beyond the dagger arcing towards them. Pansy might've screamed their name at some point – or, perhaps, several points – but amid the ever-mounting wails of distress, rising from the retreating crowd like a haunt, her voice became nigh on impossible to parse.

Eventually, Agvaldir barked, "Stop toying with them!" Evidently, he hadn't expected this to take more than a second or two.

But how long had it been exactly? By now, Ren was gasping for breath, their hair clinging to their skin in damp, matted clumps. A worrying tingle had also started in their joints, the promise that they were close to reaching their limit. Attacking had never been an option – not against this opponent – and soon, defending themself would be equally impossible. All they could do was hope they'd bought enough time.

The blond man dove for Ren again, the angle of his blade plain to see. Perhaps he was getting tired too, sloppy. *Thank the Land for that.* Ren needed the break. They swiveled out of the way, circumventing the man's dagger with plenty of room to spare – just in time to feel a white-hot lash of pain carve across their opposite side.

"What—" Ren staggered backwards, their free hand flying reflexively to their side. Hot wetness flooded out from in-between their fingers, red and sticky. *Blood*, they realized, with a disconnected sense of awareness, as if they'd been pulled out of their body and left suspended overhead, free to observe like some sort of impartial deity.

The man flashed them a smile, teeth as bright as his dagger, then lifted up what Ren had assumed was his non-dominant hand, revealing another knife, this one painted a deep, sickening crimson. "They never watch the other hand." He giggled.

Screw you, Ren wanted to say, but they were falling, dropping into the dirt like a stone. Blood pooled around them, quicker than the earth could drink down.

"Ren!" Pansy cried, shoving herself into their line of sight as she collapsed onto her knees beside them. "Oh, gods. You're— There's so much *blood*." Her fingers, doubtless attempting to apply pressure to the wound, slid uselessly across it, unable to gain solid purchase.

"'m fine..." Ren slurred, their vision going hazy around the edges. "It doesn't even hurt..."

Clearly, Pansy didn't consider this a good thing because she let out a half-choked sob, her hands, now shiny and wet, flying to her mouth in distress. Worse, Blossom seemed to agree with her assessment.

"Just stay calm," she told Ren, a flicker of panic jolting across the otherwise even cadence of her voice as she pressed a cloth against their side. A handkerchief, they realized dimly, cream-colored with tiny sunflowers embroidered into one corner. It was soaked through in seconds.

"Ugh." Agvaldir rolled his eyes. "Don't just stand there," he told his henchman. "Put the goblin out of its misery. We're not heartless animals here."

"Don't you dare!" Pansy snapped, back on her feet before Ren could even blink. She'd picked up their dagger too, discarded on their way down, and held it in front of her with trembling hands, her stance betraying every ounce of her inexperience.

"You gotta... one hand..." Ren tried to say, but their tongue had turned heavy and thick in their mouth, weighed down by the same exhaustion that had drawn over the rest of them.

Pansy, however, wasn't listening. "If you want Ren, then you're going to have to go through me first!"

"Oh, no, Miss Underburrow, we don't want that," Agvaldir said. And loath though Ren was to admit it, they agreed with him on this point. "That being said," the wizard continued after a beat, the spark of something like an idea rising to his eye, "perhaps spilling a little blood is what we need. It wouldn't be the first time an arcane lock such as this exacted such a price."

Horror swelled in Ren's breast. "No," they croaked, shoulders heaving as they struggled to sit up, a movement that sent a fresh swell of warm liquid cresting down their side. "Leave her alone . . ."

"Stay still!" Blossom hissed, pressing down harder, such that Ren had no choice but to lie flat.

Agvaldir ignored them. Snapping his fingers, he commanded, "Bring Miss Underburrow to me."

Years of unquestioning obedience to Agvaldir had left their mark. The other halflings could only watch, pinned in place by an all-too-potent variety of fear, steeped over multiple generations. Their thoughts were plain, etched into their features via a heavy hand. Against such a large adversary, what could they hope to accomplish?

The blond man, who'd had no compunctions about hurting Ren, seemed to have more restraint with respect to Pansy. Sheathing his daggers, he let out a breath more appropriate for an overworked employee laboring beneath an especially demanding boss, and promptly heaved Pansy up over his shoulder like she was nothing more than a sack of potatoes.

"Let me go!" she cried, flailing wildly in his grasp. "I'll – I'll stab you!"

He snorted, lips quirking up in amusement. "No, you won't. You can't even hold that thing properly, like your little lover over there was trying to tell you." Then, as if to prove his point, he shoved his shoulder up into her, jostling the blade right out of her blood-slick fingers.

It clattered to the floor, too far away from Ren to reach, wounded as they were. At this point, even dragging themself a mere inch seemed an impossible task, akin to scaling the steepest of mountain peaks. Plus, there was Blossom, still applying pressure to their side, her face drawn and pale. No doubt she'd rush to stop them just as swiftly as before.

Pansy's mother, however, could still do what Ren could not. She scooped up the dagger with shaking hands and said, in an equally unsteady voice, "Let my daughter go."

Agvaldir sighed. "Come now, Mrs. Underburrow. Be reasonable. You'll just hurt yourself like that. Besides, think of all the good that will come from a little sacrifice!"

"Good for you, perhaps!" she snapped, her pale face turning splotchy with steadily mounting rage. "But you're suggesting bleeding my daughter dry!"

He scoffed. "I'm not going to—"

Pansy's mother whirled around before he could even finish. "I've always been a firm believer that when someone shows you who they really are, you should believe them," she said, now addressing the other halflings, her friends, her neighbors. "And Agvaldir Starsmith is not a friend to us halflings. We all saw how quick he was to raise a hand against Pansy earlier, and now he wants to sacrifice her for his own gain! Oh, yes, he tells us it's for our benefit too, and why wouldn't he? We have swallowed that same lie time and time again, always with a smile, placing the blame that should have been his on the halflings he swept away with his tales of 'adventure' and 'protecting what matters most'. But the truth is, this is all for him. We're all just pieces on a chess board, there to be manipulated at his command. And not even death can spare us from his bottomless hunger, because if this *is* Wolf Banefoot's grave, then what is this but another halfling – part goblin or not – being shoved into his waiting maw?"

"Mrs. Underburrow, this a gross mischaracterization. All my life, I've wanted nothing but the best for Haverow and its people. You're all like *family* to me."

"Then you, sir, have a funny way of showing it!" she snapped, lips quivering as they flattened into a bloodless line. Behind them broiled a veritable torrent of emotion, scouring her voice into the thinnest of whispers. "I learned to hate my mother because of you. She came back changed, and none of us knew how to fix her. Of course, we knew what *not* to do – a list that only seemed to grow every day. No bright lights. No sudden sounds. And gods forbid you burn something even a little on the stove! It was like walking on eggshells around her. Watch what you do. Watch what you say. *If she has an episode, it's all your fault!* She let out a breath, her eyes wet and gleaming, even from a distance. "When she finally left us, it – it was a relief."

"Mum . . ." Pansy murmured, her eyes shining too.

Sniffling, her mother dabbed at the little bit of moisture that had gotten loose. "I'm all right," she said to Pansy's father, who'd wound an arm around her waist, ready to pull her close. "My point is"– her expression hardened – "we've given this man far too much to let him take any more. And if being a Haverow halfling means continuing to tolerate this man's destruction of our community, then I formally renounce my membership. It's not worth it."

"Tulip's right," said Pansy's father. "I know what my values are, and the time has come for everyone gathered here to think long and hard about theirs. Right now, we're at a crossroads, one I believe has been a long time coming. We need to decide on our community's future, and I hope that most of you, like me, have realized that the only future worth fighting for is one that keeps all of us safe. This man"– he leveled an accusatory finger at Agvaldir – "would do everything in his power to see that future dismantled."

Although the world had long since turned hazy, colors streaking together into a barely decipherable blur, the low whine building inside Ren's skull hadn't quite reached the point where it overwhelmed all else. A clamor rose from the surrounding crowd, swelling with each new voice that joined it. The tide was turning, and Agvaldir knew it.

"Councilor," he said, his voice vibrating with barely controlled fury as it sliced through the ever-building din, "I understand that the majority of people here likely weren't alive when the Blight tore through Haverow, but you remember, don't you? How so many people got sick? How all of them would have surely died without my intervention? Perhaps you could enlighten everyone else. Share your experience."

"I . . . I suppose . . ." Mrs. Millwood mumbled, her gaze flitting nervously between Agvaldir and the other halflings. She wet her lips, shuffling a few paces away from the wizard. "Though perhaps it would be best if we all return to town for now. Have a proper, civilized discussion."

"No!" Pansy snapped, her anger not dampened in the least by the precariousness of her position, still slung over the shoulder of one of Agvaldir's henchmen. "Agvaldir needs to leave and never come back! Also"– she thumped one tightly balled fist in between her captor's shoulder blades – "put me *down*! I need to— *Ren*!"

Undaunted by Pansy's desperate scrabbling, the man looked towards his employer and said, "Hey, boss, maybe we should do as they say. Cutting down a goblin is all fine and dandy, but a bunch of halflings? I don't know. Feels a little wrong, doesn't it? Like kicking a baby."

Pansy's eyes flashed. *"Baby?* I'll show you *baby."* With uncharacteristic viciousness, she grabbed two fistfuls of the man's blond hair, artfully tousled in that effortless sort of way, and yanked as hard as she could.

The man let out a high-pitched yelp along with some especially inventive swears strung together with spittle and red-faced fury. Deciding that Pansy was more trouble than she was worth, he threw her to the ground. "Forget this," he said, clutching at what Ren hoped was a brand-new bald spot. "I'm an adventurer, not a gods-damned babysitter. I'm leaving."

"You should listen to your companion and take your leave as well," said Pansy's mother to Agvaldir, her eyes blazing like twin flames as she rushed to her daughter's side once more. "If you don't, we'll make sure you become as reviled among halflings as the dark lords you've pledged yourself to fight against."

"And us goblins won't like you very much either," said a blessedly familiar voice. "I guarantee that."

Whether it was the mention of goblins or the sight of them, Agvaldir's men were quick to respond in the only way they knew how. Steel scraped against steel as they brandished their weapons, ready to put them to good use the second Agvaldir gave the order.

"Thorn," Ren managed to rasp out before Blossom shushed them, telling them to conserve their strength. In retrospect, they probably should have. The chances of their cousin hearing them over the startled shouts of several dozen halflings were slim at best. Admittedly, the sudden appearance of an equally large group of goblins – all armed, no doubt, given the contents of the message Ren had sent via raven – was bound to go over somewhat poorly when the halflings were already moderately terrified.

Thankfully, Pansy was quick to pre-empt any less-than-ideal knee-jerk response. "Thorn!" she exclaimed, her relief palpable as she staggered to her feet. "How did you—"

"Ren sent a message via raven saying you needed help. Thankfully, we were already on our way for the party, so—"

Pansy blinked. "I'm sorry. The *what*?"

Thorn nodded sagely. "Ah, yeah. I figured you might not have actually heard me last night. Poor timing on my part really, trying to talk to you when you were otherwise occupied. But goblin tradition dictates that all engagements be celebrated at the earliest opportunity – in other words, this morning. Normally, we'd have brought gifts, but once we got Ren's message, we figured we'd better swap them out for something more appropriate in the circumstances." He grinned as he hefted a large wooden club – a repurposed tree branch, most likely – over one shoulder to illustrate.

Agvaldir took what seemed to be an instinctive step back, his expression flattening into a stone-like mask. He said, "I could incinerate you with just a flick of my wrist."

"Maybe," Thorn said with an easy, unaffected shrug. "But by my count, there are – *oh*, several dozen of us, and only four of you. Also, I don't think your buddies will much like it if you start slinging fireballs in a cramped space like this. Chances are you'll blast them too. There's a reason dwarves don't use spellpowder in *populated* tunnels – or, at least, not tunnels populated by them. I'm sure your friend over there will tell you as much."

Right on cue, the dwarf's mustache twitched in recognition. However, instead of cautioning his employer like Thorn had intended, he stepped forward, dark eyes narrowing beneath the lip of his iron helm. Of course, a dwarf wouldn't allow himself to be bested by a bunch of goblins. They were too proud for that.

But pride didn't mean he'd fight fair. Dwarves never did. Fire and toxic gas were their favorite tools when it came to clearing out goblin caves – always things they could set and walk away from, as if that made their hands any cleaner. *Efficiency*, the dwarves called it. *Drill down where the earth is softest*. And, in this case, that meant seizing Mrs. Millwood with one gauntleted hand and yanking her towards him to serve as a makeshift shield.

"Don't you think you're overlooking something?" the dwarf drawled over Mrs. Millwood's half-strangled whimpers. "I know halflings are awfully small, but surely you care about their—"

Well-being, Ren imagined he meant to say. However, Thorn swung out with his club quicker than his size would've suggested, and promptly silenced the dwarf with a hard smack to the head.

Dazed, the dwarf staggered back, his hold on both Mrs. Millwood and his hammer unraveling in tandem. While the hammer dropped to the floor with a heavy *thunk*, Mrs. Millwood fled into the safety of the crowd, urged onwards by the gentle press of Thorn's palm. She stood behind him, her hands knotting in the beige knit of her shawl, desperately seeking comfort.

"Face it," Thorn said, once again addressing Agvaldir, who

seemed to have grown a touch paler. "You're outnumbered, outmatched. The pretty little lady"– he nodded towards Pansy – "gave you the opportunity to leave with a generous portion of your dignity intact. I suggest you take it. Unless you want to go the same way as your dwarf friend here. In which case, I am most happy to oblige."

"You're really going to fight alongside a bunch of goblins?" Agvaldir demanded, still scrabbling for some way to turn this around. Unfortunately for him, he'd reached the point where he was now scraping across the bottom of a barrel.

"It-it is rather unorthodox..." Mrs. Millwood said, the words jolting over her tremulous breathing. "But, I suppose, so is being accosted by armed men..."

Evidently, every halfling present could agree on that much, given the way they nodded and murmured among themselves.

"What about fighting alongside new friends?" Thorn ventured, the corner of his mouth quirking up into a lopsided grin.

"Y-yes." Mrs. Millwood nodded, a pink tinge rising to her cheeks. "I think we could all do that."

Land almighty. Had Thorn managed to *charm* Mrs. Millwood? Him – of all people? And unintentionally to boot! Ren might've laughed if the pain hadn't seized any and all amusement in a vicelike grip, smothering it before it could fully form.

Finally realizing that this confrontation had run its course, Agvaldir straightened up as best he could and barked out a curt, "We're leaving!" over his shoulder. He said nothing more as he headed back up the tunnel, pushing past goblins and halflings alike in a flurry of silken robes – though the parting glare he shot Pansy could've incinerated her just as readily as a fireball conjured from his fingertips.

Then he was gone, vanishing from sight along with his

wretched henchmen, including the still-stumbling dwarf. And Ren, certain in the knowledge that Pansy was safe, let go of the tension pulling their body taut and allowed themself to drift. Down and down into the darkness lapping at the edges of their vision, where their side ceased to hurt, until, finally, there was nothing.

19
Pansy

> Even the most immaculately kept burrows are not immune to the occasional stubborn stain. In such cases, one need only turn to our staunchest allies: vinegar and baking powder. And though they are potent tools alone, the moment they come together is when they truly shine.
>
> ELLA MERRYWEATHER,
> *HOME IS WHERE THE HEARTH IS*

All Pansy could think about as she gazed upon Ren's supine form, pale and motionless atop a ring of sodden earth, was the fact that they were dying. The person she loved most in the entire world was dying, and there was nothing she could do.

"Please," she said, desperate in a way she had never been before, as Blossom continued applying pressure to Ren's side with both hands. "Please save them. I know I haven't been a good friend to you lately. I blamed you for things that weren't your fault and unjustly punished you for them. I shouldn't have done any of that. I'm sorry, Blossom. I—"

Blossom cut her off with a gentle shake of her head. "It's okay, Pansy. Consider it all forgotten. Water under the bridge, yeah?"

She nodded, the lump in her throat bobbing with the movement, refusing to unravel.

Because Blossom's face was ashen, even in the golden light from Agvaldir's abandoned lanterns, flecked with sweat and blood. She swallowed. "I want to save them. I really do. If I had my supplies, I could make a healing potion, but—"

"Ren has herbs," Pansy said quickly, hope squeezing hard around her ribcage. "Down the hall. Take a right at the first fork."

"I don't—" Blossom started to say, her expression creasing.

"I'll take her," Thorn said, his expression, for once, serious. "I have a pretty good idea of where it is. Hard to hide the smell of all those herbs from this nose." He tapped it. "Though," he added after a beat, his gaze resting meaningfully on Blossom, still crouched in the vastness of his shadow with something like wonder reflected in her wide blue eyes, "it's surprisingly easy to get distracted by that lovely perfume of yours. Do I detect a hint of honeysuckle?"

Blossom blushed. "Freesia, actually."

"Stop . . . flirting . . ." Ren mumbled, their eyelids fluttering weakly. "At least, wait . . . till I'm dead . . ."

Pansy seized Ren's hand in hers, giving it a near bone-crushing squeeze. "You're not going to die," she said firmly, as if she hadn't been convinced of the opposite just a moment ago. "Don't joke about that." Somehow, speaking the words out loud helped, made them feel true. And this was something Pansy would give everything to make reality.

Thoroughly jolted back to earth, Blossom said, "I'll be back soon. Keep pressure on Ren's side until then. As much as you can." She waited until Pansy was in position, then removed her hands. "Lead on," she said, gesturing to Thorn, a hint of her earlier flush still clinging to her cheeks.

Thankfully, neither one dallied after that. They sprinted down the tunnel, the crowd of concerned halflings and goblins that had gathered around Ren swiftly parting to provide them passage.

"What are you doing?" Pansy asked, horrified, when Ren's hands scraped across the earth, moving as if to push themself upright. "Stay still! Didn't Blossom already tell you that?"

Ren ignored her. "You ... defended me," they murmured, the sweetness of their words undone by the wet gurgle that had preceded them. "You tried to fight a wizard for me."

"And I'll fight you too, if I have to!" she snapped, pressing her elbow to their chest in the hope that she could persuade them to abandon whatever nonsense they were trying to accomplish, without removing her hands from their present position. The movement was ungainly, awkward and, most frustratingly, ineffective.

"What're you—" Ren looked almost offended, their eyes, still glassy and unfocused, narrowing. "I'm *trying* to kiss you!"

"Well, do it later! Preferably at a time when I'm *not* trying to keep you from bleeding out."

"But I want to kiss you *now*."

"Unfortunately, we don't always get what we want!" Pansy huffed. Then, because she was nothing but a big pushover – especially where Ren was concerned – she let out half-grumbled "Fine" and briefly pressed her mouth to theirs. At least, this way they would *stay* down.

"All right, lovebirds. Make some space," Thorn said, grinning from ear to ear as he returned with Blossom. "Miss Blossom has a potion that'll fix Ren right up."

No sooner had Ren finished draining the contents of the narrow flask Blossom raised to their lips – a thick, milky-white liquid that, judging from the way their nose wrinkled, wasn't exactly pleasant on the tongue – the torn, seeping flesh beneath Pansy's palms began knitting together.

Within seconds, it was like Ren had never been injured at all, with only a thin, barely visible line of puckered skin to serve as an enduring reminder.

They let out a grunt as they sat up fully, one hand flying to their side, the skin there evidently still tender. After palming it for several moments, they asked, "Did you use bloodthorn?"

Blossom nodded. "With a touch of butterbloom, to try to mask the taste. You'll need to eat well in the coming days."

"To replace the nutrients the bloodthorn pulled to heal the wound. I know." Ren paused, their lips pressing together, as if reconsidering their words. "Thank you," they said at last. "For saving my life. I'm not sure how I can repay you."

Blossom smiled. "Think nothing of it. But if you'd really like to repay me, you can start by teaching me about every one of the herbs you've got stashed in that room of yours. I didn't even recognize half of them!"

"How about we leave that until *after* we've fixed up the cottage," Pansy interjected, her hand once again finding Ren's.

Given that she'd come so close to losing them, it was hard to deny the urge to keep them in her grasp. "I know we made do with a pretty bare-bones arrangement when we first moved in, but I do have standards. If I have to contend with splintered bits of wood in bed tonight along with those icy toes of yours, I fear I'm going to lose my mind."

Ren blinked at her, seemingly surprised. "You want to continue living here?"

"Of course! I admit it's in rather rough shape right now, but this is our *home*, Ren. I wouldn't want to live anywhere else – not without you."

A beat. Then, their voice soft and fragile, they said, "I don't want to live without you either."

This time, when Pansy leaned in to kiss Ren, the crowd around them erupted into hoots and cheers. Granted, that could have just been Thorn. Honestly, it was hard to tell; the man was loud enough to constitute a crowd all on his own.

"I suppose there's nothing left to do but get this place fixed up," Blossom said, clapping her hands together with a decisive nod. "That being said, I'm certain if we had a big, strong goblin"– her eyes flicked pointedly over to Thorn as a whisper of a smile crept across her lips – "around to help, we'd finish in no time."

It took Thorn a moment to realize she was talking about him, even though she was anything but subtle. Pansy barely managed to stifle a laugh as he pointed at himself – eyebrows rising as if to ask, *Me?* – his cluelessness not so much embarrassing as haplessly charming. Blossom certainly seemed to think so, eyelashes fluttering as she confirmed his silent query with a nod.

Suddenly it was like Thorn had never had any doubts to begin with, his chest puffing up in the most self-assured swagger Pansy had ever witnessed. Ren, however, seemed all too familiar with this behavior, judging from the way they rolled their eyes.

"Brace yourself," was all they said, keeping their voice low, when Pansy cocked a curious eyebrow at them.

"Let's get started then!" Thorn declared, all bright-eyed, wild enthusiasm as he (not-so-subtly) flexed his biceps.

Still, there was more on Pansy's mind than just repairs to the cottage, and the matter that sat right at the forefront weighed the heaviest of all. "I'm worried about Pig and Mushroom," she murmured. "There's been no sign of either of them at all. Blossom, did you and Thorn happen to see them on your way to get the potion for Ren?"

Blossom shook her head. "Sorry. No. But four sets of eyes are better than two. If we all look together—"

"Make that six," said Pansy's father, stepping forward alongside her mother. "And, of course, we'll help with the repairs, too."

"No, seven!" called out another halfling, whose voice was quickly followed by a chorus of further numbers, shouted by halflings and goblins alike. Not one person remained silent.

"And we'll pull together whatever we can to replace the garden that Agvaldir destroyed," said Pansy's mother. "No one will be going hungry this winter. Isn't that right, Councilor Millwood?" She shot the elderly councilor a weighty look, one forged of unbending iron, inviting only acquiescence – not debate.

But Mrs. Millwood, still pale and shaken from the events that had come before, didn't seem to even want an argument on the matter. She gave a quick, jerky nod, sparing Thorn one last glance before announcing, "Haverow will always be there to help its ... friends."

Warmth swelled within Pansy's chest at the councilor's words. Yesterday, at the Harvest Festival, she had been so sure that unity between halflings and goblins was nothing but a far-flung fantasy, relegating her relationship with Ren to more of the same: disapproval masked as grudging tolerance – not just from her side, but Ren's as well. How glad she was to be proved wrong! Pansy only wished someone like Agvaldir hadn't needed to serve as the catalyst – even if it was rather poetic.

After all, the man was startlingly similar to the villains that populated her vast library of Wolf Banefoot stories, selfish and cruel despite a thin veneer of respectability. Truly, it was no wonder she'd never liked him. And if this house *did* in fact belong to her beloved halfling – and goblin! – hero, Pansy couldn't think of a better place for the halfling and goblin communities to rise up together against a common enemy. No doubt, even the great hero himself would approve.

"Goblins and halflings as friends – it has a nice ring to it, don't you think?" Pansy asked with a smile.

No sooner had the words left her lips than the air around her seemed to shift, charged now with some sort of energy. Magic, she realized, as the runes Agvaldir had been so preoccupied with earlier started to glow, eerily bright even amid the still-flickering lanterns. But as far as she could tell, no one had cast a spell, and a quick glance around confirmed this fact. Everyone looked just as perplexed as she was.

At least, until the stone wall beneath the archway at the end of the hall gave a tremendous rumble, one not so much heard as felt. The whole tunnel seemed to shake with it, sending streams of freshly loosed earth tumbling from the ceiling. For a moment, it seemed like the whole thing was poised to collapse – as someone wailed from within the crowd – but then the stone wall stilled, and in one last puff of dust and debris, it gently eased aside, leaving a circular opening in its place.

Agvaldir was right, Pansy thought, eyes widening as she took note of the space that lay beyond the archway, newly revealed as a result of whatever magic had been embedded in those runes.

Though perhaps half-right was a better term. Because the cottage's latest addition, while understandably musty, given how long it had been sealed off, was not a barrow. Far from it, in fact.

"*As a child of two worlds, I here inscribe my final wish, that both halves might come together and again make whole what never should have been divided,*" Pansy said, reading out loud the words that had appeared along the archway, the inscription so weathered it seemed as though it had always been there, just hidden from view.

"So, this was Aconite's house," Ren murmured, their eyes blown wide.

Pansy nodded. "Looks like it. And it sounds like he wanted this room to be a shared space, one that halflings and goblins could use together. Maybe that's why it didn't open until now. It was waiting for our communities to finally come together as friends rather than enemies."

Ren said nothing as they rose to their feet, their initial steps unsteady enough that Pansy rushed to offer them her arm, which they gladly took. Together, they crossed the threshold first, lips parting in wonder as the full measure of the space finally hit them.

"It's *huge*," Pansy whispered, craning her neck in an effort to glimpse the ceiling, lost beneath an impenetrable tangle of ivy and other vines.

"Yeah," Ren agreed, their own gaze sweeping across the beds of mushrooms and moss that blanketed the floor at irregular intervals. "Bigger than all the cropland the clan has lost this season."

Pansy's eyes widened around an idea. "Do you think we can grow more food down here?"

"Probably. Nothing that requires sunlight, but – yes. It's possible. Though we should try our best to honor Aconite's wishes, no? Turn this place into something both of our communities can use?"

A fair point. Still, Pansy couldn't help but tease them a little. "You sure you want to invite a bunch of halflings into your home? It'll get pretty lively around here."

They shrugged, though the smile tugging at the corner of their mouth belied their apparent nonchalance. "Fine by me. I've already learned to live with one halfling, what's a few-dozen more?"

She laughed. "You say that now . . . How about a community garden, then? With a bit of space for recreation? Honestly, we have *a lot* of room to work with. And it doesn't look like we'll have to chase anyone out of their nests—"

As soon as the words left her lips, a shuffling sound, distinctly animal in nature, reached her ears. She stilled, straining to catch it once more. Though she needn't have bothered; Ren, with their superior hearing, had already determined the source.

"This way," they said, pulling her in the direction of an especially thick patch of vegetation along the nearby wall.

"What do you think it is?" Pansy asked, squatting down beside them.

They frowned. "I'm not sure, but I think it's—"

A familiar black blur darted out of the bush before they could finish, scrambling up Ren's chest in an absolute frenzy of flailing limbs.

"Mushroom." They winced, the claws seeking purchase in the fabric of their shirt evidently far from comfortable – not that the kitten cared one whit.

He trilled upon reaching Ren's shoulder, where he settled in a contented loaf, all of his earlier energy strangely absent, as if a short sprint and a scramble was all that was needed to tire him out. Ren obviously didn't believe it for a minute, leveling a narrow-eyed, sidelong look upon their shoulder's latest tenant. Granted, their misgivings didn't stop them from rubbing Mushroom lightly behind the ears, but, then again, when did anything?

Equally weak to Mushroom's charms, Pansy's hand was quick to join Ren's, stroking the explosion of fur around Mushroom's scruff. *His mane*, she thought, smiling – though in truth, Mushroom was more like a panther than a lion. "How did you even get in here?" she asked. "Is Pig with you too?"

An affirmative snort resounded from the same patch of greenery Mushroom had bounded out of, and a moment later Pig's head burst into view, flattening a couple of fronds in the process. It took a few seconds for the rest of her to follow. Evidently, the tunnel the two of them had managed to find their way into was a bit of a tight fit, especially for Pig, who, unlike Mushroom, was the very opposite of small.

Ren let out an amused huff. "Let me guess, this is where the two of you have been vanishing off to all this time. And here I was thinking there'd be a far less interesting explanation."

"What do you think dug this?" Pansy asked, pushing aside the surrounding vegetation with both hands so that she could peer into the almost-exactly-Pig-sized hole.

Ren shrugged, a motion that would have nearly sent Mushroom tumbling from his perch if not for Ren's steadying hand. "Maybe a badger. It looks like it's been there a long time."

"I wonder where it connects to upstairs..."

Ren smiled. "Well, it's our cottage now. We'll have the rest of our lives to figure it out together."

"Yes," Pansy agreed, leaning in for another kiss – Thorn's hooting be damned! "Together."

20
Ren

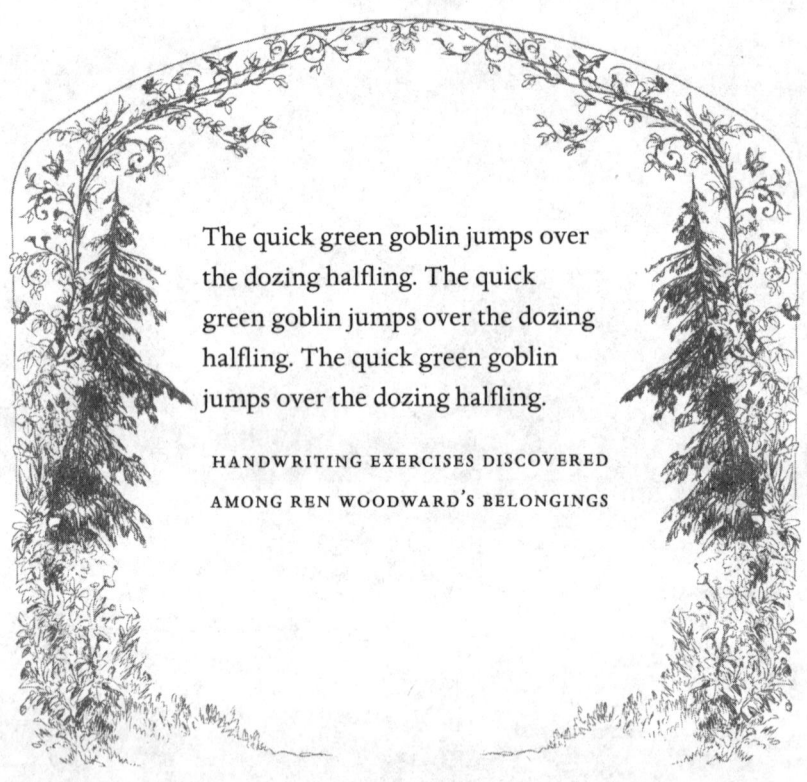

The quick green goblin jumps over the dozing halfling. The quick green goblin jumps over the dozing halfling. The quick green goblin jumps over the dozing halfling.

HANDWRITING EXERCISES DISCOVERED AMONG REN WOODWARD'S BELONGINGS

By Ren's estimates, it would've taken their clan several months to repair the damage to the cottage. For the halflings from Haverow, they were probably looking at a similar time period; maybe slightly less, given their advantage in terms of sheer numbers. But together, the job took them only a single month – and they'd managed to throw together a brand-new statue of Aconite to boot!

How the artisans responsible had come to an agreement on the hero's appearance, Ren wasn't quite sure. They imagined there must've been plenty of bickering on the matter. After all, old habits died hard, no matter how earnestly they'd been discarded. But what was the harm in a bit of arguing along the way? It had certainly worked out well enough for Ren and Pansy, as evidenced by their impending wedding. Date still undecided, of course. But soon.

First, came the all-important, extremely halfling housewarming party planned almost entirely by Ren.

"You know," Pansy said as she hefted another tray of food onto the already sprawling buffet set up at the center of the expansive room they'd taken to calling Harvest Hall, "usually one has a housewarming party shortly after moving in. We've been here almost three and a half months. Granted, it took some time to fix this place up. Plus, we were pretty busy setting up the shipping route between Haverow and your clan. So, I suppose it can be forgiven..."

Ren looked up from the mushroom farm they'd been tending to, one of several erected along one side of the space. Grinning much like the statue of Aconite standing proud just beyond the buffet – the grin the work of a goblin artisan, no doubt – Ren said, "Better late than never, right? Isn't that what you halflings always say?"

"Oh, *gods.*" Pansy groaned. "Now you're sounding like my father. Is he the one teaching you all these idioms?"

"Maybe." Ren shrugged and straightened up. "He's very talkative when we go out foraging. Also very good at identifying mushrooms. Shame you didn't inherit that trait."

Shaking her head, she let out a huff. "Introducing you two was a mistake." Yet the smile curling at the corner of her mouth, visible even though she'd ducked her head to the side, told the true story.

Their grin stretching even wider, to the point where their fangs peeked out from behind their lower lip in the way they now knew Pansy found helplessly charming, Ren barreled over to her and flung their arms around her waist. "I think you rather like it, actually," they said and pressed a somewhat sloppy kiss to her cheek.

Pansy squealed. "You better not have dirt on those hands! This dress is brand new!"

"It'll wash out. Besides, I think it'll go rather well with those acorns that rolled out of your hair this morning."

She flushed. "It's not my fault the squirrels keep mistaking my curls for a good hiding spot."

"Yes." Ren nodded sagely. "How trying it must be to have curls so thick and beautiful that all the squirrels continue to find themselves helpless against their charms." They twirled one stray lock around their finger.

"Are you a squirrel?" Pansy asked, cocking an eyebrow.

"Fine. All squirrels and one madly-in-love goblin," Ren amended, much to her apparent delight.

"Well, the goblin can stay," she said, smoothing out the front of Ren's shirt with both hands. "The squirrels, on the other hand . . . Perhaps they can join the other animals who have made their nests down here."

"On Aconite, you mean?" Ren asked, their gaze flicking over to the several nests currently balanced across the statue's shoulders and the top of his head.

"Mm. Do you think he minds?"

"I think he's probably happy for the company," Ren said, pulling their fiancée more firmly against them. "I know I am."

Then before the twinkle of protest in Pansy's eyes could build into something more, they leaned in and sealed their words with a kiss. Because not even Pansy could argue with that.

Acknowledgements

Ever since I first toddled into my local bookstore – a trip that, like the many that followed, thoroughly divested my parents' wallets of their contents – I've dreamed of becoming a published author. Now, that day is here. My debut novel is out in the world, and though writing is oft seen as a solitary activity, the act of *publishing* a book is nothing if not a team effort. And Team Goblin is decidedly robust.

First, I'd like to thank my wonderful agent, Maeve Maclysaght, for making sure my personal fan club always has at least one member. Thank you for your unwavering support and enthusiasm. I don't know where I'd be without it.

I will also be forever grateful to my amazing editors, Jenni Hill and Tiana Coven. This book would not be what it is today without either of you: no longer a charming mess, but simply charming. Thank you as well to Joanna Kramer, Anna Jackson, Nadia Saward, Serena Savini, Aimee Kitson, Nazia Khatun, Bryn A. McDonald, Lauren Panepinto, Stephanie Hess, Alex Lencicki, Natassja Haught, Kayleigh Webb, Ellen Wright, Tim Holman and the rest of the Orbit UK and US teams. None of this would've been possible without your help.

I'd also like to thank Raahat Kaduji and Sophie Ellis for giving

ACKNOWLEDGEMENTS

me the cover of my dreams. It's absolutely perfect in every way and completely deserving of the shout of delight I let out when it first arrived in my inbox.

I am fortunate enough to have several critique partners who allow me to pass myself off as a better writer than I actually am. Thank you, Jules Arbeaux and Artemis Whelan. The draft that landed in my editors' inboxes would've undoubtedly been far more embarrassing without your help.

Thank you to my parents, who nurtured my love of books and writing from the start. Sorry that the whole "lawyer" thing didn't work out. But I think you'll agree with me that "published author" is equally – if not more – cool. Dad, I hope this book is better than the slop I made you read back when I was twelve. Mom, I wish I could share this moment with you like I always wanted, but I'll just say it here: I did it!

Finally, I want to thank my wife, Candy, who's supported me from the very start. I would not have been able to realize this dream without you. You are everything to me, and I'm so lucky to have found you. Truly, there's no purer form of love than being willing to read the shittiest, earliest drafts of a novel, and you've done that for me. Not just once, but multiple times. I wish I could say it won't happen again, but it absolutely will. Here's to many more books!

Meet the Author

Jessica Hassett

JESSIE SYLVA is a recovering lawyer living in Toronto with her wife and two cats. She writes fantasy with an emphasis on queer joy, telling stories full of magic, adventure, and of course, kissing. The cozy fantasy *How to Lose a Goblin in Ten Days* is her debut novel, although her first writing commission was *The Official Dragon Age Cookbook*.

Find out more about Jessie Sylva and other Orbit authors by registering for the free monthly newsletter at orbitbooks.net.

RAISING READERS
Books Build Bright Futures

Thank you for reading this book and for being a reader of books in general. We are so grateful to share being part of a community of readers with you, and we hope you will join us in passing our love of books on to the next generation of readers.

Did you know that reading for enjoyment is the single biggest predictor of a child's future happiness and success?

More than family circumstances, parents' educational background, or income, reading impacts a child's future academic performance, emotional well-being, communication skills, economic security, ambition, and happiness.

Studies show that kids reading for enjoyment in the US is in rapid decline:

- In 2012, 53% of 9-year-olds read almost every day. Just 10 years later, in 2022, the number had fallen to 39%.
- In 2012, 27% of 13-year-olds read for fun daily. By 2023, that number was just 14%.

Together, we can commit to **Raising Readers** and change this trend. How?

- Read to children in your life daily.
- Model reading as a fun activity.
- Reduce screen time.
- Start a family, school, or community book club.
- Visit bookstores and libraries regularly.
- Listen to audiobooks.
- Read the book before you see the movie.
- Encourage your child to read aloud to a pet or stuffed animal.
- Give books as gifts.
- Donate books to families and communities in need.

Books build bright futures, and **Raising Readers** is our shared responsibility.

For more information, visit **JoinRaisingReaders.com**

Sources: National Endowment for the Arts, National Assessment of Educational Progress, WorldBookDay.com, Nielsen BookData's 2023 "Understanding the Children's Book Consumer"

Follow us:

f /orbitbooksUS

𝕏 /orbitbooks

▶ /orbitbooks

Join our mailing list to receive alerts on our latest releases and deals.

orbitbooks.net

Enter our monthly giveaway for the chance to win some epic prizes.

orbitloot.com